'A towering achievement that brings alive a ferocious landscape and a motley assortment of clashing characters. The sense of place is stifling in its intensity, and seldom has a waltz of the damned proven so hypnotic. Indispensable.'

Maxim Jakubowski, *Guardian*

'*The Broken Shore* is written with sensitivity and subtlety. All the necessary ingredients are present: a plot that works, perceptive characterisation, believable dialogue and a terrific sense of place.' *The Times*

'It's a stone classic ... read page one and I challenge you not to finish it.' Mark Timlin, *Independent on Sunday*

'Peter Temple is deservedly the leading light of Australian crime fiction and it's time the rest of the world caught on. *The Broken Shore* is a wonderful novel; riveting and unafraid to tackle major issues. The writing is lean and muscular, but also effortlessly elegant, and in Joe Cashin, Temple has created a complex and compelling central character. This is crime writing at its very best, and discovering Peter Temple has been the highlight of my year.' Mark Billingham

'The first of Peter Temple's books to be published in the UK and at last we can see why he is acclaimed as one of Australia's leading crime writers ... This is a very fine book. Characterisation, dialogue and the quality of prose are all top-class.'

Sunday Telegraph

'A truly international 21st-century thriller set in Johannesburg, Angola, Hamburg and London with an exquisite dénouement... There is a carefully measured build-up of tension and an angry hornet's nest of menace. The characters are real, the action convincing and the writing style satisf___ ___

'Peter Temple's prose is b___
his characterisation subtl___
and universal. Put simply, ___
Shore is a masterful book.'

Also by Peter Temple

An Iron Rose
Shooting Star
The Broken Shore

Bad Debts
Black Tide
Dead Point
White Dog

IN THE EVIL DAY

Peter Temple

Quercus

First published in Great Britain in 2006 by Quercus
This paperback edition first published in Great Britain in 2007 by

Quercus
21 Bloomsbury Square
London
WC1A 2NS

A CIP catalogue reference for this book is available
from the British Library

ISBN 1 84724 079 8
ISBN-13 978 1 84724 079 8

10 9 8 7 6 5 4 3 2 1

Printed and bound in Great Britain by Clays Ltd, St Ives plc.

For Horst and for Dorle
with gratitude for friendship, hospitality and kindness,
for laughter, good times and stimulating conversation

1

JOHANNESBURG ...

NIEMAND CAME in at 2 p.m., stripped, put on shorts, went to the empty room, did the weights routine, ran on the treadmill for an hour. He hated the treadmill, had to steel his mind to endure it, blank out. Running was something you did outdoors. But outdoors had become trouble, like being attacked by three men, one with a nail-studded piece of wood. The trouble had cut both ways: several of his attackers he had kissed off quickly.

Still, you could not pass into the trance-like state when you had to break off from running to fight and kill people. So, resentfully, he had given up running outside.

Niemand didn't get any pleasure from killing. Some people did. In the Zambesi Valley in the early days, and then in Mozambique and Angola and Sierra Leone and other places, he had seen men in killing frenzies, shooting anyone – young, old, female, male, shooting chickens and dogs and cows and pigs and goats.

In command, he had dealt with soldiers for this kind of behaviour. The first was Barends, the white corporal the men had called *Pielstyf* because he liked to display his erection when drunk. Niemand had executed him with two shots, upwards into the base of his skull, come up behind him when he was firing his LMG into a crowded bus. The military court found the action justi- fied in that Barends had twice failed to obey a lawful

7

command and posed a threat to discipline in a combat situation.

The second man was a black soldier, a Zulu trained by white instructors, a veteran killer of African National Congress supporters in Natal, in love with blood and the hammer of automatic fire. In Sierra Leone, on patrol in the late afternoon, the Zulu had shot a child, a girl, and then shot the old woman with her, the child's grandmother perhaps, but it could have been her mother, the women aged so quickly. Niemand had him tied to a tree, a poor specimen of a tree, had the villagers gathered. He told the interpreter to apologise for what had happened, then he dispatched the Zulu with a handgun, one shot, close range, there was no other sensible way. The man looked him in the eyes, didn't blink, didn't plead, even when the muzzle was almost touching his left eye. There was no military court to face this time. Niemand had become a mercenary by then, saving the sum of things for pay, and his employers didn't give a shit about a man killed unless you wanted him replaced: one less pay packet.

The third time was at a roadblock. A fellow-mercenary called Powell, a redheaded Englishman, a Yorkshireman, a deserter from two armies, had for no good reason opened fire on three men in a car, two white journalists and their black driver. He killed the driver outright and wounded one of the white men. When Niemand arrived, Powell told him he was going to execute the survivors, blame it on rebels. Niemand argued with him while the unhurt journalist tried to stop his friend's bleeding. Powell wouldn't listen, high as a kite, pupils like saucers, put his pistol to the man's head. Niemand stood back, took one swing with his rifle, held by the barrel, broke Powell's freckled neck. He drove the journalists to the hospital.

8

Niemand showered under the hosepipe he had run from the rainwater tank on the roof when the water was cut off. Then he lay down on the hard bed, fell asleep thinking about all the other killings, the ones that were the means to the ends. Other people's ends.

The alarm was set for 5.30 p.m. but he woke before it sounded, showered again, dressed in his uniform of denims, T-shirt, gun rig, loose cotton jacket, left the building by the stairs. The lift didn't work but even when it did, no one used it except as a lavatory or to shoot up. He walked with his right hand inside his coat, the .38 shrouded-hammer Colt out of its clip above his left hip. He stayed close to the inside wall. That way, you bumped head-on into dangerous men coming up. They always hugged the inside wall. And if you encountered one of them, then the quickest man won.

Niemand didn't doubt for one instant that he would be the quickest.

The car was waiting at the kerb, engine running, an old Mercedes, dents everywhere, rust at the bottom of the doors, no hubcaps. The driver was smoking a cigarette, looking around at the street. It was crowded, a third-world street full of shouting hawkers, idlers, street boys, garishly made-up prostitutes, black illegal immigrants from all over Africa the locals called *maKwerekwere,* interlopers who eyed their surroundings warily. This was the fringe of the old business district of Johannesburg, Hillbrow, a suburb long abandoned by all the whites who could afford to move to more secure areas. Not secure areas, only less dangerous areas. Nowhere was secure, not even buildings with dogs and razor wire and four kinds of alarms and round-the-clock security.

It had never occurred to Niemand to move. He had no possessions he valued, had been looking after himself since he was fifteen, didn't care where he lived. He couldn't sleep for more than a few hours unless he was physically exhausted, what did it matter where he slept?

Zeke saw him coming, reached across and unlocked the door. Niemand got in.

'Rosebank,' he said.

'You always look so fucken clean,' said Zeke. He took the vehicle into the street. No one driving the car would mistake it for an old Mercedes. Which it wasn't, except for the body. The driver's full name was Ezekiel Mkane. His father had been a policeman, a servant of the apartheid state, and Zeke had grown up in a police compound, a member of a client class, no respect from whites, utter loathing and contempt from blacks. A smart boy, good at languages, a reader, Zeke had nowhere to go. He joined the army, put in sixteen years, took in three bullets, two exited, one extracted, and shrapnel, some bits still there.

'That's because I'm white,' said Niemand. He had known Zeke for a long time.

'You're not all that white,' said Mkane. 'Bit of ancestral tan.'

'That's the Greek part of me. The Afrikaner part's pure white. You kaffirs get cheekier every day.'

'Ja, baas. But we're in charge now.'

'We? Forget it. Money's in charge. Took me a long time to understand that. Money's always in charge.'

Niemand's mobile rang. It was Christa, who ran the office. 'After Mrs Shawn,' she said, 'Jan Smuts, flight 701, arriving 8.45 p.m., a Mr Delamotte and his personal assistant, whatever that fucken means.'

'His travelling screw, that's what it means,' Niemand said.

'Ja, well, at the British Airways desk. To the Plaza, Sandton. He had a bad experience in a taxi last time he was here.'

Niemand repeated the details.

'Right,' said Christa. 'Then it's two restaurant pick-ups, both late. They've got your number. Zeke's due to knock off at 11. Can he stay on? Coupla hours.'

They were out of the inner city, in dense traffic heading for the northern suburbs. 'In a hurry tonight?' Niemand said to Zeke. 'Couple of hours, probably.'

'Some people have plans, you know.'

'What about you?'

'Double time?'

'Double time.'

Zeke raised a thumb. He saw a gap and put his foot down. The Mercedes responded like a Porsche.

Mrs Shawn was waiting with a shopping centre security guard. She was about forty, pretty, too much sun on her skin, slightly tipsy, a flush on the prominent cheekbones. She'd had a long lunch, gone shopping. Probably had a swim before lunch, Niemand thought, a swim and a lie in the sun. The guard put her purchases into the boot, four bags, and she gave him several notes.

'This *smells* like a new car,' she said as they queued to get into the early evening traffic on Corlett Drive. She was English, Yorkshire. Niemand knew the accent from the old days, the Rhodesia days. Lots of people from Yorkshire in Rhodesia.

'It is a new car,' said Niemand. 'In an old body.'

'God,' she said, 'that's how I feel.'

Niemand smiled, didn't say anything. He could feel that she wanted to flirt. They often did, these rich women, but it was bad for business. He'd screwed a few in the beginning but no good came of it. One took to phoning six times a day, then for some reason confessed to her husband when Niemand wouldn't take the calls. They'd lost the company's business, at least twenty thousand rand a year, and he'd narrowly escaped being fired.

That was too much to pay for a fuck you couldn't even remember.

'People down the street got hit two weeks ago,' she said. 'The car got in behind them before the security gate could close. Three men. Fortunately, they settled for money. He had a few thousand in his safe.'

'Lucky,' said Niemand. 'Mostly it's your money and your life.' He switched on the thin fibre-optic rear-view screen in the roof of the car, looked up. It was providing a 120-degree view of the road behind but it could cover 160 degrees.

'Wow,' said Mrs Shawn. 'That's technology. My husband'd crave that.'

'When we get there,' said Niemand, 'we want to be inside quickly. How does it open?'

'Remote,' she said. 'You punch in the code.'

'How far away?'

'You have to be at the gates.'

'Put in the code now.'

Mrs Shawn searched in her bag, found a device. 'I can't see,' she said. She was too vain to put on her reading glasses, held the control close to her face and tentatively pressed soft buttons.

'I *think* I've done it,' she said.

Zeke turned his head to Niemand, who kept his eyes on the rear-view screen.

The house was in a leafy street in Saxonwold, a rich part of the city. It was one of four large mock-Georgian houses built on land carved from the grounds of a mansion. The perimeter walls were three metres high, topped with razor wire. As Zeke drew up in front of the steel gates, Niemand opened his door.

'Open them,' said Niemand. 'Close as soon as you're in, Mrs Shawn.'

'It's very fast,' she said.

'Me too.'

Niemand was out, on the edge of the kerb, looking around. Early summer Highveld dusk, fresh-smelling, hint of jacaranda blossom in a broad street, no traffic, a calm street, a stockbrokers' street, a place to come home to, have a swim, pour a big scotch, shed the cares of the day. There was a sharp sound, the gates unmated, and Zeke drove into the driveway, a walled corridor leading to the doors of a three-car garage.

Niemand, walking backwards, got inside just before the gates met.

On the driver's side, a 14-inch security monitor was mounted against the wall under a small roof. Mrs Shawn handed Zeke another remote control. With Niemand leaning against the car, they went on a video tour of the house, room by room, two-camera vision. It was furnished in a stark style, steel louvre internal shutters instead of curtains, not many places to hide. Beside the monitor a green light glowed. It meant that no window and no door, internal or external, had been opened or closed since the alarm was activated.

'Looks okay,' said Niemand. 'Let's see the garage.'

There was one vehicle in it, a black Jeep four-wheel drive. A camera at floor level showed no one hiding underneath it.

Niemand gestured.

Mrs Shawn used the remote.

The left-hand door rose. Pistol out, held at waist level in front of his body, Niemand went in, looked into the Jeep, waved to Zeke. He parked behind the Jeep, and the garage door descended. Zeke took the short-barrel, pistol-handled automatic shotgun out of its clips under the driver's seat.

Mrs Shawn unlocked the steel door into the house with a card and a key.

Niemand went first, Zeke behind him.

They were in a hallway painted in tones of grey, mulberry carpet, a single painting under a downlight, a print, Cezanne. Niemand liked paintings, even paintings he didn't understand. He bought art books sometimes, threw them out after a while.

Mrs Shawn disarmed the alarm system.

'Wait here,' said Niemand.

She shook her head vigorously. 'No, I don't want to be on my own.'

Niemand in front, they went into a passage, then into every room. He opened every cupboard, every wardrobe, Zeke covering him. The beds were all box, no way to hide under them.

In the sitting room, for the second time, Niemand said, 'You can relax, Mrs Shawn.'

He holstered the pistol, didn't feel relaxed.

She went into the kitchen and came back holding a bottle of champagne, Veuve Clicquot, and a flute, a crystal flute. 'I'm having a glass of bubbly,' she said. 'This all makes me so tense. There's everything else. Beer, scotch, whatever.'

The men shook their heads. 'You're expecting Mr Shawn when?' said Niemand.

She brought her watch up to her face. 'Any time now, any time. Can you get the top of this off for me?' She held out the bottle to Niemand. He took it and offered it to Zeke, who put the shotgun on a chair.

'He does champagne,' Niemand said. 'I do beer bottles. With my teeth.'

Mrs Shawn smiled, a wary smile, uncertain of Niemand's drift, whether she'd been wrong in automatically asking the white man. Zeke stripped off the foil, removed the cage, wriggled the cork out slowly, no bang, just a whimper of gas, poured.

'Thank you,' said Mrs Shawn. 'You are an expert.'

Zeke smiled and took the bottle into the kitchen.

Mrs Shawn drank half the glass. 'Jesus, that's better,' she said. 'Let's sit.'

They sat on the leather chairs. Zeke came out of the kitchen. 'Calls to make,' he said. He left the room, closed the door. Mrs Shawn knocked back the rest of her glass, went into the kitchen. Niemand heard a cupboard open, close. Silence. She came back with a full glass and the bottle.

'Well,' said Mrs Shawn, sitting, smiling the smile, crossing her legs. Niemand knew the coke smile. He looked at her legs. They were brown legs, filling out in the thighs, the feet in soft-looking shoes. 'Home at last,' she said. 'You're very professional ... what do I call you?'

'Mike,' said Niemand. He held her eyes, smiled, looked at his watch. He had a bad feeling about this house, the kind of feeling that had sometimes come over him on patrol, brought on by nothing in particular. 'The houses next door, you know the people?'

She drank. 'Well, we're the longest survivors in the row here. What, two months, just under. Can you believe that?' She closed her eyes, stubby eyelashes. 'I was so naive when we came. I mean, I thought it'd be like Malaysia. I lived there with my first husband, we had this lovely house in KL – the poor don't bother you there. Jesus, what a shock I got. I hate this fucking country, I'd be back in the UK tomorrow ...'

Niemand was already tired of listening to her. He was forced to listen to people like her every day. To some people, he called his business Parasite Protection.

'... Bloody Brett told me it was going to be for two or three weeks. Then people are buggering him around, the deal falls through, next thing ...'

'Don't know the neighbours?' Niemand said.

She blinked, had trouble adjusting. 'Well, I see the people on that side every now and then.' She gestured with a thumb to the left. 'To wave to. They're Americans. With live-in security. An Israeli. He used to be one of the Prime Minister's bodyguards. Christ knows what that costs.'

'The other side?'

'Empty. They left a few weeks ago. Only here for a few months. Lucky them.' A phone rang, in two places. She drained her glass, went to the kitchen.

There was something wrong here.

Niemand went into the passage, looked up and down, went into the dining room, a formal dining room with a big blond table and ten chairs. Zeke was on his mobile, half-sitting on the table. He looked at Niemand, raised an eyebrow. Niemand shrugged, went back to the sitting room.

Mrs Shawn was coming out of the kitchen, glass refilled.

'My husband,' she said. 'He'll be here in a minute. He's going to London tomorrow. Won't take me. Sometimes I think he'd like to see me murdered.'

Niemand felt some of his feeling go away, went out to escort the husband in. The driveway and street outside were floodlit, bright as day, and as the man drove the Audi past him, he saw a chubby face.

In the garage, the man got out, briefcase in his left hand, looked at his watch. He was short and paunchy and even an expensive suit didn't improve that.

'Just you?' he said.

Niemand shook his head. 'My partner's inside.'

The man looked at him. He'd been drinking, face flushed. 'What colour's he?'

'Black.'

'No blacks in the house. Don't trust any black.' He pointed at the floor. 'Next time, he waits here.'

This man should be allowed to die violently, thought Niemand. He didn't say anything, walked to the door into the house and waited.

The man came over and opened the door. Niemand went in first, went through the hall, into the sitting room. The woman was standing in the kitchen doorway, champagne flute in hand. Zeke was sitting in a leather chair, the shotgun on his thighs.

Brett Shawn dropped the briefcase on a chair, was taking off his jacket, didn't look at his wife, eyes on Zeke, threw the expensive garment sideways, careless of where it fell, walked to the middle of the room, made a stand-up sign to Zeke, palm upwards, short fingers held together, flicking urgently.

'Up,' he said. 'On your bike. Don't pay a bloody fortune to have people sit on my bloody furniture.'

Zeke's expression didn't change. He stood, weapon at the end of a slack arm, looked at Niemand. Niemand nodded at Mrs Shawn. 'Thank you,' she said. 'Thank you both.'

Brett Shawn went into the passage first, Zeke behind him. Shawn was at the door to the hall, had his hand on the door handle, when the hair on the back of Niemand's skull pricked. He looked up, saw something on the ceiling behind him, something at the edge of his vision, a dark line not there before, shouted Zeke's name, spinning around, finding the pistol at his waist, throwing himself away from the line of sight, hitting the floor, rolling into position.

The man in the ceiling pushed open the inspection hatch, fired a pumpgun, hit Shawn in the side of his belly as he turned around, in the pinstriped shirt distended over the sagging gut, almost cut him in half, fired again. Zeke raised his shotgun and fired at the ceiling without turning, just his head tilted backwards, deafening noise in the corridor. Then Zeke's head blew apart, a balloon of blood and bone and pink and grey material exploding.

Niemand had the .38 out, was about to fire into the roof behind the inspection hatch, didn't.

Waited.

Silence.

A noise overhead, a bumping sound.

Waited.

A shortened shotgun dropped into the passage. Then a bare arm and a shoulder in a T-shirt fell through the hatch. A dark hand dangled.

Niemand registered the voice of Mrs Shawn screaming. He paid no attention, reached forward, got Zeke's shotgun, ran his hand over his friend's head, smeared his own throat and chest with Zeke's blood, lay back and looked at the hatch.

Mrs Shawn stopped screaming.

Behind him, the door to the sitting room opened. Niemand closed his eyes.

Mrs Shawn screamed again, slammed the door.

Niemand lay on the mulberry carpet, shotgun at his side, eyes closed, looking through his lashes at the hatch.

Nothing. Just blood running down the bare arm, down the fingers, dripping.

Mrs Shawn was shouting. She was on the telephone. She'd got through to someone. Niemand couldn't make out the words.

They'd been in the ceiling all the time. They'd come via the empty house next door, probably bridged the gap between the roofs with a ladder.

Niemand waited. His sight was going fuzzy. No sound from above.

Dead or gone, he thought.

He tensed his shoulder muscles, readied himself to get up.

A scraping noise.

The gunman's body fell through the hatch, landed in front of him, just missed his feet, blood going everywhere.

He'd been pushed.

Niemand didn't move, didn't breathe.

The other person in the ceiling didn't have a firearm, his instinct told him that. And the person was running out of time: the rest of the team would be close now, waiting to have the gates opened for them. If it didn't happen soon, they would probably desert him.

Seen through his lashes, the hatch was just a black square.

Nothing happened.

Niemand heard the door to the sitting room open.

Mrs Shawn didn't scream this time, she said, in a small voice, a child's voice, 'Oh, Jesus, God, are you all dead?'

Niemand was looking at the hatch through his lashes.

Nothing.

Feet first.

The black man came out of the hole feet first, just stepped into air, dropped from the roof like an acrobat, long butcher's knife held to his chest.

Mrs Shawn screamed, high-pitched, the scream of steel meeting steel at great speed.

The man landed feet astride his partner's body, a slightly built man, perfectly balanced, as if he'd jumped from a chair, knife hand down, the blade pointed at Mrs Shawn.

'Shut up, bitch,' he said.

He looked at Niemand lying on the floor, didn't change his grip on the knife, took a step forward, bent at the waist, took his arm back to put the blade into Niemand's groin, sever the femoral artery.

'No!' Mrs Shawn, the abrading metal shriek.

Niemand opened his eyes, raised the shotgun, pulled the trigger, heard the hammer fall.

Nothing. Shell malfunction, one in five thousand chance.

The man lunged.

Niemand brought his right leg up, kicked as hard as he could, his shin just below the knee made contact with the man's crotch, a shout of pain, he saw the knife hand move away, sat up, braced himself on his left hand, hooked his left knee around the man's right calf, rolled savagely to the left, right knee pressing in the man's upper thigh.

He felt the joint give, tendons, cartilage tearing, saw the man hit the wall with his shoulder, head turning sideways, mouth open and twisted in pain and surprise, saw the teeth and the furred tongue, the knife hand coming around, the knife huge, shining. Pain in his shoulder. He grabbed for the man's wrist with his left hand, clubbed at his head with the shotgun, laid the short barrel across his jaw and his ear, pulled the weapon back ...

The shotgun went off, a shocking concussion. Niemand hadn't realised he'd pulled the trigger.

For a second, they were frozen, two men, one black, one white, legs twisted and locked together, faces close, looking into each other's eyes.

He's strong, Niemand thought.

The man got his right hand on the shotgun barrel, had the advantage of pushing. Niemand felt the strength leaving his left arm, he was going to lose this, he wasn't the quickest this time, he could see the knife blade, see his blood on it.

No. He couldn't die here, in this bastard's house, in the service of this English prick.

He let his right arm go slack, caught the black man by surprise, pushed the shotgun barrel at him, pulled the trigger.

It worked. Eyes closed against the muzzle flash, he saw its furnace flame through his lids, felt it burn his face, felt the man go limp, felt hot liquid in his mouth and his eyes and up his nostrils.

After a time, ears ringing, he pushed the body away and raised his shoulders from the darkening mulberry carpet.

'Mrs Shawn?'

No reply.

He got to his knees.

She was on her back, one leg folded under her, one outstretched. He looked at her and knew she was dead. He didn't need to feel for a pulse. He did.

She was dead. He'd shot her in the chest. When the man was on him and he'd pulled the trigger he'd shot Mrs Shawn.

She would have been trying to help him. He remembered her shout. She'd shouted and then she would have been trying to help him.

He got up, went into the kitchen, wiped Zeke's shotgun, went back and put it into his friend's hands. He had to bend them, rearrange him. He wanted to kiss Zeke goodbye, kiss him on what remained of his face, but he didn't. Zeke wouldn't have wanted that.

Then, quickly, he kissed Zeke's throat. It was still warm.

He rang Christa, had a look around, found the coke stash, opened Brett Shawn's big briefcase, a small suitcase.

A large yellow envelope holding three stacks of American $100 bills, perhaps $20,000. Three yellow envelopes, papers, two telephone books of papers. A video cassette with a piece of paper taped to it, letters, numbers written in a slanty hand.

Niemand took the envelopes and the cassette and

went out to the Mercedes, Colt in his hand. No sign of the intruders' friends or the Israeli next door. He put the stolen goods in the safe box under the floor. Then he went back inside and did a line of coke while he waited, two lines. He thought it was a weakness to use drugs, could take them or leave them, but he couldn't bear the idea of wasting coke on the police.

He was flushing the rest down the sink when the telephone rang.

He let it ring, dried his hands, then he couldn't bear it and picked it up. Long-distance call.

'Shawn?'

'Mr Shawn's had an accident. He's dead.'

A silence.

'And you are?' An accent. German?

Niemand gave it some thought. 'An employee,' he said.

'Shawn had some papers. And a tape. You have them?'

'Yes.'

'I assume you'll be bringing them out?'

More thought. 'What's it worth?' Niemand said.

'For the London delivery, the agreed sum. Ten thousand pounds. And expenses. Return airfares and so on. Say another five thousand.'

'Twenty thousand,' said Niemand. 'And expenses.'

'Done. When you get to London, this is what you do …'

He should have asked for more.

2

HAMBURG

TILDERS RANG just before four. Anselm was on the balcony, smoking, looking at the choppy lake, the Aussen-Alster, massaging the lifeless fingers of his left hand, thinking about his brother and money, about how short the summers were becoming, shorter every year. Beate tapped on the glass door, offered the cordless telephone.

Anselm flicked the cigarette, went to the door and took the phone.

'Got him,' said Tilders.

'Yes?' said Anselm. Tilders was talking about a man called Serrano. 'Where?'

'*Hauptbahnhof*, 7.10. On the *Schnellzug* from Cologne.'

'Train? This boy?'

'Yes. Three of them now.'

'How's that?'

'There's a woman. Otto says the muscle went out and bought a case and she's carrying it.'

Serrano's bodyguard was a Hungarian called Zander, also known as Sanders, Sweetman, Kendall. These were just the names they knew.

'Call back in five,' said Anselm. 'I've got to consult the client.'

He went to his desk and rang O'Malley in England.

O'Malley wasn't in, would be contacted and told to ring immediately. Anselm went back to the balcony, lit another Camel, watched the ferry docking. The day was darkening now and rain was in the air. Above the sturdy craft, a mob of gulls hovered, jostling black-eyed predators eyeing the boat as if it contained edible things, which it did. He had a dim memory of being taken on his first ferry ride on the Alster, on the day the *schwanenvater* brought out the swans from their winter refuge. The man chugged out of a canal in his little boat towing a boom. Behind it were hundreds of swans and, in the open water, pairs began to peel off to seek out their canals. For years, Anselm thought this happened every day, every day a man brought the swans out, the Pied Piper of swans.

He heard the door open behind him.

'Herr Anselm?'

The pale bookkeeper. Could an approach be more obsequious? What made some people so timid? History, Anselm thought, history. He turned. 'Herr Brinkman.'

'May I raise a matter, Herr Anselm?' Brinkman bit his lower lip. Some colour came into it.

'Raise it to the skies.'

Brinkman looked around for eavesdroppers, spoke in an even lower voice. 'I don't like to bring this up, Herr Anselm, but you are the senior person here. Herr Baader does not seem to grasp the urgency. The landlord is making serious threats about the arrears. And there are other problems.'

'He'll be back soon. I'll impress the urgency of this on him,' said Anselm.

Baader owned the business. He was in the West Indies on honeymoon. Honeymoon number four, was it five?

'There is more,' said Brinkman.

'Yes?'

Brinkman moved his head from side to side, bit his lower lip.

'What is it?'

'Herr Baader wants me to charge certain expenses to the firm which we cannot justify as business expenditure. I could go to jail.'

Anselm wasn't in the least surprised. 'Have you mentioned your concerns to him?'

Brinkman nodded. 'He doesn't hear me.'

'I'll talk to him.'

'Herr Anselm, Herr Baader interferes in the payments.'

'How?'

'He signs some cheques. Others don't come back to me.'

'I'll talk to him. I promise.'

Duty done, fearful, Brinkman nodded. Anselm turned back to the window and thought about Baader and his lusts, his juggling of the accounts.

The tap on the glass. Beate with the cordless, again.

It was O'Malley. He whistled when Anselm told him about Serrano.

'You're sure it's his case she's carrying, boyo?'

'Yes,' said Anselm. Tilders didn't say yes when he meant, I think so. He had trained Otto and Baader had trained him and Baader had been properly trained at everything except probity in accounting.

'Not socks and shirts and the dirty underpants?' said O'Malley.

'Could be hand-carved dildos and old copies of *Vatican News* for all we know.'

'Shit,' said O'Malley. 'John, I'm desperate on this bastard. We need a look, just a quick look. Minutes.'

'Take a look,' said Anselm. 'Feel free. You have the time and place. Our work is done.'

'John, John.'

'Not our usual line of work,' said Anselm. 'You know that.'

'Nonsense, I know Baader would do it.'

He would too, thought Anselm. 'I don't know that. Ring him on his mobile.'

'Listen, you can find someone to do it, John.'

'Even if I could, these things come home to you.'

'Ten grand.'

'What do you want for ten grand?'

He told Anselm, who sighed. 'That's all? Take on a bodyguard for ten grand? The prick may take his job seriously. I am of the absolutely not opinion.'

'Twelve.'

Anselm thought about it. He knew they shouldn't get involved in things like this. But there were salaries to be paid, including his. He knew someone who might be able to arrange it for a thousand, fifteen hundred dollars. 'No,' he said.

'Twelve, that's it.'

'Fifteen, win or lose.'

O'Malley's turn to sigh. 'Jesus, you're hard.'

Anselm pulled a face. He could have got twenty, more. He disconnected and rang Tilders. 'There's something we have to do.'

'Yes,' said Tilders. 'What?'

'What kind of case did Zander buy?'

'Aluminium photographer's case.'

Anselm was silent for so long that Tilders thought the line had died. 'John?'

'Tell Otto to buy one. The same. Exactly.'

It took a call to the locksmith and four more calls, twenty minutes on the phone.

3

HAMBURG

THE *SCHNELLZUG* slid into the huge vaulted station, punctual to the second by the *Hauptbahnhof*'s great clock. Zander, the bodyguard, appeared first, blocked the doorway of his sleek carriage and didn't give a damn, looked around, took his time. He was slight for someone in his line of work, blond and elegant in a dark suit, jacket unbuttoned. When he was satisfied, he moved to his left and Serrano stepped onto the platform. He too was in a dark suit but there was nothing elegant about him. He was short and podgy, a sheen on his face, hair that looked lacquered, and a roll of fat over his collar. A laptop computer case was slung over his shoulder.

Next off was a middle-aged businessman, a man with a pinched and unhappy face who raised his head and sniffed the stale station air. After him came an elderly woman, an embalmed face, every detail of her attire perfect, then a family of four, the parents first. Once *Gastarbeiter* from Anatolia, Anselm thought, now wealthy. Their teenage boy and girl followed, citizens of nowhere and everywhere. The pair were listening to music on headphones, moving their heads like sufferers from some exotic ailment.

A woman was in the doorway. She was thirty, perhaps, in black, pants, sensible heels, dark hair scraped back, charcoal lipstick. Her face was severe, sharp planes, not unattractive.

'The woman,' said Tilders. He had a mobile to his face, a long, earnest philosopher's face, a face made for pondering.

Anselm half turned, sipped some *Apfelkorn* from the small bottle, swilled it around his mouth, felt the soft burn of the alcohol. He was on his second one. He was scared of a panic attack and drink seemed to help keep them away. He drank too much anyway, didn't care except in the pre-dawn hours, the badlands of the night. The woman was carrying an aluminium case in her left hand, carrying it easily.

'From the East,' said Tilders.

'Sure it's just three?'

'Don't blame me,' said Tilders. 'This is not our kind of work. Is it on?'

Anselm drained the tiny bottle. 'Yes,' he said. 'Blame's all mine.'

Tilders spoke into his mobile. They followed the woman and Serrano and his bodyguard down the platform towards the escalator that led to the concourse. The woman kept a steady distance behind the men, people between them. On the crowded escalator, Zander looked back once, just a casual glance. Serrano had his head down, a man not interested in his surroundings, standing in the lee of his hired shield.

When they reached the concourse, Zander paused, looked around again, then went right, towards the Kirchenallee exit. The woman didn't hesitate when she reached the concourse, turned right too, walking briskly.

The concourse was crowded, workers and shoppers, travellers, youths on skates, buskers, beggars, petty criminals, pimps, whores, hustlers.

Zander and Serrano were almost at the exit. Zander

28

looked around again. The woman had been blocked by a group of schoolchildren on an excursion. She was ten metres behind them.

'Getting late,' said Anselm. This wasn't going to work, he was sure of it.

'*Scheisse*,' said Tilders.

From nowhere came the gypsy boy, moving through the crowd at a half-run, twisting around people, a wiry child in a drab anorak, tousled black hair, ran straight into the woman, bumped her in the ribcage with his shoulder, hard, bumped her again as she went back. She fell down, hit the ground heavily, but held onto the case.

Without hesitation, the boy stomped on her hand with a heavy Doc Martens boot, thick-soled. She screamed in pain, opened her hand. He grabbed the aluminium case with his left hand but she hooked an arm around his left leg.

The boy kicked her in the neck, stooped and punched her in the mouth, between the breasts, one, two, his right hand, a fist like a small bag of marbles. The woman fell back, no heart for hanging on. He was off, running for the exit.

No one did anything. People didn't want to get involved in these things. They happened all the time and it was dangerous to tackle the thieves. Even young children sometimes produced knives, slashed wildly. Recently, a man had been stabbed in the groin, twice, died in the ambulance. A father of three.

But Zander was suddenly there, running smoothly, going around people like a fish. The boy's start wasn't big enough, the woman had been too close to Zander, it had taken too long to get the case away from her.

'*Scheisse*,' said Tilders again.

Then someone in the crowd seemed to stumble, bumping a long-haired man into Zander's path. The man went to one knee. Zander tried to avoid him but he couldn't. His left leg made contact with the man. He lost his balance, fell sideways, bounced off the ground, came to his feet like a marionette pulled up by strings.

It was too late. The boy was gone, the crowd closed behind him. Zander paused, uncertain, looked back. Serrano had joined the woman, outrage and desperation on his face, both arms in the air. Zander got the message, turned to take off after the boy again, realised it was hopeless, stopped and walked back to Serrano. Serrano was enraged. Anselm could see spit leave his mouth, see Zander recoil. Neither of them looked at the woman, she'd failed them.

Two policemen arrived, one talking into his throat mike. The woman was on her feet, nose bleeding a little, blood black in the artificial light, her right hand massaging her breastbone. Her hair had come loose and she had to brush it back with her left hand. She looked much younger, like a teenager.

A third policeman appeared, told the crowd to get moving, the excitement was over.

The woman was telling her story to the two cops. They were shaking their heads.

Anselm looked at Tilders, who was looking at his watch. Anselm felt the inner trembling, a bad sign. He went over to the newspaper kiosk, bought an *Abendblatt*. The economy was slowing, the metal-workers' union was making threats, another political bribery scandal in the making. He went back, stood behind Tilders.

'How long?'

'Five minutes.'

Serrano and Zander were arguing, the short man's hands moving, Zander tossing his head, arms slack at his sides. Serrano made a dismissive gesture, final.

Anselm said, 'I think we're at the limit here.'

A tall man was coming through the crowd, a man wearing a cap, a blue-collar worker by his appearance. The throng parted for him. In one hand, he had the gypsy boy by the scruff of the neck, in the other, he had the photographer's case, held up as if weightless.

The woman and the policemen went towards them. When they were a few metres away, the boy squirmed like a cat, turned towards his captor, stamped on his left instep, punched him in the stomach. The man's face contorted, he lost his grip on his captive and the boy was gone, flying back the way he had first fled.

'What can you do?' said the man to the woman. 'The scum are taking over the whole world. Is this yours?'

Serrano came up behind the woman. He was flushed, had money in his hand, notes, a wad, offered it. The man in the cap shrugged, uncertain. 'It's not necessary,' he said. 'It's a citizen's duty.'

'Many thanks,' said Serrano, taking the case. 'Take the money. You deserve it.'

The man took the money, looked at it, put it in his hip pocket. 'I'll buy the children something,' he said. He turned and walked back the way he'd come, limping a little from the stomp.

Tilders went on his way. Anselm forced himself to take his time leaving, found the car parked in a no-standing zone, engine running. In Mittelweg, Fat Otto, the man who had bumped the innocent commuter into Zander's path, said, 'Kid's something, isn't he? Deserves a bonus.'

'Deserves to be jailed now before he's even more dangerous,' said Anselm.

His mobile rang. Tilders, the expressionless tone. 'They got about fifty pages. Out of two hundred, they guess.'

'That's good. Get it printed.'

'The reason it took three to transport the case,' said Tilders, 'is probably the diamonds.'

'Ah.'

Anselm took out his mobile and rang Bowden International. O'Malley was in this time. 'About fifty pages. Out of perhaps two hundred.'

'Good on you. As much as could be expected. I'll send someone.' This is the moment, Anselm thought. 'We'll need the account settled in full on delivery,' he said. 'Including bonus.'

'What's this? We don't pay our bills?'

Anselm closed his eyes. He'd never wanted anything to do with the money side. 'No offence. Things are a little tight. You know how it goes.'

A pause. 'Give our man the invoice. He'll give you a cheque.' Pause. 'Accept our cheque, *compadre*?'

'With deep and grovelling gratitude.'

Anselm put the phone away, relieved. They were sitting in the traffic. 'Any takers for a drink?' he said. Fat Otto looked at him, eye flick.

'I'm offering to buy you lot a drink,' Anselm said. He knew what the man was thinking. 'Grasp the idea, can you?'

They went to the place on Sierichstrasse. He'd been there alone a few times, sat in the dark corner, fighting his fear of being in public, his paranoia about people, about the knowingness he saw in the eyes of strangers.

4

HAMBURG

IN THE closing deep-purple light of the day, Anselm turned the corner and saw the Audi parked across the narrow street from his front gate. He registered someone in the driver's seat and the jangle of alarm went through him, tightened the muscles of his face, his scalp, retracted his testicles.

He kept walking, feeling his heart drumming, the tightness in his chest. Not twice, not in a quiet street, not in a peaceful country. It wouldn't happen to him again. To him, no. Not here, not to him. No.

Just one person in the car, a man, there was another car further down, a BMW, empty.

The driver of the Audi got out. Not a man, a woman in a raincoat, shoulder-length hair, rimless glasses she was taking off.

'John Anselm?'

He didn't answer, eyes going to the BMW, back to her car.

'Alex Koenig,' she said. 'I've been writing to you.' She closed the car door, opened it again, slammed it, came around the front. 'Damn door,' she said. 'It's a new car. I was about to drive off.'

A shudder passed through him, an aftershock. He remembered the letters. Doctor Alex Koenig from Hamburg University had written to him twice asking for a meeting. He had not replied, thrown the letters away. People wanted to ask him questions about Beirut and he didn't want to answer them.

'I thought you were a man,' he said.

'A man?'

'Your first name.'

She smiled, a big mouth, too big for her face. 'That's a problem? If I were a man?'

'No,' said Anselm. 'The problem at the moment is how you got this address.'

'David Riccardi gave it to me.'

'He shouldn't have done that,' Anselm said. 'You stalk people, is that what you do?'

She had a long face and a long nose and she had assumed a chastised look, eyelids at half-mast, a sinner in a third-rate Italian religious painting. 'I'm sorry, I didn't mean to give you that impression.'

'Well, goodbye,' Anselm said.

'I'd really like to talk to you.'

'No. There's nothing I want to talk about.'

'I'd appreciate it very much,' she said quietly, head on one side.

He was going to say no again, but for some reason – drink, loneliness, perversity – he turned, unbalanced by liquor, and held the gate open for her.

In the house, standing in the empty panelled hall, taking off her raincoat, she looked around and said, 'This is impressive.'

'I'm glad you're impressed.' He led the way into the sitting room, put on lights. He rarely used the large room, with its doors onto the terrace. He lived in the kitchen and the upstairs study. 'A drink? I'm drinking whisky.'

'Thank you. With water, please.'

He poured the drinks in the kitchen, gave himself

three fingers. When he returned with the tray, she was looking at the family photographs hung between the deep windows. She was tall, almost his height, carried herself upright.

'How many generations in this picture?' she said, turning her head to him.

Anselm didn't need to look. He knew the photograph. 'A few,' he said, sitting down. He was already regretting letting her in, offering the drink. What had come over him? He didn't want to answer questions, didn't want her prying. 'What can I do for you?'

She sat opposite him, in the ornately carved wooden chair. 'As I said in the letters ...'

'I didn't read your letters. Unsolicited mail. How did you know where to send them? Riccardi?'

'No. I only met him a few days ago. I asked the news agency to forward the letters.'

'Kind of them.'

He hadn't worked for the agency since before Beirut, hadn't spoken to anyone there in a long time, five or six years, had never received anything in the mail from them. How would the agency know his address?

'Why would they do that?' he said.

She shifted in her chair, recrossed her legs, long legs. She was wearing grey flannels and low-heeled shoes. 'I'm a psychiatrist. I told them I was doing research.'

'That's a good reason is it?' He drank half his whisky and couldn't taste it, wished he'd made it stronger, the bad sign. 'Psychiatrist. Is that a special licence to invade people's privacy?'

Alex Koenig smiled, shrugged. 'I spoke to a man, I told him I was researching post-traumatic stress disorder suffered by hostages and that I very much wanted to talk to you. It was just a request. I would write to you. You could say no.'

'I didn't respond. That's no.'

'Well, I thought they hadn't forwarded the letters.'

'So you extracted my address from Riccardi.'

She laughed, not a confident laugh. 'I have to say I didn't do that. He offered the address, he said he'd ring you.'

'Well I have to say I don't have any disorder so you're wasting your time.'

She nodded. 'As you know, the symptoms can take a long time …'

'When it happens, I'll let you know. Until then there's nothing I can tell you.'

They sat in silence. Anselm felt another bad sign, the urge to disconcert, didn't care and looked at her breasts, looked into her eyes, looked down again. She was wearing a white shirt, fresh, well ironed, creases down the arms.

Alex Koenig looked down at herself, looked up at him.

'They're not very big,' said Anselm. 'Size means everything to tit men.'

He could see her slow inhalation, the slow expulsion.

'Well,' she said, 'my body aside, my research is into the relationship between post-traumatic stress disorder and the life history and personality of victims.'

Anselm felt the dangerous light-headedness coming over him, the sense of trembling inside, knew he should end this encounter. He drained his glass, went to the kitchen and half filled it, no water, came back and sat down. The light from the table lamp lit one side of her face, emphasised her nose, the fullness of her lips.

'Life history? That's what you're interested in?'

'Yes.'

'And personality?'

'Yes.'

'I've got those. Both. Two out of three. Missing only the disorder.'

Silence.

'Would you like to see my scrapbook? Stories from foreign wars? Pictures of dead people? Mutilated bodies?'

'If you'd like to show it to me,' she said.

'The shrink answer. If you'd *like* to. What would *you* like, Frau Koenig? It that Frau? Frau Doctor Koenig?'

'Alex is fine.'

'Alex is too informal for me, Doctor.' He felt himself speeding up. 'I think we need to keep a professional German distance here. Are you German? You don't look German. Some kind of *Auslander*, perhaps? A member of a lesser race? That's not quite an Aryan nose, not that I mind it, of course.'

'My father is Austrian.'

Anselm drank, a swig. 'Austrian? Of course. A psychiatrist, where else would your father be? The land of Freud, Jung and Adler. Adler never quite made it did he? A lesser light. I can't quite remember where Adler went wrong. You'd know, wouldn't you? Sorry, that might offend. Not an Adlerian are you, Doctor?'

'No.'

'Right. What about Jung? A Jungian. He was a big prick, wasn't he? Saw this huge one as a child as I remember it. This massive phallus. In a dream. Is that right, Doctor Professor?'

'I'm not a Jungian.'

Anselm couldn't stop himself. He leaned forward. 'Dream about massive phalluses too, do you? Monsters? Huge pricks with men attached?'

'I'm not an analyst.' Her smile was tight.

'No? You'd be into drugs then. Terrific. I'm with you. The best approach is drugs. Just give the crazies drugs. For fuck's sake, they're deranged, shoot them full of drugs, that'll keep the nuts quiet.'

Alex Koenig hadn't taken her eyes off him.

'Unfortunately I didn't keep a scrapbook,' said Anselm. 'And I don't remember much about my illustrious career. That's got nothing to do with post-traumatic stress. That's the result of being struck on the head with a rifle butt. But I do remember that trouble spots are all the same. Only the colours of the people change. Outside. Inside they're all the same colours. Red and pink and white. The intestines, they're a sort of blue, purply blue, the colour of baby birds, seen baby birds? Only they're wet and slimy, like big worms. Big earthworms or the worms in swordfish. People worms.'

He sat back and smiled at her. 'Well, so much for my life history. That leaves personality, doesn't it? Is that in the ordinary meaning? Or is it *persona* we're talking about? The mask, the actor's mask? Your Jung was keen on that, wasn't he? Stupid phallic fart that he was.'

He waited. The way she was looking at him, her silence, her neutrality, brought back the American military psychiatrist.

'What kind of shrink are you?' he said. 'Are you a couch-type? Plenty of couches in this house. We could talk on a couch, how's that? Both on it. Prone and supine. Which would you be?'

There was a long silence. Then Alex Koenig stood up, eyes on his, glass held in both hands, licked her lower lip, a slither of pink tongue. 'I like both,' she said. 'I like to alternate. I like to fuck and be fucked. But you wouldn't be much good either way, Herr Anselm. Your prick's useless. Even if you wanted to fuck me, you couldn't. You're not a performer. You're impotent.'

He sat in the armchair and heard the heavy front door close behind her. He stayed there, head back, massaging the fingers that wouldn't work, and after a time he fell asleep, waking beyond midnight, stumbling to his cold unmade bed in the room where his grandfather had died.

5

HAMBURG

ANSELM ALWAYS woke early, no matter how much he'd drunk, got up immediately, couldn't bear the thoughts that lying awake in bed brought. Showered, dressed, some toast eaten, he wandered the house, watched television for a few minutes at a time, too early to go to work. There was always something to look at. Anselms had lived in the house since before World War One. It had been built by his great-grandfather, Gustav. Bits of family history were everywhere – paintings, photographs, books with inscriptions, letters stuck in them to mark pages, three volumes of handwritten recipes, an ivory-handled walking stick, diaries in High German, collections of invitation cards, wooden jigsaws, mechanical toys, there was no end to the Anselm relics. In the empty, cobwebbed wine cellar, he had found a single bottle stuck too deep into a rack, 1937 Lafite. He'd opened it: corked, undrinkable.

Today, he took the tape recorder to the kitchen, sat at the table. In the damp hole in Beirut, Anselm's thoughts had often turned to his great-aunt Pauline. His first memories of her were when he was eight or nine. She was always very old in his mind, thin, wiry, always in grey, a shade of grey, high collars, strong grey hair, straight hair, severely cut. She smoked cigarillos in a holder. He had no memory of making the recordings.

They had come from San Francisco, four tapes in a box with other tapes.

He pressed the Play button. Hissing, then the voice of great-aunt Pauline.

Of course this house has seen terrible arguments.

Then his young voice.

What about?

Oh, business, how to run the business. Times were difficult before the war. And about the Nazis, Hitler.

Who argued about Hitler?

Your grandfather and your great-grandfather. With Moritz.

I don't know anything about Moritz.

There was a long silence before Pauline spoke again.

Moritz was so foolish. But he looked like an angel, lovely hair, so blond, he had the face of Count Haubold von Einsiedel, you know the portrait?

No, I don't know it.

The von Rayski portrait? Of course you do, everyone does. I remember one particularly awful evening. We were having a sherry before dinner, we always did, I was fourteen when I was included, just a thimbleful of an old manzanilla fino. Hold it to the light, my father said. See pleasure in a glass. I did. I went to that window, it was summer. They seemed to last much longer then, summers, we had better summers. Much better, much longer.

Another silence.

When was that?

When?

The awful evening.

Oh, I suppose it would have been in '35 or '36. Soon after Stuart's death. Stuart never wanted to be in commerce but he had no choice. Eldest sons were expected to go into the firm. I don't know what he

40

wanted to do. Except paint and ski. But his family, well, they were like ours. Two weeks in Garmisch, they thought that was quite enough relaxation for a year. Anselms had dealt with Armitages for many years, more than a hundred, I suppose. Many, many years. My father used to say we were married to the Armitages long before I married Stuart. He was at Oxford with Stuart's father. They all did law. That was what you did. Of course, the families had almost been joined before. My aunt Cecile was engaged to an Armitage, I forget his name, Henry, yes. Henry, he was killed in the Great War.

The awful evening.

What?

The evening of the terrible argument.

What did I say about that?

Nothing.

Yes. Let's talk about something else.

She talked about her childhood, about rowing on the Alster, birthdays, grand parties, dinners.

We always went to the New Year's Eve ball at the Atlantic. So glamorous. Everyone was there. They had kangaroo tail soup on the menu on New Year's Eve in 1940. That was the first time I went after Stuart's death. Also the last year we went. I went with Frans Erdmann, he was a doctor. Much younger than I was. He died at Stalingrad.

After eight, he left for work, closed the massive front door behind him. The temple of memory, he said to himself. The only memory missing is mine.

6

HAMBURG

ANSELM WALKED along the misty lake shore carrying his running gear in a sports bag. His knees were getting worse and his right hip hurt, but he ran home on most days. The long route on good ones, the slightly shorter one on others. The number of others was increasing.

Today, Baader was coming from the opposite direction, every inch a member of the *Hanseaten*: perfect hair, navy-blue suit, white shirt, grey silk tie, black shoes with toecaps. They all dressed like that, the commercial and professional elite of the *Hansastadt*. They met at the gates to the old mansion on Schöne Aussicht.

'Christ,' said Baader, 'I was hoping that thing was an aberration.'

Anselm looked down at his windbreaker, a nylon garment, padded, quilted, red. 'What's wrong with it?'

'It's football hooligan wear, that's what's wrong with it,' said Baader.

'I aspire to be a football hooligan,' said Anselm. 'Engage in acts of senseless violence.'

'Join the police,' said Baader. 'That way you get a uniform and they pay you.'

They walked up the driveway.

'What's this walking?' said Anselm. Baader drove a Porsche, a new one every year, sometimes more often.

'Being serviced.'

'I didn't know you did that. I thought you bought a new one when the oil got dirty.'

'Lease,' said Baader. He had a long thin face, long nose, and a near-continuous eyebrow, just a thinning in the middle. 'Lease, not buy. Deductible business expense.'

'A joke, Stefan,' said Anselm. 'A very old joke. But on the subject, Brinkman's in a state of panic. He says the kitty's empty.'

Baader stopped, eyed Anselm. 'Brinkman is an old woman,' he said. 'An old woman and a bean counter.'

'Well, he says there aren't many beans to count and some of your expenses aren't deductible. He's worried about illegality. He doesn't want to go to jail.'

Baader shook his head, started walking again. Anselm thought that he knew what was going through the man's mind: I gave this sad, drunken, amnesiac, neurotic prick a job when he was unemployable, too fucked-up even to commit suicide properly. I've put up with behaviour no sane employer would countenance. Now he's the voice of conscience.

'How was the honeymoon?' said Anselm. He should have asked earlier.

'I've had better.'

At the front door, finger on the button, not looking at Anselm, Baader said, 'When there were just three people and I did the books, I made money. Now we have to have fucking super-computers that cost as much as blocks of apartments. Maybe I should go back to three.'

'It's worth a try,' said Anselm. 'Of course, you had fewer ex-wives then and it was pre-Porsches and apartments in Gstadt.'

Baader pressed the button, waved at the camera. From his cubicle, Wolfgang, the day security, unlocked the door.

They went upstairs to the big rooms on the second floor of the grand old building that housed the firm of Weidermann & Kloster. There was no Weidermann, no Kloster and the firm was no longer the publishing house the two men founded after World War Two. Now W&K's business was looking for people, checking on people.

The biggest room was lit by a dim blue light. It held six computer workstations clustered around a bank of servers, a 1000-CPU super-computer, state-of-the-art equipment. Two tired, stale-mouthed, gritty-eyed end-of-shift people were in residence.

Anselm's office led off the room. On the way to it, he passed a shaven-headed man in black sitting on his spine, his head back, eyes closed. He was chewing in a bovine, cud-shifting way.

'You're eating in your sleep, Inskip,' Anselm said. 'Wake up and go home.'

'Home,' said Inskip, not opening his eyes, 'is where they have to take you in. That is not the situation at my lodgings.'

Inskip was new in the job, six months, but he was suited to it, not a normal person. He'd been recommended to Baader by someone who knew his father, once a lieutenant in the Army of the Rhine, now something in the British Foreign Office, probably an MI6 employee. Inskip's mother was a German doctor's daughter and he'd learned German at her knee.

Inskip had a degree in mathematics from Cambridge and his only real job had been six months as a junior lecturer at an English provincial university.

'Kicked out for GMT,' Inskip had told Anselm one night. They were standing on the balcony, smoking, snowflakes dancing in the cold light from the windows.

'GMT?'

'Gross moral turpitude. I committed an unspeakable act.'

'What was it?'

'Search me. No one would speak of it. I was off my face, drink and drugs, so I had no recollection. Anyway, I couldn't be bothered to ask, told them to fuck off. Loathed the place, all ghastly grey concrete, stuck out in these fields, students thick as sheep.'

Now Inskip opened his eyes. 'The Indonesian's on the radar. Two minutes ago.'

'Where?'

The man's name was Sudrajad. He had not been sighted in Europe since stealing four million dollars from a French construction company trying to swing a contract in Indonesia. The French wouldn't have felt so bitter if they'd got it, but it went to Americans who made a member of the Soeharto family a partner in their firm.

'Swissair 207 into Zurich from New York, 11.20.'

A list of names, dates and numbers appeared on his computer screen. Inskip began to scroll it.

'What name?'

'Hamid. The Malaysian passport.'

'Told them?'

'I'm looking for a hotel … here it is. Schweitzerhof. One night. There's a limo booked.'

'Tell them. He may go somewhere of interest on his way to the hotel.'

The clients chasing the Indonesian were a Paris firm of commercial investigators, good clients.

Anselm went into his office and read the night reports. The Serrano watchers said the woman appeared to be paid off at the station. Serrano and the bodyguard went to the Hansa Bank, where the case went into a safe-deposit box. The bodyguard left and Serrano took a cab to the Hotel Abtei in Harvesthude and had not left the premises. This information had been passed on to O'Malley in London.

In the tray was a long complaint about payment from Gerda Broeksma, the firm's representative in Amsterdam. They couldn't afford to lose her. If Anselm understood the figures, she had brought in almost 5 per cent of the firm's turnover in the past year. Holland was good for business. The Dutch were a suspicious lot. They knew that people who left their sitting room curtains open at night were not necessarily without anything to hide.

Anselm went down the short passage to Baader's office. The door was open. He was on the phone, beckoned, pointed to the Marcel Breuer chairs at the window. Anselm sat down. Baader stopped grunting into the phone and came over.

'What?'

'Gerda. She says we're three months behind. She wants to quit.'

Baader put his chin on his hands, closed his eyes. He had long lashes. 'Why does everyone go to you? The caring fucking ear. You running a complaints booth?'

'I don't encourage it, Stefan,' said Anselm. 'Believe me.'

Baader didn't open his eyes. 'No,' he said. 'Sorry. I know you don't. I'm in shit, John. Uschi's skinned me, her fucking lawyer.'

Anselm didn't feel much compassion. He'd rather liked Uschi, a failed singer. Baader had met her through someone who worked for Bertelsmann in the music business. Despite dressing like an old-school *Hanseaten*, Baader frequented the haunts of the Hamburg media types, places like Fusion and Nil and Rive that Anselm read about in *Morgenpost*.

'Then my cousin tips me off, this bio-tech company, get in big and get rich,' said Baader. 'But he didn't tell me to get out even quicker, the whole thing's just gas, a fucking Zeppelin. The prick, I'm going to kill him.'

Pause. 'I may have to sell some of the business,' he said. 'A big piece.'

'Hell of a business to sell,' said Anselm. 'Eighty per cent clearly illegal, the rest lineball.'

Baader opened his eyes. They were dark brown, something of the intelligent dog in them. Alsatian dog. 'But there's a buyer.'

For years, Anselm had been waiting for this. 'Yes?'

'An English company.'

'Yes?'

'Mitchell Harvester. Corporate risk management, that sort of thing. Take 51 per cent, give us all their work.'

'Mitchell Harvester? Is that so? They approached you?'

'Well, indirectly, sounded out, yes. They'll do it through a nominee company, no direct involvement.' Baader looked at him, didn't blink. Nothing.

Anselm stared back for a long time, waited for a sign. He got up, knee pains, left knee worse, found a cigarette and lit it with the old Zippo, disregarding the policy on smoking.

'Stefan,' he said, 'I want you to consider whether fucking teenagers hasn't destroyed important parts of your brain.'

Baader frowned, the single eyebrow dipping in the middle. 'What's wrong, don't want to work for them?'

'For that arm of the United States government, no.'

The frown disappeared. Baader smiled. He looked even more vulpine. 'John,' he said, 'I understand your position. But relax, it's not a problem.'

'No?'

'No. They want you sacked before we do the deal.'

'Fuck you.' Anselm sat down. 'Can we talk about business? I pulled fifteen grand yesterday. Against my better judgment.'

'That's my man,' said Baader, the little smile. 'Already I feel more able to resist a takeover.'

7

JOHANNESBURG

NIEMAND PARKED near the Chinese wholesaler's barred premises in a filthy side street near the market square. Two street boys appeared, danced around him, offered all manner of services. He gave them several notes to guard the car, opened his jacket to show them the gun and threatened them with certain death. To get to the door, he had to step around papers, car bits, cartons, bottles, food containers, pieces of styrofoam, a new pile of human excrement with a filter cigarette stubbed out in it.

The guard, a huge man, knew him.

'Where's the Chinaman?' said Niemand in Zulu. He called the Chinaman *uChina*.

'Deliveries,' said the Zulu. He was behind a steel gate. A shotgun was leaning against the wall, an old Remington, grip polished with hand sweat.

The Chinaman supplied Soweto hawkers, met them on the fringe to hand over goods, payment in cash, not one cent of credit. Niemand and Zeke had ridden shotgun for him for a few months before the escort service job came up. They had been held up four times: Chinaman 4, hijackers 0.

The guard opened the gate. Niemand crossed the storeroom, walked down the aisles of packaged goods that reached to the ceiling. Substandard, damaged, dangerous, mislabelled, overcooked, undercooked, production mistakes, very old, the Chinaman's stock came mostly from Eastern Europe and Asia.

At the doorway of the back room, Niemand pushed aside the curtain. The Chinaman's new wife was sitting in an armchair covered in tigerskin plush velvet, one of four arranged in a row in front of the television set. She heard the sound of the curtain rings, looked over her shoulder, barked his name and went back to watching an advertisement for miracle kitchen knives. A man with a bad hair transplant was sawing slices off a broom handle. Then he went to work on a piece of cheese, processed cheese, sliced off squares of yellow rubber.

'Try that with your favourite knife and see how far you get,' said the salesman.

The camera showed the audience clapping. Many of the people did not look like kitchen-knife buyers. They looked like people recruited from the street to applaud men with irregular hair. The camera showed the set of knives on offer. Eight knives. One of them looked like the weapon in the hand of the man who'd dropped from the ceiling.

'Cutting, chopping, slicing, dicing, they'll never be the same again,' said the salesman.

'Jackie,' said Niemand. 'I've got a video I need to watch.'

The Chinaman had told Niemand that he imported Jackie through an agency in Macau and that his resentful son, sent to take delivery of her at the airport, was screwing his father's new companion within days.

'She says she was a model,' the Chinaman had said. 'I think she model without her clothes on, know what I mean?'

Jackie used the remote to kill the knife man, went to an empty channel, just electronic fizz. 'Put it in,' she said.

Niemand went to the set. There was a video in the slot, something called *The Wedding Singer*. He plugged in Mr Shawn's cassette.

Jackie got up, her nylon dressing gown slid like water, showing a length of thin thigh. She handed over the remote and went to the back door. 'Come and have drink when you finish,' she said, staccato. 'No one to talk to here. Boring.'

Niemand sat on the edge of a chair and found the Play button. Static. It became an aerial view of wooded sub-tropical country, late in the day, shadows. Taken from a helicopter, Niemand thought, probably from the co-pilot's seat, the colour the result of filming through darkened glass.

Then the photographer was descending and Niemand wasn't sure what he was looking at, a fire, fires, an African village burning, thatched huts on fire, perhaps two or three dozen, cultivated ground around them ...

The camera went left and another helicopter could be seen, a Puma, no markings visible. Now they were on the ground and the filming was being done through the open door of the helicopter, a dark edge visible.

There were bodies everywhere, dozens and dozens of bodies. Black people.

The camera zoomed in on a group, at least a dozen people near what looked like a water trough made of steel drums sliced vertically and welded together. Black people, poorly dressed, most of them women and children, a baby, lying on the ground, hands held to their faces, some face down as if trying to kiss the packed dirt.

Men in uniform came into view, white men in combat gear carrying automatic weapons. Niemand recognised the firearms, American weapons. The soldiers were Americans. Niemand knew that because of their boots, American Special Forces boots, he'd once owned a pair.

The soldiers were standing around, five or six of them, they weren't alert, weapons cradled. The camera moved, three people in coveralls, probably civilians, talking to a tall soldier, the only one without headgear. The camera zoomed in on the group, the soldier was talking to one of the civilians, a man with a moustache. The soldier took off his dark glasses, wiped his eyes with the knuckle of his index finger. The man with the moustache said something to the person next to him, a man, short hair, a mole on his cheek. He shook his head, gestured, palms inward. The group broke up, the soldier was turning towards the camera, the screen went dark.

When the picture came back, the tall soldier was standing at the bodies lying around the water trough.

He moved a man's head with his boot.

The man was alive, he lifted his arm, his fingers moved.

The soldier shot him in the head, gestured to the other soldiers in the background.

Niemand watched the rest of the film, another two minutes, rewound it and watched it again. He retrieved the cassette and left without seeing Jackie, drove to his place and packed his one bag.

Two hours later, he was in a British Airways business class seat. Johannesburg fell away beneath him, the flat, featureless townships smoking as if bombed, smoking like the village on the film.

Could be Mozambique, he thought. Could be Angola, could be further north.

8

HAMBURG

INSKIP LOOMED in Anselm's open doorway. 'Your friend called,' he said. 'The one who won't give his name.'

David Riccardi was his name. Presumably it was the call to tell him about Alex Koenig. Many hours too late. Anselm closed his eyes at the thought of her visit.

He had known Riccardi for ten years before they were taken hostage. They'd worked together a few times, run into each other in odd places. Then they spent thirteen months together, close together. Manacled, chained to walls and beams, in the dark or half-dark, the last four months in a damp cavity beneath a cold-storage plant where they could not fully extend their legs. That was where his knee trouble had started. His knee trouble and his hip trouble.

'When?' said Anselm.

'Oh, two-fifteen, two-thirty.'

The wrong side of the night. But Riccardi's circadian rhythms were permanently disturbed, so was much else of David.

'Why doesn't he ring you at home?' said Inskip, stretching, reaching up, hands embracing, his ribs showing against his T-shirt. He was about two metres tall and thin.

'He doesn't want to wake me.'

'I see. So he rings you where you aren't.'

'Not everyone who phones you wants to talk to you.'

'I'll ponder that,' said Inskip. 'The Frogs are happy about the Indonesian, happy as Frogs can be. May I ask you a question?'

'You may *ask*.'

'What exactly *is* Bowden's business?'

'Debt collection.'

'Debt collection?'

'Say the Ukrainian government owes you five million dollars, they won't pay, you're desperate. You go to Bowden. They offer ten, twenty cents in the dollar for the debt, it depends. For you, that's better than nothing, cut your losses. Now Bowden's the creditor.'

'That impresses the Ukrainians, does it?'

'Bowdens wait until they find a Ukrainian government asset to target somewhere, maybe a Ukrainian Airways plane in Oslo, something like that. Something valuable. They bring up the legal artillery, get a court order impounding the asset. Now the Ukrainians have to fight a legal action in a foreign country to get their plane back. That or pay up the million. Bowden's bet is that they'll want to talk a settlement. Say sixty cents in the dollar. And they usually do.'

'I see. What a sheltered life I've lived.'

'All that is changing.'

Anselm went back to reviewing the logbooks. Every file had one, all checks, results, speculations, actions, all recorded in writing. As behoved parasites who lived off other people's computer systems, professional prowlers of the cyber world, W&K kept no electronic records of their own, worked only through proxy computers, and otherwise sought tirelessly to erase the traces of their electronic trespasses. If W&K was interested in you, the safest thing was to ensure that your name or names and

54

the names of anyone near you did not appear on the electronic record: no bank accounts, no vehicle registrations, no passport or visa applications, no customs records, no credit-card transactions, no plane tickets, no car hire, no hotel bookings, no bills from public utilities or department stores, no electronic commerce, no emails, no accidents, no hospital admissions, no court appearances, no nothing.

It was safe only to have your death recorded.

W&K was not the only company providing this kind of service. What set W&K apart was that, when their own efforts bogged down, Baader could ring some faceless secret servant in Munich or Moscow or Madrid or Montevideo. Then there was a chance they would get moving again. That came from fourteen years with German intelligence, the BND, the *Bundesnachrichtendienst* – ten years in Department One, Operations, and four in Department Three, Evaluation.

Most of W&K's work was commercial, companies spying on each other, on themselves, trying to find out where executives went, who they saw, who visited companies, what people said, what they wrote. But the firm took on missing persons, anything it could handle.

Just before ten, Carla Klinger knocked and came in. She used a rubber-tipped aluminium stick to walk. She was in her late thirties, thin and angular, a scar on her nose where it had been broken. The BND had sacked her because she was found to have had an affair with another female, possibly once a STASI person, Baader had been vague about the details. Then she had a car accident, broke one side of her body, arm, ribs, hip, leg. Someone told Baader about an expensively trained talent going to waste and he offered Carla a job.

'Serrano,' she said, taking the logbook out from under her left arm and offering it. 'He rang this man and they're meeting tomorrow. At the Alsterarkaden.' She always spoke to Anselm in English.

Anselm looked at the log. The man's name was Werner Kael. He lived nearby, off Sierichstrasse, in the millionaire belt, a wide belt.

'What shows on him?' said Anselm. Carla wasn't much for volunteering information, a trait she shared with Baader. Possibly something nurtured in the BND.

'Calls himself an investment consultant, holiday house in France, four weeks in the Virgin Islands in winter. He used to travel a lot, short trips. Not for a few years. Four tax investigations in the past twelve years, no action taken.'

'Tell O'Malley,' said Anselm. 'It may have meaning for him.'

She nodded, put the logbook under her arm and left.

Anselm waited, then he went down the passage. Baader was staring at his big monitor, figures.

'Werner Kael,' said Anselm from the doorway.

Baader didn't look at him. 'What's he done?'

'Arranged to meet O'Malley's man, the money man.'

Baader touched his chin with a long index finger. 'Arms, drugs, slaves, body parts. Israel, Palestinians, Iranians, Iraqis, Süd-Afs, Tamil Tigers, everyone. Sold the IRA half a container of Semtex. Then there's a fucking shipload of ethyl ether to Colombia out of Hamburg. Five thousand per cent profit.'

'What's his secret?'

'Party donor. Learned the trade from one of Goebbels' cocksuckers. Dieter Kuhn. Dieter only died last year, the year before, about ninety, the old cunt. Fascism is good for health. Hitler would still be alive. Plus Kael's got American friends, a big help in life.'

Baader swivelled. 'O'Malley's chasing money?'

'As far as I can tell,' said Anselm.

'Well, there's no knowing. Kael's got to put his dirty money somewhere, could be this man does it for him, what's ...?'

'Serrano. You don't know the name?'

'No. Tell O'Malley that as far as I know Kael doesn't talk to his clients. He's got cut-outs for that. So Serrano isn't buying or selling. Which probably means he's doing something for Kael.'

Anselm went back to his office, tried to concentrate on the task, focus on the logbook. He had to work at concentration. His mind wandered, wanted to go back to dark places, drawn as a dog was to old buried bones, rotten things, just a layer of earth on them.

The mobile on the desk rang. It was said to be secure. But nothing was secure or W&K wouldn't have a business.

9

LONDON

NIEMAND HAD a long wait at Heathrow customs. When his turn came, the dark pockmarked man looked at him for a time and said, 'Central African Republic. Don't see a lot of these. No. Quite unusual. What's the population?'

'Going down all the time,' Niemand said. 'Volcanic eruptions, human sacrifice, cannibal feasts.'

The official didn't smile, kept looking at him while he photocopied the passport page. Then he said, 'Enjoy your stay in the United Kingdom, sir. Mind the motorised vehicles now.'

Niemand changed a thousand dollars into sterling, rang a hotel, bought a pre-paid mobile phone, and took the underground to Earls Court. He didn't trust taxis, the drivers cheated you and then things became unpleasant.

It wasn't until he came up from the tube station that he felt he was in England: a cold late autumn day, soiled sky, an icy wind probing his collar, chasing litter down filthy Trebovir Road. The hotel was close by. He had stayed there before, on his way back from his uncle's deathbed in Greece. That was a long time ago and they wouldn't remember him. Besides, he had a different name now.

The woman at the desk was somewhere out beyond

sixty, crimson lips drawn on her face, high Chinese collar hiding chins, slackness.

'I rang,' he said. 'Martin Powell.'

'Did you? Just the night, dear?'

'Three.'

'Forty pounds twenty a night,' she said. 'In advance.'

'I'll pay cash.'

She smiled. 'Always happy to accept real money.'

He waited, looking at her, not producing it. He didn't care about the money but he liked to see how people behaved when off-the-record money was offered. 'What does that come to then?'

'One hundred pounds exactly,' she said. 'Dear.'

Niemand registered and carried his pilot's flight bag up the stairs covered with balding carpet. In his room on the third floor, he went through his no-weights exercise routine, twenty minutes. Then he showered in a scratched fibreglass cubicle. The water never went above warm, gurgled, died, spat into life again.

Towelling himself, he thought: A gun, do I need a gun?

He considered it as he dressed, put on clean black jeans, a black T-shirt, the weightless nylon harness that carried his valuables, a black poloneck sweater, his loose-fitting leather jacket. He didn't know who he'd be dealing with. Guns were for showing. Guns were like offering cash. People understood, you didn't have to spell it out.

Downstairs, unconsciously hugging the inside wall like a blind man, around the corner to a pub, a mock-old place with fake timbers, hungover staff, just a dozen or so customers, one sad man with a pencil moustache drinking a pink liquid, possibly a Pimm's, the last Pimm's drinker. At a corner table, he ate a slice of pizza, taste-less, just fodder, rubber fodder, he was hungry, couldn't eat much on planes, someone sitting so close to him he could hear their teeth crush the food, the drain sound of swallowing. When he was finished, he moved his plate to an empty table. He couldn't bear smeared plates, dirty cutlery, mouth prints on glasses, the cold, congealing bits of leftover food.

From under his sweater he brought out his nylon wallet and found the number. He looked around, dialled.

'Kennex Import. How may I help you?'

'Michael Hollis, please,' Niemand said in his Yorkshire accent. He had always been able to mimic accents. He heard them in his head like music, the stresses and timbres, the inflections.

'Who may I say is calling?'

'Tell him it's in connection with a package.'

'Please hold.'

Not for long.

'Hollis.' The faint German accent.

Niemand waited a few seconds. 'I have a package from Johannesburg.'

'Oh yes. The package.'

Two women came in, girls, shrieking, spiky hair, faces violated by rings, full of push and bump and finger-point.

'I'm sorry, I can't do it for less than fifty thousand, US.'

A pause. A sniff, an intake, just audible.

'What?'

'You heard.'

A pause, the sniff, another sound, a click-click. 'I'm not sure we can do that. Can I call you back? Give me your number.'

'No,' said Niemand. 'I'll give you an hour to decide. Then you can say yes or no. If it's no, the package goes somewhere else. I'll ring. Goodbye.'

Niemand went for a walk as far as Kensington Gardens, sat on a bench and watched the people. He had been there before, on his second visit to London. He was supposed to be on his way to Papua New Guinea to fight headhunters, that came to nothing, some political fuck-up. For ten days, he'd been stuck in a hotel near Heathrow with half a dozen other mercenaries – the stupid, the brain-dead, and the merely kill-crazy. Every day, early, he'd take the underground somewhere and run back, long routes plotted with a map. He got to know London as far away as Hampstead and Wimbledon and Bermondsey. Then they were paid off and given plane tickets home.

He always felt strange in England, hearing English everywhere. His father had hated the English, *rooinekke*, anyone who spoke English, Jews in particular, said it was in his blood: Niemands had fought against the British in the Boer War, been put in concentration camps, sent to Ceylon, a *koelie eiland*, a coolie island. But then his father had also hated Greeks and Portuguese, called them *see kaffirs*, sea-kaffirs. For Greeks he reserved a special loathing, having married a Greek girl and lost her because of his drinking and violence. When Niemand and his mother came back from five years on Crete, he found that his father came home drunk from the mine every day, drove the loose old Chev V8 into the dirt yard at speed, stopped in a dust cloud inches from the tacked-on verandah. One day, he braked too late, took out a pillar, half the roof fell on the Chev. He just stayed where he was, opened the bottle of cheap brandy. Niemand found him when he came home, carried him to bed, surprised at how light he was, just bones and sinew.

Niemand looked at his watch. Five minutes to go. Two young women behind three-wheeled pushchairs came from opposite directions, saw each other, cried out. Stopping abreast, they walked around and inspected each other's cargoes beneath the plastic covers, made delighted scrunched-up faces.

He dialled.

'Kennex Import. How may I help you?'

'Mr Hollis. About the package.'

No further questions.

Niemand watched the mothers talking, hands moving, talking babies, faces alive with interest.

'Ah, the package.' Hollis. 'Yes, I'm having trouble getting authorisation for the deal you suggest without seeing that the goods are as described.'

'No,' Niemand said. 'You give me the money. In cash. I give you the package.'

'It's not that simple.'

'I think it is. Yes or no.'

'We have to see the goods. You can understand that.'

Niemand didn't like the way this was going. He didn't have contingency plans. 'Now the price is sixty thousand,' he said. 'Inflation.'

'I'm sure we can agree on price when we know what we're getting. I'll give you an address to bring the package to. You do that soonest, say in an hour, thereabouts, soonest. Then we look at it, we authorise payment. How's that?'

'Forget it. You're not the only buyer. How's that?'

'That's quite persuasive. Can you give me time to discuss this with my colleagues? I'll recommend that we do it your way. I'm sure they'll agree. Call me at ten tomorrow morning?'

Niemand didn't reply for a moment. He needed to think. 'Okay,' he said.

'Good. Excellent. There's no need to look elsewhere, I assure you.'

Niemand sat for a while, not easy in his mind.

10

HAMBURG

ANSELM TOOK the firm's BMW and drove to Winterhude. He found a parking space in Barmbeker Strasse, went to the *Konditorei* and bought a small black chocolate cake, walked to the apartment in Maria-Louisen-Steig to see Fräulein Einspenner, whose service to the Anselm family began in 1935.

She came to the door in seconds. She was just bone covered with finely lined tissue paper but her eyes were bright. She seated him in the stiff sitting room on a striped chair, took the cake to the kitchen and came back with it, sliced, on a delicate plate, on a tray with cake plates and silver cake forks.

They talked about the affairs of the day. She knew about everything, watched the news and current affairs on television, her eyes not up to reading the paper.

'How is Lucas?' she said.

'Well. He's well.'

'When is he coming to live in his house?'

'I don't know. He has a house in London.'

'Then he should give the house to you.'

'Perhaps his son will live in it one day.'

Fräulein Einspenner thought about that for a while, nodding. Then she said, 'Your German is very good.'

She always said that to him at some point. She had said it to him for thirty years.

Fräulein Einspenner separated a tiny piece of chocolate cake with her fork, put it to her mouth slowly. There was no perceptible chewing movement. She was ingesting it.

Anselm waited until he thought she had swallowed.

'Moritz,' he said. 'Do you remember much about him?'

She was looking at her plate, making another incision in her thin slice of cake with the side of her fork.

'Moritz?'

'My great-uncle.'

'I was a servant,' she said.

'You do remember him?'

She finished the cut, didn't impale the fragment, didn't look up, began another separation.

'I saw him, yes. He came to the house.'

'What became of him? Do you know?'

More work on the cake.

'Became of him?'

'What happened to him?'

She rested the fork on the plate.

'The war,' she said, looking up.

'He was killed in the war?'

'A lovely cake. When will you come again? I so look forward to seeing you. I see your father and your grandfather when I look at you.'

This meant she was tired. She walked to the front door of the building with Anselm, holding his hand, two fingers of his hand, and there he stooped to kiss her papyrus cheek.

She smelled as she had thirty years before, when she had stooped to hug him, kiss his cheek.

'Remember when we used to go to Stadtpark together?' she said. 'The birds. You loved them so much.'

He walked back to the car, stopped to buy cigarettes, drove down Dorotheen Strasse and into choked Hofweg.

Turning down to Schöne Aussicht, he saw the last light of day on the silver lake. Three small boats were tacking towards the Pöseldorf shore, on their sails a colour the palest rose.

In the building, Baader was gone, returned to his child bride, and the shifts had changed. Inskip was back.

'There may be life outside this place,' he said in his languid English voice, not looking at Anselm. 'Have you considered that?'

'Movement, yes,' Anselm said. 'Life is another matter.'

'I'll settle for movement,' said Inskip. 'Up and down. You may or may not be pleased by some initiative I've shown. A Ms Christina Owens came up on the Continental database. The Campo woman checked in as C. Owens at a hotel in Vancouver six years ago. Someone in Canada found that out for the client.'

'Yes?'

'Christina Owens is staying at a hotel in Barcelona. The security man's given me some pictures.'

'Let's see.'

Inskip tapped, they waited, the screen began running a jerky hotel lobby surveillance film, four cameras: entrance, reception desk, seating area, lifts.

A couple came in the door, a woman with shoulder-length hair and a man walking just behind her. They saw him at the desk collecting a key. At the lifts, waiting, she turned her head to him, a younger man, said something, curt, impatient. He shrugged, raised a hand. The lift doors opened and they entered.

'Again.'

The couple came into view walking through the doors from the street.

Anselm raised a finger.

Inskip froze the film. She was head-on to the camera.

Anselm made the enlarge sign.

It was a taut-skinned face, perky nose, eyebrows pencilled in, full lower lip.

'Save it.'

The box file was at Inskip's elbow. Anselm opened it, took out the top photograph: a woman, mid-twenties perhaps, hair pulled back, long nose, glasses. She had the face to play a librarian in a Hollywood film and she bore no resemblance to the woman in the Barcelona hotel surveillance video.

Anselm looked at the name and date pencilled on the back: Lisa Campo, October 1990.

'What's the nature of her malfeasance?' said Inskip.

'She's an accountant. Worked for Charlie Campo, a Midwest pizza prince. She became Mrs Campo, stashed around six million dollars offshore for Charlie. Skimmed money. Then she took off. Our client says there's five million moved, vanished. And all Charlie's got is this old driver's licence shot.'

'Sad, really.'

'Send the pic and the whole video to the Jocks, marked Rush. They may still be upright, capable of responding today.'

The firm sometimes used people in Glasgow, experts in facial recognition, academics making a buck on the side, putting taxpayer-funded research to good use.

Inskip said, 'You're suggesting that these totally different women might be the same person?'

'I'm just running up the bill.'

He nodded. 'How uncommercial of me. What do the Jocks do? Apply haggis-fuelled intuition?'

In spite of his considerable hacking skills, Inskip pretended to technological bewilderment, an upper-class English attitude of puzzlement and disdain.

'This'll be over your head, old fruit,' Anselm said, 'but they use something called PCA, principal component analysis. You establish a person's eigenface, then you compare any other face's eigenvectors, beginning with eyes, nose and mouth. It's well established but the Jocks have come up with a few tricks of their own.'

Inskip rolled his chair back, ran fingers through his hair. 'Eigenface? Why do the English think a German word is more serious than an English one? I mean, really, what has *Doppelgänger* actually got going for it?'

'Didn't register anything except the one word, did you? Send the pics.'

Anselm was reading the logs when Inskip loomed in the doorway. 'John. The sporran-swingers say 100 per cent positive.' He wrinkled his brow. 'I cannot believe that.'

Anselm looked at him for a while. 'Her eigenface. Plastic surgery couldn't hide it. Nothing they can do about the distance between her pupils. Her eye sockets. Booked in for how long?'

'Didn't notice.'

'Notice, James. Check it.'

Inskip sniffed, disappeared. Anselm signed a logbook, went back to the big room.

'It's three nights, two to go,' said Inskip.

'The man to ring is called Jonas. Campo's lawyer. The emergency number's in the file. If I remember, Charlie Campo offers twenty-five grand if he gets to confront her. Half for us.'

'My God.' Inskip was looking for the number. 'Who gets it?'

'Our policy,' said Anselm, 'is to give half of our cut to the finder.'

'The other half?' He was dialling, tapping on his keyboard.

'Distributed to the needy. For example, to someone who needs a new wife or a new Porsche.'

'Vulgar vehicle,' said Inskip. 'Do you want to speak?'

Anselm shook his head. You didn't want to deny people the pleasure of bearing good news. Inskip put on his headset. Anselm listened to the crackling from space, the crisp sound of a phone being picked up.

'Jonas.' Vague voice.

'Weidermann & Kloster in Hamburg, Mr Jonas. Sorry about the time. It's the Campo file.'

'What?' A cough, cigarette cough.

'The airline's found your client's luggage.'

'What, you found the name?'

'No, we've identified the actual luggage.'

'You're kidding?'

'No.'

A cough. 'Listen, fuck this spy shit, it's Lisa?'

Inskip looked at Anselm. 'We believe a hundred per cent positive,' he said.

'The face?'

He looked at Anselm again. Anselm nodded.

'The face. One hundred per cent.'

'Christ. Where?'

'Barcelona. Last night. Booked in for two more nights.'

'Barcelona, Spain?'

'Yes.'

'That's a hundred per cent?'

Inskip raised an eyebrow. Anselm nodded again. The Scots were never wrong. Eigenfaces didn't lie.

'Yes.'

'Ten years,' Jonas said, 'Charlie'll come in his pyjamas. Listen, Barcelona, some cover there, local knowledge, you can get that?'

Inskip looked at Anselm, opened his hands. Anselm took the headset off him, put it on. 'Mr Jonas, John Anselm. We can arrange that but it's expensive.'

Jonas cleared his throat, not a sound to wake up to.

'Fuck expense, John,' he said. 'Lose this fuckin fish, I'll die. Do it now.'

'Can you transfer fifteen thousand US immediately?'

'Check your balance in thirty.'

Anselm said, 'Give us your flight details when you have them and you'll be met.'

'Tonight,' said Jonas. 'We fly tonight. Barcelona, Spain. Some place quiet, we need that, you with me?'

'The person who meets you will have arranged that.'

Jonas made a sound like a snore. 'This works, I'm comin around, drinks, dinner. Fucking breakfast. For days.'

'And lunch?'

Jonas laughed. 'For wimps, man. Remember that movie?'

Anselm reminded him about the bonus and said goodbye. Inskip was looking at him, mouth open a little, teeth showing. He was more than interested, a little excited. 'Cover?' he said, no sign of languor now. 'What's that mean?'

'Make sure she doesn't vanish again.'

'We can do that?'

'We can do anything. Record this in the log.'

Anselm sat down at the workstation next to Inskip and rang Alvarez in Barcelona, exchanged pleasantries in Spanish, told him what was needed.

'Expensive,' said Alvarez.

'Within reason, Geraldo.'

'In advance, a thousand? Perhaps.'

'Because this is short notice, yes. I'll send it tonight.'

Anselm was heading for the door when Inskip said, 'What'll happen to the woman? Lisa?'

Anselm looked over his shoulder. 'What do you think? Charlie gets his money back, they fall in love again, go on a second honeymoon. Eat pizza.'

Inskip nodded a few times, licked his lips, turned back to his screen.

11

LONDON

NIEMAND OPENED his eyes, out of sleep instantly, disturbed by something, some irregularity, some change in the background noise he'd listened to as he drifted away on the too-soft bed.

Listening. Just the night-city sounds: wails, growls, whines, grates, squeals.

It had been a sound from inside the hotel. Close by.

Listening. Thinking: a hard sound, metallic, like a hammer strike. What could make a harsh metal-on-metal sound?

He knew, threw the sheet and blanket aside, was out of bed, wearing just his watch and running shorts.

Someone had opened the fire-escape door.

He was at the back of the building, last room in the corridor, a door away from the short passage that led to the fire-escape exit. Someone had pushed on the lever of the steel fire-escape door, found it reluctant to come out of the latch, applied more force, too much. It had come out, hit the restraining pin above it hard. That was the sound, a ringing, metallic sound.

Someone inside the hotel had opened the fire-escape door to let someone else in.

More than one?

He looked at his watch. 1.15 a.m.

If they're coming for me about the tape, he thought,

there'll be a big one to break open the door, then they'll want to be finished in seconds, down the fire escape inside a minute.

He pulled the bed covers straight, they'd look there, that might give him a second, they were hardly rumpled by his few hours of sleep. He looked around for anything useful – the chair, a flimsy thing, better than nothing.

Stand behind the door? His instinct said: No, see what I'm up against, don't get slammed against the wall by a door shoulder-charged by a gorilla.

He stepped across the worn carpet and stood to the left of the door, back against the wall, holding the chair by a leg in his left hand.

Waiting in the dark room, wall icy against his shoulderblades, listening, all the city sounds amplified now. Calm, he said to himself, breathe deeply, icy calm.

No sound came to his ears from the passage.

Wrong. He was wrong. Too jumpy, the fire-escape latch just an invention of a mind looking to explain something, something in a dream probably. They couldn't have found him. How could they find him, they didn't even have a name? He dropped his head, felt tension leave his neck and shoulders.

The door came off its hinges.

A huge man, shaven-headed, came with it, went three steps across the room with the door on his right shoulder, his back to Niemand.

Close behind him was a tall, slim man with a silenced pistol in both hands, arms outstretched, combat style. He saw Niemand out of the corner of his eye, started to swing his arms and his body.

Niemand hit him in the head and chest with the chair before he had half swung, broke the chair back to pieces, hit him again with the back of the seat, more solid, caught him under the nose, knocked his head back.

The man stepped two paces back, his knees bending, one hand coming off the pistol.

The big man had turned, stood frozen, hands up, hands the size of tennis racquets.

Niemand threw the remains of the chair at him, stepped over, grabbed the gunman's right hand as he sank to the floor, blood running down his face, got the pistol, pulled it away, pointed it at the big man.

'Fuck, no,' said the big man, he didn't want to die.

Maori, maybe, thought Niemand, Samoan. He shot him in each thigh, no more sound than two claps with cupped hands.

'Fuck,' said the man. He didn't fall down, just looked down at his legs in the black tracksuit pants. Then he sat on the bed, slowly, sat awkwardly, he was fat around the middle. 'Fuck,' he said again. 'Didn't have to do that.'

The gunman was on his knees, lower face black with blood. He had long hair and it had fallen forward, hung over his eyes, strands came down to his lips. Niemand walked around him, pushed him to the carpet with his bare foot. There was no resistance. He knelt on the base of the man's spine, put the fat silencer muzzle into the nape of his neck.

'Don't even twitch,' Niemand said. He found a wallet, a slim nylon thing, in the right side pocket of the leather jacket. Took the mobile phone too. In the left pocket were car keys and a full magazine, fifteen rounds. That's excessive for taking out one man, Niemand thought. He stood up.

'Scare, mate,' the gunman said. 'That's all, mate, scare.'

It was hard to pick the accent through the blood and the carpet but Niemand thought it was Australian. An all-Pacific team.

'How'd you find me?'

The man turned his head. He had a strong profile. 'Just the messenger here, mate. Bloke gave me the room number.'

'What's your car?'

'What?'

Niemand ran the pistol over the man's scalp. 'Car. Where?'

'Impreza, the Subaru, at the lane.'

'Don't move.'

Niemand went to the doorway, now a hole in the wall, looked down the dim corridor. Nothing, no sounds. The room next door was empty, he'd seen the white-board in the reception office.

He went back. 'Unlucky room number,' he said to the man on the floor and, from close range, shot him in the backs of his knees. Clap, clap.

While the man keened, thin sounds, demanding, Niemand dressed, stuffed his things in his bag. The big man was lying back on the bed now, feet on the ground, making small grunting noises. If he wanted to, Niemand thought, he could have a go at me, just flesh wounds, like cutting your finger with a kitchen knife. But he doesn't want to, why should he? He's just the battering ram, the paid muscle.

Like me, all I've ever been, just the paid muscle. And always stupid enough to have a go.

'Give me your mobile,' he said to the big man.

The man shook his head. 'No mobile.'

Niemand went down the fire escape, not hurrying, walked down the alley, saw the car, pressed the button to unlock the driver's door. He drove to Notting Hill, light traffic, rain misting the windscreen, feeling the nausea, the tiredness, not too bad this time. He'd never driven in London but he knew the inner city from his runs, from the map. Near the Notting Hill Gate underground, he parked illegally, left the car unlocked with the keys in it, Three youths were nearby, laughing, one pissing against a car, he saw the joint change hands. With luck, they'd steal the Subaru.

On the underground platform, just him, two drunks and a woman who was probably a transvestite, he took out the gunman's mobile, flipped it open, pressed the numbers.

'Yes.' Hollis.

'Not a complete success to report,' Niemand said. 'Those boys you sent, one's too fat, one's too slow. I had to punish them. And I'm going to have to punish you too, Mr Hollis.'

'Hold on,' said Hollis. 'There's some ...'

'Goodbye.'

Niemand put the mobile away. One of the drunks was approaching, silly slack-jawed smile.

'Smoke, mate?' he said.

Glasgow. Niemand knew what people from Glasgow sounded like, he'd spent time with men from Glasgow. He turned side-on to the man, moved his shoulders. 'Fuckoff, throw you under the fucking train,' he said in his Scottish accent.

The man put up his hands placatingly, walked backwards for several steps, turned and went back to his companion.

12

HAMBURG

'WHAT'S SERRANO'S business in Hamburg?' said Anselm. He was uneasy, his scalp itched. The other people in the restaurant seemed too close, he felt that they were looking at him.

They were in Blankenese, finishing lunch at a table in the window. Below them flowed the Elbe, wide, grey, unhealthy. Two container ships attended by screeching flocks of gulls were passing each other. The huge vessels – clumsy, charmless things bleeding rust at the rivets and oozing yellowish liquids from their pores – sent small waves to the banks.

'Moving money, papers,' said O'Malley. 'He shifts stuff all the time. Can't keep any computer records. No paperless office for Mr Serrano.'

'The pages any use?'

'The ones we can understand don't help us. We sold them to a firm in Dublin, so we'll get a bit of our money back. In due course. We don't demand cash on delivery. Unlike some.'

'Cash flow problems. The boss's been away on honeymoon.'

'Why does he have to marry them?'

'Some Lutheran thing. What's Serrano want with Kael?'

'We'd like to know.'

'You came over to tell me that?'

'No. I've got other business here. Mention this matter to Baader?'

'Yes. He says Kael's a man of parts.' Every time Anselm looked around, he thought he caught people staring at him.

O'Malley looked pensive, chewing the last of his *Zanderfilet*. He was big and pale, a long patrician nose between sharp cheekbones. He looked like an academic, a teacher of literature or history. But then you looked into his bleached blue eyes, and you knew he was something very different.

In the disordered and looted album of Anselm's memories, Manila was untouched. Manila, in the Taproom at the Manila Hotel. The group came in laughing, O'Malley with a short, bald Filipino man, two elated young women who looked like Rotary exchange students from Minnesota, and dark and brooding Paul Kaskis. O'Malley was wearing a *barong tagalog*, the Filipino shirt worn over trousers. The Filipino was in a lightweight cream suit, and Kaskis was in chinos and a rumpled white shirt.

The Filipino ordered margaritas. Anselm heard him say to the blondes that he'd started drinking them at college in California. At Stanford. They shrieked. They shrieked at the men's every utterance. It struck Anselm that if they were on an exchange, it was an arrangement between Rotary cathouses, an international exchange of Rotary harlots.

There was a moment when the shrieking women had gone to the powder room and the Filipino was talking softly to Kaskis and O'Malley was standing next to Anselm, paying for cigars.

'I think I know you,' said O'Malley. 'You're a journalist.' He was Australian.

'No and yes,' said Anselm.

'Don't tell me, you're with …'

'I'm a freelance, not with anyone in particular.'

O'Malley's washed-out blue eyes, remarkable in his sallow face, flicked around the room. Then he smiled, a smile full of ruc. 'Not CIA then?'

'No. I don't think they'd have me.'

'Fuck it,' O'Malley said. 'Met two today, I was hoping for a trifecta. Well, have a drink with us anyway.'

Anselm ended up having dinner with them. At one point, shrieking Carol, the taller and bigger of the American women, put an accomplished hand on him under the table, seemed to look to O'Malley for guidance.

Now O'Malley asked for guidance. 'What's Baader say about him?'

'Arms, drugs, possibly slaves, human organs. Untouchable. He has friends.'

'Just another Hamburg businessman then.'

'I suppose,' said Anselm. He had a cautious look at their fellow-lunchers, members of Hamburg's haute bourgeoisie, serious people noted for being cold, tight-lipped and very careful with a mark. Most of them were in middle age and beyond, the men sleek-haired and hard-eyed, just on the plump side, the women lightly tanned and harder eyed but carrying no excess weight, taut surgically contoured faces many of them, bowstring tendons in the neck.

'Baader says Kael doesn't talk directly to his own clients,' said Anselm, 'so he may be a client of Serrano's. Kael's money's all dirty and Serrano may be helping him with it.'

'This meeting tomorrow,' said O'Malley. 'Can that be covered?'

'Outdoors, it's a put-and-pluck on Serrano,' Anselm said. 'With possibilities of disaster. Want to wear that?'

'I'll have to.' O'Malley ran a hand over his tightly curled greying black hair, touched the collar of his lightweight tweed suit, the knot of the red silk tie. 'The world used to be a much simpler place, didn't it? There were things you could do, things you couldn't. Now you can do anything if you can pay for it.'

'Nostalgia,' Anselm said. 'I was thinking the other night. I've never asked. What happened to Angelica?'

'She doesn't work any more. She paints. She married an Englishman and now there's an American.'

'People you know?'

'The Pom, yes. I liked him. Eton and kicked out of the Guards. Rooting the CO's batman probably, much worse than rooting the CO's wife, he doesn't fuck his wife. The American's rich, inherited. I had dinner with them in Paris, in their apartment, the Marais can you believe? They have a cook, a chef. But there's hope, she's really distant with the hubby. Not surprising, he's an Egyptologist, the place's like a tomb and he could bore Mormons stiff.'

O'Malley drank the last of his wine. 'Still interested?'

'Just curious.'

'I could bring you together. Accidental meeting.'

'We only actually kissed once. While very drunk.'

'I remember. The Angel didn't kiss casually, though. Not a serial kisser.'

'I may be too late for accidental meetings. I may have had my ration of accidental meetings.'

'No, there's always one left.'

A youth in white had appeared to take away the plates. Close behind him came another young man, dark, Italianate, long-fingered. He fawned over O'Malley, suggesting the dessert trolley or something from the kitchen, anything, any whim. O'Malley ordered cognacs. He had the accent identified with Cologne, somehow frivolous in the intonation. North Germans found it annoying.

The waiter gone, O'Malley sighed. 'Well, a business lunch. What's a put-and-pluck cost?'

'As an estimate, plenty.'

O'Malley was looking away, watching three sailors on a Japanese container ship taking photographs of the shore. He said nothing for a while, drank some riesling, nodded in answer to some inner question. 'Yes,' he said, 'I thought it would be in that vicinity.'

They sat in silence until the cognacs came, more fawning. O'Malley rotated his fat-bellied glass and sniffed the small collar. 'If angels peed,' he said, and sipped.

Anselm felt the unease returning, wanted to be out of the place, away from people. He saw O'Malley's mouth rolling the liquid, his upward gaze, the calibrating.

'Nice lunch,' said Anselm. 'Thank you.'

O'Malley landed his glass on the heavy white linen. 'My pleasure. You eat quickly, not so much a diner as an eater.'

'I usually eat in the street,' Anselm said. 'Vendor food. You get into habits like that.' The unease was growing. He steadied himself. 'I have to go.'

On their way out, O'Malley stopped and bent over a handsome woman in dark business clothes, alone. 'Are you stalking me, Lucy?' he said. 'How did you know I'd be here?'

Anselm kept going, he wanted to be outside. A flunky was waiting to open the door. He went out onto the pavement, closed his eyes, breathed deeply, said his mantra.

In the taxi, O'Malley said, 'That woman, she's English, a very smart maritime lawyer based here. Froze a Polish ship for us in Rotterdam. I hope she's going to do the trick again.'

'I'm sure the courts look kindly upon her.'

'She's persuasive. They say she blew a judge when she was starting out in England. That's the gossip. Judgment overturned on appeal. Black mark for a judge.'

'At least he's got his memories,' Anselm said. 'Keep her wig on?'

O'Malley shook his head. 'How can you be so ignorant of legal decorum?'

13

LONDON

HALLIGAN, THE deputy editor, presided over the news conference. Caroline Wishart was nine minutes late, just behind skeletal Alan Sindall, the chief crime reporter.

'Welcome,' said Halligan. 'I'm thinking of making this meeting's time more flexible. We'll just run the fucking thing from 2 p.m. to whenever, open-ended, pop in whenever it suits you.'

'Sorry,' said Sindall, eyes down.

Caroline said nothing, eyes on the styrofoam cup of coffee she was carrying.

'Came together did you!' shrieked Benton, the small, fat deputy news editor, clapping his hands in front of his glasses. 'Came together!'

'Shut up, Benton,' Halligan said, 'we don't have to be *like* our readers. We *purvey* smut. That does not require that we ourselves be amused by childish double entendres.'

'Just a joke, Geoff,' said Benton, eyes down.

'Pathetic. Since by the grace of something or other the chief criminal reporter and the stand-in to the power of three for the editor of Frisson or Pissoir or whatever it's called are now here, let's hear it. About Brechan, Marcia?'

'Where's Colley?' said Marcia Connors, the news editor, a sharp-faced woman in her late thirties. 'Does he still work here? Does anyone know?'

Colley ran the paper's Probe team.

'He's accounted for his absence,' said Halligan. 'What's happening?'

'Nothing,' said Simon Knight, the chief political correspondent, slumped, looking over his glasses, chins rolling into a loosened collar already dirty. 'Brechan apparently doesn't have a care in the world.'

'The question was addressed to me,' said Marcia.

'Oh,' said Knight. 'Well, go for it, old dear.'

Marcia eyed him briefly, touched a canine with a short-nailed fingertip. 'Brechan gave us the slip last night.'

'And the catamite?' Halligan was looking at her hopefully.

She shook her head.

'Can't find him?'

'No.'

'Marcia, someone is going to find out about this and find the prick. We heard it first. You're saying it's not going to be us?'

'We can't find him.' She ran a hand over her hacked-short hair. 'Simple as that. If someone else can, good fucking luck to them. Gary vanished on Tuesday, there-abouts. His ex-boyfriend, this little poof is more vegetable than animal, into very serious substance abuse, he *thinks* Gary rang at some time around Tuesday to say he was going into a private clinic somewhere. He *thinks*. And he's never heard of Brechan.'

'Somewhere?' said Halligan.

'Somewhere. We've tried, believe me, we've tried. Could be in fucking Montevideo.'

'Have you tried Montevideo?' said Simon Knight.

Marcia didn't look at him. 'Oh fuck off, you fat ponce,' she said.

Halligan waved his hands placatingly, swivelled his

chair to face the window. 'How did we come to stuff this thing up so comprehensively? Handed to us on a plate.'

'Don't know about handed anything,' said Marcia. 'It was only a tip-off.'

'Perhaps it *is* a pack of lies,' Simon Knight said. 'The man's got more enemies than Thatcher at her peak. And he's only the Defence Minister in waiting.'

Halligan came back to face the room, deep lines across his forehead. 'Bugger it,' he said. 'I told the boss we'd get the story. He was beside himself with joy. His favourite position.' He shook his head. 'Well, what is there for the front then?'

'Public schoolboys selling drugs,' said Marcia.

'That's news?' said Merton, the industrial affairs editor. 'What about pubs selling beer?'

'And fuck you too,' said Marcia.

Caroline put up a hand.

'Yes?' said Halligan.

'I've got pictures,' she said.

Silence in the room.

'What?' said Marcia.

'What?' said Halligan.

'Pictures.'

Marcia showed teeth, both top and bottom. 'I think it's too early in the day for you, darling. Up all night with the braying coke snorters. Tell us about your shitty little shots when we get to the rubbish end of the paper.'

'I've got pictures of Brechan and Gary,' Caroline said to Halligan.

A silence lay on the room, a religious silence. Halligan clicked his nails on the table. Nails too long for a man, Caroline thought. Her father would have thought so, anyway.

'Brechan and Gary?'

'Yes. And Gary's story.'

Marcia leant towards her. 'What kind of pictures? Doing what exactly?'

Caroline looked pointedly at the woman's bleached moustache, savoured the moment. She'd heard that Marcia had once had an affair with Halligan. 'I'm talking to Geoff,' she said. 'When I want to talk to you, I'll give you a sign. I'll indicate.'

'Doing what?' said Halligan.

Caroline took the lid off her coffee cup, had a tentative sip. 'Christ, the coffee's terrible around here,' she said. She wanted to make them wait. Since her first day on a free suburban rag in sodden Birmingham, all her life really, she had wanted a moment like this.

'Well?' said Halligan. His mouth was open and, with his pendulous jowls, he looked like a dog about to drool. 'Well? Doing what?'

Caroline had another sip of coffee. 'We should probably talk in private,' she said.

'Meeting adjourned for ten minutes,' Halligan said. 'Don't stray too far.'

Everyone got up and filed out except Marcia, who was lighting a cigarette.

Caroline waited until the door closed behind the last person before she looked at Marcia. 'You too,' she said. 'Out.'

Marcia was about to draw on the cigarette. She took her hand away, her mouth frozen and fish-like. 'Who the fuck do you ...'

Halligan raised both hands to her, palms outward. 'This won't take a moment, dear ...'

'Don't you fucking call me dear you spineless shit.' She got up. At the door, she said, 'This is going to be a defining moment in both your lives. I'll make fucking sure of that.'

She slammed the door.

Halligan pulled at his nose with thumb and forefinger. 'Now,' he said. 'The pictures.'

'Gary and Brechan fucking.'

'Fucking,' he said. 'Each other? Is that right?'

'Yes.'

'Taken by?'

'I don't know. It could be a remote thing.'

'You've got the pictures in your hands?'

'Yes. And Gary's story on tape. The full story. I've promised him thirty thousand pounds.'

Halligan looked at the table, tapped his pink forehead with his knuckles. 'Chickenfeed,' he said. 'Wait till the boss hears. Unbelievable. This is terrific. Terrific. You are terrific.'

Caroline took the folded sheet of paper out of her inside pocket, gave it to him.

He read it, looked up at her. 'Yes, you can leave the Frisson section immediately. Yes, you can be off-diary. Yes, you can have an office. But as for the rest of this, Caroline, it's ridiculous ...'

She stood up and started for the door. 'Read the story in the *Sun*.'

'Caroline my dear, sit down, let's talk,' he said.

14

HAMBURG

LIGHT DRAINING from the world, the coming winter on his skin, knee joints pleading, Anselm ran home, not stopping till he stood at his gate in the silent street, slumped in the shoulders, seeing his ragged breath in the air.

He was in the kitchen, about to drink bottled water, weak, unshowered, when the knocks sounded on the huge front door. He froze. There was a bell, it worked, someone chose to knock. Pause – again the hollow knocking.

He spoke to himself, calmed himself, and went down the cavernous passage into the hall, switched on the outside light. A shadow lay on the front door's stained-glass window.

'Who is it?' he said.

'Alex Koenig.'

Anselm opened the door. She was formally dressed, a pinstriped suit, dark, a white shirt with a high collar, dark stockings. She looked severe and striking.

'I came to apologise,' she said. 'I was wrong to come here uninvited and what I said was unforgivable.'

Anselm shook his head. 'You don't have to apologise. No one who deals with me ever has to apologise.'

'You will accept my apology?'

'Of course, but ...'

'I won't bother you again.'

She turned and went quickly down the path. He wanted to call after her, ask her to come back, come inside, show her that he was not the savage and unpleasant person he had presented to her.

But he did not. He was scared of her. Of what she knew about him.

Alex Koenig didn't look back, the gate clicked behind her. A wait, then a car drove away, its sound lost in the murmuring city.

Anselm went back to the kitchen, down the flagstone passage so wide he could not touch the walls with outstretched arms. He put the bottle of water away, opened a beer and downed it in two long-throated drinks, the clean tawny smell filling his nasal cavities. He poured a glass of white wine, sat at the pine table. Just to sit there comforted him. The great, worn table in the kitchen always comforted him.

In Beirut, fighting against claustrophobia and pain and panic, his memories of the house on the canal, of the kitchen and the garden saved him. He had forced himself to think about the house and his childhood, his family: being woken by his brother in the middle of the night and seeing adults in the garden throwing snowballs; walking by the canal with his grandfather, autumn leaves underfoot; in the kitchen helping Fräulein Einspenner to shell peas, peel potatoes, knead dough. The kneading he had remembered most clearly: the feel of the dough, the life in it, the resistance building beneath his hands, the sensual, silky, breast-like resilience.

And he remembered the roses one summer – the ones the colour of burnt cream in the big pots on the terrace, the three or four shades of pink around the front gate, the dark satiny reds that smothered the boundary wall.

Later, after he had been beaten, after the panic when

he began to discover the holes in his mind, the blank spaces, the lacunae, it began to gnaw at him that he didn't know the names of so many things. For a long time, he could not distinguish between what he had never known and what he had forgotten. And when he thought he could, he was filled with an aching despair that he would die without knowing the names. In that hopeless space, always dark, the world was gone, the whole world of sky and earth and trees moving in a cold wind. Gone.

And with it the names.

Now, sitting at the table in the flagstoned room, he remembered clearly the ache to know the names, to be able to say them to himself. The need to know names.

The names of so many things.

'Do you know the names of any roses?' he had asked.

'What?' Riccardi, a whisper.

'Roses.'

'Roses?'

'Yes. Roses. Their names.'

And so it began. In that foetid hole, black, a shallow grave, two men lying so close together they could not be sure whose breath they smelled, whose body sounds they heard, whose heartbeat they felt – they began to name things. In three languages. Roses. Trees. Give me ten trees. Dogs, name twelve dogs. Fifteen saints. Twenty mountains. Flowers, stars, saints, rivers, seas, singers, capitals, wars, battles, writers, songs, generals, paintings, poets, poems, actors, kinds of pasta, ocean currents, deserts, books, trees, flowers, desserts, architectural periods, cars, American presidents, parts of speech, characters in books, prime ministers, volcanoes, hurricanes, bands, waterfalls, sculptors, American states, meat dishes, actors, breads, wines, winds, women's names from A to Z, men's, towns, villages, statues, operas, kings, queens, the seven dwarves, engine parts, films, directors, diseases, biblical figures, boxers, names for the penis, for breasts, the vagina, for eating and shitting and pissing and kissing and fucking and pregnancy and telling lies.

But not words for dying.

No, not words for dying. They didn't need words for dying. They were going to die.

The tape recorder was on the table. He went to the study and fetched the box of tapes. He went back and forth on the one with 2 written on it, circled.

You were talking about Kate yesterday.

Oh. Yes. Kate was a Jew.

Who's Kate?

Our cousin's wife. I'll show you her photograph. Beautiful girl, lovely. A Jew. Nominally. Her family. Not in a religious sense. I don't think they had any religion to speak of. We, of course, we thought of ourselves as Christians. But all we did was observe the traditions. We only went to church on Christmas day, to the Landeskirche, just a family tradition. And of course we had the most wonderful Christmas Eves, the Feuerzangbohle, *the presents, my dear, the wonderful presents.*

What about Kate?

Moritz was abominable. Isn't that a lovely word? Abominable. English is a lovely language. Stuart used to call all kinds of things abominable. Do you know about the creature of the snows? In the Himalayas? Where do you place the stress in that? I've never been comfortable with the word.

About Kate? Moritz?

Moritz said we should put the Stürmer *sign on the entrances to the family businesses. Such a stupid and dreadful thing to say ...*

What sign?

Oh, you know, Juden sind hier nicht erwünscht. *He was talking about how Germany needed to be cleansed of Jews, it was a matter of hygiene, nonsense like that, he had obviously been drinking.*

Kate heard that?

Your great-grandfather didn't like that kind of talk. We dealt with many Jews. He was an old-fashioned person. Well, he was old. Not that old, I suppose … as old as I am now, I suppose. Good heavens. I would need to work that out. How old he was. One forgets.

This was just before the war?

You looked like Moritz when you were a boy, do you know that? A little bigger, he was thin. But your eyes and the hair and the chin.

No. *Did many people you knew feel the way Moritz did?*

About Jews? People said things. But the Nazis, we had contempt for their rubbish. We all did. The people we mixed with. The old merchant families. We had all travelled, you see, we were … worldly, I suppose that's the word. 'That Man', that's what we called Hitler. That Man. A vulgar person. They were all vulgar, the women were all … well, I shouldn't. He was Austrian too, not German.

Moritz. What happened to him?

I remember when you came to this house the first time. Lucas was quiet, he didn't move from your mother and you just ran around madly and Einspenner was so taken with you, she took you into the kitchen and showed you the cellar …

Before he went to bed, Anselm made a cheese omelette, ate it with toasted five-day-old bread. He wasn't hungry, just a duty the mind owed the body. In the study, he saw the American Defense Secretary on television. He was behind a desk, Michael Denoon, a hard-faced man, boxer's scars on his jaw and right cheekbone. Through the pancake, the lights caught them, thin lines where skin and flesh had been jammed against bone and split open. But his nose was straight, no one had got through to his nose.

A CNN woman came on, lots of hair, eyes wide open, and a big cone-shaped mouth. She said:

Pressure on US Defense Secretary Michael Denoon to enter the presidential race intensified today when Newsweek *reported that an informal poll showed 155 of 222 Republican members of the House of Representatives would support Denoon's candidacy.*

Republican Senator Robert Gurner is thought to be unelectable since the disclosure three days ago of his two-year homosexual relationship with New York actor Lawrence Wellman.

Denoon again. He put his head to one side, ran a hand across his hair, modest, straightened, looked at the camera.

Of course I'm deeply honoured by this expression of confidence by people who speak for millions of ordinary Americans. I'm humbled too. This nation bears deep wounds from the great sacrifices it has made in faraway places to fight evil and promote freedom and democracy. Now we need calm, peace and prosperity. We need to renew ourselves, to put America first, to see clearly our place in the world. But whether I am fit to take up this great challenge is a matter for long and careful thought.

Anselm went to bed and thought about America. He tried to remember what it had been like to feel wholly American, to look at the world as an American. He knew he had once but he could not recapture it. Over the years, moving from war to war, horror to horror, his nationality had been bled from him. The more he saw of the world's conflicts, of people dead, wounded, mutilated, raped, dispossessed of what little they had, the more unreal America seemed, the more the cruel naiveté of America embarrassed him. That was partly why he was drawn to Kaskis. Kaskis didn't expect America to behave sensibly and so he wasn't disappointed when it didn't. He remembered sitting in a dark bar in San Francisco with Kaskis. It was the mid-1980s. He was about to go to Pakistan and Afghanistan, Kaskis had just come back.

'The CIA wants to fight this one to the last dead Afghan,' Kaskis said. 'More CIA in Islamabad than in fucking Langley. Bill Casey's got this hick from Texas, he's the point in Congress. The prick's been up in the hills hanging out with the mojahedin. He thinks we give them the right stuff we can do a reverse Vietnam. And for nickels and dimes. This time we stay at home and our proxies kill Russians. Lots of Russians. Fifty-eight thousand would be a nice number.'

Kaskis had stubbed out his cigarette, fished for another. 'I weep for my fucking country,' he said. 'Everywhere we go we sow dragon's teeth.'

On the long slope towards sleep, he saw Kaskis, saw his face as he was taken away, the look back, the lift of his dark-stubbled chin, the wink. Anselm tried to shake the image away, dislodge it, but it clung, tenacious.

The dark eyes of Kaskis, the flash of his teeth. In all of it, Kaskis had never shown a sign of fear.

Before dawn, Anselm woke in a foetal clutch, straightened his body and lay on his back, stretched his arms and legs. I haven't woken myself by crying out loud for a while, he thought. I haven't woken wet with sweat to find tears on my face.

15

LONDON

THE MAN on the front page of the newspaper was over-weight, middle-aged, naked. He was looking at the camera, standing, flabby. Sagging teats, hairy belly out, engaged in a sexual act with someone lying face down. The detail had been obscured. A big headline said:

WELL, I'LL BE
BUGGERED,
MR BRECHAN!

Niemand took the newspaper from the next table when he sat down with his breakfast on a styrofoam tray. The story was about a politician called Brechan, filmed having sex with someone called Gary. Gary was quoted as saying: 'Look about fifteen, don't I? That's why they like me. I'm twenty-two. Believe that? Anyway, Angus passed me on to this other bloke. Not a clue till I saw him on telly. Oh my God, I said to ...'

Niemand ate the scrambled eggs, powdered eggs, and the small tasteless meat patty and the piece of extruded bacon. He didn't mind food like this. It was assembly-line cooking, reasonably clean. They couldn't risk people getting ill. Counter-productive. Easier to be hygienic. Just like the military.

He turned the page. The story went on. Three politicians were involved but the others weren't named. The writer said they would be: tomorrow.

The writer's name was Caroline Wishart. There was a picture of her above her byline. She had long hair and her nostrils were pinched as if she were drawing a big breath, sucking in air. He sat and thought, eyes on the street. London was much dirtier than he remembered, more poor people, more junkies.

A face. Inches away, beyond the glass, bulging hyperthyroid eyes stared at him, a woman in a knitted hat, dirt marks on her face, ash smears, darker marks. She tapped on the glass, a hand in a cotton gardening glove with its fingers cut off at the second joint.

Niemand looked away. The woman tapped again, angrily, then gave up. He watched her go. Her crammed plastic bag was splitting. Soon her possessions would begin to fall out, just more rubbish on the street.

He couldn't deal with Kennex Imports. They wouldn't send a fat and a slow the next time. He was well ahead, he had Shawn's money. He should cut his losses, take a ferry to France, Holland, Belgium, anywhere, post the tape to a newspaper or a television station.

But he didn't like being thought of as something they could simply squash, a capsule of blood, like a tick. They had tried to get the tape for nothing. Next to nothing. The price of hiring a fat and a slow.

What was the tape worth?

He found the newspaper's telephone number in the middle of the paper, on the opinion page. They kept him on hold for a long time. He had to listen to a news radio station. Then she came on.

'Caroline Wishart,' she said, a voice like the women on English television, the newsreaders who could talk without moving their lips.

He used his Glasgow accent again. 'I've got something that will interest you,' he said. 'A film. Much more important than that article today.'

'Really,' she said, dry. 'I get a lot of calls like this.'

'A massacre in Africa.'

'A lot of that goes on.'

'Soldiers killing civilians.'

'What, the Congo? Burundi?'

'No. White soldiers. Americans.'

'American soldiers killing civilians in Africa? Somalia?'

'No. This is ... it's like an execution.'

'You've got a film?'

'Yes.'

'What's your name?'

'Doesn't matter. Just give me five minutes of your time.'

He heard her sigh. 'You'll have to come here. Not today, today's impossible.'

'Has to be today.'

'Are you, ah, offering this film for sale?'

'Twenty thousand pounds.'

Caroline Harris laughed. 'I don't think you've come to the right place.'

'See it and decide,' said Niemand.

She laughed again. 'Are you a crank? No, don't answer that. Let me see, ah ... twelve noon.'

She gave him the address. 'Tell reception you've got an appointment. Give me a name.'

'Mackie,' he said, seeing in his mind's eye the little redheaded killer, the empty blue eyes, the big freckles. 'Bob Mackie.'

16

HAMBURG

ANSELM SAT in the driver's seat of the Mercedes and watched the ferry heading for the landing. It was a windy day, tiny whitecaps on the water, windsurfers out, three of them, insouciant, skidding over the cold lake on a broad reach.

'Noisy,' Tilders said. 'May not work.' He had a scope suspended from roof brackets trained on the boat. It was an English instrument made for military use with an image-stabilised lens, 80x magnification. A small LCD colour monitor sat on the console. He fiddled with the plug in his ear. Its cord ran to a black box on his lap.

They had nailed Serrano inside the hotel. He was alone, bodyguard no longer needed. In the lobby, a frail-looking old man crossed his path, stumbled and fell. For a moment, it looked as if Serrano was going to walk around him, then he bent down, put out a helping hand. The old man got up shakily, leaned on Serrano for a few seconds, thanked him profusely. Serrano continued on his way to the restaurant for breakfast.

Outside, in the car, they waited. Tilders was looking upwards, pensive. Then he closed his eyes, nodded.

'Working,' he said. 'Orange juice, eggs Florentine.'

Serrano was now wearing a micro-transmitter.

'Working,' said Tilders.

In the BMW, watching the ferry, Anselm raised his

right hand, the hand that worked fully, mimed. Tilders raised the volume.

Serrano, speaking German: ... *this ferry. What's the problem?*

Kael: *Nothing's safe any more.*

Serrano: *I can get seasick just looking at boats. In a harbour.*

Kael: *Tell me.*

Serrano: *Werner, I just heard from Hollis, they fucked the business up.*

The transmission went fuzzy, fragmented for about five seconds, abrasive sounds.

Serrano: ... *contact him.*

Kael: *He fucking hopes. Why should he do that? This is the most hopeless ...*

Serrano, a laugh: *Well, Lourens is dead, that's ...*

Sound lost again, for seconds the rough abrasive sounds.

Kael: ... *Can you grasp that? If this prick's got the papers and the film, whatever the fucking film is ... How did Lourens die?*

Serrano: *In a fire. Chemical fire. Not even teeth left.*

Kael: *Well, that's something. Shawn?*

Serrano: *Shot by blacks. So it appears. The business is strange. Werner, the question is what do we do now?*

Kael: *You ask me, you idiot? We'll have to tell the Jews. They'll blame us.*

Serrano: *You're the one who went to the Jews. You're the one who did what they said. I thought we weren't going near them again? I thought you took a holy vow?*

Silence. Sounds, bumping sounds, the ferry hitting the chop as it passed another vessel.

Kael: *You should wear a hat in Provence in summer.*

Silence. A noise. Anselm thought it was Serrano clearing his throat.

Serrano: *Well, fuck you. Maybe you need a smarter person. Have you got one?*

Silence, the bumping sounds, a cough.

Kael: *Don't be so sensitive. Hollis? What does the cunt say?*

Serrano: *He's shitting himself. He thought he was doing the right thing.*

Kael: *He should. He should shit himself. I'm going to kill him personally. Tell Richler.*

Serrano: *What?*

Kael: *What do you fucking think? Just tell him. They're up to their balls in this. If the Ashken stuff is in the papers, well …*

The ferry was docking, they could hear the sounds of movement, the voices of passengers.

Kael: *I walk from here. Thomas will take you.*

'Good bug,' said Anselm. Tilders nodded.

Kael's Mercedes, dark blue, was waiting about fifty metres from the landing, the driver standing at the rear passenger door. He was a big man in a dark suit, feet wide apart, hands at the buttons of his jacket. Tilders got him on the monitor. The shutter release was silent.

Serrano and Kael were the first passengers off the ferry. Anselm looked at the monitor. The two men were on it, Tilders was looking at the screen and taking pictures.

Silence until the men were at the car. Anselm saw Kael give Serrano something.

Serrano: *What's this?*

Kael: *Ring the number and leave a time, five minutes before the ferry I've marked leaves.*

Serrano: *Extreme, this is extreme.*

Serrano got into the Mercedes and was driven away. Kael walked off in the direction of his house. The last passenger off the ferry was a fat man in a suit carrying a briefcase. Anselm watched him come in their direction. When he was near you could see that he was a dispirited man, in him no satisfaction at the end of the working day, no expectation of ease to come. He walked past them with his head down.

'Otto will go to Hofweg,' said Tilders. 'I don't know if all this is worth it.'

'They pay for a full record,' said Anselm. 'We don't have to ask whether it's worth it.'

17

HAMBURG

ON THE OUTER fringe of Barmbek, once a working-class suburb, O'Malley was waiting for him, beer on the counter.

Anselm looked at the brown walls, brown carpet, brown curtains, the dead-faced barman.

'Impressive venue,' he said.

'Well, you're not Bavarian,' said O'Malley. 'This is a Bavarian hangout. Beer fresh from the cask. Stick around, you'll be singing old Bavarian songs.'

'Songs wildly popular in the 1930s, no doubt,' said Anselm. He was rubbing his dead fingers, bending them, turning his hand. He wanted to be outside.

The barman brought another beer without being asked.

O'Malley paid.

'I thought the Marriott was more your speed,' Anselm said, casual voice, he could do that, he got better at it every day. 'Full of rich and dubious people. Still, I can see they know you here.'

O'Malley drank, ran an index finger along his lower lip. 'I'm the customer,' he said, 'with all the rich meaning the word holds. And I like the beer. Also I'm staying nearby. How'd it go?'

'Well.'

'Listen?'

'Part of the service.'

'So?'

'Serrano told Kael about someone that's gone wrong. They talked about people now dead. Kael told him to tell a person called Richler. He could be an Israeli. Serrano's coming back tomorrow.'

'Dead people?'

'Shawn. Lourens. Something like that.'

A card game in the corner detonated, exclamations of disbelief.

Anselm went rigid, every muscle, tendon.

Four players. War babies, in their fifties, leather-faced men in leather jackets. Brown leather jackets.

Anselm drank. The beer had the feral-yeast taste. That and the men in playing cards brought a hotel on the Ammersee into his mind. Had he forgotten it? He hadn't remembered it for a long time. The woman's name was Paula, an artist, he'd lived with her in Amsterdam for a while. They'd gone on holiday, had an argument that night about another woman. Seated in the hotel's dining area, the locals looking on, she'd punched him in the mouth, a full swing across a table. Her little walnut fist drew his blood but a bone broke in it. Worth it, she said to him later, in pain, unrepentant.

'We may have to go on,' O'Malley said.

Anselm found a cigarette, put it on the table, let it lie. Any delay in lighting up was good. Some tension left him. 'I would warn of expense. If that's of consequence.'

O'Malley raised his hands, not high, big and pale strangler's hands. 'Discount for repeat business?'

'Second time's much harder.'

'Yes, women have said that to me,' said O'Malley. His eyes went to the door.

Anselm looked, tight muscles in the stomach, shoulders, thighs.

Two young men came in from the street, one tall, one average, short haircuts, soft and expensive leather jackets, not brown. They were not at their ease, eyes going around, over O'Malley and him.

The barman didn't care for them, just a small and telling shift of hips and shoulders.

O'Malley drank his final centimetres, leaned closer. His expression was amused. 'Well, got to go, a dinner date,' he said. 'These boyos ...'

Anselm didn't look at the two men. 'Is there an anxiety you haven't told me about?' He held O'Malley's eyes, smoked, sipped beer.

'You never know,' said O'Malley. 'Serrano's a dangerous man. Give me something else.'

Anselm felt in the inside pocket of his jacket. Condoms, a packet of condoms, old, some forgotten optimism in the purchase. 'I'm going to give you something worth much more than any tape,' he said.

O'Malley nodded, smiling, teeth showing, the O'Malley smile that meant nothing, not pleasure, not fear. 'I'm parked about twenty metres down, left.'

'Cowbarn beer, Bavarian nostalgics, now it's intrigue. Anything else?'

'Give it to me, mate.'

Anselm slid his hand out of his coat, put it palm down on the table. O'Malley smiled, covered his hand, gave him a pat, a gesture of friendship from a large hand, scar tissue on all the knuckles.

'*Compadre*,' said O'Malley.

Anselm removed his hand and O'Malley pocketed the condom packet.

'I liked Manila,' said Anselm. 'Can we go back?'

O'Malley shook his head. '*Ein ruheloser Marsch war unser Leben.* All the fun people are gone, Ferdie's gone, Imelda's gone, Bong-Bong's gone.' He paused. 'Angel's gone too. So am I. Anyway, you can't go back, anywhere.'

Anselm saw Angelica for a moment, the tiny tip of pink tongue, the swing of dark-red hair half curtaining an eye. 'That theory,' he said, 'has it been properly tested? Scientifically, I mean.'

O'Malley shook his head in wonder, got up, left. The inner door closed loudly on its spring. Anselm put the glass to his lips and looked around. The two newcomers were in mid-glance at each other. The taller one shrugged, looked at the barman, raised a hand to get attention.

'*Zwei Biere, bitte,*' he said in an irritated tone, not a Bavarian accent. '*Ist das tatsächlich möglich?*'

Anselm got up. At the door, he turned his head. The two men had no interest in him. He went outside, into a cold early winter evening perfumed with vehicle fumes and cooking smells, walked to where O'Malley stood beside an Audi.

'My condoms for this tape.'

'I don't know,' said O'Malley, 'I could use these frangers. The night is young.'

'Unlike you and the condoms. Will she wear her wig? It excites me, the thought.'

O'Malley smiled. 'Really, John, that's pathetic. You need more exoticism in your life. I like women in full surgical gear, green smock, rubber boots, the cap, the face mask.'

'You're sick.'

'The exact point, my good man.'

18

HAMBURG

ANSELM TOOK the car back to the office. He was looking at the logbooks when the phone rang.

'We go on,' said O'Malley.

'So be it.'

He finished his reading, signed, changed and set off for home, running in the cold dark, hearing the city humming like a single organism. There was no wind. The lake was still and the lights of the far shore all came to him in silver lines, followed him as he moved: he was the focus, the point of intersection.

As he ran, he thought about coming back to the house that day, after Beirut. It had been spring, late evening, the house empty and shuttered, almost everyone who had lived there dead. He was mostly dead too, and he had begun to cry when he opened the gate, saw the roses in bloom. He was half drunk, and he wept, sitting on the steps, his head in his hands, tears pooling in his palms. He knew that he was home, as close to home as he would ever be.

Inside the house, the power was off, the heating had not been on for years, the air smelled of dust and ancient lavender furniture polish and, somehow, faintly, of cigar smoke, of the Cuban cigars smoked by his grandfather – his great-grandfather, for all he knew. He had walked through the ground-floor rooms, opened the curtains, heavy as wet canvas, pulled the shrouds off the furniture.

That day he took the whisky out of his bag, chose a glass from dozens in the pantry, rinsed it in one of the porcelain sinks in the scullery, the water running dark for a good while. He sat on a huge, deep embossed-velvet sofa looking out at the terrace, the overgrown darkening garden, took the tablets and drank himself to sleep. At some point, he drew up his legs, becoming as small as he could.

The next day, he was woken by the pounding of the knocker on the front door. His brother, Lucas, fresh, pink-cheeked. They embraced, awkwardly, they had no easy way to touch each other, there was no fit of body, arm or hand. Anselm had felt his stubble scrape the smooth cheek of Lucas, pulled back. They drew apart.

'This is stupid,' said Lucas. 'For God's sake, we were worried, this is not a good idea, John, you're coming to stay with us, you can't stay here. Lucy's adamant, I'm adamant, for God's sake ...'

'Just for a while,' Anselm heard himself say. 'Get myself sorted out.'

They went inside. Anselm followed Lucas, his older brother grown small, as he walked around inspecting things. Lucas owned the house. It had been left to him.

In the kitchen, Lucas said, 'Are you sure? About staying here?'

'Yes.'

'I'll say it again, you're more than welcome in London. There's also the cottage in ...'

'No. Thank you. Thank Lucy. I want to be here.'

The relief in Lucas showed in his eyes, in a movement of his mouth. He took out his telephone. 'We'll need some German efficiency. Yes. Get things liveable here. I'll talk to a man I have dealings with. Deutsche Bank.'

By late afternoon, lunch had been delivered, the power was on, the phone connected, a new refrigerator was cooling in the pantry, a plumber had been, a new water-heater installed, six people had cleaned the house, cartons of food and drink delivered by a small van had been stored.

At the gate, the taxi's diesel engine thumping, Lucas said, 'Listen, I'd like to stay but I've got to be in New York tomorrow, we're in a shitfight with Murdoch's people.'

Anselm said, 'Thanks, I appreciate ... all this.'

'I'll have your stuff from San Francisco sent. It's in storage, I did that, I thought ... well, need anything, just call the number. It's on the pad. Next to the phone? I wrote it down. They'll get me. Any time, it doesn't matter.'

Anselm nodded.

'The time doesn't matter. Okay?'

His brother put out his right hand and touched Anselm's cheek, found himself doing it, crumpled his hand, tapped Anselm's face with a loose fist.

'You will,' he said. 'John, you'll call me, won't you?'

Anselm said, 'Yes. Thanks. For everything. Give my love to Lucy. And the boy.'

He'd forgotten the boy's name.

'Hugo, it's Hugo.'

'I know that. You don't always name things. You don't always have to say the name.'

He saw wariness in Lucas's eyes.

'No,' said Lucas. 'Of course. I know you know Hugo's name. I wasn't suggesting otherwise.'

They tried to hug again, failed miserably, and Lucas was driven away, a hand at the window.

Tonight, as he ran, Anselm remembered going inside and walking around, standing in the kitchen. He had been close to Riccardi for so long, so close. He had dreamed of being alone, of walking on an empty beach, no one near, and now he was alone and it frightened him. He had sat down at the table and rested his forehead on the lined scrubbed wood, cool, and he had begun to cry again.

Now, in his street, almost walking, sweat cooling on him, that day seemed close. He thought that he was only marginally different now. In some ways, he was worse now.

He went inside, showered, drank, watched television. He hoped the phone would ring. It didn't. He went to the kitchen, sped across tape number 3, sampling, looking for a mention of Moritz, his own teenage voice strange to him. He caught the word:

Moritz. What happened to him?

It's a lovely day. We could go for a walk. Are you bored here? With an old woman? Two old women.

I'm not bored. I like being here. I want to know about the family, my dad doesn't say much so it's ...

It was the summer he was seventeen, the five weeks he had spent with his great-aunt, the two of them and Fräulein Einspenner in the huge house. Next door, a girl lived, Ulrike, a year younger. She wore a big straw hat when she was out in the long garden that ran to the canal, and she was pale in a way no American girl was pale. He lusted after her. Once, after they were introduced, they sat side by side on the terrace. She leant forward and he looked into the big, loose armhole of her summer blouse and saw that she was not wearing a bra. He saw the full hanging curve of her right breast. Even paler than her face. Pale and veined like graveyard marble. His blood changed course. He made an excuse, went upstairs to his bedroom and stood looking down at her, penis in hand.

Einspenner has always been besotted by you. From the day you came here, a little American boy who spoke German.

What happened to Moritz?

He didn't come back from the war.

He was killed?

Well, the war.

A silence.

Afterwards, we tried to forget the war, you know. It was so unfortunate. Such a mistake. Your great-grandfather went into a decline. The business was ruined. All those years, the tradition. Destroyed. Gone. Your grandfather tried to pretend it wasn't happening. He would not accept it. For him, London was closer than Berlin or Munich, he went to England five or six times a year. He talked about going to London as we would talk about going to, going to Mönckebergstrasse. He had old friends from Oxford. And the people we dealt with of course. He knew Chamberlain, do you know that?

No.

And there was his mistress in London.

Chamberlain's mistress?

No, your grandfather's mistress, that drew him to London. Of course. She lived on Cheyne Walk.

You knew about his mistress?

It was no secret. We all knew. I met her after the war. A woman of great charm. And dignity. She was not a kept woman, she had her own money. He was a very attractive man, my brother. He hadn't been close to your grandmother for a long time. They were friends, but they weren't close. You know what I mean. She had her own interests.

Didn't the war ... I mean, what did his mistress feel about Germans then?

Silence.

She understood that Hitler didn't speak for all Germans. But lots of English people admired Hitler. It made your grandfather so angry. That Mitford girl who hung around Hitler. Her father was an English lord.

About Moritz, didn't you ...

What do they teach you at school? Do you read the great works?

Well, we have to read a lot of ...

My father loved English poets. Milton and Wordsworth. They were his favourites. And Blake, he liked Blake. He used to read them to us. Thackeray and Dickens he liked too. And Gibbon, he used to take Gibbon on holiday to the sea.

So was Moritz ...

And Shakespeare, he loved Shakespeare, the tragedies. He used to say that Shakespeare didn't write the tragedies, a German must have written them and had his work stolen because no one except a German could be so ...

Sitting at the kitchen table, Anselm listened until the end of the tape, lulled by Pauline's quiet voice talking about people whose blood ran in his veins and who were now just faces in faded photographs. He heard himself ask about Moritz again and receive no answer.

19

HAMBURG

IN THE morning, Anselm spread out the family tree his great-aunt had drawn up on pieces of paper, taping pages together as the record widened and lengthened. He had found it, carefully folded, in a desk drawer in the small sitting room. Unfolded, it was half the size of a single-bed sheet.

Pauline had traced the family back into the German primeval forest. The Hamburg branch had come to the city in 1680. From then on, she had recorded in her minute script the occupation of every member who achieved some distinction. Here a senator, here a consul, aldermen, physicians, a writer, a judge, attorneys, scholars, a composer. The rest were presumably just merchants. There was a French connection too, Anselm noticed. Pauline had written *Huguenot* in parentheses after the French names of people two Anselms married in the late 1600s.

Anselm found his grandfather, Lucas, and siblings Gunther, Pauline and Moritz. The birth dates, marriages and offspring of the first three were recorded, as were Lucas's death in 1974 and Gunther's in 1971. For Moritz, there was only his date of birth: 1908.

What became of Moritz, who looked like Count Haubold von Einsiedel? Did he marry? Were there children? When did he die?

Anselm remembered his father talking about Gunther. In 1940, the three children had been sent to live with Gunther and his American wife in Baltimore and they never really went home to Hamburg. But his father had never mentioned Moritz.

Time to go to work. Beginning to run in the morning was like starting an old machine, like pulling the cord of a lawnmower never oiled, the moving pieces reluctant, grating.

When he was warm, moving without pain, Manila came to his mind: Angelica Muir, the side-on look of her, the small nose, her teeth, the taste of her.

After the first lunch, he had many meals – lunches, dinners, late breakfasts, early breakfasts – with O'Malley, Angelica and Kaskis. They went to all kinds of gatherings and parties, everything seemed to turn into a party. O'Malley floated in the culture, spoke fluent Tagalog, knew everyone from millionaire Marcos cronies to penniless hardline Communists. He never stopped paying, no one else was allowed to pay. And, when things were moving at some party, he broke into song – country & western songs, Irish songs, operatic arias, songs from the War of Independence against the Spanish, Neil Diamond's greatest hits, Cuban revolutionary songs.

O'Malley had called himself a financial adviser. His firm was Matcham, Suchard, Loewe, two secretaries and an elegant crew-cut Filipino with an American accent and a wardrobe of Zegna suits.

After he had filed his last story from the Philippines, Anselm had dinner with O'Malley and Angelica and Kaskis. She was wearing a green silk dress that touched her only on the shoulders, her nipples, her sharp hipbones. By midnight, fifteen people were in the party. At 4 a.m., they were in a garden, smoking the weed from the mountains, drinking out of the bottle, San Miguel, vodka, anything, fifty or sixty people, talking politics, breaking off to join O'Malley in songs about heartbreak, revenge, and dying for freedom. Around 5 a.m., under a tree in the heady night, he told Angelica that he was in love with her, it had come to him suddenly, no, a lie, from the moment he met her.

In the shadows, she kissed him, his head in her hands, her tongue in his mouth, touched his teeth with her perfect teeth, moved them, a silken abrasion felt in the bones of his face. It went on for a long time.

That kiss was in Anselm's mind as he ran down the home stretch, a cold wind coming over the Alster, his eyes watering. He remembered the soft, damp night, the feel of the tropical tree against his back, against his spine, Angelica's hipbones, her pubic bone on his, that he wanted to kiss her forever. If necessary, they could be fed intravenously while they kissed.

And then, at 5.30 a.m., he had to leave, the day already opening, a sky streaked from edge to edge with pale trails as if some silent armada of jets had passed in the darkness. Angelica put her hands into the taxi, ran them over his face like a blind person, said, 'You should have spoken.'

She put her head in, one last kiss, their lips bruised, puffy, like boxers' lips.

O'Malley appeared. 'The right thing now, boyo,' he said. 'Go home and tell them to pull the plug on the miserable old cunt.'

Taking off, looking down at the hopeless tilting shanties, children, dogs, his numb fingers trying to direct the nozzle's airstream onto his face, his eyes, it came to Anselm.

On the first night in the Tap Room, the Rotary harlot with the hand that lay on him like a big spider, O'Malley had believed that he was CIA and he had never changed his mind.

Years later, on that morning in Cyprus, two clean men, soaked, scrubbed, shampooed, cleaner than they would ever be again, after the doctors took off their gloves and left, Riccardi said something.

'Why me?' Riccardi said, not looking at Anselm. 'Why am I the one they didn't hurt?'

A hundred metres to go to the gates, no wind left, aching.

He couldn't run it out, stopped, stood with his hands on his hips, feeling sick. Walked the rest of the way, trying to regain composure.

Eyes on him. He felt them and he looked.

Inskip was on the balcony, black T-shirt, shaking his head. He drew on a cigarette. A second, then smoke came out of him like his spirit escaping.

20

LONDON

SECURITY RANG and she went to the bare, functional room and looked at the man downstairs. The equipment was good quality, big colour monitor, and there were two angles, full frontal, close up, and full length, left profile.

He was tall, dark hair flat on his head, cut short. He looked French, Mediterranean, a long nose, broken, no twitches or quick eye movements, that was a good sign, coat with a leather collar.

'Bag?' said Caroline Wishart.

'All okay metalwise,' said the security man.

'Send him up.'

He was standing when she came into the interview room, nodded at her, eyes grey-green, the colour of the underside of poplar leaves, the poplars at the bottom of her grandmother's garden.

'Caroline Wishart,' she said. 'I've only got a couple of minutes.'

He took a video cassette out of a side pocket.

'Sit down,' she said.

She took the tape. A slip of paper was taped to the side with numbers written on it in a strong vertical hand: 1170. Slotted it into the machine, and found the remote control. She switched the set on, pressed the Play button. Just static. She pressed again, pressed anything. Numbers appeared at the bottom of the screen.

'Fuck this,' she said. She looked at him. He was sitting with his hands on his stomach. Most men would have been twitching to intervene. Either he was different or he was even more technologically incompetent that she was.

He said nothing. He didn't look at her.

'Can you do this?' she said, hating to have to say it.

He held out his hand. She gave him the remote. He switched off the set, switched on, pressed a button, pressed another.

The film began.

The sub-tropical plain, dark.

When she saw the bodies, Caroline felt sweat start in her hair and she began to feel sick, a small wave of nausea, a ripple. She glanced at the man, Mackie. He had laced his fingers.

At a certain point, Caroline closed her eyes. She turned her head slightly so that Mackie couldn't see.

'That's it,' he said.

She opened her eyes and watched him retrieve the tape. He didn't sit down again, stood looking at her. She didn't know what you did with something like this. This wasn't politicians fucking rent boys. That was simple, just an extension of the story that got her to London, her breakthrough story: *Mayor Denies Brothel Payoff*. She should get Halligan in ... no, he'd simply take over, it wouldn't be her story any more.

'They tried to kill me,' he said.

'Who?'

He shrugged. 'Sent people to my hotel.'

'And?'

Another shrug. 'I'm here.'

She realised. 'You offered it to someone else?'

'And now I'm offering it to you.'

'Could be faked,' she said because she couldn't think of any other response. Distrust, suspicion – they were always sound responses in journalism. 'I'd have to show it to other people here, they'd check it out … then we could talk about money.'

He said nothing, just picked up his bag and walked. She hadn't expected that, he was going. She felt something slipping out of her hands, got up, went after him, touched his sleeve, grabbed his arm.

'Settle down, hold it,' she said. 'Just hold on for one second, will you, I'm not …'

Mackie stopped, turned his head. 'What?'

'I don't have the authority to buy something like this.' She stood close to him, still holding his sleeve, looked into his eyes, it often worked. 'I'm sorry I said that about, about being faked. I'm sorry. Will you leave the tape with me? A copy? I promise I'll give you an answer today.'

He moved away from her, just a small distance. 'No,' he said, 'this was a mistake.'

Caroline knew she should plead. There was a time for pleading. It was any time you saw the shimmer of a story that would go on the front page without argument, would require no exercise of editorial judgment by any drink-befuddled executive prat, would speak for itself in short headline words an eight-year-old could understand.

'Listen,' she said, holding on to his arm. 'I don't need a copy, an hour, two hours, that's it, two hours, that's all I need, I'll talk to people. An answer in two hours. No bullshit. Give me a number.'

He looked at her for so long that she let go his arm and blinked.

'Please,' she said. 'Trust me.'

'One o'clock,' he said. 'I'll ring you at one. Just say yes or no.'

His accent wasn't Scottish now. It was South African.

'Mr Mackie, we might need a contract, a legal document, you know, we could do this through lawyers, you'd be protected and we'd ...'

'Just say yes or no. Twenty thousand. I'll tell you where to send it.'

When he was gone, she went to her tiny cubicle, her first day in it. She rang security and asked for prints of Mackie, sat back and thought for a long time about what she should do. This was her story: the man had come to her because of her byline on the Brechan story. But it was too big for her. He wanted cash for something that might be worthless.

It wasn't. She felt it in her marrow. Her instinct said this was a big story. And her instinct was good. It had taken her to three big stories in Birmingham.

But Halligan would take it away from her. The story would disappear into the inner sanctum without her.

She had to deliver it personally, the way she'd delivered Brechan. Brechan had been the most wonderful luck. She would be writing lifestyle crap now, ten hottest pick-up bars in the City, if someone hadn't decided to give her Brechan's rent boy.

'We know your work from Birmingham,' the gaunt man in the pub in Highgate said. 'We think you're the person to expose this.'

Luck, just pure luck.

It didn't happen twice.

Who to go to now? Who to trust? Who could get the money?

Colley. He was the only one. She'd been introduced to him in the pub and he'd bought her drinks and made lewd suggestions. Her boss in the permanent catfight that was the Frisson section had told her that Colley ran his own mini-empire. He kept his own hours, only came to conferences when he felt like it.

She went to his office, not a cubicle, a proper office with floor-to-ceiling walls, and knocked.

'Enter,' shouted Colley.

He was sitting at a large desk covered with files and newspapers-looking at a laptop, a cigarette burning in an old saucer. She thought he looked like someone who had lost a large amount of weight quickly.

'Caroline Wishart,' she said. 'We met in the pub?'

'I remember. Some things I remember.'

'I need help.'

Colley looked at her. His eyes were heavy-lidded and he was squinting as if caught in a spotlight. 'First you pinch the Brechan story from under my nose,' he said, 'now you come crawling for help.' He pointed downwards. 'Under the desk, you upper-class slut. Unzip me with your teeth.'

Caroline sat down. She had to tough this out. 'I thought your generation still had button-ups,' she said. 'Button-up flies are hard on teeth. All I need is the benefit of your experience.'

He smiled, thin lips, yellow teeth. 'All? Took me thirty years to get where I am. Cost me my liver and my hair, most of my brain. You ruling-class gels walk in, you pout and shake your little tits and they make you editor of some new fucking rubbish section. Grovel to me.'

'I've just seen a film. Soldiers killing civilians. White soldiers killing blacks. A man wants to sell it.'

She told him about Mackie, about the tape labelled 1170.

'Well,' he said, 'probably South Africans, won't surprise anybody. Killed blacks like flies. That's not news any more.'

'He says the soldiers are American. They're shooting people lying on the ground. Seems like a whole village. It's like an execution. Kids too.'

Colley moved his head around, light catching his dirty glasses. 'What was the name again?'

'Mackie.'

'And he says people tried to kill him in his hotel in London?'

'Yes.'

'What's he want?'

'Twenty grand.'

'That's it? Comes in, shows you the film, says he wants twenty grand?'

'Yes.'

'Generally, there's a bit more mystery and foreplay. What's your feeling about the film?'

'Real. And awful. Some of the people might be identifiable.'

'Soldiers?'

'There's a group near helicopters. Might be two civilians. He says someone who wanted to buy the film tried to kill him. When I said I needed time, he walked.'

'Bluff.'

'He was walking,' said Caroline. 'He was going. No doubt in my mind.'

'Well, the walk. I've had walkers. Let them piss off, get to the lift. Where'd you let him get to?'

'Okay, I'm learning,' Caroline said. 'He's ringing at one, he wants a yes or no. Should I take it to Halligan?'

She watched Colley scratch his head, a delicate operation. He'd had two kinds of hair transplants and a surgical procedure involving strips of his scalp being moved around, with strange results.

'Yes,' he said. 'My view is that the proper thing to do is take this to Halligan immediately.'

'Well,' she said, 'if that's your advice.'

'No,' he said. 'It's not. Twenty grand's nothing. Is this a joint venture then?'

'It is.'

'Give me an hour. We can deliver this without Halligan and the fucking lawyers.'

21

LONDON

NIEMAND FOUND a car hire firm in Clerkenwell, used his passport, the international licence, paid for seven days in cash, a ridiculous sum. He would be gone much sooner, but his instinct said to leave a margin. Hired killers had come for him in the night and he didn't know how they found him.

He drove around for a few hours, places he knew from his runs. He wanted to be gone, London was full of rich people, he didn't care about that one way or another, but the poor and the desperate were shame-faced, hiding in alleys and under bridges when they should be in the open, shaming the rich.

He parked and waited for 1 p.m., mobile on the passenger's seat. He would go to Crete and stay with his cousin. Dimitri was like him, they looked alike, all the relatives said that when they'd come to look at him and his mother after their arrival from Africa. It had been late afternoon when they reached the village in the hills. The taxi dropped them in the square. His mother went somewhere and came back with two men, who took their suitcases. They'd all walked down some narrow broken streets and then it was all old women in black, men with moustaches, staring children, everyone seemed to pay more attention to him than they did to his mother. They didn't look at her in the way they looked at him.

He knew now they were looking at the other blood in him, they didn't see a lot of strange blood.

Dimi became his friend quickly, in hours, no one ever wanted to be his friend before. Dimi had to be dragged away that evening, was at the door the next morning to take him away, show him things. Dimi taught him how to fish, taught him the Greek swearwords, how to deal with the bigger boys at school, and how you could see the woman undressing if you crept out late, went over the roofs, dead quiet, like cats, and leaned dangerously over a parapet, holding on to a television aerial. He remembered the wait, the agony, the way she came and went, and the final delirious moments when she stood in their full sight, the pull of her petticoat over her head, the slither, the release of her big breasts, their lift and sag, the long dark nipples and the loaded bottom-heavy swing as she turned, tossed her hair, black hair, coffin-black and shiny.

Did she know they were watching?

He looked at his watch, his mind still on Crete, a boy leaning over a parapet in the warm barking night, engorged, pulse beating in his head, erection pressed against the rough surface like a spring – painful, pleasurable.

It was just on 1 p.m. He considered his plan. Careful was seldom wrong, everything he'd been through told him that. He found the piece of paper with the number, switched on the phone, and dialled.

'Yes.' The woman, Caroline Wishart.

'It's Mackie,' he said. 'Yes or no.'

'Yes.'

'Cash. I'll need cash. Today.'

'That's very difficult,' she said.

His didn't like the sound of that, his hand needed something to do, opened the glove compartment. A

McDonald's packet, scrunched up, greasy. They had rented him an uncleaned car. He would buy a roll of shit-paper and block the air intake before he gave it back.

'I'm going. Yes or no?'

'Mr Mackie, the answer is yes but you must give me until tomorrow to get the money. I will get it, I promise you but I can't until tomorrow. It's very difficult to get a sum like that quickly in cash. But I will. I will. Please bear with me. Will you?'

Niemand hesitated but he believed her. 'Okay, I'll ring you tomorrow at twelve, at noon. Have it in a bag, a sports bag. In fifties. Give me your cellphone number.'

She gave it to him.

'Mr Mackie, how can we be sure ...'

He told her where to be.

22

WASHINGTON

ABOVE THE tree line, the mountain was a cone of purest white and the sky behind it was grey, grey with darker streaks, the colour of the puffs of smoke that issued from the trees – a ragged line of puffs, one, two, three, four, five. When the sound of the incoming shells came to the ears of the men and boys watching in the village, they took shelter, casually, it wasn't done to hurry, show any anxiety, not in front of the cameras, the journalists.

Scott Palmer looked at his empty whisky glass, didn't resist the temptation. He went to the drinks table and poured two fingers of whisky and one of mineral water. There was no sleep without whisky, precious little with it. Sleep had gone with Lana. Before, really, he hadn't been sleeping much for a long time.

The television camera was moving around trying to find artillery shells landing on the village, it found a hole in a roof, possibly an old hole, went to two men with cigarettes under their moustaches.

'Don't stay up all night.'

His son was in the doorway, head on one side, hair falling over an eye. Palmer looked at him and he felt the pulse of love in his throat. The boy was hopeless, twenty-four and still taking useless college courses, talking eco-nonsense, playing his guitar, surfing.

'Finishing up, son,' he said, showing the glass. 'Long day.'

Andy came over and put his hands on Palmer's shoulders.

'Don't work so hard,' he said. 'Where's it get you? We ever going to play golf again? Feels like years.'

'Soon,' said Palmer. 'Soon. We'll take a decent break, go to the Virgins, play golf, sail.'

'Count me in,' said Andy. He ran a quick hand over his father's hair. 'Just that one, right? Then you go to bed.'

Palmer nodded. When he looked around, Andy was at the door, looking back at him.

'I used to say that to you,' Palmer said.

Andy nodded, didn't smile, a sadness in his look.

'Goodnight, Dad.'

'Goodnight, boy. Sleep tight.'

He put his head back, held whisky in his mouth, thought about Andy, about the day Lana drove the Mustang under a car transporter on Highway 401 outside Raeford, North Carolina, 2.45 in the afternoon. She was alone, leaving a motel, lots of drink taken.

Everyone knew who. Two years later, drinking with Ziller, they were old buddies, they'd been through shit together, Ziller said, 'That day. Who was it?'

'Seligson. But you know that.'

'Never thought of killin him?'

'Wife and a kid, a girl. What's the point of two dead? And me doing life. Who'd look after Andy?'

The phone on the side table rang.

Palmer looked at his watch. He muted the television sound, let the phone ring for a while, cleared his throat.

'Yes.'

'General, I'm sorry if I've woken you. It's Steve Casca.'

124

'One forty-five? Asleep? Who does that?'

'Sir, may I ask you to ring me back?'

Palmer put the phone down and dialled the number showing on the display. Casca answered after the first beep.

'Thank you, sir. Sir, a minor Langley asset in London has contacted their resident. The asset's been offered a film. US military personnel in action. Said to be filmed in Africa, some kind of massacre. That's the asset's term.'

'Taken when?'

'Not known, sir.'

'What else?'

'The tape has the numbers One, One, Seven, Zero. Eleven seventy, that is. On a label.'

Palmer closed his eyes. Eleven Seventy. No.

'We can find nothing on that,' said Casca. 'We thought to ask if this might have meaning for you.'

The television was now showing a building with a third-floor balcony hanging away from the wall, hanging from one support. The double doors leading out to it had blown off. In the street, a crowd had gathered, policemen in *kepis*. It was a French city, possibly Paris.

'Probably best not to take it any further,' said Palmer. 'Leave it with me. I'll talk to some people.'

'If you say so, sir.'

'I'll need the names, the asset and so forth.'

'I can give you that now, sir.'

Palmer listened and wrote on the pad. 'That's fine,' he said. 'Steve, I don't think you need to log this call.'

'What call was that, sir? Apologies about the time.'

'Sound instincts.'

'Goodnight, sir.'

'Goodnight, Steve.'

He'd always thought well of Casca, even after the serial fuck-ups in Mogadishu. He'd behaved well in Iran, he'd showed his worth. Palmer put the television sound on again. The building was the Turkish embassy in Paris. Mortared, four rounds, possibly five. Mortared? An embassy in Paris? The whole world was turning into Iraq.

He muted the set again and dialled a number. Eleven Seventy. Would it never go away?

'Yes?'

It was the boyfriend.

'I need to speak to Charlie.'

'I'm afraid ...'

'Palmer.'

'Please hold, Mr Palmer.'

It took a while. People had worried about Charlie being a fag. But no one was going to blackmail Charlie. Anyway, faggotry had an honourable history in the service. British fags were another matter altogether.

'Sir.'

'Serious situation, Charlie,' said Palmer. 'Some things have to happen. I want you to arrange it now and I want you to go tonight and make sure everything's neat. Neatness is important.'

'Yes, sir.'

23

HAMBURG

BAADER RAISED his eyebrows and puffed his cheeks. After a while, he expelled air and said, 'You're asking me?'

'No,' said Anselm. 'I'm just going around exposing my personal life to anyone who's breathing.'

'When did you last ask anyone for advice?'

'I had the idea I should change,' Anselm said. 'Clearly a very stupid idea.' It was. He was already full of regret.

Baader looked unhappy. 'Well, change, you're almost normal these days. Except for the fingers. Just hungover. Christ knows how you run with a hangover. I can't walk with a hangover.'

'It's my way of punishing myself,' said Anselm. 'You get women to cane you. I run. Should I talk to her?'

'I should cane myself. No, that doesn't work. Like massage, can't massage yourself. Can you buy a caning machine? Do they have that?'

'Everything. They have everything. Are you hearing me?'

'Jesus, John, talk to her. What does she look like?'

Anselm hesitated. 'Not like Freud,' he said.

A smile from Baader, the sly-fox look. 'Attractive, that's what you're saying, is it?'

'The academic look, not necessarily my taste. The scholar. A certain primness.' He used the word *geziertheit*.

'Glasses?' Baader was interested.

'No. Well, yes.'

'I like glasses. Black frames?'

'Me, we're talking about me. Less about you.'

Baader looked away, bent his head, scratched an ear. 'To be serious,' he said, 'what the fuck would I know? The things that happened to you, I can't begin to ... Well, are you feeling okay?'

'I'm feeling fine.'

'The memory?'

'Bits come back. It doesn't bother me as much as it used to.'

'Well, talking can't hurt. You've never talked to me. Who did you talk to?'

'I'm sorry I mentioned this. Paid Gerda? If not, I'm looking for another job.'

A hand in the air, a stop sign, gentle. 'John, relax. Gerda's paid, the landlord's been paid, everyone's been paid. We're up to date on payments. I'm personally skinned but everyone's been paid.'

Anselm went back to his office. Talked to anyone? What was there to say? How did you talk about fear, about cringing like a whipped child, about pissing in your pants, other things, sobbing uncontrollably, other things?

Carla Klinger knocked. 'The new file,' she said. 'The chemist. He flew to London. Now I've got him on a flight to Los Angeles from Glasgow, took off an hour ago.'

It was a second before he placed the chemist. Yes. The chemist's company in Munich thought he was planning to defect to the competition. Five years he'd been on a research project, they were close.

'That's good work, Carla. Tell the client.'

She smiled her cursory smile, nodded, turned on the stick.

Good work? Thieves, contract thieves, spying, stealing to order, stealing anything for anyone. Anselm thought about the woman they'd found in Barcelona, Lisa Campo. He remembered his reply to Inskip's question.

What do you think? Charlie gets his money back, they fall in love again, go on a second honeymoon. Eat pizza.

For all they knew, Charlie Campo wanted to find his wife so that he could torture her and kill her. For all they cared. Just a job with a success bonus. Good work? He'd enjoyed it at the start, four of them using Baader's purloined software, learning how to search the waters for a single rare fish, the net ever expanding, dropping deeper. Sitting in a quiet room, in the gloom, watching the radar, waiting for the blip, waiting for the coelacanth. He'd felt removed from himself, a relief from the running introspection, the endless, pointless internal dialogue. Just the quiet lulling of the electronic turbines, the hard drives spinning, spinning, spinning. But now ...

Anselm went down the passage to Beate's office. She wasn't there. He was grateful not to have to endure her remarks about health as he went onto the balcony to smoke.

A cold day but dry, patches of blue coming and going in the high, wispy cloud. In line with Pöseldorf, a ferry with a ragged tail of gulls was cutting through the chop. Kael and Serrano would be off their ferry by now.

Alex Koenig.

He could ring her to say he would talk to her about what had happened to him. Within limits. He could set limits, things he wouldn't talk about, the parameters of their talk.

What was the point of that? How could he set limits? What would they be?

Beate tapped on the glass. Anselm flicked his cigarette

end into the garden below – not a garden, just balding lawn and unpruned leaf-spotted roses, no one cared.

This would be Tilders. He went inside. Beate smiled her beatific smile.

'I'd have brought the phone but I saw you were almost finished with that vile thing.'

'You're never finished with vile things,' said Anselm.

24

LONDON

THE STORE was warm and fragrant, like a palace in a dream. As Niemand wandered around, the expensive scents of the women shoppers brushed his face, clung to him. On an escalator, he stood behind three youngish Japanese women in grey, sleek as pigeons, eyes rounded by the knife. They appeared to be crying.

When he'd finished looking, riding the escalators, he left by a back exit and walked around the block. He found a spot to watch the front doors and dialled. Caroline Wishart answered on the third ring.

He told her where he was, where to go.

He didn't see her go into the store, there were two entrances, the pavement was crowded. After a while, he crossed the street, went into the store through the right-hand doors, turned right and climbed the stairs to the third floor. He went through jewellery and handbags, around four Asian women talking in undertones, rings on their fingers flashing like lights. At the escalator, he dialled again.

'Yes,' she said.

'I got bored,' he said. 'I'm on the fourth floor looking at the toys. Come up the escalator next to the stationery, in the corner, know where that …'

'Yes,' she said. 'I know.'

He waited, saw her pass. Waited, watched the people, dialled her again.

'Sorry,' he said, 'you'll have to come down again. To the second floor.'

'Don't mess me around,' she said. 'This isn't a spy film.'

He looked at his watch, stepped onto the up escalator.

Caroline Wishart didn't see him until the last second, when he was offering the package. She opened her mouth to speak, closed it, held out the bag with one hand, took the package in the other.

Niemand took the bag.

'Goodbye,' he said.

He walked up the escalator, three people ahead of him, bag in his left hand, three steps at a time, glanced back. She was off the escalator, half hidden by a man in a dark suit. Another man was in front of her, facing her, close.

When he turned his head, looked up, he saw a woman at the top of the escalator, back to him, a young woman in black, dark hair on her shoulders, talking on a cellphone held in her right hand, her head back.

Niemand thought: Who do these people phone? Who phones them? What do they have to say to each other? He looked down, watched the metal belt slide beneath the shiny steel plate, he'd always felt some unease at the moment; in his life he had been on escalators no more than a few dozen times.

He was taking the step to solid ground, to safety, when the woman on the cellphone raised her left hand, fingers spread, her hand moving, her fingers speaking.

She had hair on her knuckles, dark hair.

She turned, less than two metres from him, smiling, a nice smile, big mouth, dark lipstick, brought the cellphone away from her head, looking at it, chest-high.

Niemand took a pace and dived at the man in drag.

He was in the air when he saw the two short black barrels protruding from the top of the phone.

He heard nothing. Saw only a lick of flame.

The blow was high in his chest, no great pain.

Fuck, he thought, why didn't I expect this?

Then he had his left hand on the weapon, brought his right hand down the man's face, clawed his face, nails just long enough to gouge flesh from forehead, eyebrows, eyelids, cheekbones. He made a screeching noise, then Niemand had his fingers hooked behind the man's lower lip, nails beneath the teeth, wrenching.

The man in drag was not prepared for this kind of attack, this kind of ferocity, this kind of pain. Blood running into his eyes, blind, he let Niemand drag him to his knees. Niemand got the weapon away from him, no resistance, let go the jaw, kneed him in the head twice, three times, the man fell sideways, head hit the carpet, the wig was half off, near-shaven skull revealed, pale, shocking.

Niemand jumped on his head, kicked it, looked around, grabbed the sports bag, suddenly aware of the people, shouting.

Go down, said his instincts.

He went up, ran up the escalator, hurting a little in the chest now, not much, people getting out of his way on the moving steel ramp. On the next floor, he told himself, Walk, be calm, no one here saw anything, no one heard anything. Seconds, it lasted seconds.

Walk, just walk.

He walked through games and dolls, toys, saw a stairway, no, not that one, a section full of plump women, maternity wear, shoes, children's shoes, children standing around looking bored, rich children buying school uniforms, veer right, through a doorway, stairs. Yes.

He went down, as fast as he could go without causing people to look, not many people coming up the stairs, he was bleeding a lot, he could feel the warmth of his own blood on his skin now, but the pain was bearable.

Bearable, he said to himself, you're not dying, this is not a terminal wound, not a lung shot. No, definitely not a lung shot. He'd seen enough lung shots, he knew lung shots. The sound, the strange bubbling sound. Nothing like that. He was breathing fine, just pain and blood, that was nothing.

Sonny, you die when I fucken tell you to and not a fucken second before.

They were the words mad Sergeant Toll shouted at him when he lay in an erosion gully, bruised all over, arm broken, at the School of Infantry obstacle course. Niemand used the same words to the curly-haired boy, Jacobs, whose blood was lying like red mercury on the ancient dust of Angola. But Jacobs hadn't obeyed. He'd coughed blood and he'd died.

Floors, he'd lost track of floors, surely this was the ground floor. No, one to go, shit no, more than one. He wasn't feeling well. Not a good idea this, he should have left Mr Fucking Shawn's cassette where he found it.

More stairs. Another floor? No, he remembered this section, the smell, perfume, somehow not women's perfume, too much lemon and bay, this was the ground floor, carry on down, he'd be in the basement.

An exit, right there, to his right, he hadn't noticed it. He walked towards the doors. Upright, don't hunch, the tendency was to hunch when hurt, why was that? It didn't help, didn't take away any pain.

He looked around, not feeling alert. Where were they? They hadn't sent one man to kill him. One man in a dress and a wig. They'd sent two men to the hotel, that hadn't worked. Second try, this place would be crawling with killers, a full fucking platoon of them.

He went past the doorman, who stared at him, then

onto the pavement, lots of people, they were hard to avoid, all carrying bags. He bumped into a woman, said sorry. Daylight fading. Cold day, cold on his face, he felt warm inside, that was a good sign, they always talked about feeling cold when you were hit badly. The old hands. He was an old hand now. But he'd never taken a bad hit. Just the piece out of his side, the flesh wound in the bum and the grenade slivers in his arm and his chest.

He knew where he was. The underground was just around the corner. Catch the tube as planned.

The pain was in his jaw now, why was that?

He crossed the side street, walked to the corner, turned into the busy street. No, he shouldn't catch the tube, he'd be trapped down there. He walked past the station entrance, halfway down the block. Cross, better to cross, he thought. Crossing the street, traffic stalled, walking between the cars. This was a silly thing to have done, you didn't want to die for this kind of shit.

Too late to think about that. Anyway you didn't want to die protecting parasites in Joburg, that would be a really seriously stupid way to go.

'You all right?'

Someone was speaking to him. Someone on a motorbike, sitting in the traffic, a yellow helmet, waiting for the lights

'Need a lift,' said Niemand. 'I'm hurt.'

'Get on,' said yellow helmet.

Niemand got on, bag on his lap, held the sides of the rider's leather jacket. He looked back. Two men in dark suits were on the corner outside the store, looking around.

Then, through the cars, he saw another man in a dark suit coming, running around cars.

Coming to get him. Make sure this time.

He couldn't move, couldn't get off the bike.

What was the point? He couldn't run.

The man was fifteen metres away, a pale face, dark hair, coming quickly.

Fuck, he thought. Stupid.

With a roar, the bike pulled away, went between a car and delivery vehicle. Niemand's head went back and when it came forward he couldn't stop it, it came to rest between the rider's shoulder blades, wanted to stay there.

This wasn't good. How much blood had he lost? He took a hand off the rider's jacket and felt his shirt. It was wet, soaked.

Too much blood.

25

LONDON

'YOU TELL me what's going on,' said Caroline Wishart. 'Two bastards sandwich me, take the package. Stolen goods, the one says. Then someone attacks Mackie.'

'Close the door, will you?'

Colley was holding a plain cigarette in long ochre fingers, tapping it on his desktop, tapping one end, turning it over, tapping the other. 'I'm buggered,' he said. 'Who knows how many people he's swindled.'

'Where'd you get the money?'

'The money?'

'Yes, the money.'

He lit the cigarette with an old gas lighter, many clicks before the flame and the deep draw, belched smoke, did some coughing. 'Chalk this one up to character building,' he said. 'Some you win, some are fuck-ups. That's life.'

'Who'd you tell?'

'Tell? Who'd you tell?' He put on a high-pitched and squeaky voice, his idea of an upper-class girl's voice.

Caroline wanted to strangle Colley, go over to him and slap his face and put her hands around his mottled neck.

'Leaving aside the pathetic quality of your imitations,' she said, 'where'd the money come from?'

He smiled, a pleased expression. 'It wasn't actually real money.'

'What?'

'The top and the bottom ones, yes. The middle ones ... shall we say Middle Eastern?'

It was dawning on Caroline that she was missing something. 'Well, shall "we" tell me what the fuck's going on here?'

Colley formed his lips into an anus and blew tiny, perfect smoke rings. She saw the pale, vile tip of his tongue. The grey circles met the thermal from the ground-level heating duct, rose, dissolved.

'You came to me for help, remember,' Colley said. 'You could've gone to Halligan, but no, you thought he'd pinch your story, make you sorry you screwed him with your non-negotiable demands.'

She could not contain herself. 'Well, not doing that, that was probably a big mistake.'

Carefully, Colley rested his cigarette in a saucer, finger-shaped nicotine stains around the edges, looked up at her. 'Listen, sweetheart,' he said, 'your big scoop, it happened to you, you didn't happen to it. Now you've got to produce another one. And you gels, you can't actually do that, you can't actually do anything, and once you stop giving the working-class old farts cock-stands, once the next little upper-class tart comes along, well then you're back to writing your lifestyle crap.'

He was telling her something but she couldn't quite grasp what it was.

'Still,' said Colley, 'you can always get daddy to set you up as an interior decorator, can't you?'

'So what do I do?' she said.

'Nothing. Move on, this never got off the ground, no harm done, we just forget it. We don't put it in the CV and we don't entertain the pub with the story.'

'That's it?'

Colley took off his glasses, looked for something to

clean them with, found a crumpled tissue and breathed on the filthy lenses. 'Well,' he said, not looking at her, rubbing glass, 'some good can come out of a cockup. You never know.'

She waited. He didn't look up, started on the other smeared lens. He wasn't going to say any more, she was dismissed.

She left, feeling the tightness in her chest, the sick feeling.

One day she would kill Colley. Tie him to a tree in a forest, torture him and kill him. No, torture him and bury him alive, shovel damp soil alive with worms onto his head, into his mouth, watch his eyes.

But she knew that what she hated most was not Colley.

No, she hated herself for being so stupid as to go to him, to trust him.

26

HAMBURG

HE FOUND her on the university website.

Dr Alexandra Koenig, Dr. med., Dr. phil., Dipl.-Psych. Clinical psychologist. Research: Empirical validation of psychoanalytical concepts; psychophysiology; post-traumatic stress disorder.

A homepage carried a photograph, properly severe. He went to her curriculum vitae. It listed at least two dozen articles. She had been a visiting fellow at the Harvard Medical School. She was on the editorial board of the *Journal for Trauma Studies*.

There was an email address. Anselm stared at the screen for a while, then he opened the mailer, typed in her address. Under Subject, he put: Rudeness, contrition.

In the message box, he typed: We could meet, for a walk perhaps. John Anselm.

He felt relieved after sending the message and went back to the logbooks. The phone rang.

'It's done,' said Tilders. 'Some luck too. Two for the price of one.'

'Not a concept known to this firm,' said Anselm. He didn't know what Tilders was talking about. They must have got the bug on Serrano earlier than expected.

His email warning was blinking. He clicked. Alex Koenig.

The message was: A walk would be nice. Does today suit you? I am free from 3 p.m.

Anselm felt flushed. He couldn't think of anywhere to meet her, and then he thought of his childhood walks with Fräulein Einspenner in Stadtpark. He hadn't been there in thirty years.

She was waiting in front of the planetarium, formally dressed again, wearing her rimless glasses. There weren't many people around, a few mothers with prams or pushers, lovers, older people walking briskly.

She saw him from a distance, didn't look away, watched him approach.

'Herr Anselm,' she said, long and serious face. She held out her right hand. 'Perhaps we start again?'

'John,' said Anselm.

'Alex.'

They shook hands.

'Shall we walk?' she said.

They walked on the grass, away from the building. There wasn't much left in the day. A wind had come up, serrated edge of winter, hunting brown and grey and russet leaves across a lawn worn shabby by the summer crowds.

'Well,' she said, not at ease. 'You know what I do for my living. You are not still a journalist.'

'No,' he said. 'I'm in the information business.'

'Yes?'

'We gather it and sell it.' That was true, that was what they did. He didn't want to tell this woman the sordid truth but he didn't want to lie to her, he'd told a lot of lies, most of them to women.

They were at the road. She stopped and turned. He turned too and they looked back at the planetarium: it was big, solid, domed, towering over the parkland, a faintly sinister presence, alien in its setting.

'That's an Albert Speer kind of building,' Alex said. 'Hitler must have liked it. It says, look at me, I'm huge.'

'Well, I don't want to stand up for Adolf's taste in architecture but if you have to have water towers, it's not too bad.'

'Water tower? I thought it was a planetarium.'

'Now it is. It think it was built as a water tower. We could have coffee, something.'

He needed a drink, he hadn't had anything to drink all day, nothing at lunch time, he usually drank beer from the machine in the basement.

'Yes, good. Do you know where?'

'I think so. It's been thirty years, almost that.'

They set off again, crossed the road. She took big strides, he'd always had to shorten his stride with women, the women he remembered walking with. That was not many. He remembered one. He remembered walking in Maine with Helen Duval, she complained constantly about being bitten by midges, then she tripped over a root and claimed to have sprained her ankle. They were within sight of the cabin he'd hired. That was as far as they ventured.

'You're a medical doctor,' he said. 'As well.'

'In theory,' she said. 'In practice, I can't even diagnose myself. I get flu and I think I'm dying. You came to the park when you were young?'

'I was brought to see the birds. They used to have wonderful exotic birds and all kinds of fowls, these huge fluffy things, golden pheasants, I remember. May still be here somewhere. Do you enjoy what you do?'

She had taken off her glasses. He hadn't noticed her do that.

'I suppose so.' She looked at him, looked away. 'Yes. Well, I do what I do and I don't give much thought to whether I enjoy it. It's not that ... it's not a question that arises. It's my work.'

She was not used to being asked questions. *She* asked the questions. They walked in silence for a time, gravel hissing underfoot, the wind tugging at them, lifting their hair. Then they saw a sign and went down a path and found the café. There were more people in it than in the park, people rewarding themselves for taking exercise.

'Hot chocolate with rum,' said Anselm. 'That's what we should have.'

'Right.'

'The woman who brought me here always had one. She used to give me a teaspoonful. That's where it all began. My decline.'

A waitress in black with a white apron came and he ordered two, stopped himself ordering a drink as well, asking her whether she wanted a drink.

'What brought you to hostages?' said Anselm.

He wasn't looking at her, he was looking at the people. He had been doing that since they entered, doing an inventory of the people in the big room. Then he realised she would notice that and he looked at her. She's pretending she hasn't noticed, he thought, she's wary. She thinks I'm capable of repeating last time's performance.

I am.

'Well, most of the post-trauma research in this area has been on large groups,' said Alex. 'I'm interested in the dynamics of survival in small groups.'

'What about personality and life history?'

She smiled. 'You didn't take well to that. May I say that?'

Anselm nodded. 'Certainly. To my shame. Did it come under the heading of an extreme reaction?'

'Mild, I'd class it as mild.'

'On the extreme scale.'

Alex laughed. Some of the wariness was leaving her, he felt that. The drinks arrived. She sipped.

'Wonderful. I haven't had one of these in years. Not since Vienna.'

'Does research like this have a use?' said Anselm.

'That's a journalist's question,' she said. 'Academics hate questions like that. It might have a use one day. Everything has a use one day, doesn't it?'

'That's not a very academic answer,' said Anselm. 'I thought the idea was to present your research as vital to the survival of the universe?'

She held up her hands, the long fingers, no rings. 'I know, I should say that. Vital to the survival of my career would be more like it. Let's say my project is part of the giant mosaic of research, we can't quite see the pattern in it yet. But ...'

'You're not very German,' he said. 'You don't take yourself seriously enough.'

'If I'm not very German it's because I'm Austrian-Italian. A quarter Italian. My mother is half Italian. Her family is Italian-Jewish. Jewish-Italian. Atheists until they think they're dying. How do you describe yourself?'

'Once I thought I was American. American-German. But I don't know now. My mother was American but her father was British.'

There was silence. She looked away.

'Not being sure about what you are, that wouldn't be a trauma symptom, would it?'

Alex looked at him impassively, she had a judge's face, and then she smiled. 'Everything's a symptom of something,' she said.

She finished her drink, a pale collar of froth left around the glass. Anselm drained his.

'I could drink many of these,' she said. 'But I have to see a doctoral student, a frighteningly earnest young man. How did you travel here?'

He told her he was parked off Ohlsdorferstrasse.

'I'm near there. We can walk together.'

He paid and they walked back, light failing fast, shadow pools around the trees, streams of shadow under the hedges, the planetarium brooding, like a monument to something. He sometimes thought that everything old in Germany was a monument. The past had suckers, it attached itself to everything. There was no need to visit the sites or the *denkmäler*. Places spoke, whispered, smoked of what had been. The old railway lines held in their steel the weight of death trains, the city streets knew black boots, the songs, the slogans, the jeering and the tears. And lost hamlets and dripping cowpatted country lanes held voices, not always the voices of murderers and haters but of simple men and boys dead for the Führer in frozen landscapes far away, the tanks bogged in mud set like concrete, the soldiers' last thin intakes of air not reaching their lungs, going back into the huge grey world, then the rattle and then nothing. Just snow and ice and useless metal and human innards cooling, cooling, freezing. And over it all the sky of lead.

'It's a little menacing,' she said.

'Yes.'

They talked, it was easier now, leaves playing about their feet, they talked about the city, the traffic, the weather, the coming of winter, of *Winterangst*, of the need for sunlight, for Vitamin D, about where she lived. She lived in Eppendorf. She volunteered that she had been married. Her ex-husband was in America.

At their parting, she ran a hand over her hair and he thought he heard the sound it made.

'So,' she said. 'Will you talk to me?'

He put his hands in his pockets. He was reluctant to part from her. 'If you think it'll help you get better. Come to terms with your life.'

She bit her bottom lip, looked down, smiling, shook her head.

'It might,' she said. 'There is the possibility also that it could save the universe.'

'Just added value, a bonus.'

Anselm drove back to Schöne Aussicht, met Baader on the stairs.

'I saw you smile,' said Baader, pointing at the lobby below. 'Down there. At the door. Feeling okay?'

'Facial tic,' said Anselm. 'That's what you saw.'

27

LONDON

'HEAR ME?' the voice asked.

Niemand opened his eyes, raised his head, didn't know where he was.

He was still on the motorcycle, leaning against the rider, who was talking to him, head turned, mouth close, inside the helmet.

He looked around. Rubbish bins, cardboard boxes, walls close.

'Yes,' said Niemand. 'I hear.'

He straightened up, lost his balance and fell sideways and backwards off the motorcycle. It didn't hurt when he hit the ground, it was like being very drunk, nothing hurt.

Where was the bag?

'The bag?' said Niemand.

The yellow helmet was standing over him, holding the bag. 'Got it. You need a doctor, I'm ringing for an ambulance, okay?'

'No,' said Niemand. He was trying to concentrate, it was difficult, he didn't want to go to a hospital, they would find him there, they had no trouble finding him anywhere.

'No, hold on,' he said. 'Just a sec ...'

He put his hand into his jacket and found the harness, found the nylon wallet in his armpit. There was a card in it with numbers, five numbers, Tandy's number was there, Tandy was a pethidine addict but he was a good doctor, for a mercenary he was a good doctor, he knew a gunshot wound when he saw one.

He wasn't going to be able to unzip the wallet, find the card, his fingers were too fat, he'd developed fat fingers, no feeling in them.

'Listen,' he said to the yellow helmet. 'Inquiries. Ring and ask for a Doctor Colin David Tandy, T-A-N-D-Y, Colin, that's the one. Tandy. Tell him Con from Chevron Two … needs a favour.'

'Tandy? Chevron Two?'

'Colin Tandy. Tell him Con from Chevron Two. A favour. I've got a phone here in my pocket, you can …'

'Just lie there,' said the helmet. 'I'll ring from inside. I live here.'

'Listen,' Niemand said. 'Tell him … tell him Con says blood's a … a bit short. Might need some blood.'

'Jesus,' said the helmet. 'Don't die.'

He lay there. It wasn't uncomfortable. A bit cold, but not uncomfortable. He knew what uncomfortable felt like. This was easy. His neck was cold and his hands and feet but it wasn't bad. He thought about getting up. The car was in the parking garage, wasting money. Money. Shit, the bag? Where's the bag?

He felt for it, both hands, both sides, but his fingers were too fat and his arms were fat too, heavy, fat arms and fat fingers, it was very difficult to …

When he woke, he was on a bed and someone was standing over him, doing something to his arm, two people there, he wanted to speak but his lips felt numb.

'… fucking lucky prick …' said a voice, he knew the voice. Tandy. Tandy had taken shrapnel out of him.

He woke again and he was alone, on a bed, naked, tape on his chest. He raised his head, and he could see a railing, like a railing on a ship. He was on some kind of platform, it wasn't daytime, there was light coming from below, white light, artificial light. Banging, he heard bangs, not loud, chopping?

The bag, where was the bag? But he was too tired to keep his head up and he went back to sleep.

The third time he woke, he was clearer in the mind. He was on a big bed, a sheet over his legs, a black sheet. The bed was on a platform, a platform at one end of a huge room. He could see the tops of windows to his right, five windows, he counted them. Steel framed windows. Big.

'Awake?'

He looked left and saw half of a woman, cropped white hair, spiky, a black T-shirt. More of her came into view, she came up the stairs, she was all in black.

'The guy on the bike,' said Niemand. His mouth was dry. The words sounded funny, not like his voice. 'What happened to him?'

'I'm the guy on the bike,' she said. 'I have to give you an injection. Your friend left it. You have really useful friends.'

'Are you Greek?' She looked Greek, she looked like one of his cousins.

'Greek? No, Welsh. I'm Welsh.'

Niemand knew a Welshman, David Jago. He was dead.

'Thanks very much,' he said. 'Picking me up, everything. Tandy. I'm feeling a bit strange.' He was feeling sleepy again.

'He told me to say the bullet seems to have chipped your collarbone and gone out your back. You've missed paraplegia by a centimetre. He's says he's given you a battlefield clean-up, he takes no responsibility, don't mention his name to anyone and don't call him again. Ever.'

She came closer. 'I've got to inject you,' she said.

Niemand focused on her. Welsh. She had a Greek look. The mouth. The nose.

'What's the chance of a fuck?' he said. 'In case I'm dying.'

She shook her head and smiled. It was a Greek smile. 'Jesus, men,' she said. She held up the syringe. 'Listen, I'm the one with the prick. Do you need to pee?'

28

HAMBURG

VOICES IN the background, scuffling noises, other sounds. Tilders was watching a display on the small silver titanium-shelled machine.

'Alsterarkaden,' he said. 'Having coffee. The first bit's just small talk, ordering.'

Anselm was looking at the photographs of Serrano and a dark-haired man. They were sitting at a table in one of the colonnade's arches on the bank of the Binnenalster. In one picture, the man had a hand raised.

'What's his name?'

'Registered in the name Spence,' said Tilders.

'Looks like joints missing on his right hand,' said Anselm, showing the picture.

Tilders nodded. He was moving the tape back and forth. Serrano's voice, speaking English: ... *anxious, you can imagine.*

Spence: *It's very unfortunate.*

Serrano: *You would be able to get some help locally.*

Spence: *Things aren't what they used to be, you understand.*

Serrano: *Surely you've still got ...*

Spence: *We don't enjoy the same relationship, there's a lot of animosity.*

Serrano: *So?*

Spence: *The other party may have to be told.*

Serrano: *You understand, it was a long time ago, we feel exposed, we're just the sub-contractors.*

Spence: *You were his agents, not so?*

Serrano: *Agents? Absolutely not. Just in-betweens, you should know that.*

Spence: *I only know what filters down. I'm a bottom-feeder.*

Serrano: *His agents never. A dangerous man. Unstable.*

Spence: *You're worried?*

Serrano: *You're not? You should be worried. The Belgian's one of yours.*

Spence: *I don't know about that. I don't work in the worry department. That's a separate department. So I don't have that burden.*

Serrano: *This isn't helping, I hoped …*

Spence: *You lost him. If you'd come to us this needn't have happened.*

Serrano: *Well, it's happened, there's no point …*

Spence: *His assets, you know about them.*

Serrano: *We gave some financial advice but beyond …*

Spence: *Beyond bullshit, that's where we should be going. I'll say one word. Falcontor. Don't say anything. It's better we clean this up without the principal party being involved. They make more mess than they take away.*

Serrano: *So?*

Spence: *The person can be found. Marginalised. But we need all the financial details. The Belgian's too. We would want control of everything now.*

Serrano: *I'm sorry, you don't know who you're dealing with. We don't disclose things like that.*

Spence: *You came to us. I'm saying it's the only way to guarantee your safety.*

Serrano: *Well, perhaps we'll let this take its course, see what happens. See whose safety we're talking about.*

Spence: *That's an option for you. A very dangerous option, but, you want to be brave boys …*

Serrano: *A threat? Are you …*

Spence: *Don't worry about money, worry about life. Know that saying? We need to know your position quickly.*

Tilders pressed a button, opened his hands. 'That's it. Spence goes, doesn't wait for the coffee.'

'The service is bad everywhere,' said Anselm.

'Same place in two days.'

'Kael's all paranoia,' said Anselm, 'but Serrano doesn't seem to give a shit.'

Tilders nodded, flicked back a piece of pale hair that fell down his forehead, separated into clean strands. 'It appears like that.'

Anselm took the photograph of the man with the missing finger joints down the corridor, knocked. Baader swivelled from his monitor.

Anselm held out the photograph. 'Calls himself Spence.'

Baader glanced. 'Jesus, now you're playing with the *katsas?*'

'Katsas?'

'His name's Avi Richler. He's a Mossad case officer.'

'Thank you.'

Anselm went back to his office. Tilders put another tape in the machine, watched the digital display, pressed a button.

Serrano: *Richler wants the details. He knows about Falcontor. Bruynzeel too.*

Kael: *The cunts, the fucking cunts.*

Serrano: *I said that to him. He says it's about our personal safety.*

Kael: *They must have holes in their fucking heads if … Jesus.*

Serrano: *Well, who brought in the Jews? This boat is making me sick.*

Kael: *Don't be such a child. What could be in the papers?*

Serrano: *Lourens said to me at the Baur au Lac in '92 when we were meeting the fucking Croatians, he was snorting coke, he said people who betrayed him would have a bomb go off in their faces. He was paranoid you understand ...*

Kael: *In the papers? What?*

Serrano: *I don't know. I told Shawn to take anything he could find. There could be instructions. Notes maybe, things he wrote down. There's nothing on paper from us. Not directly.*

Kael: *What do you mean not directly?*

Serrano: *Well, obviously he would have had proof of some deposits I made.*

Kael: *Your name would be on them?*

Serrano: *Are you mad? The names of the accounts the deposits came from.*

Kael: *How secure is that?*

Serrano: *As it can be.*

Kael: *And this film?*

Serrano: *I told you. He said he'd found a film, someone came to him with a film, it was dynamite. He said, tell them it's Eleven Seventy, they'll fucking understand. That was when he wanted us to go to the Americans to solve his problem.*

Kael: *Eleven seventy? And you didn't ask what it meant?*

Serrano: *He was shouting at me, you couldn't ask him anything. And he was on a mobile, it kept dropping out. I couldn't catch half of what he said.*

Kael: *You set this up, you're the fucking expert who's left us turning in the wind, you should fucking know better than ...*

Serrano: *Christ, Werner, he was your pigeon. You brought him to me. You're the one who said the Süd-Afs were like cows waiting to be milked, stupid cows, you're ...*

Kael: *You should shut up, you're just a ...*

Serrano: *Calm down.*

Kael: *Don't tell me to calm down.*

A long silence, the sounds of the ferry, something that sounded like a series of snorts, followed by laboured breathing.

Silence, sounds of movement, a cough.

Kael: *Paul, I'm sorry, I get a bit too excited, this is a worrying ...*

Serrano: *Okay, that's okay, it's a problem, we have to think. Richler wants an answer today.*

Kael: *You know what they want to do, don't you?*

Serrano: *Maybe.*

Kael: *They want to tidy up. And they want the assets.*

Serrano: *These boats, I'm not getting ...*

Kael: *Tell him we agree but it'll take time. Seventy-two hours at least.*

Serrano: *Where does that get us?*

Kael: *They'll have this prick by then. If what he's got is bad for us, we're possibly in trouble. If not, we haven't handed them our hard work on a plate.*

Serrano: *You don't actually think he'll believe me?*

Kael: *Of course he won't. But they won't take a chance.*

Tilders switched off. 'That's it,' he said.

'Good bug,' said Anselm. 'You're doing good work.'

'Another put and take ...' Tilders shook his head.

'If you can't, you can't. We don't want to spook anyone.'

Tilders nodded. His pale eyes never left Anselm's, spoke of nothing.

29

LONDON

'THERE'S MONEY in my account I know nothing about,' said Caroline. 'Ten thousand pounds.'

Colley was looking at her over the *Telegraph,* narrow red eyes, cigarette smoke rising. 'Wonderful, darling,' he said. 'I'm surprised you noticed. Perhaps mummy popped it in.'

'The bank says it's a transfer from the Bank of Vanuatu. An electronic transfer.'

'Electronic money. Floats in cyberspace, falls anywhere, at random. Like old satellites. Finders keepers. Congratulations.'

'I'm declaring it to Halligan, I'm handing it over.'

He lowered the paper. 'Are you? Yes, well, that's probably a sound thing to do. In theory.'

'In theory?'

'Well, it may be a bit late to develop principles. After you've played the bagwoman.'

Caroline wasn't sure what he was saying. She had no anger left, it had taken too long to get the bank to tell her where the money had come from. The blood drained from her face. She was no longer certain that she knew what had happened. But she had a strong feeling about what was happening now and she felt cold.

'I've been set up,' she said. 'You know about this, don't you?'

Colley shook his head. He had an amused expression. His strange hairs had been combed with oil and his scalp had a damp pubic look.

'No,' he said. 'But if you're unhappy, that probably stems from something unconnected with the present situation. It could come from realising that you're just a pretty vehicle, a conduit. Something people ride on. Or something stuff flows though.'

She had no idea what he was talking about. 'I've been set up.'

'You've said that, sweetheart. Remember? Not too much nose-munchies with the public schoolboys last night? All I know is you came to me with a proposition involving paying someone for something that we could make a lot of money out of. I told you that the right thing to do was to go to Halligan. I said I wanted nothing to do with your proposal.'

He opened a drawer, took out a flat device. 'You're out of your depth here. Like to hear the tape?'

Caroline felt the skin on her face tighten, her lips draw back from her teeth of their own accord. She turned and left the room without saying anything, went down the corridor, through the newsroom. In her cubicle, door shut, she sat at the desk with her eyes closed, clenched hands in her lap.

Out of your depth.

Her father had said those words, those words were in her heart. The image came to her of her toes trying to find the bottom of the pool, toes outstretched, nothing there, the water in her mouth and nose, smell of chlorine. She could still smell chlorine anywhere, everywhere, smell it in the street, anywhere, any hint of it made her feel sick. Her father had used the phrase that day when she was a little girl wan from vomiting and he had repeated it every time she failed at anything.

She shut the memory out, stayed motionless for a long time. Then she opened her eyes, pulled her chair closer to the desk, and began to write on the pad.

Out of her depth? Go to Halligan and tell him the whole story? Who was going to be believed? Colley had a doctored tape. She had no hope.

Out of your depth.

No. Death before that. The phone rang.

'Marcia Collins. You probably don't remember me. I'm the features editor now. Does your personal arrangement with the executive branch permit me to ask what the hell you're doing? Am I allowed to ask that?'

'No, you aren't,' said Caroline. 'Don't call me, I'll call you.'

A silence.

'I suppose you've heard they found your little Gary. Dead of an overdose. Been dead for days.'

30

HAMBURG

WHEN TILDERS had gone, Anselm went out on the balcony and smoked a cigarette, watched him drive away. He looked down at the unloved roses and thought about his first days in the family house.

On his second morning, he had woken in fright from a drunken sleep and did not know where he was. He had been fighting the top sheet, twisting, it was tight around him. He'd lain back and felt his hair. It was wet with sweat. He got up. The pillowslip was dark. He stripped it from the pillow. It gave off a chemical smell, the smell of the pink fluid the doctor gave him to drink before he left the hospital.

In the huge tiled bathroom, pissing into the rusty water in the toilet bowl, the same smell had risen, richer now, it sickened him.

He showered, standing uncertainly in the huge bath. Water fell on him, a warm torrent, he was inside a rushing tube of warm water. He did not want to leave it. Ever. But eventually he went downstairs. There was bread and butter and tea, tea in bags, a box of leaf tea. He made toast and tea, that was an ordinary thing to do.

An ordinary thing on an ordinary morning.

Tea brewed in a china pot. In a kitchen. Toast with butter. He had thought it gone forever.

He'd made two slices of toast, put them on a plate, and put the pot of tea and the toast and butter and a bowl of sugar on a tray and gone out onto the terrace. There was an old, dangerous chair to sit on and a rusty garden table. He'd gone back and forth to the kitchen and, in all, eaten seven slices of toast, toast with butter, just butter. He drank three cups of tea from the English china cup, roses on it.

Just eating toast and drinking tea, sitting in the sunshine in the wobbly chair, massaging the two fingers on his left hand, he could not remember more peace in his life.

Then he was sick, he could not reach the bathroom.

He had not left the house for two weeks. There was enough food and drink for ten weeks, more. He did nothing, existed. The milk ran out, he drank black tea. He sat in the spring sun, dozed, tried to read *Henry Esmond*, found on his great-aunt's bedside table, drank gin and tonic from before midday, ate something from a tin, slept in an armchair smelling faintly of long-dead dog, he had a memory of the dog, a spaniel, one eye opaque. He'd woken dry-mouthed, empty-headed, drunk water, poured wine, watched television in the study, not very much of anything, often went to sleep in the chair, woke cold in the small hours.

His brother had rung every second day. Fine, said Anselm, I'm fine. I'm pulling myself together. He had no idea what together would look like. There were terrifying blanks in his memory of the years before the kidnap – big blanks and small blanks, with no pattern to them. They seemed to go back to his teens. It was hard to know where they began.

He'd exhausted his clean clothes. Where was the laundry? He'd remembered a passage off the kitchen leading to a courtyard. The washing machine was unused for a long time, the hose disintegrated, water everywhere. He washed his clothes with old yellow soap in the porcelain sink, found a pleasure in it, in hanging the washing in the laundry courtyard.

And every day, he'd walked around the garden, looking at the roses, smelling them. One morning, when he woke, he'd known what he was going to do. Before noon, he left the house for the first time.

He knew where the bookshop was. He had been there on his last visit to his great-aunt, on his way to Yugoslavia. He had bought her a book.

He walked a long route, up Leinpfad to Benedictstrasse and down Heilwigstrasse and through Eichenpark and on to Harvesterhuder Weg and through Alsterpark. He walked all the way to the Frensche bookshop in the Landesbank building. In the crowded shop, he was assaulted by fear bordering on panic but he found the book. It was waiting for him, twelve years old, never opened, an encyclopaedia of roses. He paid and left, sweating with relief.

He walked down to the Binnenalster, bought a sausage on a roll from a street vendor, sat on a bench in the sun and opened the book. His was the hand that cracked its spine. He looked at the pictures, read the descriptions, while he ate. Then he walked all the way home, too scared to catch a bus, and, exhausted, went around the garden trying to identify the roses. It was more difficult than he had imagined. He was sure about Zephirine Drouhin at the front gate, *Gruss an Aachen* on the terrace, Madame Gregoire Staechelin on the wall, and three or four others.

But that wasn't enough. He wanted to know the name of every rose in the garden, and there were so many he couldn't be sure of – the pictures were fuzzy, the descriptions too imprecise.

Like his memory.

Beate knocked on the glass. Anselm finished the cigarette and went in.

31

HAMBURG

BAADER CAME into Anselm's office and slumped in a chair. He put a new case cover sheet on the desk.

'I gave this to Carla,' he said. 'You were busy with Tilders.'

Anselm looked at the form. The subject was someone called Con Niemand aka Eric Constantine, South African, occupation security guard, last seen London.

'Lafarge Partners?' he said.

Baader was looking down, fingers steepled. 'Credit check's okay. Corporate security. How many corporate security consultants does the world need?'

'Demand and supply. Ever think about what happens to these people after we find them?'

Baader closed his eyes, shook his head. 'John, please.'

'Do you?'

'This is a business.' He still didn't look up.

Anselm went ahead, knew how stupid he was being. 'These people, they can pay. That's all we care?'

Baader lifted his fox head. 'Care? Care about what? Lafarge. Probably run by Catholics. If you like, we could ask the Pope to give them a moral clearance. On the other hand, the Pope cleared Hitler.'

He looked away, not at anything. 'John, either we provide this service for anyone who can pay or we don't provide it at all. You're unhappy with that, I'll give you a very good reference. Today if you like.'

Silence, just the sounds from the big room, the hum of the internal fans cooling sixty or seventy electronic devices, the air-conditioning, noise from a dozen monitors, a phone ringing, another one, people laughing.

'I'm really tired,' said Baader. 'I've sold the shares, the car, the apartment. I'm moving to this shitty little apartment, two rooms, all night the trains run past, eye level, ten metres away, the noise, people look at you like you're in Hagenbeck's fucking zoo.'

He got up. 'So I'm not receptive to ethical questions right now. Next year perhaps.'

'I'm sorry,' said Anselm. He was.

'Yes, well, when you're in trouble, you too can sell your dwelling. Then you can buy your own island, buy Australia, it should get you enough to buy Australia, world's biggest island, live happily ever after.'

'My brother owns the house,' said Anselm. Baader knew that, he just didn't want to believe it.

Baader was at the door, he stopped, turned his head, said, 'War criminals from three wars, Pinochet's number two executioner, a Russian who leaves five people to die in a meat fridge, a man who swindles widows and orphans out of sixty million dollars, a woman who drowns two children so that she can marry an Italian beachboy. And the fucking rest.'

They looked at each other.

'Count for something? Yes? Yes?'

'Yes,' said Anselm. 'I'm a prick, Stefan. I'm a self-confessed prick and contrite.'

'Yes,' said Baader. 'Anyway, it's too late to change. We can't. You can't. I can't. The fucking world can't.'

Anselm stared out of the window for a long time, just a sliver of lake view, a slice of trees and water and sky, endless sky, the water fractionally darker than the sky. He still had the dreams, dreams about sky, about lying on his back, he was on a hilltop looking at a huge blue heaven, birds passing high above, twittering flocks so large their shadows fell on him like the shadows of clouds, and then the real clouds came, the mountains of cloud, darkening the day, chilling the air.

After a while, his thoughts went to Alex Koenig. It was not a good idea. She wanted something from him. A paper in a learned journal. He was a scalp. No one else had interviewed him. On the other hand ...

He started at the knock.

Carla Klinger.

'Cut your hair, I see,' said Anselm. 'I like it.'

She blinked twice, moved her mouth. 'Two weeks since then but thank you. The new British file, Eric Constantine, Seychelles passport, he hired a car from a Centurion Hire in London.'

'When?'

'Yesterday. Seven days hire. Paid cash. To be returned to the place of hire.'

'Centurion Hire? How big are they?'

'One site.'

'And they're online?'

'No. I looked at the big hire companies, nothing, so I thought about what all the small car-hire businesses would have to do. One thing is insure, they have to insure the cars, and I asked an insurance person. In the UK, three insurance companies get most of the hire car insurance. They don't just insure all of a company's vehicles, blanket cover. Every hire, they want a record of who the hirer is. Inskip and I opened them up and we found the name.'

She licked her lower lip. 'Not a great problem,' she said.

Anselm shook his head. 'Not for you maybe. For people like me, a great problem. Why didn't anyone think of it before? Can we run all the British currents through it, see what happens?'

'Inskip's doing that now. Then we'll see what we can do in the States. I don't know the insurance position there.'

'You should be in charge here.'

'Then who would do my work?'

She left. Walking with a stick didn't make her any less attractive from behind. From any angle.

He went back to looking out of the window. He had said it. He wasn't necessary. Carla could do her job without him and probably do Inskip's too.

Baader could save a lot of money by showing him the door. It would cross the mind of someone who'd had to sell his shares, his Blankenese apartment, the Porsche, now lie awake in a two-room post-war walk-up listening to the trains' electric screech vibrate his window.

Baader could have got rid of him a long time ago.

Baader was his friend, that's why he hadn't done it.

It was thirty minutes before his meeting with O'Malley. Anselm got up and put on his good overcoat.

32

HAMBURG

A FERRY was on its way to the Fährdamm landing. Anselm paced himself to get there to meet it. The lake was choppy, north wind raising whitecaps. He got off at the Fährhaus landing and walked back along the shore towards Pöseldorf, along the gravel path through Alsterpark, not many people around, some old people and women with prams, two junkies on a bench, workers sucking up leaves, the devices held at the groin, big yellow whining demanding organs.

A high sky, a cold day slipping away. Anselm thought about how his father had told him that Alsterpark was only as big as it was because so many Jewish families had lived on the west side of the lake and had been dispossessed. They were gone, gone to horrible death or exile, when the Allied bombers came in the high summer of July 1944. Then people walked into the lake to escape the unbearable heat of a city set on fire by teenage boys dropping high explosive bombs, incendiary bombs, napalm and phosphorus bombs. Aunt Pauline talked about it early on the first tape.

I went to the coffee factory that day. Otto, our driver, took me. We had two coffee factories. I used to do the accounts, I couldn't bear to do nothing. I hated sitting around the house, I begged to be allowed to do something, it was difficult for women to do anything in families like ours, you understand. Marriage, children, the domestic world, that was the domain of women, my mother never questioned that for one second, she could not understand that women might want something else. I didn't have children, of course, so I think she made an exception for me, not a full exception, she always hoped I'd marry again. I tried to tell her … what was I saying?

The bombing.

Oh. Yes. I was at the factory in Hammerbrook, in Bankstrasse. I used to work until late, after 9 p.m., it was summer, it had been terribly hot for weeks. We were driving back when we heard the sirens and then the bombs started to fall. And we stopped and got out and we ran to some trees, I don't know why. After that, you can't imagine. The whole world was alight. Buildings fell down. The flames went up forever, the sky was burning, it looked as if the clouds were on fire. Burning clouds, like a vision of Armageddon. The heat. There was no air to breathe. The flames burnt up all the air. And the people ran out of the buildings, the screams of the children. The tar melted, people stuck in the tar. The car windows melted. Things just burst into flame. We were lying down against a wall trying to get air from the cobblestones. I was absolutely sure that I was going to die, that we were all going to die. And then the Feuersturm *began, it was like animals howling, the wind, so strong it pulled me away from the wall and Otto grabbed my leg and hung onto me.*

Operation Gomorrah, it was called. How did they choose the name? Whose idea was that? Gomorrah, one of the cities of the plain. The Hamburg fires burnt for nine days. Forty thousand people died, most of them women and children. Nine days of hell, the dead lying everywhere, rotting in the heat, black swarms of flies over everything, and then the rats, thousands of rats eating the bodies. Anselm remembered reading the planner of the raids' words:

In spite of all that happened in Hamburg, bombing proved a relatively humane method.

Air Vice-Marshall Harris.

Relatively. What was the Air Vice-Marshall thinking of? Relative to what? Auschwitz? Were there relatively humane ways of killing children? Relatively speaking, where did Bomber Harris's raids rank on the table of twentieth-century horrors that had at its head the cold-blooded annihilation of Jews and Gypsies and homosexuals and the mentally infirm?

Not a cheerful line of inquiry, Anselm thought. Turn to other things. What would Alex want to know? What would he tell her? He didn't want to tell her anything. This was a mistake, the product of loneliness. His life was full of lies, he could lie to her. But she was trained in lie-detection, she would know. Did that matter? Wasn't lying the point? You were supposed to lie. The truth was revealed in your lies, by what you tried to conceal. Telling the truth ruined the whole exercise. There was nothing under truth, beyond truth. Truth was a dry well, a dead end. You couldn't learn any more after you knew the truth.

Anselm walked down Milchstrasse, feeling dated, dowdy. Pöseldorf was as smart as it got in Hamburg. The *Zwischenzeiten* was over now, the people were in winter gear. Shades of grey this year, grey flannel, grey checks, grey leather, soft grey shirts, grey scarves. Grey lipstick even.

Eric Constantine, wanted man, he'd bring the hire car back in a week; people would be waiting. What would happen to him?

Too late. Baader was right.

In the café, O'Malley was at a corner table, in a grey

tweed suit, in front of him a small glass and a Chinese bowl holding cashew nuts.

'More to your taste than Barmbek?' he said.

It was a French sort of place, darkish, panelled, a zinc bar, dull brass fittings, freckled mirrors, paintings that impoverished artists might have traded for a few drinks, new-shabby furnishings.

'It's marginal,' said Anselm. 'It's better than all brown. What's that you're drinking?'

'Sherry. A nice little amontillado fino. Want one?'

'Please.' He'd only had two beers and an *Apfelkorn* all day. He looked around. The man behind the counter was talking on the phone. He had a cleft in his chin and highlights in his blonde hair.

Without moving his head, O'Malley caught the man's eye. He pointed at his glass, signed for two.

'So, what are these blokes talking about?'

'We got an earlier conversation. With the Israeli. The *katsa*. Want it?'

O'Malley finished his sherry. 'That's extra, is it?'

'Well, yes. Five hundred, that's in the basement. We'll throw in the pictures.'

'And steak knives?'

The barman arrived with the sherries. He said to O'Malley in English, Irish in his English, 'You must try the dry oloroso, it's exceptional, very nutty.'

'I have no doubt I will,' said O'Malley. 'Again and again. Thank you, Karl.'

When the man had gone, Anselm said, 'You're a stranger here, then.'

'He's a computer bloke, made a few quid in Ireland, now he's realised his dream, come home, opened this little bistro.'

'German?'

'Certainly. From Lübeck.'

'Ireland. Isn't there something wrong with that story?'

O'Malley shook his head. 'Change, John, the world's changed. Narratives don't run the same way any more. All the narratives are at risk.' He drank some sherry. 'Of course, you're in the cyberworld most of the time, that's not real. How are my blokes?'

'They're worried. This Spence who is actually Richler is threatening them. The deceased Lourens in Johannesburg apparently left something dangerous behind. Kael is agitated. May I ask what you actually want from these people?'

O'Malley looked at him for a while, rolling sherry around his mouth, his cheeks moving. He swallowed. 'No,' he said, 'you may not. But since you take secrets to the grave, I'll tell you. My clients are looking for assets, thirty, forty million US Serrano and Kael handled in the early nineties. Falcontor. Did they say that name?'

'Yes. Richler.'

O'Malley looked interested. 'Richler?'

Anselm tried the sherry, drank half the small flute. He remembered the British embassy in Argentina when the Falklands business was beginning, his first war, standing in a high-ceilinged room in Buenos Aires, drinking sherry with the press attache. She had narrow teeth and she talked about the international brotherhood of polo. 'It's so unfortunate because of course we're both polo-playing nations so there's always been a real affinity ...'

Later she made a pass at him. He took the pass. Her husband was an art dealer, that was all he remembered. That and the bites on his chest, tiny toothmarks like the attack of a crazed ferret.

'Whose money?' Anselm said.

O'Malley smiled, the canines showing. 'Well, that's an awkward one, boyo. This is money without provenance, without parentage. Conceived in sin, sent out to make its own way in the world. It doesn't belong to Serrano, that much is certain.'

He chewed a cashew nut, picked up the bowl, turned it in a big hand. 'They found bowls like these in a Chinese galleon lying on the bottom of the sea, hundreds of years old, I forget how many. Amazing, no?'

'I'm not sure,' said Anselm. 'Amazing's not what it used to be. I presume these people are all lying to each other.'

'It's a way of life for these blokes. Their relationships are based on porkies. Darling, promise me you'll never tell me the truth.'

Four people came in, three young women, tall, anorexic, bulemic too probably, and a small man, plump, no trouble keeping food down. It was all shrill laughter, hair moving, hands moving, waving, shrieks, going over to the owner and kissing him on both cheeks. Anselm felt the need to be outside. Not an urgent need, just a strong wish to be in the open.

He put the small tape case on the table. 'I suppose we can skip the condom routine here. If you want to go on, tell me tonight. This isn't getting easier. It may have to be on Kael and he's hypochondriac.'

'I'll ring,' said O'Malley. 'I'll have a little listen and ring. And since when do you know who's a *katsa* and who isn't?'

'Everyone knows.'

Anselm walked to Fährdamm and the luck was his again, the ferry was coming in, nosing in to the jetty, a bump, two bumps. He sat on deck and smoked, cold wind wiping the smoke from his lips. The dark came suddenly and the shore lights came through the trees and lay on the water like strips of silver foil, bending, turning.

33

LONDON

THE MAN opened the door within seconds. She knew he had heard the gate's small noise, not so much a screech as a scratch. It was not a timid opening. He opened the door wide.

'Yes?'

'Good evening. Sorry to bother you,' said Caroline.

'Well then don't.'

Nothing of the courtly doorman about him, not a smiling doorman this. Just a big bald man in shirtsleeves, a wide man, downturned mouth, pig-bristle grey eyebrows.

Caroline had her card ready. She offered it to him. He looked at it, held it up to his face, looked at her, no change in expression.

'Yes?'

'It's Mr Hird?'

'It is.'

'Could we talk? It won't take long.'

'About what?'

'Something that happened at the store yesterday.'

'Don't talk about what happens at work. That's company policy. Goodbye.' Hird didn't move.

Caroline took the chance. 'Can I bribe you?'

He touched his nose with a finger, pushed it sideways, sniffed. 'No.'

'Is that a no or a maybe?'

'It's a no. Come inside.'

They went down a cold short passage into a cold room that looked unchanged for fifty, sixty years, a sitting room from around World War Two. The armchairs and the sofa had antimacassars and broad wooden arms. Two polished artillery shells flanked the fireplace. Above the mantelpiece was a colour photograph of the Royal Family – King, Queen and the two little princesses. A collection of plates and small glass objects stood on mirror-backed glass shelves in a display cabinet with ball-and-claw feet.

'Havin a glass of beer,' he said. 'Want one?'

'Yes, please.'

'Sit down.' He left and came back with two big glasses of beer, tumblers that bulged at the top.

'Well, what?' he said, sitting down.

Caroline sat and drank a decent mouthful. She moved to put the glass down, didn't for fear of marking the chair arm.

'Put it down,' Hird said. 'Not a museum. Looks bloody like it but it's not.'

She put the glass down, opened her bag. 'A man was shot in the store yesterday. On the third floor.'

Hird looked at her, drank beer. It left a white line on his upper lip and he didn't remove it. 'Entirely possible,' he said, 'I'm down on the ground, noddin and smilin.'

A black cat came in, fat, gleaming, silent as a snake, glided around the room, around chair legs, around Hird's legs, brushed Caroline's ankles. She failed some feline test and it left.

Caroline took out the security camera photographs of Mackie, held them out. 'He might have left through your door,' she said, she didn't know that. 'Can you remember seeing him?'

Hird put down his glass, took the pictures, held them

on his stomach. He looked at them, gave them back to her, said nothing, drank some beer.

'Recognise him?'

'Busy store. How many people d'ya reckon go through my door every day?'

'He's on camera going through your door. The question is whether you remember him.'

'They send you around here?'

'No. Only my mole knows I know.'

She was lying. She had no mole. Store security denied all knowledge of the incident.

Hird kept his eyes on her. He had a big drink of beer. Caroline matched him. Their glasses were down to the same level.

'A mole in security?'

'Yes.'

'He'd tell you what's on the street cameras.'

'There's some problem there.'

'So how'd you know where to come?'

'It's my business to find out.'

'Right,' he said. 'Right. Saw your name in the paper. That Brechan. Shafted the bastard, din you. Shafter shafted.' He laughed, he enjoyed his joke. 'Bloody rag, your paper.'

Caroline shrugged, said, 'I gather the Prime Minister reads it.'

He laughed again. 'Bloody would, wouldn't he? See which Tory prick's been up a kid's bum last night. Course the lovin wife'll give the bastard an alibi, won't she?' His voice turned to purest Home Counties. 'We were at home all evening, officer, just the two of us, a quiet dinner, watched some television, had an early night.'

'So you saw this man,' said Caroline as a matter of fact.

Hird nodded. 'This an interview? Read me name in the paper?'

'No. Just background. No name. Nothing that can identify you. I promise.'

He studied her, drank some beer. 'Just looked odd,' he said. 'Then I saw his hand up to the chest, blood comin out between the fingers.'

In her heart, she felt the spring of pleasure uncoil at her cleverness.

'Did security see him?'

'Nah, been called away.'

'You didn't tell them?'

Hird studied her. 'What's your mole say?'

'He says he's not aware of any report.'

'Well, there you have it.'

'So the man went out the door and ...'

'I went out, just to the corner to have a look-see. Deserted me post. Sackable offence. Still, had a customer's welfare at heart, din I?'

'And?'

'Well, he was pretty normal, not wobbly, but he wasn't walkin too straight. Bit of bumpin. Went into Brompton, thought he might be heading for the tube. Then these two fellas come along, they were lookin for him, that's for sure.'

'And?'

'Well, he keeps goin up the street, then he crosses and he gets on the back of this motorbike.'

'Waiting for him? The motorbike?'

Hird shook his head. 'In the bloody traffic, couldna been. He just stood there, then he got on the back of the bike. Another fella come from somewhere, he was runnin at them, then off the thing went like a rocket. Yellow helmet, one of them big helmets, spaceship helmet. Know what I mean?'

'And the men?'

'Buggered off.'

'Didn't get the number of the bike, did you?'

'Too far.'

Caroline nodded, finished her beer, got up. 'Thanks, that's a big help.'

Hird stood up, not easily. 'Can't see how.'

'You'd be surprised,' said Caroline.

They left the room. He went first. On the way down the passage she found a fifty, rolled it up. He opened the front door. She went out, turned.

'Well,' she said. She tapped the side of her nose with the rolled note, offered the roll. 'We were at home all evening, officer, we watched television ...'

Hird laughed, gave her the nod, nod, wink, wink, took the note and put it in his shirt pocket.

'Keep insertin it up the bastards,' he said.

34

HAMBURG

INSKIP WAS watching the vision from some pale anonymous formica-walled airport terminal, views of queues, of passengers, close-ups of faces when their turns came at the counter. He jumped from queue to queue, face to face.

'Real time in Belgrade,' he said. 'It's a feed to the people who sold them the system. Quality control purposes.'

'Very nice,' said Anselm. 'What's our interest?'

'Intellectual, for the moment. Another breakthrough in techniques of invasion. I thought that earned praise.'

'It does. You're a promising person.'

Inskip sniffed. 'That's a theatrical sniff,' he said.

'Don't get to the theatre much.'

'Moving on, I have the new London subject's hire car in a parking garage near Green Park. Bills mounting, they've run a check on it.'

Eric Constantine. The name stuck in his mind.

'Probably a dead end then,' said Anselm. 'I'm going home.'

'Do you do that?' said Inskip.

Anselm was packing up when the phone rang.

'It's yes,' said O'Malley.

Anselm rang Tilders.

'Yes,' said Tilders. 'They understand this is going to be difficult?'

'Yes.'

'Wish us luck.'

'I do. Luck.'

Anselm had no urge to run home, walk home. He went out into the cold, misty night and, for the first time, took the sagging BMW car home. Outside the house, he got out and opened the wooden gates. It was a fight. Bolts and rusted hinges contested his wishes. He parked in front of the garage. No car had stood there for a long time, on those brick pavers.

Standing on the dark threshold, looking for the key, and inside, when he was sitting in the kitchen, glass in hand, he thought again about his Moritz: pro-Nazi. An anti-Semite. He looked like some count painted by von Rayski. And I look like him.

Anselm went to the photographs on the wall, the photographs Alex had looked at on the first night. There were dozens, going back more than a century – formal portraits, groups, weddings, dinners, sailing pictures, pictures taken at balls, in the garden, on the beach at Sylt, pictures of children, children with dogs, him with his parents and Lucas, Gunther and his wife, him with his grandfather in the garden, both with forks, big and small. No photograph of anyone who could be Moritz.

Surely Moritz could not have missed every single photographic occasion?

He went back to the kitchen, sat down. Alex. He should telephone her and say that he had changed his mind, apologise for wasting her time in Stadtpark. He had enjoyed talking to her, he could say that, but he didn't want to talk about the past.

The telephone rang and Anselm knew. He let it ring for a while and then, suddenly fearful that the ringing might stop, he went to answer it.

*

Alex's apartment was the size of a house, on the third floor of an old building in Winterhude, built between the wars, an *Altbauwohnung*.

Anselm said, 'May I lie on a couch? Or have I suggested that before?'

Alex Koenig smiled. 'You have and you may not. I've got coffee. Or brandy and whisky. Some gin left. I like to drink gin in summer.'

She was all in black, a turtleneck sweater and corduroy. Her hair was pulled back. Anselm thought she looked beautiful and it made him even more uneasy.

'You can't drink gin after sunset,' he said.

'Yes? Is that a British rule? It sounds British.'

'I suppose so.'

'But you're not British.'

'My mother's family are English.'

'Ah, mothers. They like rules. Impose order on the world, that's a mother's primary function. There is also beer and white wine.'

'White wine, thank you.'

She left the room and he went to the window. The curtains were open and he looked out at the winter Hamburg night, moist, headlights, tail lights reflected on the shiny black tarmac skin. The streetlamps made the last wet leaves on the trees opposite glint like thousands of tiny mirrors. He turned, noticed the upright piano, an old Bechstein, went across and opened it, he could not resist. His right hand played. The piano was badly in need of tuning. So was his hand, he thought.

'You're musical,' she said.

Anselm turned around. 'Playing "Night and Day" doesn't make you musical.'

'It makes you more musical than I am.'

He took a glass from her. 'Thank you. Interesting furniture.'

'The chairs?'

'A passage lined with chairs. About twenty chairs in this room. Yes, the chairs.'

'Kai's obsession. My ex-husband. Did I say his name? He likes things people sit on. Very much. He seeks out chairs.'

'Would you say he craved chairs?'

She tilted her head. 'Chairs he doesn't have, yes. There is an element of craving.'

'He must miss them.'

'I don't think he cares about them after he's got them. It's the thrill of getting them. He wants them but I don't think he cares about them.'

'Napoleon was like that,' Anselm said. 'So were the Romans, I suppose. Whole nations they didn't care about and wouldn't part with. Did this chair thing bother you?'

'Very much. It kept me awake. And then again, not at all. Are you sure you've eaten?'

'Is this going to be taxing? Do I need to be in shape?'

'Let's sit down.'

They sat, a narrow coffee table of dark wood between them, a modern piece. On it was a tape recorder, a sleek device.

'May I record this?'

'My instinct is to say no,' said Anselm. 'But why not?'

'Thank you.' She touched a square button. 'To begin,' she said. She wet her lips with wine. 'Can I ask you about your memory of the events? Is it clear?'

'It's fine. It's earlier and after that's the problem.'

'After your injury?'

'Yes. I don't remember anything for about a month.'

'And earlier?'

'There are holes. Missing bits. But I don't always know what's missing. There are things you don't think about.'

'Yes. So, the beginning. Your experience in trouble spots, that would have prepared you to some extent?'

'Well, by '93 Beirut wasn't really a trouble spot. Southern Lebanon, yes. Anyway, I thought we were dealing with GPs.'

'GPs?'

'Gun pricks. Paul Kaskis coined the term. Long before. A prick with a gun.'

'Ah. You would fear them surely? Gun pricks.'

Gun pricks. She said the words with a certain relish.

'There's a survival rule,' said Anselm. 'Paul invented that too. DPGP. Don't Provoke Gun Pricks. He didn't but they killed him anyway.'

'So you were scared?'

'I was scared. I thought you were interested in personal history?'

'I am. But I need to know about the specific circumstances too. Does it bother you to talk about them?'

He had come in trepidation and had been right to. He didn't want to talk about Beirut, it was stupid to have agreed to. She wasn't that interesting, appealing, she wasn't going to be the answer, an academic, they bled most of them of personality before they gave them the PhD. But he wanted to behave well, he had a bad history with her, he didn't want her to think he was disturbed.

'Well,' said Anselm, 'you should always be scared around GPs. The first few minutes, there's usually a lot of shouting, all kinds of crap, you just hope it dawns on them killing you might not be smart. Or that someone more intelligent or less drugged will come along, tell them to back off.'

'So you thought it would soon end?'

'I hoped. It's new every time. You hope. You pray. Even the godless pray. You shut up. Keep still, try to breathe deeply.'

'When did it change?'

Now was the moment to go. He felt the pulse beating in his throat, he knew that pulse, that sign, the blood drum.

She said, 'Your glass is empty. Can I?'

He nodded, relieved. She went out and came back in seconds with the bottle, filled his glass.

She'd known, she'd felt his pulse.

Anselm drank, lowered the level by an inch. 'They taped us,' he said. Then, quickly, 'Wrists and ankles, across the eyes, put hoods on, I couldn't breathe.'

He had said it. *I couldn't breathe.*

'And that scared you even more?' she asked, voice soft.

There was no turning back. 'Yes.'

Silence. He didn't look at her, wanted a cigarette badly. There was an ashtray on a side table. After a while, he looked at her and said, 'What did Riccardi tell you?'

'He was ... a little emotional.'

'What did he tell you?'

'He said you were silent in the beginning.'

'I had tape over my mouth.'

'After that, in the first place they kept you.'

'Riccardi is a vocal person. It's like having the radio on. I'm surprised he noticed.'

'He says he talked because you were both silent.'

'Riccardi doesn't need an excuse to talk. He talks in all circumstances. He'd talk over the sermon on the mount, the Gettysburg address. What else did he say?'

'He says he never thought it was political.'

'Everything's political. Anyway, you wouldn't want to make Riccardi your judge of what's political. He's a photographer. Born to take snaps. I was with him in Sri Lanka for a month and in the plane on the way back he said, "So what was all that about, anyway?"'

'He says it was never clear to him what you and Paul Kaskis were doing in the Lebanon.'

'Kaskis wanted to talk to someone. He asked me to go with him, I had nothing better to do.'

'Talk to someone? About what?'

'I don't know. Paul never told you anything. How does this line of inquiry further post-trauma research?'

She frowned. 'I'm sorry, I'm just curious. You have to be in my work.'

'Riccardi might have asked me before he opened his heart to you.'

As he said the words, Anselm heard the whine in them. He sounded like a betrayed lover

'He didn't think he was doing any harm,' Alex said. 'He's your friend. He admires you very much. And he finds relief in talking about a painful experience. Most people do. Is it that you don't?'

'Can I smoke?'

'Of course, I should have said. This place was full of smoke when Kai was here. Pipe smoke. I rather liked it. It reminded me of my father.'

He fetched the ashtray and lit a cigarette, blew smoke at the distant ceiling. 'I was more than scared when they put the tape over my mouth, the hood,' he said quickly. 'I panicked. I lost control of myself.'

'Your body?'

'Yes.'

There was relief. Why had the thought of that moment of helpless indignity been so clenched in him? He knew. Because, at that moment, John Anselm reporter, John Anselm detached observer, was no more. He had become a victim. He wasn't the storyteller any more. He was in the story. He had joined it. He was a foul-smelling minor figure in an ancient story, no different from any civilian casualty of war, from any red-eyed, black-garbed crone pushing a barrow of sad possessions down a rutted road on the way from precious little to much, much less.

He remembered too that, in the aftermath of that moment, it had come to him with complete certainty that there would be no return to safety and a shower, to drinks and a meal, more drinks, reminiscences, laughter, to a long sleep in a bed with sheets.

'I think I have to go,' said Anselm. 'I think I've changed my mind about talking. I'm sorry.'

Alex shook her head. 'It's not to be sorry about. This is painful for you, I understand that. We can talk about something else.'

'I have to go.'

At her front door, he turned, awkward. 'Goodbye. I've wasted your time.'

She put out a hand, seemed to hesitate, then she touched his arm, just above the elbow. 'No. Not at all. Can I ask you one more thing? A personal thing.'

'Yes.'

'Would you like to see me again? Not professionally?'

35

HAMBURG

TILDERS LOOKED tired. His eyes half closed, he talked more than usual. Anselm listened but his mind was elsewhere, on Alex Koenig.

'This is the end,' says Tilders. 'We had to put it inside his raincoat sleeve. We had no choice. It's a bad place, desperation. Dangerous. You will hear. He kept pulling at his cuff, he crosses his arms.'

'Yes,' said Anselm. 'Let's hear it.'

Serrano: ... *didn't get excited. He's very reasonable.*

Kael: *That's a bad sign. They're looking for this ...*

Serrano: *He says they've called in a few favours ... Shawn had been ... the British possibly.*

Kael: *Well, the prick ... anything for ...*

Serrano: *... ever mentioned the film.*

Kael: *Did he?*

Serrano: *I can't recall. I used to turn off ... say ... when he was like that, on drugs, drinking. He said ... Bill Casey when he was ... the CIA, that kind of thing. Knew everyone. North. Sharon ... when he was a soldier. Fucking Gaddafi even ...*

Kael: *What else does Richler say?*

Serrano: *The worrying thing, he says he hopes fucking Shawn did a good clear out ... this special office, the Süd-Afs, they're looking for assets ... target now.*

Kael: *Shit. Still, he could be lying. Second nature to them.*

Serrano: *Also fucking Bruynzeel, he says that's a priority. They want to know what we have.*

Kael: *He can wait.*

Serrano: *I was thinking last ...*

Kael: *Glad to hear there is thinking.*

Serrano: *I'm getting really annoyed ...*

Kael: *Thinking what?*

Serrano: *He talked about buying property, a house in England I think, other places ... there might be something there.*

Bumping and scratching noises.

'We thought the thing had fallen out,' said Tilders.

The sounds went on for at least fifteen seconds. Then Serrano was heard.

Serrano: *Possibly.*

Kael: *This is your business, you understand. I'm too old to have to deal with shit ...*

Serrano: *My business? Excuse me, Werner, excuse me, who benefited most from this? I'll tell you. I'll tell you ...*

Kael: *... down. We're expendable, do you fully understand that?*

Serrano: *What about your friends? Your friends won't ...*

Kael: *The world changes. Your friends get old, they forget, they die.*

Anselm made the gesture, Tilders touched the button. Anselm gave him the slip of paper. 'Put it in his hands. I'll ring him now.'

Tilders rose, gathered up his possessions.

'You're tired,' said Anselm. 'How many jobs do you have?'

Tilders smiled, a wan thing without humour or pleasure. 'Only as many as it takes,' he said.

36

LONDON

CAROLINE WISHART knew what to do. Charcoal-suited Dennis McClatchie had taught her, sixty-five years old, pinstriped cotton shirts with frayed collars, full head of slicked-back hair, breath of whisky and cigarette smoke and antacid tablets. She should have thought more about Dennis before going to Colley.

Early on, someone told her McClatchie had been a famous reporter, sacked from every Fleet Street paper.

'What happened, Dennis?' she asked him one day, shivering in the cold, shabby office, grey northern light coming through the bird-crapped window panes.

'Bad habits, darling. For one, the horses, bless 'em, blameless creatures, innocent, with these ruthless, terrible blood-sucking humans around them.'

He drew on his cigarette, pulled in his cheeks, let the smoke dragon out of his nostrils. 'Punching editors, that was of little career assistance. But. No regrets there. Well, perhaps. One or two I should have nailed more thoroughly. Just laziness really. And I didn't like hurting my hands. I had nice hands once.'

He'd lit a new cigarette from his stub, stifled a cough.

'Married a lot too,' he said. 'Can't recall some of 'em. Women I hope. Damn lawyers sent me demands from people I'd never heard of. Had to get a death certificate forged in the end.'

He looked at her, turned the head, the skull, she thought she heard his spine creak. 'All of it drink-related, I should say in my defence,' he said. 'All my crimes have been drink-related. All my life has for that matter. I'll call my autobiography *A Drink-Related Offence*.'

One day in her first week, she felt the eyes of Dennis on her when she was sitting frozen with anxiety. She had been expelled from school, sacked from Sotheby's, asked to leave Leith's cooking school, told lies to get this job. Now the slovenly Carmody, class-hate written all over him, had given her an assignment, spat a few words from the side of his mottled mouth.

'What's the cheerless cretin want, darling?' said McClatchie.

'A story on community services. I'm not quite sure where to start.'

McClatchie looked at her, looked at his hands for a while, the nails, the palms. A plain cigarette burned between two long fingers the colour of old bananas. She knew that he knew that she'd lied about her experience.

'I always start with a proposition,' he said. 'A headline. Gets you going. Pope Hid Nazi War Criminals. Moon Landing Fake.'

She hadn't grasped the point. Her eyes showed it.

'Community Leaders Slam Burnley Services,' said McClatchie.

'Do they?'

'No idea. Probably. There's no gratitude in the world. Get on the blower and ask 'em.'

'Who?'

'Start with that Tory prat. He'd like to cull the poor but he'll give you the compassionate bullshit. Tell him you're hearing a lot of complaints about services. Baby clinic, that sort of thing?'

'Is there one?'

'Not the foggiest. The phone book, darling. Peek at that. Under Council. Something sexy like that.'

Start with a proposition. She sat in her cubicle office far away from Birmingham, McClatchie mouldering in the wet ground now, thought about what she'd seen and what Mackie had said in their first conversation.

'*A massacre in Africa.*'

'*A lot of that goes on.*'

'*Soldiers killing civilians.*'

'*What, the Congo? Burundi?*'

'*No. White soldiers. Americans.*'

'*American soldiers killing civilians in Africa? Somalia?*'

'*No. This is … it's like an execution.*'

So, the proposition, the headline:

US troops in Africa massacre.

That would do to go on with. It would help explain why Mackie thought the film was worth twenty grand and why other people thought it was worth killing him. She knew that for a fact.

Just looked odd. Then I saw his hand up to the chest, blood comin out between the fingers.

She thought about Colley, how she was tricked. She wanted to kill him.

Colley's time would come, that wasn't important for now.

Africa. Where in Africa?

Southern Africa? Mackie was South African.

American troops in Southern Africa?

Had there ever been? Where? When?

She logged on, put the words *US troops southern africa* into the search engine. Hundreds of references came up, fifty at a time. She rejected, read, printed, the morning went by, she ate a sandwich, the afternoon advanced, her eyes hurt.

The phone. Halligan.

'Marcia's upset. She's got some right to know what you're working on. In her new position.'

Caroline tried to compose the right response. She was tired.

'I'm sorry she's upset. Such a nice person. I simply explained to her the terms of my contract.'

'Yes. Entered into under the gun. Leaving fucking Marcia aside, what the hell are you doing? You report to me, remember? So please report. ASAP.'

Caroline took her career in her hands. 'Bigger than Brechan,' she said. 'Just an estimate, mark you.'

She thought she heard Halligan swallowing, his throat's slimy clutch. Just imagination.

'I'll calm the woman down,' he said. Decisive. 'Report to me soonest.' Pause. 'When would that be?'

'Soonest.'

Silence. She heard the silent sound of his chagrin and his regret.

'Yes, well,' he said. 'Posted. Keep me.'

'Of course. Geoff.'

She went back to the screen. She now knew more about American involvement in Africa since the 1950s than anyone needed to know. And she knew very little of any use to her in understanding Mackie's film.

What would McClatchie do? She saw McClatchie in the eye of her mind. She saw his burial, the half dozen of them around the pit, the soil that had come out of it under pegged plastic, half a dozen people standing in the drizzle at the edge of the flat, wet necropolis.

Get on the blower and ask 'em.

Who?

She went back to the screen.

37

LONDON

'WHAT'S HE say?'

'He says congratulations on the good work, love you. What do you think? He says find him or die. We're going to carry this like nail holes in our fucking palms, you know that? Ten to the woman, twenty to the fink, six hundred in the bag. Plus we have to pay these idiots. And for what? *Caddyshack*. We get an ex-rental video starring Chevy fucking Chase. I hate the cunt. Is he still alive?'

'He's alive. It's his hair that's dead. The biker, I don't understand. That doesn't make sense.'

'Now this boy knows he's dealing with incompetents. Be comforting, wouldn't it? To know you're dealing with pricks? Two of them run out after him and they don't get the bike number. I still cannot believe that.'

'Hire for a week, next day you park in a garage, your intention is not to come back, you're going to be picked up by a bike. No.'

'The hospitals?'

'Nothing local. They're going wider. On a bike, could have gone anywhere.'

'He won't stick around. If he's alive, he's running. Just make sure these fucking Germans don't miss some fucking ferry, charter flight to Ibiza, balloon, something.'

'We could ask for help. Ask Carrick. They'll find him.'

'Find him, they find the fucking film. The bike, that's what we need. Find the bike, we nail the cunt. Ring of steel, now that would have helped.'

'Just around the City, no use. Although ...'

'What? What?'

'I read they were trying out cameras in other parts for when Bush was here ...'

'Who would know? Who would know?'

'I don't know, how would I ...'

'Ask the fucking Germans, ring the fucking Krauts, they're supposed to know everything.'

'How much can you tell them?'

'Just tell them everything we know. Okay? We're hanging out here. Time, the bike, the place, two people, the fucking direction, anything you can think of. Now. Please?'

38

LONDON

NIEMAND WOKE, an instant of bewilderment. Then he knew where he was. It was night, there was light coming from downstairs.

He needed to piss, urgently. He sat up, put his feet on the floor. His shoulder felt stiff but there was little pain.

He stood up, went to the bathroom naked. There was a mirror above the toilet and his face looked pale. He went back to the bed, wrapped the sheet around his waist and went to the top of the staircase. Looking down made him feel dizzy. Below was a big room with a long trestle table at one end under a row of windows. On the table stood several models of buildings and what looked like a model of a town, a village with a church in a square.

She was not in view. He didn't know her name.

Niemand started down the steep stairs. The woman appeared, a knife in her hand.

'Not you too,' said Niemand.

She frowned, then she realised. 'I'm cooking,' she said. 'I'm chopping vegetables.'

'How long has it been?'

She looked at her wristwatch, a man's watch. 'Nearly twenty-four hours.'

There was no point in hurrying. They'd have found him before this if they could.

'My clothes,' Niemand said. 'I have to go.'

'You can't wear what you came in. Except for the jacket, that's okay.' She pointed to her right. 'In there, there's a cupboard. You might find something to fit you.'

He was at the bedroom door, when she said, 'Or you could just carry on wearing that sheet. Won't raise an eyebrow around here.'

He liked the way she spoke. It was a musical sound, it had tones. In the bedroom, a wall of cupboards was full of men's clothes, one man's clothes, jackets, suits, shirts, shoes. He found underpants, a pair of jeans, they looked a bit short in the leg for him, too big in the waist. They would do. He took a grey T-shirt, too big, that didn't matter, found socks.

He went back upstairs and showered in the big cubicle, wetting the bandage. When he went to soap his side, he felt a sharp pain at the collarbone, in his back.

The clothes didn't look too bad. His shoes were under the bed. He put them on and went to his bag on the dressing table. The money was in bundles held with rubber bands. He opened one, saw the fakes immediately, only the top notes looked real.

'Bastards,' he said without venom. It didn't surprise him. It had been nothing but betrayals since the beginning. Plus he had been stupid.

He examined all the bundles. Probably five hundred pounds in real notes. His jacket and his nylon holster were hanging over the back of a chair. Blood had dried on the jacket lining. He put the real money in the holster, took the bag and went downstairs.

The kitchen was a counter along one wall. She had her back to him, doing something with a pot.

'Did I say thank you?' he said. 'Thank you.'

She turned, not surprised, she had heard him on the stairs. She was a good-looking woman, a strong face, dark eyes.

'Quite all right,' she said. 'I often pick up wounded men. It's a service I provide to the community. Are you hungry?'

Niemand thought for a moment. He should leave. 'Yes,' he said. 'Please.'

'It's a kind of stir fry. Chicken. Sit down.'

She put out two plates, cutlery, napkins, two wine glasses, a bottle of red wine, not full. She poured wine without asking.

The food was good. She wasn't bad to eat with either. No noises, she kept her mouth closed when she was chewing, she didn't talk with food in her mouth.

'Your name's Con,' she said. 'I'm Jess.'

He waited until he'd swallowed. 'Jess. Where are we?'

'Battersea.'

He knew where it was. He pointed at the trestle table to his left. 'Is that your hobby?'

'I'm a model maker. I do it for a living. A very bad living.'

'Make models?' It had never occurred to him that there could be such an occupation.

'For architects. Usually. The village there, that's a development in Ireland. A typical Irish village for millionaires. Americans.'

They carried on eating. Then she said, direct gaze, 'Who shot you?'

Niemand finished chewing, swallowed, wiped his mouth with the napkin. He drank wine. He liked red wine, it was the only alcohol he liked. 'A man dressed as a woman,' he said.

Jess drank. 'I'll put that again. Why did you get shot?'

She had probably saved his life. She had a right to ask.

'I was stupid,' he said. 'I was selling something to people I didn't know.'

'Drugs?'

'No.'

'They shot a dealer around the corner the other day. In his car. Two men. One from each side.'

'I'm not a drug dealer.' He didn't have strong feelings about dealers in drugs, the whole world was built on addictions, but he didn't want her to think he was one. 'I'm not a drug dealer,' he said again.

'Point made.' She finished her wine and stood up. 'I have to go out,' she said. 'I'll be back around ten, ten-thirty.'

He stood up too. 'I'll be gone. Thanks. I'll wash up.'

There was a moment of awkwardness.

'You should stay quiet for a few days, the doctor said,' she said. 'He doesn't really have a bedside manner, your doctor.'

He heard the sound upstairs. Pivoted.

Christ, no, not again.

'It's the cat,' she said. 'Climbs up the pipes, gets into the bathroom. Always knocks something over. Deliberately. It's not even my cat, thinks it owns the place.'

'Just the night,' said Con. 'Would that be okay?'

There was a pad and pen beside the phone. She wrote. 'My cellphone number. Ring if you come over weak.'

He nodded. 'What floor are we on?'

'Third. There's another one. It's empty.'

'How'd you get me up here?'

'In the lift. This was a factory. The fire-escape door's in the corner over there. They made radio parts, valves and condensers, stuff like that.'

'How do you know about old radios?'

'My dad,' she said. 'He wanted a boy, so he taught me how to fish and shoot and change a fuse and hotwire a car.'

Niemand sat down. 'I wish I'd met you earlier in my life,' he said.

39

HAMBURG

THEY RAN on the river path, saw the backs of the houses across the water, here and there a rowboat pulled onto the bank, fowls strutting and pecking, a man hanging washing. There were few runners, many people on bicycles. The sun came and went, gave no heat.

Anselm had not run with anyone since college, since his runs with his room-mate Sinclair Hollway, who went on to become a Wall Street legend for putting twenty-six million dollars on a nickel play. The unauthorised money lost, Sinclair was found dead in his house on Cape Cod a week later.

'Anselms have been in Hamburg for a long time,' she said.

He looked at her. Her hair was pulled back and she was wearing anti-glare glasses, the kind target shooters wore, yellow. She looked different.

'What do you know about Anselms?'

'I looked them up. I suppose you know all the family history.'

'Some.'

'Pioneers of the Hanseatic trade with America, it said.'

'That's quite possible. How old are you?'

The yellow eyes. 'Thirty-seven next month. Why?'

'No reason.'

'You simply wanted to know?'

'Yes. Simply wanted to know. Innocent inquiry. Or isn't it?'

'I have no opinion.'

'No innocent inquiries. Is that it? Nothing is innocent.'

'A question about age, that could certainly be innocent, yes.'

'But you don't think this is?'

'I didn't think you had any curiosity about me. This is really a conversational cul-de-sac. What kind of books do you enjoy? Do you read novels?'

'I read novels.'

Once he had read two or three a week, on planes, while eating, waiting for something, someone, somewhere. He never went anywhere without at least two, usually three, buying five or six at a time and leaving them where he finished them. He had donated books to planes, airports, trains, railway stations, left them in parks and bars and hotels and coffee shops, government offices and embassies, taxis and buses and hire cars. Once he left a book in a brothel, the woman had seen it in his coat pocket, asked for it.

They ran. He looked down and saw how shabby his running shoes were, bits were peeling. No German would run in such shoes.

A family on bicycles was coming at them, two abreast. He dropped behind Alex. The plump mother said thank you, three children each said thank you, the father said another thank you.

Running behind her, he admired her backside. He also admired her action. No show to it, no big knee lift or arm action. She just ran, everything straight. When he went up to join her, they touched, just a brush of upper arms, a sibilant friction.

'DeLillo,' she said. 'Do you like him?'

'I read the earlier books, the Oswald book, that was the last one I read.'

'You liked that?'

'I don't know. I must have, I finished it.'

'You give up on books easily?'

'Yes. It's an American thing. Gratify me or be gone.'

'You don't want to live in America again?'

In the beginning, in the early days in the old house on the canal, he had sometimes thought about going back to America. But the idea disturbed him, made him weepy. Go back where? He had no home, the people he had loved were gone, father, mother gone, he was alone. Lucas was all he had, if he had Lucas, they could not even touch properly and Lucas lived in London, he was English now. Go home to the place he left to go to Beirut? To Kaskis's tiny apartment on the hill? It would belong to Kaskis's family since Beirut. And later he came to think that Hamburg suited the way he felt, his condition. He was of it and not of it. He belonged and he didn't. The Germans had partial memory loss and so did he. They had chosen what pieces to forget, but then perhaps so had he.

'America overwhelms me,' he said. 'There's too much of too little. Why would you think I don't have any curiosity about you?'

The yellow eyes looked at him, away. 'I should not have said that. A silly thing to say. What else do you read?'

'Mostly, I get drunk and go to sleep in front of the television with the cable news on.'

It was true. He sat with a book in his lap, a glass in his hand and on the television an endless loop of death, destruction, pain, fear, famine and misery. Often he came back and watched again when he woke far out on the wrong side of the night, wet with sweat from his dreams.

They ran.

'I also listen to music while I'm getting drunk watching the news,' he said. 'A multi-media experience.'

They ran. Anselm's knee was beginning to hurt, the pain that started as dull, like a memory of a pain, gradually turned to fire in the joint.

'You're not interested in the music I listen to?' he said.

They ran. He thought that this would probably be the only run they would ever take together and he did not know how to prevent that from being so.

'People like you probably listen to Wagner,' she said. She did not turn her head.

'Wagner?'

He had no idea what she meant, he had no view on Wagner, his father had hated Wagner, the Wagners as a whole. But he also disliked her tone, it send a current of annoyance through him and, for an instant, he wanted to bump her into the canal – it would be easy, hip and shoulder. Splash. There would be no coming back from that and it would be over. He would go home. Resume his life without shrinks. She could crawl home, wet, have her own post-traumatic stress.

'People like me?'

She said nothing, didn't look at him.

They ran and he kept looking at her. 'What kind of person am I?'

She still didn't look at him. 'You're an adrenalin addict,' she said. 'You like percussion. You're a seeker after percussion.'

'I was a hostage, that's all you know about me. Where do you get all these other opinions from?'

'Just intuition. Professional intuition. You say you were often scared but you never stopped looking for chances to be scared.'

Anselm heard bicycles coming up behind them. He fell

back to let them pass, thin androgynous people in latex outfits, helmets, thin dark glasses. Alex slowed for him.

'That's not a terribly clever thing to say,' he said. 'That was my job. That was what I did. I didn't go to these places on holiday.'

'Did you take holidays?'

The sun went. His knee was getting worse, soon he would be showing it, favouring it, he would be pathetic. This was why you didn't run with other people.

'Time to turn,' he said. 'I've got to be at work in an hour.'

They turned. He tried to slow the pace but she wouldn't be slowed. She wanted to push him, he felt that.

'Holidays,' she said. 'Did you take holidays?'

He didn't want to answer. He couldn't remember. He remembered the artist who hit him, that was all. It was possible that he hadn't taken other holidays. Then he remembered sailing with Kaskis in the Bahamas. That wasn't really a holiday. Kaskis was doing something there, some story on money laundering and corruption. He rang, said come over and we'll have a sail, I'll hire a boat. They took the boat out the morning Anselm arrived. There was a strong wind to begin with. It got a lot stronger and it changed direction. His experience was on smaller boats and this one was a pig. They should have expected that, it was a cruising boat, not meant for heavy conditions. Kaskis didn't want to make for harbour. He also didn't want to take down the mainsail. He agreed only after they dug in and, for a few seconds, it seemed as if they would pitchpole. Taking down the mainsail, Anselm was almost knocked overboard, cut his head. Under power with just the jib up, the boat threatened to breach in the troughs. Getting home took a long time. Kaskis loved it, he lit up with pleasure. You could see how he'd made Special Forces in the army.

'I took some holidays,' said Anselm.

The knee was not good. It was sending signals up and down. He looked at her. She was looking at him.

'What kind of holidays do you shrinks take?' he said. 'Or do you just stay at home and introspect? Keep in touch with your inner selves. Do some mental scoping.'

'Scoping?'

'You could scope your anima. Do an animascope. An animoscopy. That's got a nice medical sound to it.'

'So you didn't take holidays?'

'What is this about holidays? Since when were holidays the measure of people? Did Marie Curie take a lot of holidays?'

'I don't know. Do you?'

'I don't care.'

'Your memory loss. Has that been permanent?'

'How did we get on to that? What's permanent? Permanent is a retrospective term. I'm still alive. Just.'

More cyclists, no leanness or androgyny here, a group of overweight women, bikes wobbling, breasts alive, jostling inside tracksuits.

'Precision,' said Alex. 'It is important. Do you still experience the loss of memory? Correction. The absence of some memory.'

'Some. Yes. I've lost all the good bits, the holidays. I'm left with the crap.'

Both knees were hurting now. He would have to stop, walk the rest of the way. He did not want to do that.

They ran for another hundred metres.

'I'm tiring,' she said. 'Can we slow?'

He felt relief, he'd outlasted her, he didn't have to be humiliated. 'It's just a kilometre,' he said. 'I was thinking we should pick it up.'

The yellow glance, a shrug. 'If you like.'

She went away from him without effort, no sign whatsoever of fatigue. He watched her backside and could make no effort to go after her. The path turned and she was gone.

Anselm stopped, walked. She had tried to be kind to him, to spare him embarrassment. She had pretended to a weakness she didn't have. His response, wired into his brain, was to go for her throat.

She was waiting at her car, grey tracksuit on, yellow glasses off, breathing normally.

'I found a reserve of energy,' she said.

'I noticed.'

They didn't speak until she stopped outside the office gates. She didn't look at him.

'Perhaps that is not a thing we should do together,' she said. 'It might not bring out our best natures.'

Anselm took his bag from the back seat. 'I don't have a best nature,' he said. 'Least worst, that's my best.'

40

LONDON

THE REQUEST from Lafarge to find a motorcycle was on his desk. He was tired, not just his knees hurt now, his left hip sent splinters of pain up and down. He summoned Inskip and explained.

'It's Mission Hopeless,' he said, 'but they're paying. Carry on, Number Two. Or is that Number One? No, I would be Number One, surely?'

'Number two,' said Inskip, 'is a crap in toddler talk.'

Anselm nodded. 'I shouldn't distrust my instinct for the language. Carry on, Number Two.'

In mid-morning, Inskip stood in the door, his egg head to one side. Anselm thought he saw a faint flush of blood in the pale skin. Also, Inskip was wearing a red T-shirt. He hadn't noticed that earlier. Had fashion changed? Was red in the ascendant?

Inskip said, 'Would you like to listen to something, Number One? Number One being a piss.'

Anselm nodded, rose and went to Inskip's workstation, sat beside him.

'I've found this person,' said Inskip. 'In a company that's doing closed-circuit TV trials in London. Roads, stations, shopping malls. The football. A minion of the coming total surveillance state. I haven't been entirely straightforward with him. Forgivable, is that?'

Anselm looked into the black eyes, looked away.

Inskip touched the key.

Asked and we could've fucking looked, couldn't we?

They didn't know. Inskip's voice.

Asking's how you find out what you don't fucking know.

They didn't know to ask.

What? Is this fucking philosophy? This what I fucking missed by not going to fucking Oxford?

George, what could you have told them?

What? Every fucking pushbike and Porsche and cunt on a skateboard that went through the check, that's what.

Can we get that now? It's a small window, five, ten minutes.

I'm waiting. We serve you lot, don't we. Only to ask. Say again?

Four-fifty on. The passenger might be leaning on the rider. He might have a bag, a sports bag, that would probably be on his lap, hard to see. No helmet, the passenger ...

No helmet. That's where you start, sunshine. Hang on.

I've got an offender here, five-three, that's a nice bike, he looks like he's gone to sleep, the bumboy, not at all alert, no helmet, shocking disregard for the law.

Plate? Can you run that?

Running, my lord ... Yes, this is your person ... I can give you an address, see how fucking easy it is when you simply ask?

Point taken. A salutary lesson, George. Name and address?

'He thinks you are?' said Anselm.

Inskip put a hand to his naked scalp, lay fingers on it. 'MI6,' he said.

'You may go far in this line of work.'

'And owe it all to my teachers.'

'Give it to Lafarge.'

41

LONDON

SHE FOUND a person to start with, at the London School of Economics, in the School of Oriental and African Studies.

They sat in a small study that smelled of cigarette smoke. He was an overweight man in his fifties, head shaven, black polo-necked shirt. He looked like a Buddhist monk gone bad, in thrall to things of the flesh, the ascetic life a memory. His eyes were red, he smoked Camels in a hand that trembled a little, and he jiggled his right foot without cease.

'Well,' he said, 'Americans are not strangers to the region.'

'But massacres?'

'Massacres? A difficult term. Massacre. Imprecise. Like genocide. Used very loosely.'

'Killing civilians. Lots of them.'

He started to laugh, coughed, kept at it for a while, produced an unclean red handkerchief, crumpled like a tissue, tore it open and covered his mouth.

She looked away. He recovered.

'Sorry. Terrible tickle in the throat. Dust. Place never gets cleaned. So, yes. Killing of civilians? Common practice in the region. For about three hundred years.'

'But not by Americans.'

'Depends. Depends on what you think is the causal chain, I suppose. In Angola, for example.'

'For example?'

'You're not connected with television, are you?'

'No.'

'I do quite a lot of television. You may have seen me?'

'I thought your face was familiar.'

'Really?' He ran a hand over his scalp, a pass, quick. 'Yes. Well, I've been too busy recently, books and whatnot, can't drop everything because some television producer calls. They expect that, you know, incredible arrogance.'

'About Angola, you said ...'

'Lots of atrocity rumours about Angola in the eighties. One a month. What you'd expect from a superpower war-by-proxy, I suppose.'

He studied her, scratching an eyebrow. 'Wishart. Are you the person who wrote that Brechan story?'

He had assumed a prim expression. He looked like a Pope now, some Renaissance Pope whose portrait she'd seen somewhere.

'Not the headline,' she said. 'That was in poor taste.'

'Thoughts of Wilde crossed the mind. None so hypocritical about buggery as the unexposed buggers.'

'Yes. To get back to Angola ...'

She had to wait while he lit another cigarette. He had a big lower lip, red, and when he blew out smoke, it turned down and he showed paler flesh inside, the colour of tinned tuna.

'Angola,' he said. 'A resource war, one of the late-century resource wars. Many more to come. I'm considering a book on the subject ... working on it, actually. I've done a lot of work on it. I'm well beyond considering it.'

'Atrocities ...'

'Well, there's always talk. I remember a story about a village disappearing off the face of the map, in some American rag.'

'Would you know which one?'

'This is so long ago.'

'This is very important,' Caroline said. 'When you say American rag …?

He seemed to be galvanised, sat back in his chair, ready to speak to camera, chins up.

'Well, American rags. There've been a few. America's got this tiny left fringe. The right's a huge great heaving pit of snakes – but energetic. The left's always been quite pathetic, sad. No life and no theory at all. Well, a little, just the simpler bits they can half understand. Gramsci, they half understand bits of Gramsci. The hegemony stuff. But deep down the right loonies and the left share the same conspiracy mania, it's rooted in a small-town America paranoia. There's a plot out there to take things away from them, democracy, freedom of speech, a man's guns, a man's right to fuck his pig, there is no, I mean absolute zero, understanding of structural …' He tailed off, seemed to have lost course, blinked at her with stubby eyelashes.

She said, 'A village in Angola disappeared off the map?'

He focused. 'Of course, you have to be *on* the map to disappear *off* it, don't you? The logical precondition. God knows how they could tell it had vanished.'

'And you say there were others? Atrocity stories?'

'Many. Both sides. Raped nuns are always good value. The atrocity story is a staple of modern conflict. It illustrates what utter monsters the other lot are. As in the ex-Yugoslavia. Take for example …'

'So they said this Angolan village had been destroyed?'

'Something like that. Dimly recall, mark you. Dimly. It was a longish piece. Quite well done.'

He closed his eyes. 'Ah,' he said, 'got it. *Behind Enemy Lines.*'

'Yes?'

'California, I think. Published in some little place in California. *Behind Enemy Lines*. I liked the name.'

'No chance of you having the clipping?'

He shook his head. 'My dear, long gone, I've moved on. The thing didn't live beyond four or five issues, they never did. I subscribed to everything in those days. Remotely promising, I sent off my money. They probably owe me twenty quid. Do you get a penny back when these rags collapse with ten issues owing on your subscription? My arse. Try the library here. Hopeless though it is.'

The library had never held *Behind Enemy Lines*. But a librarian clicked keys at speed, interested frown. He found the complete *Behind Enemy Lines* for sale, a rarity, seven issues, good condition, twenty pounds, from an address in Portsmouth. Southpaw Books. Email, telephone, fax.

She went outside and rang. A man with a bad cold answered. She said fifty pounds if he would go through *Behind Enemy Lines* and fax all items involving American involvement in Africa.

'Go through them?' he said. 'Darling, basically, we sell the stuff. That's the business.'

'Sixty quid,' she said. 'How's that? And you keep the magazines. Inside an hour.'

'Time's money,' he said. 'I'm a slow reader.'

'A hundred. The contents pages too. I'm stopping there.'

'Credit card transaction, is this?'

'What else?'

'What's your fax number?'

42

HAMBURG

O'MALLEY RANG.

'I'm sitting here just down your very pleasant little road. Where the boats are. A word, perhaps?'

Anselm went out, didn't bother with a coat. It was much colder than when he had come to work. The sky was an army blanket, dirty grey, a shade lighter than O'Malley's BMW, which, in turn, was a lighter grey than O'Malley's suit.

'Flitting to and fro, you should open an office here,' said Anselm. It was warm in the car and there was the smell of leather and newness. 'Think of the fares you'd save.'

O'Malley shook his head. 'What would save some real money, mate, is buying your business. But I'm not flitting, I'm having a little stay, a sojourn. Did I not say that? No? Before the courts tomorrow, trying to get the attention of some naughty Poles. They have products we wish to render immobile. In a warehouse down by the river. Your beer, your ballbearings, your smoked hams, your binoculars, your pickled cucumbers, beetroot, artichokes. Even your Polish condoms, a container load. In packs of fifty, the weekend packs they're called.'

'For football teams, surely?'

'Aimed at the single male. These people are not called Poles for nothing. The brand is *Ne Plus Ultra*.'

Anselm put his head against the headrest. 'The old-fashioned Polish condom makers. I didn't know there were any left. Knew their Latin, history of the Peninsular Wars. Craftspeople in rubber.'

'Latex. Moving on, another task.'

A police car was coming towards them, slowly, no hurry, a shift to get through. Both occupants, men, gave them the lingering eye.

'Ceaselessly vigilant in the interests of the rich,' said O'Malley. 'Whereas out in the gloomy industrial hinterland, the lower orders have to beg and beseech the *Politzei* to come to their assistance.'

'I didn't realise you were familiar with the conditions of the German working class.'

'A lifelong interest. Like Engels in England.' He looked at Anselm's shirt. 'Winter's setting in. I could probably find an old coat to send you.'

'I'd be grateful. *Winterhilfe* usually toss a few warm garments my way. But not exactly Zegna.'

O'Malley was getting a slim notecase off the back seat. 'Mine wouldn't be Zegna. It would be hand sewn by my little man. Crouch is his name.' He opened the leather box, flipped through papers. 'Doesn't have the ring of Zegna, Crouch. Ermenegilda Crouch. No. This matter concerns something called Falcontor. Remember?'

Falcontor. Richler on the tape:

I'll say one word. Falcontor. Don't say anything.

O'Malley found an A4 envelope. 'From Serrano's case, at the station. Your excellent if expensive work. We can't make much sense of this stuff. The cross-trained bloodhounds you employ may have more luck.'

'I thought you said Serrano was still in the paper era?'

'He is. But the places he parks the ill-gotten stuff may not be.'

'What do you want?'

O'Malley scratched an eyebrow. 'Well, you know. Anything. The main interest is assets. But anything. Don't spook anyone, that's paramount. And speed. And the name Bruynzeel. Keep an eye out for that.'

'Flemish, I presume?'

'I would too. Sounds like a nasty symptom the nanny should report.'

A couple appeared on the jetty, began to take off the cover of a boat.

'I was like that once,' said O'Malley. 'Weather was no impediment. Serrano, the hotel, can you keep that running?'

'Yes.'

'Good on you. How many ways do I love a crisp affirmative? Concludes the business. Oh, and notice I've got a new number. The old one was boring me.'

Anselm put his hand on the door latch. 'You won't forget the coat?'

'No,' said O'Malley. 'Consider it in the mail. And this coincidence will amuse you. An email in my box from Angelica. The American bore. It's over. Taken his Egyptian artefacts, gone. She's holding on to the apartment in the Marais pending the legal nastiness. Sadly, the chef's been terminated.'

'I'm sure you can arrange food parcels. When you say speed?'

O'Malley looked at him. 'Yes. We'd be grateful. Things that are solid can melt into air.'

'I wouldn't be too hopeful.'

'In me, the hopeful genes. In all the O'Malleys. Globally. The O'Malley diaspora of optimistic genes.'

'Probably inherit the earth,' said Anselm. 'O'Malleys and cockroaches. Still, the evolutionary day has only just begun. Give us a few hours.'

'Hours, certainly. Not even units of time in the evolutionary day.'

Anselm felt the pressure fight the car door as he pushed it closed. It was even colder now. It felt like snow, the air still, the feeling of something pendant. Waiting for its time. But it was much too early in the year. Its time was nearer Christmas, when it would fall at night, the magic flakes hushing the discordant city.

In the blue gloom, Carla was at her workstation, text on her right-hand screen, green code on the black screens to her left. She saw Anselm coming and swivelled, her useless leg thrust out. He showed her the case folder.

'Some time?' he said. 'It's a priority.'

She nodded. He gave it to her. She read the cover sheet, opened it and looked at the pages inside, flipped them. Two columns to the page. Letters, numbers, names handwritten in ink.

'This has meaning?'

'Not to the client. Serrano, remember Serrano? These are his notes. The client is interested in something called Falcontor. Also the name Bruynzeel.'

He wrote them on her pad. 'Something might occur to you. I promised a preliminary report soon.'

She put the file down and laced her fingers, turned the palms outward. He heard her knuckles crack, a sound that always disturbed him, for no reason that he knew.

He went back to his office and the paperwork. Jonas was a happy agent. He had paid the bill, plus the $25,000 bonus. Pizza baron Charlie Campo and his runaway wife Lisa were reunited at last. In romantic Barcelona. All forgiven – a terrible, impulsive mistake. Sherry and tapas in a little bar off the Ramblas. Soft light, the bottles on the shelves glowing blood and oranges and rust. Glances. Touches.

Anselm thought of a woman with tape over her mouth, tied to a bed. Screaming through her eyes.

He went back to work, wrote an authorisation for

Herr Brinkman to pay Inskip and Carla the equivalent of $6250 each.

Blood money. They were bounty hunters. The woman could be dead. He could find out, but he didn't want to.

Through his slice of vision, Anselm looked at the sky, the lake, both still. The day was darkening. Perhaps it would snow. An early snowfall. It wouldn't be a proper snowfall, though, just tiny flakes that turned into slush when they touched the ground. The earth wasn't cold enough yet. When he was about twelve, he had been in the garden helping his grandfather fork over the vegetable patch.

'Weather experts, they know nothing,' the old man said. His hair was the colour of the sky. 'The earth tells the clouds when it's time for snow.'

Thinking about his grandfather, about cold earth, a day came into his mind like a ghost. He remembered the hotel, the down mattress that buried you, folded over you. Rising early, long before first light, walking down the creaking corridor to the bathroom where the pipes shrieked and keened and moaned and hammered. Hours later, climbing, climbing in the elderly Mercedes, first gear most of the way, they came around the side of a mountain. Suddenly they were above the mist. It lay below them, seething, stretching away, a savage sea, and, poking out of it, dark mountaintops like steep and inhospitable islands.

Where was that?

A cough from the doorway. Carla.

'You look ... distant,' she said.

'Visions from the past. Come in, sit down.'

Unusually, she did. She kept her bad leg straight when she sat down, took her weight on one arm, then the other. 'This is difficult,' she said. She did not quite meet his gaze.

Anselm nodded. 'Nothing easy from Bowden.'

'I can find a Luxembourg bank. That is it so far.'

Carla had the sad, lip-biting air of a child who

thought she had disappointed. Bad marks, failed to win the race or didn't jump high enough, far enough.

'Well,' said Anselm, 'you'll find something sooner or later.'

Carla refolded her hands. He hoped she wouldn't crack her knuckles. They were hands too big for her thin frame, elegant, long fingers, the nails well kept, rounded for typing. Erotic hands.

'Kael,' she said.

'Kael?'

'Serrano is connected with Kael, not so?'

She didn't know about the bugging of Serrano and Kael.

'Yes.'

'The connection includes these papers?'

'Probably.'

'Kael isn't an investment consultant. You know that?'

'I know that.'

She shifted again. 'Kael. Herr Baader could possibly … I don't know …'

It hung. He knew what she was saying.

'Wait.'

Anselm went down the corridor to Baader's office. He was on the phone, a knee against his desk. His head movement said, come in. Anselm sat down. Baader was answering someone with yes and no. Then he said: *'Na klar. Die Sache is erledigt. C'est fini. Schönen Dank. Wiedersehen.'*

He looked at Anselm, shaking his head. 'My life is moving beyond intolerable. Into a new phase.'

'You can't go beyond intolerable.'

'You can. You're not German enough to understand that. What?'

'O'Malley's interested in dealings connected with Werner Kael. Carla's on it.'

'So?'

'She thinks you could help. She's embarrassed.'

Baader's head went to one side. He ran a finger back and forth over his upper lip, over the day's regrowth. Anselm could hear the faint sawing sound.

'I had dealings with Kael,' said Baader eventually.

'Dealings?'

'I knew him.'

'I thought you were an analyst?'

'I did other things first. You earn the right to become an analyst.'

'I'll file that. Carla's idea?'

'It's not a favour I want to ask.'

'Okay.' Anselm got up.

'Kael's file is sanitised. I told you, he's got friends.'

'Well, O'Malley's worth a lot to us. But ...'

'Find another direction. What have you got? Have you got banks? So-called banks?'

'One, I think. Luxembourg.'

Baader slid his chair back, pushed off the desk, spun around, feet off the ground, like a child on a roundabout. 'Give me the bank,' he said. He kept spinning. 'I'm more at ease approaching from that side.'

Anselm watched him going around. 'Stefan,' he said, 'if you ever feel the need to talk to someone, you know where to find me.'

'Damaged,' said Baader. 'Both of us, we're damaged goods. Return to sender.'

'Address unknown, no such number, no such phone.'

Baader smiled, a happier fox now. 'A man who knows his Elvis cannot be damaged beyond repair.'

Anselm went back to Carla. 'No,' he said. 'We'll see what we can do with the bank. Give me the details. And have a try at Bruynzeel.'

She nodded and left. Anselm rang O'Malley.

'This is not proving easy.'

'I was rather hoping your distinguished head of chambers might weave his magic.'

'He may yet.'

'Carry on, Hardy. Ring me tomorrow. In the p.m. With luck, I'll be celebrating with my learned friend.'

'Eating your smoked ham with your pickles, beetroot, drinking your Krakow pils. And making use of your ...'

'Not another word.'

43

LONDON

SHE HAD been gone for a while, perhaps half an hour, when the phone in the kitchen rang.

Niemand was watching television, the news, a dark-haired woman and a man with glasses taking turns reading it. The woman was finishing an item about illegal Kurdish immigrants found in Dagenham.

He let it ring. Her answering machine came on. Her calm voice saying, 'Thank you for calling Jess Thomas Architectural Models ...'

On television, the man was talking about calls for new crowd-control measures at football grounds, a teenager had died in Belgium, crushed.

Niemand pressed the mute button on the remote.

'... and leave a message,' said Jess's voice on the machine.

The tone.

'Get out now,' said Jess, quick, urgent. 'Just go. I don't know how long you've got.'

He was up, took his valuables holster, his jacket, stuffed them into the bag, went for the fire-escape door. He was there when he remembered and he went back and tore the page off the pad, her cellphone number.

The steel door's bar resisted, not opened for a long time, rusted, painted over, many times, he couldn't get it to move. He dropped the bag, put both hands to the lever, pushed down.

It wouldn't move. Did not give at all. Solid.

Take your time, said the inner voice. The voice of his first instructor, in time his own voice. The careless, languid voice: Take your time, chicken brain.

Jolt it free.

Hit it.

With what?

He looked around and he looked across the kitchen, across the big space of the sitting room and workroom to the far wall.

Three shadows.

He saw three shadows flit along the bottom of the big industrial window. Gone in an instant, just bits of grey behind the wire-impregnated security glass.

Tops of heads.

Three heads, quickly, stooping but not stooping low enough, the lights from outside throwing shadows upwards.

Niemand hit the lever with his clenched hands, brought them down, used them like a flesh hammer, the pain was instant. In his hands, his back, his shoulder.

The big lever jerked free, upwards. He grabbed the bag, swung the steel door inwards, went out into the cold, drizzling night. Closed the door. He looked for a way to bolt it from the outside. No bolt. Stupid. It was a fire escape.

They would know where he had gone.

Of course they would know. Where else could he go?

Third floor. He looked down. An alley, bins, wet cobblestones, a streetlight at one end, a long way away. Straight lines of drizzle, a nimbus around each light. Where would they wait? At each end. That was what he would do. Someone at each end. Wait for him to come down, choose a direction.

He couldn't see the alley's end to the right. Dead end? Suicide to go down.

What the hell. He went up. Treading lightly, wet metal stairs, keeping against the wall, looking down at the alley. The night was loud, sirens, music from somewhere nearby, two sources of music, vehicle noises.

The roof was flat. He could make out a tank and a square structure, probably the lift housing, three chimney-like things, ventilation intakes, vents, something like that.

Light from the alley below. Niemand went to the parapet, looked down with one eye.

Headlights at each end of the alley.

They didn't care. They knew they had him.

Six metres below him, a black figure was on the fire-escape landing, Jess's landing, a weapon upright in one hand – machine-pistol. He could see the fat silencer tube.

A gun. He should have bought a gun. You never needed one until you didn't have one.

He walked over the wet roof to the tank. It was on four legs. He ran a hand over it. Wet. Old. Rusty. He tapped the bottom, tapped the top. Full of something.

The legs were bolted to the concrete. A long time ago. One was bent under its burden. He kicked it and it gave without hesitation, the tank tilted.

He went around, stood clear, kicked another front leg. It didn't move. Just hurt his toes. He looked around, eyes adjusted now, he saw a piece of pipe: thick, not long, it lay in a pool of rainwater. Left when the building was converted, a shoddy conversion, the pipe sawn off from some old plumbing.

The burst of gunfire hit the tank, above him, well above his head. He heard only the percussion, an ear-jangling thwang, saw sparks like fireworks in his brain.

He fell. And as he fell he reached for the length of

pipe, got it – wet, slimy, hard to hold. Heavy. He lay, looking back, pain from his shoulder.

A penis-head above from the stairs. All black, head in a black balaclava, tight like a stocking mask, the man's eye sockets and eyelids blackened.

In the middle of London. Full fucking nightfighting shit.

'Don't move,' said the man, voice clear. 'You won't get hurt. We don't want to hurt you.'

This was better. They wanted him alive this time. For a while. Until they'd watched the film, made sure it wasn't Chevy Chase again, the holiday in Europe one.

Niemand rose to his knees. He held up his left hand in surrender, weakly, and he kept the pipe behind him. By its weight, it was cast-iron.

The man rose, he was on the roof, the weapon pointed at Niemand.

'Hands in the air, please,' he said.

'Don't point that fucking thing at me,' said Niemand. The man bent his forearm, held the machine-pistol upright, pointed it at the heavens. He was confident. He knew that Niemand had nowhere to go, back-ups on the stairs.

Niemand threw the pipe.

Stood and threw in one movement.

He threw it with his arm below shoulder level, threw it as he would a grenade, he didn't want the weight to snap his elbow, he expected pain. And it came, from his chest, his neck, it seemed to come from his whole upper body.

The man saw what was happening, brought the barrel down. But he didn't want to fire.

The pipe changed its angle, side-on it hit him in the head. He went down, axed, the weapon in his hands slid away, across the wet concrete.

Niemand found the machine-pistol, picked up the

cast-iron pipe, went over and struck the other front tank leg. At the third blow, it gave.

The tank fell gracefully, hit the roof with a dull sound, and released a thick liquid. Lots of liquid, and it flowed, flowed past the still man in black, the roof tilted towards the fire escape, and the liquid ran and spilled over the edge.

Niemand sniffed the fluid, found the matches in his holster. The first match didn't strike.

The second one did, flared. He touched the fluid, the flame died. A sound from the stairs, scratch on metal.

The back-up boys.

The third match wouldn't strike.

He would have to go now.

Go where?

He scraped another match. It flared, held, burnt bright. He applied it to the liquid.

Nothing. He blew gently.

'HANDS IN THE AIR!'

Fire under his hand, jumping at him, burning the hairs in his nose.

Heating oil.

He saw the dark head at the fire escape, the weapon, saw the fire whipping down the stream, a blue-red flame reached the fire escape, went over the edge.

Liquid fire. A waterfall of fire.

One long agonised scream. Then screams, screaming. The other back-ups on the stairs.

Niemand walked to the other side of the roof, he wasn't in a hurry now, looked down at the lane below. There was a car in it, blocking it, doors open, inside light on.

A big pipe ran down the side of the building, beginning three metres below. All the plumbing shared a pipe. He did not wait, put the machine-pistol in the bag, slung the bag around his neck so that it hung on his back.

He went over the side, face to the building, didn't hang, dropped blind to the pipe's first joint, hit it with his right knee, kept falling, caught the tight-angle bend with both hands, took his full weight with his hands and shoulders. The pain almost caused him to let go, it blotted out his sight for an instant. Then he went down the pipe without his feet seeking purchase, just hands holding, a controlled fall, hands slowing him, like going down a rope.

He hit the concrete hard, legs not ready for it, knees not bent, sat on his backside, jarred the bones. He got up, ran around the right side of the car, looked.

Keys in it.

Bag off, into the car, reach to close passenger door, a manual, thank Christ, turned the key.

A tortured sound. The motor was already on, running, they'd left it running, so quiet he hadn't heard it.

Reverse where it should be?

Shit no, forward. He hit the brakes, tried again.

Backwards down the lane, twenty metres, engine screaming. Into the street. Braked, looked, nothing coming, a tight left turn.

First gear. Missed it, got into second, pushed the pedal flat, it didn't bother the engine, the motor could handle second-gear take-offs. An old man in a raincoat looking at him. Down the rainslicked street, right at the first corner. Going anywhere, going away.

Slow down, chicken brain, said the inner voice. Take your time. Being picked up by the cops now would be silly. Stolen car.

Alive.

Jesus, alive.

Third-time lucky.

You didn't get more than three.

44

... LONDON ...

THE FAX was there when she got back: three stories. Two were short, just a few paragraphs. The third spread over three pages. It was called: 'And Unquiet Lie the Civil Dead'.

The date was February 1993. The byline was Richard Monk. She read quickly and she drew a line beside a section:

> As for Namibia, the white South African regime regarded it as a fief. Soldiers killed with impunity. It was sport. One regiment was on horseback. They rode down running humans, teenagers many of them, just ill-nourished boys. The soldiers galloped alongside them and they shot them between the shoulder blades with automatic shotguns. And the riders laughed at what they saw. There were no consequences. Later, Mozambique was the same, a place to corral starving two-legged animals: blow them up with grenades, sizzle them with flame-throwers. But this had limited training value; it was too easy.
>
> And then came Angola, sad, ravaged Angola, cursed with oil. At least 300,000 people – many of them civilians – have died in the civil war since Holden Roberto of the FNLA first took the CIA's coin in 1962. Together, Holden and the agency held a small war and the whole world

225

came: the US, South Africa, China, the Soviet Union, Cuba. South Africa was invited in by the US and it came with alacrity. In August 1981, given the nod by a Reagan Administration foaming at the mouth over the Cuban presence in the country, it invaded southern Angola. The South African force of 11,000 men, supported by tanks and aircraft, laid waste to Cunene province. Some 80,000 Angolans fled their homes. How many died is unknown. The South African army settled down for a long and murderous stay.

From 1981, the US used both military power – South African troops (and their proxies) and Savimbi's UNITA forces – and economic pressure as it set out to destabilise countries in the region. As a result, some estimates put deaths by starvation at more than 100,000 in 1983 alone. Along the bloody way, there have been many chances to end the Angolan conflict. But, until last month, the US turned its face against any settlement that did not fully replace Soviet with American influence.

The CIA and the Defense Intelligence Agency will miss Angola and the nearby countries. They like the region a lot. It has been good to them, a wonderful place to train staff, hundreds of them (even black officers, although the South Africans didn't approve). It has also been a chance to provide extravagantly paid work for the agencies' loyal friends – the little 'civilian' airlines and the freelance specialists of all deadly and corrupt kinds.

As for the warm and loving community who live by selling arms, the misery of Angola has been a bonanza. Millions of dollars of US weapons have gone to the South Africans and their ally, Savimbi's UNITA.

And hasn't Angola been fun for America's so-called mercenaries, the live-action fringe of the gun-crazies. Almost every bar they infest has some thickneck who can tell you stories about high old times killing black people in

Angola (with the odd rape thrown in). In Tucson recently, a man called Red showed me his photographs. In one, he was squatting, M16 in hand, butt on the ground.

Behind him was an obscene pile of black bodies, one headless.

'Soldiers?' I asked.

'Niggers,' he said. 'Commie niggers.'

Some of these men even claim to have fought Cubans, but that is highly unlikely. In Angola, the Cubans fired back.

Sick American porn-killers are bad enough but there is the possibility of much worse.

In early 1988, CIA and DIA propagandists began feeding the media stories about Cuban troops using nerve gas in Angola. (Angola was always 'Marxist Angola', the Cubans were always 'Soviet-sponsored', and Savimbi was always 'the US-backed freedom fighter'.) Highly dubious 'experts' were always cited. Of course, their South African and other connections were never mentioned.

Fragments of evidence now suggest that this campaign was in response to rumours in South Africa of a village in northern Angola being wiped out.

Wiped out by which side? How? We don't know. But should the rumours have spread outside South Africa and been investigated and confirmed, the CIA-DIA misinformation artists had done the groundwork for blaming the Cubans.

Richard Monk. Who was Richard Monk?

Caroline found the contents page. The Notes on Contributors said: 'Richard Monk is a freelance journalist who is no stranger to the world's trouble spots.' That wasn't going to help. She typed *richard monk* into the search engine.

An hour later she had nothing.

She circled the editor's name: Robert Blumenthal. Where would he be decades later?

Another search. Hundreds of Robert Blumenthal references came up. She went back and added *editor behind enemy lines*.

Half a dozen. The first one said:

> ... *veteran radical editor Robert Blumenthal, 69, collapsed and died Saturday while giving the William j Cummings Memorial Lecture at the University of Montana's School of Journalism ... Behind Enemy Lines ...*

She went to the source, *The Missoulian,* daily paper of Missoula, Montana. Robert Blumenthal was long gone. The Saturday he died at the podium was a Saturday in 1996. The story mentioned *Behind Enemy Lines* among seven or eight publications Blumenthal had edited. They had names like *The Social Fabric, To Bear Witness, Records of Capitalism.* It said he had lived in Missoula for ten years with his partner of twenty-two years, the photographer Paul Salinas.

Go home, lie in a bath with a big whisky, eat scrambled eggs for supper. Watch television.

Colley. The bastard. He'd treated her with contempt, casually used her. She didn't know why or how. But he had betrayed Mackie to someone who wanted to kill him, tried to kill him.

Mackie might be dead.

She might have killed him by going to Colley instead of going to Halligan.

Get on with it.

It took another hour to find a phone number for the right Paul Salinas. When she had the number, it rang but no one answered, no machine.

She waited. Tried again. Again. The fifth or sixth time, she was going to go home, it was after 8 p.m., the receiver was picked up. 'Salinas.'

'Mr Salinas, my name is Carol Short. I'm ringing from Sydney, Australia. I'm a publisher's permissions person and I'm hoping you can help me.'

She carried on lying, told him a story about wanting to publish Richard Monk's piece in an anthology of political writing.

'Publisher? Sorry, did you say that?'

He was wobbly, she could tell. He might have been asleep, the phone ringing unheard.

'Yes. It's called The Conviction Press. It's new, no money, no track record. We're not acceptable politically.'

'Australia?'

'Yes. Sydney. I don't suppose you know, but there are radicals in Australia.'

Salinas laughed and she could hear that it took a lot out of him.

'We were in Australia in '75, late '75,' he said. 'Met a lot of people. Amazing people. Byron Bay, we went up there. That was really good stuff they were smoking. Big year for you Aussies, wasn't it, '75?'

She had no idea what he was talking about.

'People seem to have thought so at the time.'

Would that response pass?

Salinas laughed and he sounded stronger.

'That's what Bob loved about Australians. Give nothing away. *Not bad.* See something, read something, it's excellent, you love it. What do you say? *Not bad.* Bob adored that. He adopted that. It was our joke. Shakespeare? *Not bad.* Picasso? *Not bad.* You like this food, exotic ingredients, three hours in the making? *Not bad.* He had a time, any shit descended, he'd say, Paul, let's go live in Australia.'

Salinas had a deep voice. Each word had its space. She saw a big man with a beard, black hairs on the backs of his hands.

'We need to get Richard Monk's permission to publish,' she said. 'But I can't find a writer or journalist by that name on any database.'

'Doesn't surprise me,' said Salinas.

Silence.

'*Behind Enemy Lines* was Bob's last fling. Not that he knew it.'

'It doesn't surprise you that I can't trace Richard Monk?'

'Hell, no. Write for anything Bob published, brace yourself for wiretaps, mail intercepts, the short-haired men in the brown suits having a quiet word with your neighbours.'

'You're saying that wouldn't be the writer's real name?'

'Not if you can't find him.'

'Well, they say it's such an interesting piece. We'd be sad not to republish it. But if we can't, we can't. If I can't ask him, that's that.'

'Yeah, pretty much.'

Caroline sensed something. 'I feel like a failure,' she said. 'I am a failure. Can I ask you for advice?'

'Sure.'

'If you were some dumb publishing assistant and you wanted to find out who Richard Monk was so that you could ask him, what would you do?'

There was a moment of nothing, just a hollow sound on the line. 'I'd ask the person I was talking to.'

'Who is Richard Monk, Mr Salinas?'

'Hold on, I'll get Bob's secret ledgers.'

She held. The lonesome sound. This would all be worthless. Nothing would come of this. He came back inside two minutes. 'I'm sorry, I didn't retain your name?'

'Carol Short. The Conviction Press. Sydney. The number is 61 2 7741 5601.'

Please God, don't let him say, I'll ring you back.

'Doesn't seem to be here. I'll have to ring you back.'

Gone.

'At any time,' she said.

McClatchie wouldn't have fucked this up.

'Let me ring you back,' she said. 'There's no need for you to pay for the call.'

'No, wait. Here it is, this is it ... the last issue ... *And Unquiet Lie* ... here we are. Money order, address in San Francisco. Not much. Still, he would've been doing it for the cause.'

'There's a name?'

'John Anselm.'

45

LONDON

WOULD THEY report the stolen car to the police? They'd tried to kill him three times. Tonight was just a delayed execution. They were not ordinary citizens who reported things to the police.

Three times in this huge city they'd found him. How had they done that? Once by the mobile, perhaps, he had worked that out, there was no other way.

But after that?

He had hurt three of them. Possibly badly. Possibly kissed them off.

Air. He needed air. He found the button, his window descended.

Cold London winter air. Exhaust fumes. A wet smell, like the smell in a cupboard where damp clothes had been hung.

Go where?

He was on a main street now, lots of traffic, bright shops, crowded pavements, no idea where he was. He saw a parking space, pulled in behind a Volvo. Sat, trying to think, too much adrenalin in the system to think straight.

'Lookin for me?'

Niemand jerked away, his right elbow coming up in defence.

'Relax, relax, mon. Need to calm down, chill out. Smell the roses. What can I get you? I'm your mon.'

A black man stooping, standing back from the open

window. Not big. Shaven head, goatee beard. Tight leather jacket. Three strands of golden chains.

'I need a cellphone,' said Niemand. 'Quick.'

The man looked at the car, side to side, exaggerated movements of his head.

'Got any ID, officer?'

'Fuck you.'

The man looked at him, weighed him up.

'Sixty quid,' he said. 'Bargain. Today's special. Nokia, brand new. Okay for a week. Guaranteed. Well, say six days from today. Be safe not sorry, hey, mon?'

'Okay.'

'Wait.'

He was gone. Niemand looked around for something to identify the car's owner. Nothing in the glovebox, on the tray. He felt behind his seat, in the footwell.

Something.

A nylon jacket? No, too heavy.

It was a BB, a belly-and-balls bulletproof waistband, hips to solar plexus, fastened at the side with Velcro, tied between the legs. Niemand had owned one. Never mind the chest shot, what worried soldiers was the gut shot, groin shot, balls shot off – those were the major worries.

There was a pocket across the back, sideways. It held a Kevlar knife, like a piece of thin bone, a fighting knife. Weighed no more than a comb and you could carry it through a metal detector.

Niemand put the corset into his bag.

The man was coming back, weaving down the busy pavement. He came close, showed the device.

'State of the fuckin art, mon,' he said. 'The 6210. Internet. Voice diallin. Four hours talkin time to go.'

Niemand found a fifty and a ten. 'Where's the owner?'

'On holiday. Won't know till he comes back.'

They did the exchange.

'Where is this?' said Niemand.

'This?'

'Here. Where am I?'

The man shook his head. 'Battersea, mon. Thought it might be sunny fuckin Hawaii, did ya?'

Niemand watched him go down the crowded pavement, slick as a fish through kelp. He took his bag and got out, left the car unlocked, keys in the ignition. He walked in the opposite direction to the phone seller. Cold drizzle, smells of cooking oil in the air. It took a long time to find a cab.

'What is your desire?'

The driver was an Indian, a balding man with a moustache, a stern, worried face.

Jesus Christ, where to?

'Victoria Station.' It came to mind. What did it matter? At least he knew where Victoria Station was.

He leant back, felt his muscles let go, watched the world go by. Into a main road. Night traffic, heavy both ways. The driver said nothing. They crossed a bridge. Presumably Battersea Bridge. He must have come this way on the back of Jess's bike. On the other side of the bridge, the traffic was bad.

Who were these people trying to kill him? How did they find him? He should give them the film in exchange for letting him leave the country. Ring the woman who'd betrayed him. No. That wasn't the way it worked: they wanted the film and they wanted him dead. They knew he'd seen the film, he couldn't be left walking around.

Jess. They would kill her too.

They would think she was in this with him. Why shouldn't they think that? She'd picked him up on her bike. She'd taken him home. Of course, they'd think that.

'Pull up anywhere you can,' he said. 'I'll get out here.'

'Well, this is not hardly worth my while, you said explicitly you wanted ...'

Niemand found a twenty, showed it. 'Just pull up,' he said.

The driver didn't look impressed, pulled to the kerb. Niemand didn't say anything more, got out. It was the Kings Road, he recognised it, knew where he was. He leaned against a wall, got out the cellphone, found Jess's number.

It rang. And rang. The little electronic sound.

It wasn't going to be answered. He knew that.

He should have done this before. She had saved his life. Taken him onto her bike, into her house, organised his doctor.

And she had phoned him in time to save his life, save it for the second time.

There had been nothing in it for her. Nothing. She had simply done it for him. For another human being.

All I said was, Thanks very much. What kind of a person am I? Ringing. Ringing.

The sound of being picked up. The button.

He closed his eyes for an instant. Thank God.

'Yes?'

'Jess?'

'Who's that?' A woman.

It wasn't Jess.

Jess was dead. He knew it.

'A friend. Is she there?'

Silence. He thought the line had gone.

'Con?'

Niemand let his breath go.

'Yes,' he said.

'Are you all right?'

'Fine,' he said. 'They tried to kill me again.'

'Where are you?'

He told her. He should have said thank you again and goodbye and sorry about your building, but he told her.

46

HAMBURG

THE PHONE.

'Mr Anselm?'

'Yes.'

'David Carrick from Lafarge in London. Does that mean anything?'

'It does.'

The man had the kind of English voice Anselm disliked. Eton and the Guards. He'd come across a few of them. The pinstriped suits with a white stripe. Not blue, not red. White. When had he come across them?

'Wonderful,' said the man. 'Good. We're secure here, are we?'

'What can be done has been done.'

'Of course. That's Latin, isn't it? Totally rotten at Latin. I wonder if I can ask you to run a credit check? Someone new to the UK.'

Customs.

'Name?'

'Martin Powell.' He spelled the surname. 'Recent arrival, we would think. And we'd also like a general search, anything that turns up in the name. May I say that this could not be more urgent.'

'You may. We'll give it priority.'

'Thank you. The numbers, you have them?'

In his segment of view, Anselm could see that the day was darkening.

'We do.'
'Immediate contact, please.'
They said goodbye.

47

LONDON

'LET ME be clear. I'm tired, I don't want to be in this shithouse town. We have the place, the cunt is there alone. Now one man is dead and two are in hospital with burns and the cunt is gone.'

'Well, in essence.'

'In essence? That means?'

'Yes. Mr Price.'

'So keep your fucken Limey talk for your old private school pals. This's a fuck-up of some size, not so?'

'Yes. It is. But we had ...'

'Who hired these people?'

'We've used them before, Charlie, they've done ...'

'You hired them?'

'Well, ah, Dave ...'

'Don't be a prick. Don't fucken shift the blame. Who's the seller? In fucken essence?'

'We're not sure right now. We'll be ...'

'That's so fucken reassuring. You don't even know who the cunt is. We're trying to kill some cunt, we don't even know who he is.'

'Haven't had very long. This thing kind ...'

'*Very* long? *Very* long? You want *very* long? Oh, well, sorry to rush you. Listen to me. You now have *no* fucking long. You have absolutely *zero* long. You are in *negative* long.'

'We're doing everything we can.'

'I need to say to you, any more fucked up than this, you boys, you get skewered asshole to Adam's apple. Cooked like fucken barbecue pigs. All night long, meat falls off the bone. Only the pigs, they kill the fucken pigs first.'

'If I can say something, Mr Price ...'

'Say. Just say.'

'This is England, we can't just ...'

'Wow, you fucken Limeys are somethin. Dunkirk, fucken retreat, fucken disgrace, your finest hour.'

'It's the Battle of Britain actually.'

'What?'

'The Battle of Britain. That's England's finest hour.'

'That right? Excuse my fucken ignorance. Well, listen to me, goes for you both. Things don't get better quick your fucken worst hour's gonna happen real soon. Your fucken worst minute. Anyway. Now. Where the fuck are we?'

'Mr Price, someone shot two men in a hotel in Earls Court the night before last. In the legs. The room was in the name Martin Powell. No sign of him. The men have told a story – met a man in a pub, he invited them to his room to have a drink, he turned ...'

'Just the fucken ending.'

'Mackie said people tried to kill him in a hotel, he told the woman that. Wishart. This Powell could be our man.'

'You heard this when?'

'An hour ago. We've got people on it.'

'So pleased to hear that. The motorbike rider? It's the one picked this Mackie up?'

'Yeah. The address we got for the bike, it's her old address. We sent someone, parcel to deliver, you know. Wrong address, this other woman, she gave the new address ...'

'And your people went around there and shot themselves in the balls. Jesus, Martie, I cannot fucken believe ...'

'They say they heard the phone ring inside. Hit the front door, he was already gone.'

'Who's carrying the can for this?'

'No problem. They're, ah, reliable. Good.'

'Are you fucken mad? One man. One solitary fucken individual. On a plate. First, your reliable cunts decide to take him out in the most public place they can find, make this brilliant fucken decision, you don't put them straight.'

'Can I say, I didn't ...'

'Fuck that up, then they set a building alight, own casualties minor. Just one dead, two in hospital having emergency skin grafts ...'

'Private clinic, it's ...'

'Shut the fuck up.'

'Ah, there's no chance of any ID, not the vehicle either. It should be ... okay. Yes. Safe.'

'Should be? Safe? Boy, who the hell trained you, you ask for your money back. Plus fucken interest. This Powell? When you gonna know?'

48

HAMBURG

'I'VE GOT a Martin Powell on entry.'

Anselm looked up.

Inskip, languid in the doorway.

'Yes?'

'Heathrow. Four days ago. Central African Republic passport. Age thirty-six, occupation sales representative. Flight from Johannesburg. Hand luggage only.'

He crossed the room and put a copy of the file note on the desk.

Anselm took the pad, got up and went to the filing cabinet, found the folder, the page. He wrote the key on the pad. 'Run this,' he said.

'Immediately, Minister. In my pigeonhole today I found a cheque.'

'Should keep you in black T-shirts for life. Or red.'

'You noticed. It crossed my mind to spend some of it on a decent dinner. Hamburg haute cuisine. Might invite you.'

'Very generous. Put most of it aside. When my anti-dining phase ends I'll take you up.'

Anselm thought he saw something, hurt perhaps, in Inskip's eyes.

'Take me up, take me down, just as long as you take me.'

Inskip left.

Anselm found the Lafarge file. The number rang twice.

'Lafarge International. How may I help you?'

'Mr Carrick, please.'

'Carrick.' The clipped tone.

'Weidermann and Kloster.'

'Right, yes. Hello.' Some anxiety in the voice.

'Is this a good line?'

'Go ahead.'

'The person entered from Johannesburg at Heathrow four days ago. Central African Republic passport. Age thirty-six, occupation sales representative.'

'Any background?'

'Not yet.'

They said goodbye. Anselm went to Inskip's station in the workroom.

'In,' said Inskip. 'Amazing. How can we do this?'

'They bought Israeli software.'

'Meaning?'

'Meaning it's got a rear entrance. Run Jackdaw.'

Shaking his head, Inskip clicked on an icon, a stylised bird with a D for *Dohle* superimposed on it. A box came up.

'The name?'

'The name,' said Anselm.

Inskip typed in *Martin Powell* and clicked.

Three sets of letters and figures appeared.

Anselm said, 'Select and click. And whatever you do, don't print anything. Take notes. Go back to Jackdaw when you're finished and erase.'

'Sir.'

Anselm went across to Carla, stood behind her. She had code on two monitors. Her eyes were on the screens, her fingertips were stroking the keyboard, not pressing keys, thoughtful, just running down, making small clicking sounds. He looked at her hands for a while before he spoke.

'Any luck?'

She swivelled slightly, put her head back, looked up at him. Her sleek hair touched his hip. 'Herr Baader's friends have not been very helpful. But now I think the bank's encryption, it may be out of date. I have someone in Canada testing it. A secure person.'

'Good.' Without thinking, he touched her shoulder, pulled his hand away. She showed no sign of taking offence. He thought he saw the embryo of a smile on her lips.

At his desk, Anselm worked through the files, made notes for operators, dictated instructions for Beate. Alex was always at the edge of his thoughts. She came to mind too often, he thought about what she might be doing, what her day-to-day life was like. The apartment full of chairs. The ex-husband in America. Alex when she was waiting for him at the car, flushed face and neck: pink, sexual pink. She had prominent collarbones and a deep hollow between them.

The internal phone rang.

Inskip.

'I've got something.'

Anselm went back to the blue room, to Inskip's station. He sat on the chair next to him. Inskip pointed at his main monitor. A column of names, one high-lighted.

'Here's a Martin Powell on a list. The date on it's 1986.'

He scrolled down the column.

'It's alphabetical,' he said.

'I see that.'

'Here's the list that follows, dated a month later.'

The new column had names with figures beside them,

amounts of money in rands, the South African currency. Inskip scrolled down it. R10,000 was the smallest sum. There was no Martin Powell.

'List number two,' said Inskip. 'Some kind of payroll. Notice that this list is *mostly* alphabetical. Five names from list number one have gone and in their places are five new ones.'

'Mostly alphabetical,' said Anselm. It took him a second to grasp the meaning. 'The new names are all in the alphabetical positions of the missing ones?'

'You're quick, Master. That's right. My assumption is that whoever made up list number two changed names but didn't bother to re-sort alphabetically. Just cut and pasted in the new names.'

'Payments,' said Anselm. 'Could be the five used false names on list number one, assumed names, but were then paid in their real names.'

'And Martin Powell is gone.'

Inskip selected a name. 'And in his place is this man.'

The name was: NIEMAND, CONSTANTINE.

Anselm was staring at the screen. 'What's the year?'

'1986.'

'Go to the top and scroll.'

Anselm looked at the names. He knew what the lists meant. He didn't know how he knew, but he knew. 'These people are mercenaries,' he said. 'This is the gang assembled for a coup in the Seychelles. Organised in England. The South African government backed it, then they betrayed it to the Seychelles government. Paid off the troops.'

Inskip turned his shaven head, blue in the light. He raised his eyebrows. 'How do you know that?'

Anselm got up. 'I know it because the world is too much with me. As for you, this is bonus-quality work. But there isn't a bonus.'

'Your approval, I'm content to bask in that.'

'While you're warm, run the Niemand name.'

Anselm went to his office and rang the number in London.

'Carrick.'

'W and K.'

'Hold on.'

Clicks.

'Go ahead.'

'We have something.'

Anselm told him.

'Your operator's very good,' said Carrick. 'We need that name checked. Soonest.'

Inskip, holding up a notepad. His eyes were bright.

'Hold on a moment, please,' said Anselm.

'Got him,' said Inskip softly. 'Got Niemand.'

Anselm said to Carrick, 'We have something on Niemand. I'm putting the operator on.'

Inskip came in, took the handset, cleared his throat. He looked at his notes. 'A man and his wife and a security guard were murdered by black burglars in a house in Johannesburg four days ago,' he said. 'Another security man killed the attackers. His name is given as Con Niemand. His firm says he's an ex-soldier.'

He listened. 'No. This is from the Johannesburg *Star*. British. The name is Shawn.'

Anselm was looking at his desk, sightless. He didn't register immediately.

'S-H-A-W-N,' said Inskip. 'Brett and Elizabeth Shawn. Ages forty-seven and forty-one.'

Sitting in the Mercedes with Tilders, Kael and Serrano on the ferry, the voices from the crackly bug:

Well, that's something. Shawn?

Shot by blacks. So it appears. The business is strange. Werner, the question is what do we do now?

49

HAMBURG

TOWARDS HOME in the cold night, late, Anselm walking, the far shore's lights lying broken in the lake.

Reading the names on Inskip's list, he had felt a sense of recognition and it had come to him: the farcical plot to stage a coup in the Seychelles, he had found out about it in late 1986. He remembered going to London from Paris, staying at the hotel in Russell Square. He'd stayed there often, he knew it well: the cramped bedroom, the tiny floral wallpaper pattern, the corner shower that steamed up the whole room, the small dining room where only breakfast was served, always eggs, bacon and sausage, pigeon-sized eggs cooked hard, bacon that was mainly fat, a single sausage like a pygmy's little finger.

He talked to the man in a pub, it was winter, December, near Christmas, the pub wasn't far away from the hotel, on a corner. They sat at a table in a corner of the saloon bar. The man wanted revenge on people, his superiors, he was sixtyish, bland-faced, a thin scar beneath his right eye. An accident in childhood, perhaps. Struck by a swing.

Anselm tried to remember whether he had written a story about the Seychelles business. The clipping would be in the cartons sent from San Francisco at Lucas's instructions. Some time in the first week, he had cut the tapes on one. Grey-blue document boxes, stacked neat as bricks. He remembered opening one and reading a clipping with his byline datelined BOGOTA, TUESDAY. It had meant nothing to him; something written by a stranger from a place he did not recall. He sat there for a long time, blinking away tears. He did not open the boxes again.

Two people were coming towards him: men, one medium, one shorter, they moved apart, he felt an alarm – they wanted him to pass between them. He moved to his right, the right-hand man shifted.

Guten Abend, and they were gone. The taller man was a tall woman. Her perfume brushed his face like a cobweb. He carried it a long way, he knew the scent, he knew it well. For a few moments, he wanted desperately to know who wore it, tried to will his mind to tell him.

The pulse in his throat quietened. He could not remember ever going to Bogota. He remembered his first trip to Beirut ... since when did he remember that? Sleeping on the floor of the Dutch photographer's small apartment in Ashrafiyé near the Place Sassine. The bakery called Nazareth. Henk introduced him to the crepes, the cheesy crepes. He remembered the impossible traffic, the insane driving, cocks crowing from gutted buildings, vegetable patches in the ruins, the feeling of people pressing upon you.

He could probably always have remembered his first time in Beirut. He simply hadn't thought about it. You didn't know what you remembered until you thought about it.

Nonsense.

Why were so many things coming back? Was everything going to be restored? An unbroken thread? A complete chronology? Would he remember his life again as one piece? Would he be whole again, remember people now unknown to him – people he had loved, people he had slept with? Were they all going to appear without warning, rise silently through the black mud and matted weed like peatbog men?

The thought made him uneasy. Perhaps it was better to be without the memories. What did it matter? What did holes, gaps, matter? Life didn't make any sense, it wasn't a story, it wasn't a journey. It was just short films by different directors. The only link was you. You were in all of them. You missed a plane and your life changed. You misheard a place name, went to the wrong bar and then you spent two years with a woman you met there. You were leaving for Europe and the agency rang and instead you went to Colombia. The difference was five minutes. Kaskis rang and then you almost drowned in the Caribbean. Kaskis rang again and if you'd been in Bogota you wouldn't have spent a year lying in holes in Beirut and you'd have missed the experience of a red-eyed teenager recircuiting your brain with the butt of a Kalashnikov.

Enough.

Shawn.

Waiting to cross Fernsicht, he thought about the man called Shawn murdered in Johannesburg. Kael and Serrano had some connection with him. And Lafarge in London were looking for a man called Martin Powell, whose real name was probably Constantine Niemand, and who was probably on the scene when Shawn died. Niemand, an ex-soldier who killed Shawn's killers.

Anselm thought that he was at the intersection of these things and he had no understanding of them. There was a film involved, Kael had talked about a film.

Kael: … *Can you grasp that? If this prick's got the papers and the film, whatever the fucking film is … How did Lourens die?*

Serrano: *In a fire. Chemical fire. Not even teeth left.*

Kael: *Well, at least that's neat. Shawn?*

Serrano: *Shot by blacks. So it appears. The business is strange. Werner, the question is what do we do now?*

His street was calm and wet, the traffic noise muted here, most of the leaves down now, the tree limbs silver in the light from streetlamps and front porches, their shadows on the ground like dark roadmaps of densely settled places.

The laundry had been delivered, neat packages on the porch. In the house, the answering machine's red beacon called to him as he passed the study. He poured a drink first, whisky and mineral water, not too strong. He was trying not to have three or four neat whiskies when he came home. It was a fight. He craved the quick hits.

He put on the heating and took the clean, ironed sheets upstairs and made the bed. Then he went down and made another drink, took it to the study, switched on the desk light, sat down in the leather armchair and pressed the machine's Play button.

John, Lucas. I've had a call from a woman, a journalist. She's been trying to find you. Says it's very urgent. Life and death. Her words. Persuasive woman. Something you wrote in, hold on … it's called Behind Enemy Lines. *One of your left-wing rags, no doubt. Her name's Caroline Wishart. W-I-S-H-A-R-T. I told her I'd pass on her number. It's a direct line, London …*

Anselm found a pen, played the message again and wrote down the number.

Life and death. A figure of speech.

Behind Enemy Lines? It meant nothing. Probably after 1989, that was where the major fault line seemed to run. There seemed to be bigger gaps after 1989. How could the brain be so arbitrary? He drank whisky and said the name over and over. Nothing.

Ring Caroline Wishart? About something he'd written. He hadn't written anything since Beirut.

Who would say the words 'life and death'? Journalists. Journalists would say them. Say or not say.

They would say or not say anything. It was a trade of omission, implication, suggestion, allusion, half-lies, other fractions of lies. The challenge was to find a way to get people to tell you things. It was just technique – that was what he had said to himself then, in that life.

Lying even to himself.

The sound of water in the drainpipe outside. When the rain was steady, the house's drainpipes made special sounds, irregular, surging sounds. The gutters seemed to hold the water, then let it go. Silence, then a rush. You could count the time between flushes if you said *and* between each count. Three, sometimes four seconds. He had first noticed this when they came to Hamburg for his grandfather's funeral. Lying in the bedroom upstairs, in his father's childhood bedroom, in his father's childhood bed, Lucas asleep across the room – Lucas went to sleep instantly, anywhere – he had fallen asleep counting the pauses. How old? Ten or twelve.

The house had its own life, its own ways. When he came from Beirut, it was mute. He heard nothing, no sounds, a silent house. Then, gradually, it seemed to relax, accept him. One by one, sounds appeared. The house began to groan and creak, it moaned quietly in the wind. There were sounds of friction in the roof, strange rubbing sounds. Pipes began to choke and hammer, the heating whispered, the stair-treads released squeaks in descending or ascending order seconds after his passage.

Caroline Wishart.

He dialled W&K. Wolfgang answered.

'*Anselm. Herr Inskip, bitte.*'

'Inskip.'

'Anselm.'

'I thought you'd gone home.'

'I've done that. Now I'm bored. Run a Caroline Wishart, will you? A journalist. London. Nothing fancy.'

He spelled the name, waited. He heard keys clicking, the humming of the blue room. He finished the whisky. Only the second drink of the night. Remarkable.

'She's a hot new talent,' said Inskip. 'An exposé person. Exclusive. Minister Buggered Me Says Rentboy. Pictures.'

'Is that a complaint?' said Anselm. 'I thought rentboys understood what the job entailed.'

'He could be referring to the Minister's stamina. It could be a compliment.'

'Yes. Thank you and goodnight.'

Anselm fetched another whisky. He vacillated and then he dialled W&K again, Inskip.

'Put this through for me, would you?'

He would be giving her his number if he dialled direct. He put down the phone. It rang within seconds.

'Caroline Wishart.'

'John Anselm.'

He heard her sigh.

'Mr Anselm, I'm so pleased you've called. I'd almost given up hope.'

It was an upper-class voice.

'It's about what?'

'You wrote a piece for *Behind Enemy Lines* in 1993. Called "And Unquiet Lie the Civil Dead"? Under the name Richard Monk.'

Anselm didn't say anything. The title meant nothing to him. Nor did the name Richard Monk.

'I'm trying to follow up on something in it about a rumour that a village in Angola was wiped out.'

Blank.

'What makes you think I'm Richard Monk?'

'The person the publisher paid for the article was John Anselm. A cheque was sent to him to an address in San Francisco.'

San Francisco?

'What address?'

She told him.

Kaskis's apartment.

'Who told you that?'

'The publisher's friend told someone who told me. Robert Blumenthal's friend.'

He saw a man with hair like a dark, curly frame around his face, bright brown eyes. The look of an intellectual lumberjack. He remembered a voice, low, husky, quick speech.

That was all he remembered.

'I'm sorry,' said Anselm. 'I had an accident in 1993 and my memory's bad. I can't recall the piece. Not at all.'

She was silent. She doesn't believe me, he thought. Well, a person who seeks out rentboys who say they were fucked by a British Cabinet Minister, she'd probably be of a sceptical bent.

'Mr Anselm, it's terribly important,' she said. 'I wasn't being melodramatic when I said to your brother it was a life and death matter.'

He didn't say anything.

She made a small sound. Not a cough, a sound of embarrassment. 'I'd really like to say more,' she said, 'but I'm … I'm not comfortable speaking on the phone. You'll understand, I think.'

Anselm thought he heard something in her voice. Truth, you sometimes knew it when you heard it. Truth and fear and lies, they had their pitches and cadences and hesitancies.

'It's a long shot,' she said. 'I'm a bit desperate. Very. I've probably bothered you for nothing. Wasted your time.'

Anselm looked at his drink. Bob Blumenthal? How did he know him, know his face so well? What short film was that? Did he like or hate the Bob Blumenthal whose face he could see.

'I'll call you again,' he said. 'Give me some time.'

'Tonight?'

'I don't know. Possibly.'

'Please. I'd be … it's … well, it's not a story I'm chasing, it's something more. Anyway, I've said that. So …'

'Yes. Goodbye.'

Anselm sat for a while, smoked a cigarette. The room had warmed. He sipped the whisky, finished it, went to the kitchen and poured another one. People interested in his past, things he knew. Alex, this woman. Sniffing around him. He was a source. A repository of something. They thought he had something they could use.

But why did that make him uneasy? He knew about cultivating people, getting people to trust him, to tell him things.

Forget Caroline Wishart. She wanted something and there was no knowing what it was. It was unlikely to be what she said it was.

The life of question and answer. How had he fallen into it?

You're got an inquiring mind. Not many people have. Consider yourself blessed. His mother had said that to him. He couldn't recall anything else his mother said. So, from all the years together, all the nurturing, he came away with three sentences.

No.

He remembered something else. Her telling him, in this house, that she was leaving his father. He was seventeen. On the terrace of this house, sitting in the wicker chairs, losing their paint even then and never painted again.

The chairs were still on the terrace, the exposed surfaces bare of paint. His father had remembered them from before the war, before he was sent to America.

The last Anselm to sit in the chairs, look at the garden, at the canal. He would be that one.

The day she told him, it was autumn. He remembered the big drifts of leaves lying in the garden, in hollows, at trees. Leaves liked to cluster.

He had trouble recalling his mother's face. In Beirut, in the coffin for two, her smell had come to him in dreams, lingered in his nostrils when he woke as if it were actually in the air. Not a perfume exactly, cologne and something else, a talcum powder perhaps. The smell had filled him with a sadness and a longing so unbearable that he would gladly have died to extinguish it.

That day on the terrace, she said, she had a matter-of-fact way, she said: *Darling, your father and I are getting on each other's nerves. We're going to take a little break from each other. A sort of holiday, really. It'll be good for both of us. Don't look at me like that. It won't change anything. And you're both grown up now.*

She joined Médecins Sans Frontières. He went to college and she died in the Congo. His father said on the telephone that it was quick and painless, a fever, she lost consciousness. Some exotic viral infection, he couldn't remember what it was called.

What did people mean when they said *grown up*?

Anselm rubbed his eyes, finished the whisky. He went to the big stone-flagged room off the laundry, the boxroom, floor-to-ceiling shelves. In the corner, stairs went down to the cellar. Frau Einspenner had taken him down those steep stairs, a little of the exquisite apprehension came back to him.

The cartons from San Francisco stood on the floor, only one opened.

His life before Beirut lay in the boxes. He felt no attachment to that life, no curiosity about the missing pieces of it. He should leave the material remains alone.

He began with the open carton.

50

LONDON

'HIS NAME is Constantine Niemand. South African, an ex-soldier, a mercenary, worked as a security guard in Johannesburg. Two days before he arrived here, he was on the scene of an affair in Johannesburg, a burglary gone wrong, five people killed, three blacks, one a security guard, the other two ...'

'Losin me, boy.'

'A white couple were killed. Brett and Elizabeth Shawn, British passports.'

'Your Krauts running that name?'

'Yes.'

'The woman, what'd you do there?'

'There's a watch on the place. She hasn't shown.'

'And the old address?'

'The old address?'

'Your reliable pricks heard the phone ring. Then he wasn't there. Who the living fuck do you think called him? And how the fuck did she know to call him? Hasn't crossed your brain has it? And don't say *in essence* to me again, I'll strangle you with my own hands.'

'With respect, Mr Price, I'm not prepared ...'

'Sonny, deal with me or deal with the devil. There's much worse coming up behind me. I'm the good cop. You want to walk from this fucken Waco you created, get the fuck out. And wherever you go, get on your knees every morning, noon and fucken night and pray the Lord to take away the mark on your fucken forehead.'

'We'll cover this stuff, Charlie.'

'I truly hope so, Martie. I truly do. Or we're talking missing in action.'

51

HAMBURG

IT WAS in the second carton. In the top box.

A flimsy magazine with a sombre cover of light grey type on a black background.

Behind Enemy Lines. A Journal of Argument.

February 1993.

Four articles were promoted on the cover. The top one was: 'And Unquiet Lie the Civil Dead'.

Anselm took the magazine to the study and sat behind the desk to read it.

From the first words, he knew that he had not written it. No matter how battered the brain, there was something in it that knew what it had created, and he had not created this. It was vaguely familiar but it wasn't his.

He found what the woman was talking about, the village in Angola.

Fragments of evidence now suggest that this campaign was in response to rumours in South Africa of a village in northern Angola being wiped out.

Wiped out by which side? How? We don't know. But just in case the rumours spread outside South Africa and were investigated and confirmed, the CIA-DIA misinformation artists had done the groundwork for blaming the Cubans.

Nothing. It meant nothing. Why had someone told

Caroline Wishart that he had been paid for writing the article? And given her his San Francisco address as the place the cheque was sent to?

He paged through the rest of the magazine. On the last page was an offer for back issues of the magazines and three others:

The Social Fabric
Records of Capitalism
To Bear Witness
To Bear Witness

That was it, he knew the name, that was how he knew Bob Blumenthal. He pictured his face again. A café in San Francisco. In the afternoon. Long ago.

Anselm was looking for a cigarette when it came to him: he had written a piece for Blumenthal on the CIA and European intelligence services. That was what they talked about that day. In 1990. Blumenthal had rung him. Kaskis and Blumenthal went back a long way, Blumenthal had taught Kaskis at college after Kaskis left the army. Kaskis had written stuff for him.

Anselm thought about living in San Francisco, in Kaskis's tiny apartment on the hill. Kaskis knew the people who owned the building, Latvians, friends of his family. Kaskis never spent more than a few days at a time in San Francisco. Anselm remembered him staying for a week once, that was the longest. They went out at night, went to bars where journalists hung out, drank a lot. Kaskis always had somewhere to go later. Someone he had to see before the night was over.

Anselm remembered the piece. It was published in *To Bear Witness* and it was called 'American Spider: Global and Deadly'. It would be in the document boxes.

Why should he help this woman, this muckraker? Because he'd heard something in her voice. Perhaps it was a matter of someone's life and death. He rang Inskip again, got connected to the London number. She was close to the phone. Was it a work number?

'John Anselm,' he said. 'I found the article. A man called Paul Kaskis wrote it. He had the magazine pay me. He owed me money.'

A long sigh. 'Paul Kaskis, do you ...'

'He's dead.'

'Oh. Shit. The name, I think I remember it, he was kidnapped with you ...'

'He was murdered in the Lebanon.'

Another sigh. 'Well, thank you. I think I'm at the end of this road. As a matter of interest, what was he doing in the Lebanon?'

'He wanted to talk to an American soldier, an ex-soldier. A Lebanese-American.'

'You wouldn't remember his name?'

'Diab. Joseph Diab.'

He hadn't told Alex that. Why was he telling this woman?

'Did you know what it was about?'

'No. Paul never told you anything.' Anselm's eyes fell on the photograph albums on the bookshelf beside the door, three big leather-bound albums, he remembered looking at them when he was a child, Pauline pointing out people.

'Look,' she said, 'I'd really appreciate being able to ring you if I get any further with this. Is that possible?'

Anselm hesitated. Then he gave her the W&K number. 'Leave a message if I'm not there.'

He took the photograph albums from the study to the kitchen. He poured wine and opened an album. The pictures were in chronological order, little notes in ink under most of them identifying people by names and nicknames, giving places, dates, occasions. There was a photograph of Pauline and a young man sitting on the terrace. Fräulein Einspenner was standing behind them, the maid. She was young and beautiful. In the first album, the captions were in red ink. In the other two, they were in green, in Pauline's hand.

There were pictures missing, taken out of their corners. The captions were crossed out and cross-hatched in green ink until they were illegible.

The phone rang again.

'I feel I need company,' Alex said. 'I've had some news, I'm feeling a little ...'

'Come over,' he said. 'Can you do that?'

52

VIRGINIA

THEY WALKED in the day's cold ending and stopped beside a pond, silver, sat on a wooden bench bleached white as bone by sun and rain and snow.

'Got a smoke? I'm not allowed to.'

Palmer reached into his coat. 'Allowed? Fuck, who's running things here?'

They lit cigarettes, sat back. Smoke hung around them in the still air, reached the earth, curled. High on the wooded hill behind the pond a cluster of maples blazed amid the brown oaks, seemed to be sucking in the light.

'Pretty spot,' said the shorter man. 'The prick's hard to kill, is he?'

'He's quick.'

'And they're dead.'

'Yup. Messy. I sent Charlie Price to sort it out. They told him they'd use pros next time.'

Three ducks came around a small point in the pond, ducks keeping close together, missed the mass exodus to warmer places, just the three of them left.

'He's been in the trade,' said Palmer. 'Now he's riding shotgun. He drove this Shawn's wife home, the arrangement was that he stayed for the husband to get back. I think he just lucked onto this.'

'Shawn had the film?'

'Looks like it.'

'What about him?'

'Well. A known quantity. Courier mainly. They say Ollie North used him.'

'You wouldn't want that to be the high point of your career.'

Palmer shot his cigarette butt towards the water. It fell well short, lay on damp leaf mould. 'I gather he took Ollie. Like everyone else.'

Silence. The other man shot his butt. It almost made the water, died in a puddle.

'So who would be using him?'

'We're checking.'

'I was given to understand this history was history.'

Palmer put both hands to his head and scratched all over – back, top, sides. 'Burghman was in charge, we can't ask him. The film – well, that's something else. No one knew about a film then.'

'Not a huge cast of suspects.'

'No. Trilling says Burghman told him, he thinks it was in '93. Burghman said there'd been a problem but it was fixed and the slate was as clean as it needed to be.'

A deer had appeared from the thicket on the far shore of the lake. It looked around, advanced with delicate steps to the water's edge, lowered its head and drank.

'Never saw the point of killing animals like that.'

'No,' said Palmer.

'I might have another smoke.'

A breeze had come up, worrying the trees, worrying the water. Palmer lit a cigarette, handed it over, lit another.

'As it needed to be. That's not the same as clean.'

'No.'

'This guy's tried the media. Could try again.'

'We'll hear, we'll have some notice,' said Palmer.

'It's late to be caught in the rain, Scottie.'

They heard the sound of a jet on high, the booming hollow sound, filling the world, pressing on trees and water, on the throat. The deer started, was gone.

'Won't happen,' said Palmer. 'But we may have to go on with the Brits. I wanted to ask you.'

'Don't let Charlie near them. Subtle's a Mossberg up the arse.'

'I'll go myself.'

'Good. Time. Going back tonight.'

Out of the wind, on the path, deep in shadow, their heads down, feet disturbing the leaves. The other man looked at Palmer and Palmer looked at him, and they both looked away.

The man said, 'Well, judgment. Live or die by your judgment. Comes down to that.'

Palmer nodded.

'But you know that, Scottie.'

'I do. Sir.'

They walked, smoking, smoke hanging behind them like ragged chiffon scarves, the dark rising beneath them.

53

WALES

WHEN THEY were on the motorway, he told her to drop him somewhere, anywhere, a petrol station, but she said no, they were going somewhere safe, he could decide what to do then.

Niemand didn't argue. He tried to stay awake but the car was warm and quiet, the smell of leather, soft classical music on the player, and his head lolled and he fell asleep. He woke several times, registered nothing, and then they were entering a village on a narrow road with houses on both sides.

'Almost there,' said Jess.

He was asleep again before they were out of the village. He woke with the car going uphill on a stony dirt road, tight bends, their headlights reflecting off pools in the wheel ruts and turning stone walls silver.

They stopped.

An entrance, an old wooden gate.

'Here,' she said. 'This is it.'

She was looking at him.

'Where?' he said.

'Wales.'

'Right,' he said. 'Gate.'

He got out, shaky legs, no feeling in his feet. Wet air. Cold, a wind whipping. Dead black beyond the beam of the lights and the only sound the expensive hum of the Audi.

He expected resistance but the gate swung easily, old but maintained, no squeaks, grease in the hinges.

She drove through. Niemand closed the gate. He walked to the car, hurting in many places, the balls of his feet. He didn't mind. He was glad to be alive. There was a Greek saying for what he felt, for gratitude for life outweighing pain and suffering. He reached for it, the tone of it was in his head, the way it was said, but the words didn't come.

He got in. They went up a narrow, steep driveway, turned left. The headlights caught one end of a low building, a long cottage, small windows, and they went past it and lit up another building, a stone barn, a big building with brace-and-bar doors and a dormer window.

Jess stopped and got out, the engine running, the lights on. She stretched, arms to the sky, fingers outstretched, then she bent to touch her toes. She was smaller than he remembered her to be.

'Let's put it inside,' she said. 'I feel like I'm looking after someone's baby.'

'Me,' said Niemand. 'I'm the baby.' He said the words without thought but he didn't regret them, wanted to apologise more fully, thank her.

Jess didn't reply. She went to the doors, fiddled with keys and unlocked two padlocks. Niemand opened the doors, new doors. The Audi's lights lit a large space, new concrete floor. A vintage Morris Countryman was to the left, the one with a wooden frame. On a rack against the back wall were big tools: snipper, chainsaw, hedge-trimmer. In front of them stood a stack of bags of fertiliser. To the right, in a line, were an ordinary lawn mower, a ride-on mower, two trail bikes, a mulcher, all new-looking and clean.

Jess parked the Audi.

Lights off. Pitch dark.

The cabin light came on, she got out, opened the back door and removed their bags, closed the door. Dark again.

They didn't move for a moment, silence.

'Good gear,' said Niemand. 'And neat.'

'Doctors,' she said. 'They're rich. He's a slob but she loves order. She wants to come and live here for a few years, grow things.'

He took the bags, closed the doors, and she padlocked them. They walked around the house to the front door, crunching the gravel.

'No electricity,' said Jess.

Inside, she found a candlestick close to the door and lit the candle with a plastic lighter. They were in a small hallway, coats and hats above a bench. Three doors opened off the room. She went first, through the left-hand one into a big low-ceilinged room. He could make out armchairs, a sofa, an open hearth.

'There's a generator,' she said, 'but the lamps will do tonight.'

He followed her through a door into a kitchen. There were Coleman lamps on a shelf. She lit two, she knew what she was doing, how to pump them. The grey-white light brought back memories for him, other places far away and long ago.

'You need to eat,' she said.

'No,' Niemand shook his head. 'No thanks.'

In the car, he had woken each time with the nausea he always felt after fear, after firefights, any violence, the sick feeling, and with it the physical tiredness, as if some vital fluid in his body had been drained.

'Are you ...?'

'Yeah, fine.'

His whole torso hurt, felt battered. It wasn't a new

feeling. The first time was at the School of Infantry, he had boxed against men much bigger, much stronger, badly overmatched, taking heavy body punches, to the ribs, the shoulders, low blows too.

'Sure?'

'Sure.'

'Sleep then. It's late.' She pointed. 'Through there. A bedroom, down the passage there's a bathroom, I'll light the water heater.'

Niemand looked around the room. He didn't want to say it.

'Jess,' he said, 'this place, they can connect it with you?'

'Nice to hear you say my name,' she said. 'Con, who are they?'

'I don't know. The owners are your friends?'

'Yes. I was at school with her sister.'

He was tired, he had trouble standing, legs weak, he had the feeling of not having feet. He put a hand on the back of a chair. 'Who would know you could get the car, come here, this house?'

Jess touched her hair, pushed it back, he could see the tiredness in her.

'I've been here with the owners,' she said. 'They're in America. I keep an eye on their house in London. I don't think anyone knows I've got these keys.'

Niemand tried to think about this but he gave up.

'Listen, Jess,' he said, 'tomorrow I'll go and you stay here and I'll make sure they know you're not with me, you're not involved.'

'Will you tell me what's going on?'

'Yes. In the morning. What I know.'

'Go to bed,' she said. 'We'll talk in the morning.'

For a moment, they stood looking at each other. Then he took a lamp and went to the bedroom, stripped. He walked down the narrow, short passage holding the lamp, almost bumped into her coming out of the bathroom, lowered the lamp to cover himself.

'It's too late for modesty,' she said, smiling. 'I've seen everything you've got.'

He showered, trying to keep the water off his bandage. Then he went back to the bedroom, dressed again and lay on the bed under the eiderdown, lay in the dark and listened.

Noise of the wind, hollow sound, lonely. He thought about the Swartberge, the survival course in the mountains, eyelashes frozen in the morning, lip cracks opening, the way human smells carried in the clean cold air.

They could find them here. There was no point in thinking otherwise. In the morning, he would ring the Wishart woman, tell her Jess knew nothing about the film, had never seen it, was only involved by accident. He would catch a bus, a train, go somewhere where he could work out how to get another passport.

The Irishman would help him. That was a possibility.

He drowsed, drifted away, not peaceful, exhausted.

54

HAMBURG

'I'M REGRETTING this,' said Alex. 'I was regretting it before I got into the car. It's stupid of me. An imposition.'

She was holding two bottles of red wine and she offered them to Anselm.

'To drink,' she said. 'Tonight.'

Even in the dim light, he could see that she was flushed. She had been crying and he thought she looked beautiful and desirable.

'Welcome to the house of remorse,' said Anselm. 'Here we regret almost everything we do.'

He took the bottles, showed her into the study and went to the kitchen. It was a choice between a 1987 Lafite and a 1989 Chateau Palmer. He drew the corks of both bottles and went to the pantry for good glasses. He'd broken many Anselm wine glasses, glasses his great-great grandfather might have drunk out of. But there were enough left to see him out.

In the study, Anselm said, 'This is kind of you but this wine's too good for me.'

'From my ex-husband's collection,' said Alex.

'It's nice of him to donate it.'

'He killed himself in Boston yesterday.'

Anselm poured the Lafite. They sat in silence, each in a cone of lamplight, the wine dark as tar in their glasses.

'I don't know why I'm upset,' said Alex. 'For a long time I hated him. And then I came to terms with my feelings.'

'How did you find out?'

'A colleague of his rang an hour ago. I felt so ... fuck, I can't express it.'

'Why would he do it?'

'Apparently the woman he lived with left him about a month ago. His colleague says he was depressed, he'd been drinking a lot, not going to the university, missing classes.'

More silence. She finished her wine and he refilled her glass. She leaned her head back, half her face in shadow. 'He rang me about two weeks ago,' she said. 'I didn't let him speak. I told him I had nothing to say to him.'

Anselm wanted to say that it wouldn't have made any difference but he could not bring himself to. 'Would you have taken him back?' he said.

'No. Never.'

'I wouldn't dwell on it then. How long were you married?'

'Six years. He left me for the American woman.'

Anselm rolled wine around his mouth, swallowed. 'You can keep coming around with this stuff,' he said.

'Kai wouldn't open a bottle except to impress. One day he brought his head of department home for a drink, a fat man, a medievalist, so self-important you wanted to kill him. But you would not be able to get your hands around that pig neck. And Kai opened a fifteen-year-old burgundy. The man couldn't believe it. *Life's too short to drink inferior wine*, Kai said. This is from a man who bought house wine from that little place next to the canal in Isestrasse, do you know it? You take your own bottles, he fills them with terrible Bulgarian liquids full of brake fluid. Whatever that is.'

She looked at him, she licked her lips, drank a lot of wine.

'I took the marriage seriously. That was the end of serious relationships for me.'

She drank. 'It had been going on for a long time before I found out. More than a year. He had all these trips, London, Copenhagen, seminars, that kind of rubbish. I believed him.'

All betrayals were the same, thought Anselm. The only tragedy was that, in the instant in which they became known, the life drained from everything that had gone before – like colour photographs turning into black-and-white.

Alex held out her glass. He half-filled it, added some wine to his. Her quick drinking made him nervous. He was the quick drinker, that was his escape.

She studied the wine against the light, took a big mouthful. 'He'd done it before,' she said, not looking at him, looking around the room.

'Done what?'

'Left one woman for another without any warning.'

He knew what she was going to tell him.

'He left his first wife for me,' she said. 'He sent her a telegram.'

Anselm went to the desk and found a cigarette. He could remember his grandfather sitting behind the desk smoking a cigar. The big brass cigar ashtray was still in position, to the right of the blotter in its embossed-leather frame.

He leaned against the desk. 'Well,' he said, 'he probably intended to tell her in person, never got around to it.'

'He was twelve years older,' she said. She swilled the last of her wine, looking at the scarlet whirlpool, drained it. 'More, please.'

Anselm poured the Lafite, left an inch in the bottle, there was sediment.

Alex drank. 'It tastes better and better,' she said.

'Twelve years,' said Anselm. 'An older man.'

'When he left me, I worked out that I was the same age his first wife was when he left her. He told me she was frigid, didn't like being touched, he thought she was a repressed lesbian, she was always kissing and hugging her women friends.'

'That could be a sign, yes.'

'No. I saw her with a man at an exhibition. He looked like a biker. She couldn't stop touching him, she rubbed herself against him like a cat.'

'What did that tell you? Clinically speaking? With hindsight?'

Alex finished her glass. She held it out and shifted in her chair, crossed her legs, a hint of languor in the movements.

It felt as if the atmospheric pressure had fallen. Anselm poured the Palmer into clean glasses.

'It told me, clinically speaking, that he'd lied to me from the start,' she said. She sat back. 'Talking about it makes me feel better. Have you betrayed many partners?'

'A few, I suppose.'

'You don't remember?'

'Some I remember. I remember the reverse too.'

'And how did you respond to that?'

There was something edging on the flirtatious in her voice, the way she was sitting, in the carriage of her head. It wasn't the manner of a bereaved person.

'I didn't bear grudges.'

'Would you say you were a forgiving person?'

'No. I think I just didn't care enough.'

Anselm looked away. He hadn't intended to say that, he hadn't wanted to admit his emotional callousness to anyone. He hadn't admitted it to himself. Much of his adult life had been spent in pursuit of things, including women, but in the moment of possession, they had lost some of their value. And, later, he had not felt any lasting pain at losing them.

'Are we talking about before or after Beirut?' she said. 'Or both?'

'Before. Things have been quiet in the partner business since.'

She tilted her head and her hair fell onto a shoulder. In the lamplight, her lipstick was almost black. 'Not enough big-breasted women around? For a tit man like you?'

'I was lying,' said Anselm. 'I'm really a leg man. Legs.'

Alex recrossed her legs, ran a hand over a thigh. 'I'm not quite sure what that expression means,' she said. 'Does it mean legs like dancers' legs?'

'Well, for some. We legmen are not all alike.'

'And you? Personally?'

'I like runners' legs.'

She smiled. 'I'm a runner.'

'Yes.'

'It's warm,' said Alex. She unbuttoned her waistcoat, leaned forward and took it off, threw it onto an empty chair. She turned her head to Anselm. 'Would you like me to keep going?'

Anselm's mouth was dry. He sipped wine. 'Yes,' he said.

She unbuttoned her shirt. She was wearing a white bra.

55

HAMBURG

'LAFARGE RANG,' said Inskip. 'They've added a name.'

Anselm took the file. He was feeling light-headed.

Jessica Thomas, born 1975, an address in Battersea, London. Inskip had filled in her electronic record.

'It's the woman on the motorbike,' said Inskip. 'The one who picked up Niemand. We could have been running her long ago.'

'Orders,' said Anselm. 'We await orders.'

'I thought initiative was what you liked?'

'After the orders, that's when I like it.'

'Tilders left this for you five minutes ago.'

A sealed pouch. A tape.

'May I know what Tilders does?'

'Outdoor work. Heavy lifting.'

'Thank you. Another veil lifted. Whatever he does, it gives him an air of sadness.'

'He comes across a lot of saddening things. Also he's tired. That can give you a sad air.'

Anselm went to Carla's workstation. She swivelled her chair and rested her hands on her thighs. 'We have had some luck,' she said.

Behind her two monitors had lines of green code on their black screens.

'Serrano's bank. Very careless for people who deal in

secrets. Everything's outdated. I find on their log that four years ago they transmitted a large amount of data to a bank in Andorra. Gonzalez Gardemann.'

'Why would they do that?'

'Back-up, I suppose. I can't find any links but Gonzalez may be the same operation under another name.'

'Even so, you'd normally send information like that by hand from one stand-alone system to another.'

Carla shrugged. 'As I said, careless. Perhaps a sales-person convinced them the encryption was safe. Or someone inside the company wanted to compromise their data. There are other possibilities.'

There would be. Someone from the BND would know that. Deceit without end. Seamless deceit.

'The point is,' said Carla, 'Gonzalez are equally stupid. Instead of moving the data to a stand-alone, they have left it where we can reach it. Their firewall is a joke, their encryption is hopeless. First generation. My Canadian cracked it like a walnut.'

She raised her arms above her head, entwined her fingers, stretched.

Anselm waited for her knuckles to crack. She was looking at him, she had a look about her lips. She knew he was waiting for the sound.

She smiled. Her fingers slid apart, her arms came down.

'The numbers on the documents you gave me,' she said. The pages from the *Hauptbahnhof*, from Serrano's case.

'Yes?'

'One set worked. It must be the bank's code for Serrano.'

'And?'

'It's one big file, hundreds of transactions. Some small, some big. I need to put the figures we have through them.'

'How long?'

'An hour perhaps. This has taken time. You may wish to tell the client.'

'Yes. Your work is greatly valued. As always.'

She looked down, the glossy hair fell across her forehead like a dark comb sliding. 'Thank you. And may I say thank you for the bonus?'

'No, not me. It's the client's reward for your work.'

She turned her head to the monitors and she said, *'Nun, wir sollten uns eine Flasche Champagner teilen.'*

Anselm didn't register for a moment that she'd spoken to him in German. She had never spoken to him in German since the introductions on her first day.

She hadn't turned her body away from him, only her head.

She was asking him out. The words, the language of her body.

'So bald wie möglich,' he said.

Carla turned her head and looked into his eyes and nodded. No smile.

He went back to his office and opened Tilders's pouch. An audio-tape and a sticker with the logbook code DT/HH/36 1/02 and the words: *Bruynzeel & Speelman Chemicals.* It was Serrano at his hotel. A direct line.

Yes?

Serrano.

Yes?

This is worse than I thought. Our friend, have you got any anxiety there?

Me? Anxiety? What about?

Records he might have kept.

From me, nothing. Otherwise, how would I know?

Speaking in German, neither of them native speakers.

Would he keep his own records?

Well, he wasn't mad then.

He wouldn't?

I don't know. He might have. He was semi-government. Governments like records.

I must ask you again. This film, does it mean anything?

A silence.

I could guess but I don't want to.

What are we talking about?

Nothing.

You know what it could be?

What are you? The tax department? Forget it.

The Jews are putting pressure on us. They want our dealings with you too.

Silence. Then Serrano said:

Are you there?

They want what?

Records. Anything. Everything.

You have records?

No.

Well, just shut up. It's all bluff. These things pass. Just keep your mouth shut. Trilling's connections, there's no problem.

You can talk to him?

I'll see. Things in the past, no one wants to talk about the past.

This is in the present. Talk to him. About the Jews, I thought you were close to them?

Silence again, then the other man said:

Werner Kael gets close to his customers, does he? Who's spoken to you?

He's using the name Spence.

Yes, I know him. Kael would know him.

Kael says they want to rub us out and they want the assets.

Probably correct. If the Jews think something can damage them, they scorch the earth. But first they take the wheat. They must think you are hiding the wheat.

Nonsense. Talk to Trilling. I'll ring later.

Ring tonight. Don't worry so much. People are in deep here, it has to go away.

Serrano sighed.

We don't want to be put away.

The other man laughed.

You personally can relax. They never put the accountants away. They should but they don't.

Anselm rang O'Malley on the new number. In his view, he could see that the sun was out, the lake was strewn with glitter. A glass tourist boat caught the light.

56

LONDON

THREE MEN kidnapped in Beirut in 1993. Paul Kaskis and John Anselm, American journalists, David Riccardi, Irish photographer.

Caroline read the clippings again. *The Times* described Kaskis as 'foreign correspondent and former military affairs correspondent for the Washington newsletter *Informed Sources*'. Anselm was a 'freelance veteran of news flashpoints from Somalia to Sri Lanka'. Riccardi was called an 'award-winning battle zone photographer'. The kidnappers were thought to be 'anti-American Hezbollah extremists'.

John Anselm said Kaskis was murdered. Caroline skimmed. There was no mention of the death of Kaskis. The last clipping, dated 17 July 1994, said Anselm and Riccardi had appeared at the US embassy in the early morning of the previous day.

So Anselm and Riccardi were never interviewed, never told their stories, didn't write about them.

Caroline closed her eyes. The time to stop this was now. She had fobbed off Halligan for the last time. Now she should tell him it had looked promising and then it had evaporated.

It would be humiliating. More humiliation, after being treated like a hooker – fucked over and given money.

She caught herself rubbing her hands, something she did without thinking when she was feeling stressed. Her cook's hands. Her father once said her brother had pianist's hands. Richard had no musical ability, couldn't whistle 'Happy Birthday'. After Sotheby's sacked her, her mother suggested cooking school. Her father was reading the paper, from behind it, he said, 'Good idea. The Digby women all have cook's hands.' The Digbys were her mother's family. After that, she took every chance to study the hands of the Digby women but she saw no sign of domestic-staff uniformity.

No more humiliations. She'd had her share. Think.

A man in drag had tried to kill Mackie. Only Colley knew about the meeting. She had set up the meeting and a man in drag had tried to kill Mackie.

And money appeared in her account. Colley could mock her because he had a doctored tape of their meeting. No one would believe her story.

The time to stop this thing? Colley arranged the money, arranged for the money in the briefcase the slight, dark woman gave her.

But Colley didn't arrange for Mackie to die at the head of the escalator. Colley was a slimy old hack who picked through celebrities' garbage and followed up-market call girls to see who their customers were, but he wasn't an arranger of killings.

No. For personal gain, he had told someone about the film and that someone had arranged to get it and kill Mackie and compromise her.

Who had Colley told?

There were no answers that way. The film, she'd seen the film, the whole thing was about the film. People would kill to get the film.

A village in Angola. Americans. That was still the way to go.

Anselm said Kaskis intended to interview Joseph Diab, an ex-soldier, Lebanese-American, in Beirut. In the Lebanon anyway, which was mostly Beirut as she understood it.

Did the paper have a correspondent in Beirut? She never read the foreign news pages.

It took five minutes to find out. They had a stringer called Tony Kourie who worked for a Beirut paper, a moonlighter. He answered the phone. A faint East End accent.

He said he knew her name, he'd seen the Brechan story. They compared weathers. Then she asked him and he whistled.

'No shortage of Joe Diabs here. Had a go from the American end, have you? US Army?'

'No. I will if I have to.'

'I'll have a try. Anything else might help?'

It came to her from nowhere.

'Okay,' he said. 'Get back to you.'

The phone. Halligan.

'Caroline, we're at the end of the road here, darling.'

'I need a little more time,' she said, confidence gone.

'Full account. Pronto. Today. In writing, in detail.'

'I think I've shown ...'

'Shown? You won't mind me saying turning up Brechan's bumboy, that's now looking less spectacular. A lot less clever of you. In the light of information received.'

The skin of her face felt tight. Information received?

'I'll get back to you,' she said.

'You will. Soonest. And the contract, well, study the fine print.'

Minutes passed. She realised she was rubbing her hands together. The phone again.

'Caroline, Tony Kourie. Listen, I've got a likely Joe Diab. Joseph Elias Diab, age thirty-six, born Los

Angeles, parents both born in Beirut. Former US Army senior sergeant.'

'Yes?'

'And dead. Outside the house of his cousin, six shots to the body.'

'When?'

'Night of 5 October, 1993.'

'Thanks, Tony. Really, thanks. Repay you if I can.'

'Tell the bastards to run some more of my stuff.'

'I will.'

Caroline looked at the printouts, but she didn't pick them up for a while. She knew. Anselm, Kaskis and Riccardi had been kidnapped on the night of 3 October, 1993.

57

HAMBURG

SHE WOULD be full of regret.

Then again, she might not be.

He was going through the day before's logbooks, rendering them billable, thinking about Alex, thinking about what happened next.

The phone whispered. Beate.

'Herr Anselm, a Caroline Wishart. Yes?'

He thought to say no, he wanted to say no, but he had given her the number. She would try again.

'Yes. Thank you.'

Beate said, 'Mr Anselm will take your call.'

They said hello.

She said, 'Mr Anselm, I'm really sorry to bother you again.'

He waited, he didn't mind being rude to her, he didn't want to talk to her, let her feel that in his silence.

'It's about Paul Kaskis.'

He didn't want to talk about Kaskis or about Beirut, to this woman, to anyone.

'Ms Wishart, I don't know what you're working on, I know nothing about you except that you caught a politician with his pants down. And life and death is just a phrase. So, with regret, no.'

A pause.

'Mr Anselm, please, please just listen to me,' she said,

rushing. 'It's not just a phrase. A man showed me a film of people being murdered. In Africa. By American soldiers. He wanted to sell the film. Then I saw someone try to kill him. I also want to ask you whether you know that Joseph Diab, the man Paul Kaskis was in Beirut to see ...' She ran out of air. 'Joseph Elias Diab was murdered the same night you were kidnapped. He was executed.'

A film.

Anselm barely heard the rest.

A man called Shawn murdered in Johannesburg. And Lafarge in London looking for a man named Martin Powell, now thought to be Constantine Niemand, who was there when Shawn died and who killed Shawn's killers.

Kael had talked about a film.

If this prick's got the papers and the film, whatever the fucking film is ... How did Lourens die?

'What's the man's name?' he said. 'The man with the film?'

'Mackie. He called himself Mackie. Bob Mackie.'

Not Powell or Niemand.

'I'll call you back in a few minutes, said Anselm. 'Give me your number again.'

He went through to the workroom. Inskip wasn't at his station. The man next door, Jarl, the Scandinavian and Baltic specialist, pointed to the passage door and drew on an imaginary cigarette. A longing imitation.

Anselm followed Jarl's finger, braved Beate's eyes, and then it took muscle to open the glass door against the wind, then to prevent it slamming. Cold. It would be cold even with a coat. The north wind was running a rabble of clouds across a pale-blue sky. Across the road, the trees were stripped for winter now, shivering.

Inskip had his back to the view, to the lake, to the

wind, lighting up. He handed over the cigarette and lit another. They hunched against the wind.

'A holiday,' said Inskip. 'I'm thinking, let's fly away to ten days of sun. Sun and naked skin.'

'Why waste money,' said Anselm. 'You can get the exposure here over two or three years. For naked skin, we have St Pauli.'

Inskip didn't look at him. He drew on the cigarette held high in his fingers, near the tips.

'My, you've thrown my thoughts into disarray,' he said. 'I had in mind a concentrated experience, two or three years of sun in ten days. And I was thinking of my own skin. My own etiolated skin.'

Anselm blew smoke. The wind's grab reminded him of a holiday in the Hamptons in winter when he was a teenager, smoking in the dunes, the wind-whipped grass, the stinging sand, grit on teeth.

'Those South African lists?' he said. 'Remember your piece of detection?'

'Indeed. The aborted coup gang.'

'Write them down?'

'In the file.'

'Of course.'

They smoked. Below them, on Schöne Aussicht, two police motorcyclists appeared, riding abreast. A police car followed, then three dark-grey Mercedes Benz saloons. A second police car and two more motorcycles completed the convoy.

'Who's this?' said Inskip.

'Some nonentity. No mine detectors, no helicopters, no foot soldiers.'

Inskip rubbed his beard stubble. 'Pardon my inquisitive nature but I've wondered about something. Does this firm make enough to have premises a few spits from the Senate guesthouse?'

Anselm took a last draw, cartwheeled the butt into the sad garden below. 'It's complicated but the short answer is No. I need that file.'

They went inside, crossed the room, raked by the cold fire of Beate's disapproval. Anselm collected the file and took it to his office. He looked at the lists and then he went back to Inskip's station and gave him the name.

Ten minutes later, Inskip came in with a piece of paper.

'A charming woman in the newspaper's library,' he said. 'She looked it up for me. They still have actual paper clippings and file cards with names.'

'Quaint,' said Anselm.

He looked at the sheet of paper, then he put it in the file. He rang Caroline Wishart.

'I can't help you,' he said. 'The name Mackie means nothing. And Diab's death, that was just a coincidence. People got shot in Beirut all the time then.'

She was silent.

He didn't wait, said sorry and goodbye.

The file was open on the desk, the names of the brigands assembled to stage a coup in the Seychelles.

Just above POWELL, MARTIN on the first list.

Just above NIEMAND, CONSTANTINE on the amended list.

The name MACKIE, ROBERT ANGUS.

Robert Angus Mackie was a mercenary, killed in Sierra Leone in 1996 said the newspaper library in Johannesburg.

The man who showed Caroline Wishart the film, the man Lafarge were hunting, he wasn't Bob Mackie.

The man was Constantine Niemand.

58

LONDON

CAROLINE LISTENED to her voicemail. It had gone unattended.

Listen you homophobic bitch, you think you can crucify this man because he …

Next.

Hi, Caroline, my name's Guy and I think we should meet. I've been fucked by names, you would not believe, I'm talking about big names, I'm talking show business, I'm …

Next.

Caroline, I'm Tobin Robinson's producer. Tobin would very much …

Next.

Listen, sweetie, I really like your face, you have that kind of thin cocksucker …

Next.

We had a little chat, glass of beer, you came to see me. Remember?

It was Jim Hird, the doorman who saw Mackie.

I was talkin to a bloke today, he wrote down the number of that bike, know the one I mean? Some blokes come around askin but he didn't like the look of 'em, kept mum. I thought you might have a use for it.

He read out the number.

She was out of the door in seconds but she had to wait

five minutes for Alan Sindall, the chief crime reporter, to get off the phone before she could ask him.

'You'll have to buy me a drink,' he said. 'I've got something urgent on at the mo. I'll send it around. Soonest.'

59

LONDON

THE MAN's name was Kirkby. He raised his wine glass to the light, studying the yellowish liquid like a pathologist with an unusual urine sample. 'We always try to help,' he said. 'Where possible.'

'It's finding someone,' said Palmer.

They were in a wine bar in the City, in a long room with tables under high windows. Casca had arranged it. Casca said MI6 suggested a meeting, and that meant something.

Kirkby put the glass to his beaky nose, sniffed deeply, sipped, took in air like a fish, closed his eyes, rolled wine around his mouth, swallowed. 'Helen Turley,' he said. 'A genius. One of yours.'

'What?'

'She made this drop. The proprietor here managed to get two cases. Exorbitant price. But.'

Palmer saw that Kirkby had caught the eye of the man behind the counter of the wine bar, a huge red-bearded, red-faced person wearing an apron. Kirkby toasted him wordlessly. The man nodded and raised his own glass.

Palmer drank. He liked wine. He'd come late to it. His father's view had been that wine was one of many European curses on America. For some reason, he regarded it as an Italian curse. Probably because his father disliked Italians even more than he disliked the

Irish. 'The only good thing about the Irish is that they're not Italian,' he said when Palmer told him he planned to marry someone of Irish descent.

'We'd like to know if he leaves, of course,' said Palmer. 'But he's with a local. That's where we'd appreciate help.'

Kirkby looked at him, a neutral gaze, looked away, looked back. 'Yes?'

'She may be the easiest way to find him.'

'And she's not ... helping?'

'Out of sight too.'

'Inquiries, who's been ...?'

'A private firm. Lafarge.'

Palmer knew that Kirkby knew about Lafarge.

'Private. Yes.' Kirkby touched his oiled hair, smiled, raised his glass to his lips. He seemed to hold wine around his gums before swallowing.

'It's urgent,' said Palmer. 'We wouldn't ask otherwise.'

'No, of course you wouldn't. I'll, ah, I'll have a word with someone. Ask them to get a move on too.'

Palmer took out the card and held it edgeways on the table. Kirkby took it, delicately, at a corner, put it in his top pocket without a glance.

'We'd like to know where she might go, friends, that kind of thing,' Palmer said. 'Without alarming her.'

'Yes,' said Kirkby, 'that's more or less what I thought you'd like.'

He finished his wine, licked his lips, took a doubled envelope from an inside pocket and gave it to Palmer. It wasn't sealed.

Palmer took out his reading glasses. He hated having to do that.

Three pages. Phone-tap transcripts.

Palmer read, and he had to stop himself sighing.

'You can keep those,' said Kirkby.

'Thanks.'

'Well connected, unfortunately. The father.'

Palmer nodded. It was over and they got up and went to the counter. He paid. Exorbitant was about right for the wine, he thought. At the door, they shook hands.

'I'll make a call from here,' said Kirkby. 'Get things moving.'

60

HAMBURG

ANSELM WENT to the basement and got a beer from the machine. Soon they'd take the machine away. The room was empty, the heating off, damp blistering the paint on a wall. No one used the place any more except to sneak a smoke, avoid going out into the chill. In the first years after his arrival, the room always had people in it, financial charlatans from the top floor, advertising people from the annexe, people drinking liquor and coffee, smoking, eating their packed lunches. Flirting. The truck had come to refill the beer machine every afternoon. He'd never lingered, nervous, hanging out, just got two beers, gone outside, drained them in minutes.

He sat on the formica-topped table, put his feet on a chair. The television in the corner was on, an old Grundig, the colour uncertain. Beyond midday and he was only on his first beer. What did this mean? He took a measured swig and lit a cigarette. Drink and smoke, the fatal, sweetest combination.

Constantine Niemand had a film of something terrible in Africa. He tried to sell it to Caroline Wishart and later she saw someone try to kill him.

Kael and Serrano sent Shawn to Johannesburg to look for papers, documents, anything that involved them. Shawn found a film too. Then he was murdered.

Niemand was there, and then he had the film and the documents.

Lafarge were looking for Niemand and someone called Jessica Thomas.

Caroline Wishart wanted to connect Kaskis's one-paragraph reference to a rumour about an Angolan village to the film Niemand showed her.

Anselm thought about San Francisco, about Kaskis calling from somewhere, a message on the machine:

A few days in Beirut, it's on me, my grandpa's money's come through, to spend not on myself but in the interests of truth and justice. I need a witness, a reputable witness, but you'll have to do. And a photographer. Got one handy? Footloose and fancy-free?

On the plane two days later, Kaskis was just himself, giving away nothing, you didn't bother to question Kaskis, he told you what he wanted to tell you. It was a free trip to somewhere where there were always saleable stories to be found.

What had Kaskis said about Diab?

He's a bitter man, a wronged man, the army done him wrong ...

He couldn't remember when Kaskis had said that. At the hotel in Beirut perhaps. Riccardi arrived after them, the morning after. Kaskis and Riccardi went for coffee. How much did Riccardi know about the job? Who was he there to photograph? Stills or video? Black and white? Colour? So much photographic equipment hung off Riccardi that people in the street had been known to point and ask: How much for that?

But surely Riccardi already knew when he arrived in Beirut? Kaskis would have described the job when he rang him in Ireland. Told him who, why, the point of the exercise.

There was no certainty of that. Riccardi often forgot to

ask the most basic questions. He simply didn't care. And Kaskis always had the *this-is-your-commanding-officer-and-I'll-tell-you-what-you-need-to-know* air. Presumably that came from the army. He joined at seventeen, became a Green Beret, ended up in Delta Force. He didn't talk about it much. Once he had said the army didn't want you to go beyond a certain stage of maturity:

'If you've got the brains to grasp that, then baby, it's time to saddle up and ride. The ones who don't, well, they're kids forever. Playing this fucking wonderful game with really dangerous stuff. And I'm not talking just the grunts, the cannon fodder. There are kids right at the top – the fucking Pentagon's full of them.'

Anselm stubbed his cigarette, tested the can for beer, wobbled it, drained it.

The television showed a heavily built man getting into a car, Secret Service protectors around him. The woman on television said:

In spite of strong rumours, American Defense Secretary Michael Denoon today continued to avoid declaring that he will next year seek the Republican Party nomination for the American presidency. Gerald McGowan reports from Washington.

A solemn-looking man came on, standing in front of the White House. He put his hands into the pockets of his black overcoat and said:

White House insiders are today saying that Secretary of Defense Michael Denoon is hours away from resigning his position to begin his late run for the presidency.

Since the collapse of the Gurney campaign, Denoon is said to have been urged to take the field by powerful interests. These include the US military, which he left twelve years ago as a much-decorated four-star general, and the Republican Party's most powerful business group, Republicans at Work.

Anselm was on the stairs when he thought about the flight to Beirut. Business class. Free drinks. He had been drowsing, cabin lights dimmed. Kaskis had taken a photograph out of his briefcase, adjusted the overhead spotlight to look at it. An 8 x 10 print, a group of men, perhaps a dozen, posing like a team, standing, some squatting or on one knee. Young men in casual clothes, jeans, T-shirts, some baseball caps. He remembered signatures – they had signed across their chests with a broad-nibbed pen, a felt-tipped pen, not full names, first names. He remembered thinking some of the signatures were childlike, immature. He also remembered thinking they all looked like bodybuilders. The thick necks, the big, veined biceps.

Anselm went to his office and found a file. He took it into the humming workroom. Inskip was reading an airline passenger list.

'When you've got a moment,' said Anselm.

'This'll keep.'

Anselm sat down and wrote the name 'Joseph Elias Diab' on Inskip's pad. 'I need a US Army service record. National Archives and Records Admin database. They run something called CIPS, Centres Information Processing System. To get what's called a NARS-5 record, you need a user ID and a password. Users are federal agencies. And you can only access the record groups used by the agency you represent.'

'Naturally,' said Inskip. He looked at the ceiling and rubbed his chin stubble. 'Just sticks in the mind does it, this sort of stuff?'

'Veterans Affairs are easiest. They're allowed to see most things.'

'I'm going to need some handholding here.'

Anselm found what he was looking for in the file. He wrote it on the pad. 'The procedure's here. Carla did this one a couple of months ago.'

'Perhaps she could do it again?'

'She's busy. And you need to learn. The problem is the agency's password changes every ninety days. No indication when this one was issued. Could be outdated. Very likely. Then you start from scratch.'

'I love scratch. What's the US Government's view on such invasions?'

'On conviction, death or worse.'

'Ah, choice. The American way. With or without fries?'

Carla rolled into view, rolled from behind her partition on her chair. She was looking at Anselm, her head back, pale forehead free of hair, an unlined expanse of skin.

'Falcontor,' she said. 'When you're ready.'

He went over.

Carla had pages of notes in her clear, spiky handwriting.

'It's complicated,' she said. 'But what we seem to have is Serrano's business accounts going back to 1980. There are many, many transfers into the main one.'

'From?'

'What you would expect. Caymans, Panama, Hong Kong, Netherlands Antilles, Jersey, Liechtenstein, Andorra, Isle of Man, Vanuatu. The black money places.'

'Big money?'

'In total, yes, millions. But many are small, a few thousand. Lots of regular transfers. A possibility is that he has set up accounts for clients and pays himself fees from them. Then there are loan accounts.'

'Loans to Serrano?'

'Yes. One of them is called Falcontor. Big money – forty million dollars, thereabout, in big amounts. Six million dollars three times, one of seven million. All from a bank in the Antilles over two years. But others as small as 250,000 US. My experience says these will not be genuine loans.'

Anselm studied her. 'No?'

'No. The bank, well, to call these paper constructions banks is nonsense, the bank is owned by a blind trust in Hong Kong. It is very likely Serrano's own trust, his own bank. He pays interest on these loans – that would be strictly for tax purposes, a precaution. His place of permanent residence is Monaco, I doubt whether he has ever been audited anywhere. So. He lends himself money and pays himself interest. And he also makes loans.'

'Loans? From Falcontor?'

'No. There are transfers from Falcontor. Big sums. No details, just dates and amounts. I gave up on that and then I thought about it again and I thought these are probably internal bank transfers, so I looked for a password, tried a few dozen obvious ones, you can get lucky. And then I tried the name Bergerac.'

She looked at him, she was smiling a small, pleased smile, she wanted to be asked.

'Bergerac?'

'People like their names, they often look for ways to use them.'

Anselm got it. 'Cyrano de Bergerac.'

Carla laughed, he couldn't remember her laughing, it was a real laugh, deep. 'Correct,' she said. 'I tried it. It didn't work so I ran the anagrams. Raceberg opened the door. I got the account number. And the dates and amounts, they match.'

Anselm smiled and shook his head. He felt her delight, her pleasure lifted him. He knew the buoyancy of the moment when intuition intersected with luck. The lift-off. He wanted to put out a hand and touch her, complete a circuit.

He didn't.

'That's clever,' he said. 'That's very clever.'

'Amazing luck.'

'The clever are luckier.'

'In some things.'

She held his eyes, and then she said, 'It's called Credit Raceberg. It makes loans.'

'Not real loans either?'

'I would be surprised. Astonished.'

'The borrowers?'

She shrugged. 'Banks and account numbers. But some of the banks, well, if we can't open them we should be in another type of work.'

'I'll tell the client what we've got.'

'More in perhaps an hour.'

'I'll say that.'

Anselm went to his office and rang O'Malley. 'We're on our way with the inquiry,' he said. 'Another hour or two. We should meet.'

'I'll bring some Polish beer. Anything else you'd like? From Poland, I mean? I have your pickled …'

O'Malley had his injunction.

'Like that, is it? Just some ballbearings. I'll call you.'

Forty-five minutes later, Carla was at his door, uneven on the sticks.

'I can come to you,' he said and he regretted it. He put fingers through his hair. 'That was not something I should have said, was it?'

She smiled. 'I'm not sensitive about being the way I am. Also, I like the exercise. Come and look.'

61

LONDON

THE MAN on the phone ended the call and stood up.

'Mr Palmer,' he said, 'didn't expect you so soon.'

Palmer nodded to him, went to the corner window. Outside, the day was the colour of pack ice, low cloud, a wind tearing at two flags on a rooftop. He looked down at the river, slick and grey as wet seal fur. A feeble sun came out for a few seconds and caught the oil streaks.

'Where's Charlie?'

'Just stepped out. Get something to eat.'

'Call him.'

'Right away, yes.'

Palmer waited, eyes on the river, listened to Martie make the call.

'Charlie, Mr Palmer's here.'

He put the phone down. 'He'll be here pretty soon.'

Palmer turned, looked at Martie. Martie returned his gaze for seconds, then he looked down, touched the collar of his blue shirt.

'Not the best run of operations this, would you agree, Martie?'

'No, sir. Ah, yes, sir. Not the best, no, we've had some ...'

'Don't say bad luck, Martie.'

'No, sir.'

'These contractors.'

'Agincourt Solutions. Carrick knows the boss. Ex-army, ex-MI6.'

Palmer looked at him for a while. What to do with clowns? 'That's like saying ex-Mossad,' he said. 'There's only Mossad and dead. Why'd they shoot this guy?'

Martie stopped running his tongue over his teeth under his upper lip. 'Well, it's the back-up man, he's there if something goes wrong with the handover. He says the guy just got to the top of the escalator, looked at him, dived at him, he fired. Instinct.'

'Instinct of an arsehole,' said Palmer.

'Yes, sir.'

Palmer turned back to the window. In the building next door, on the third floor, he could see a man moving down a long white table. It was a restaurant. The man was putting out the cutlery, the implements flashed like fresh sardines. He had the precision and economy of a casino dealer.

He heard the door close. Martie coughed.

'Mr Palmer, this's David Carrick.'

Palmer turned. Carrick was medium-height, pale smooth hair, in a dark suit. He was going to fat but he held himself like a gasoline pump.

'Any other contractors you'd like to recommend, Mr Carrick?' said Palmer. 'Any other old friends?'

He noted Carrick's swallow, the bob in his short neck above the striped shirt.

Soldiers, dogs, kids. Kick 'em and forgive 'em. His father's dictum. That had been his father's ranking order too. Soldiers first. Dogs before children.

Palmer turned back to the window, to the river, stood rubbing his palms together, hands held vertical. His palms were dry and the sound was of water moving on sand, a tropical sound. Australia. Never mind the Virgins. The

Great Barrier Reef. After this, with the boy. Golf, sailing. He hadn't sailed enough with the boy, they worked well together. You never had to tell him anything twice.

Kick 'em and forgive 'em.

The door.

'Scott.'

Charlie Price, in a dark-grey suit, grey shirt, no tie. From across the room, Palmer could see the blood in his eyes.

'I don't want to run this down the chain of command, Charlie,' said Palmer. 'I want you three to hear it from me. This business, it's maybe a bit more important than I've managed to get over to you. And it's getting more important and more fucked up by the minute. Now it isn't just this South African and the woman, now it's ...'

Carrick's mobile trilled. He looked at Palmer, who nodded.

'Carrick. Yes. Yes. A second, please.' He went to Martie's desk and wrote on a pad. 'Thank you. Well done. Stay on it.'

Carrick pocketed his phone.

'Progress,' he said. 'The woman used a card to buy petrol on the A44. We're back on track.'

62

LONDON

'SHE DOESN'T live here any more and I don't know where she lives,' said the woman and slammed the door.

Caroline stood in the thin rain and thought about trying again. Then she went back to the car and got the phone book out of the boot. 'You can never find one when you need one,' McClatchie once said. 'I used to keep 'em in the boot. Whole of Britain. You never know.'

There were any number of J. Thomases and a Jess Thomas Architectural Models in Battersea. She tried that on the cellphone.

An answering machine message – a woman with a faint Welsh accent.

Caroline fetched the Yellow Pages. There weren't many architectural model makers. She rang the first one. A man answered.

'Hi, this is a really strange thing to ask but I'm trying to get hold of a model maker called Jess who rides a motorbike and ...'

'Jess Thomas,' he said. 'She's in the book.'

'Great, thanks, you wouldn't know anyone who could tell me something about her work, would you?'

'Her work? Why don't you ask her to nominate some clients?'

'I'd really prefer to do it before I approach her.'

'Well, she's pretty much in-house for Craig, Zampatti, you could ask them.'

'I will. Thanks very much.'

It took a long time to get to Battersea and it was wasted. No one answered the bell of Jess Thomas's place of work and dwelling. There was mail in the box. When she looked up, she saw a man watching her from the other side of the street. Something made her go over.

He was old, ancient, small, lifeless grey hair needing a cut, in a long raincoat, pyjama pants showing above battered brown shoes.

She introduced herself, told the truth.

The man looked at her through glasses smudged and scratched. He dropped his top teeth and moved them sideways. She looked away.

'I'm looking for Jess Thomas. She lives in the building.'

'Hasn't come back since the fire,' he said. 'Up on roof. Run away, the boogers.'

'Who?'

More teeth movements. He looked around, took a hand out of a pocket and waved it vaguely. There were bits of sticking plaster on his hand, dirty strips.

'What?' he said.

'Who ran away?' Caroline prompted.

'Before fire brigade come,' he said. 'Burned uns. Two of 'em. I seed 'em, put 'em in the van. They come in a van. And a car. Burned. The two. I seed 'em.'

'And Jess, the one with the bike?'

'Bike?'

'The girl with the bike? Was she at home?'

'Home?'

'The girl on the motorbike.'

'Never in my day. Girls.'

Caroline bent over him. He had a sour dairy smell, like old spilt milk.

'Was she there, at home. Was the girl there when the fire happened?'

He shook his head with some vigour.

'Went off before, always hear the motorbike. Bloody racket. Nice girl. Never rode motorbikes, girls, no, never, not my day. On the back, mind you, now that ...'

'Has she come back?'

'Hey?'

'The girl?'

'Nah. Always hear the motorbike, never rode motorbikes in my day, girls ... one booger come down the pipe, seen him. Off he goes in the car. Like bloody lightning.'

'Whose car?'

'Car?'

'The one who came down the pipe? Whose car did he go off in?'

He shook his head, as if she'd said something stupid.

'Well, their bloody car, what else? Come in a van. And a car. Booger come down pipe, he's off. Bloody lightning. I can tell you. Down there, in that lane. The car.'

She thanked him, gave him a ten-pound note. He looked at her as if she were not quite right in the head.

Someone fleeing? Escaping? Mackie? Had Jess Thomas brought him here and people had tried to kill him again?

She sat in the sluggish traffic, sky leaking, windscreen fogging. She felt weak, tired, scared, a little, perhaps. This is not for me, the inner voice said, this is too serious for me. I'm not responsible for people trying to kill Mackie, villages in Africa, I'm involved by accident, he saw my byline, I owe him nothing. And there's nothing in this for me. There's no page one here.

There probably wouldn't be another page one.

... *turning up Brechan's bumboy, that's now looking less spectacular.*

The woman who rang her. The woman who said she had lived in Birmingham and admired her for uncovering corruption and had a friend who was being harassed, he was really scared, he thought he was in danger, and he needed to talk to someone in the media. A person who could be trusted.

And then being run through the obstacle course. The no-shows, the phone calls, having to sweet-talk Gary's friend. Finally, finally, after two days, the meeting in the park, in the dark. And, before the handover of the film and the tape, Gary saying, quickly:

On this, there's just me talkin on this, right? Solo. Only it's like an interview, know what I mean? Tony asked me the questions, only he's not on the tape, that's wiped. Okay? So you can put in the questions. Say you did this interview with me. Anyone asks me, we had an interview, that's what I'll say. Cause I don't have the time to actually do that. So this is the same, know what I mean?

She had gone to the conference late, you had to be late on a day like that. She had waited, so high, so sure that she had it. She had sat there, the pulse felt in her throat, not really hearing what other people said, it didn't matter. She knew that she was going to be the star, they were just supporting acts before she came on.

Waiting to be the star. And for once she was. She remembered the silence. And Marcia's mouth frozen open.

The moment went a long way to balancing other memories. The one of running down a path towards her father, her brother behind her. Her father was coming home. They had been waiting all day. Her father held out his arms and she held out hers.

She remembered the feeling of complete delight. For the feeling, there was no adequate word. She ran to him and then her father's arms went over her head and took her brother, lifted him, tossed him into the air, caught him.

And she ran into her father's legs, was left clutching her father's legs, his long, thin, muscular legs.

That had come back to her soon after the wonderful moments, the screwing of Marcia, it had come in the midst of the euphoria, not in any distinct form, just a shiver. That night she woke dry-mouthed with the thought that she had done something terribly stupid when she thought she was being lucky because she was deserving. 'You earn your luck.' Her father's words. Things came to those who deserved them.

But why her? What had she done to deserve Gary? Halligan had said: *A lot less clever of you. In the light of information received.*

It was beginning to dawn on her what that meant. Colley had said something strange too:

...just a pretty vehicle, a conduit. Something people ride on. Or something stuff flows through.

Driving the small car in the electric city, the thought settled on her, dark fingers across a darkening day.

She had been a dupe.

She had been used to bring down Brechan. Someone had the tape and the film. Someone chose her to be the vehicle, the conduit. Not because she was smart. No, because she was dumb. Dumb and eager.

She should have come out with it: said that she never interviewed Gary, only Tony, the youth who said he was Gary's friend, was acting for him. She should have told Halligan the whole story about the woman whose telephone number suddenly ceased to exist. Along with dark-eyed, quick-talking Tony and his number.

I suppose you've heard they found your little Gary. Dead of an overdose. Been dead for days.

How many days? Was he alive when she got the film and tape from the man in the park who said he was Gary? They had been unable to determine the day of Gary's death, never mind the time.

She rested her forehead on the steering wheel for a second. She had to go on with this. Mackie. She had to find him before her role in the Brechan story was fully revealed.

63

HAMBURG

'FALCONTOR. Forty million dollars in two years, 1983–1984. Six million dollars three times, one payment of seven million. All from a bank in the Antilles.'

O'Malley tapped the side of his nose with a long finger. The envelope with Carla's report lay on the table unopened. 'More,' he said, 'tell me much more.'

They were in the pub off Sierichstrasse, sitting in the corner. It was the post-lunch lull, only four or five other tables in use, young men in suits drinking the last of their wine. O'Malley was wearing a dark-grey suit and a blue shirt and a red tie dotted with tiny black castles.

'It's not simple,' said Anselm. 'Money in the Antilles bank goes into Falcontor. Money goes from there to the account of something called Raceberg Credit. Raceberg lends the money moved from Falcontor to five accounts. One is a Dr C.W. Lourens, one account in Johannesburg, one in Jersey.'

Anselm waited. O'Malley blinked, didn't comment.

'This is the Lourens of whom Serrano and Kael speak so warmly,' said Anselm. 'I presume that. Dangerous drug fiend. Now departed.'

O'Malley looked away, at the window, at the street beyond, at nothing. He had a half-smile, like someone hearing music he liked.

'Presume away,' he said.

'Then there's a South African company called Ashken Research, also a big receiver, Johannesburg bank account. And a Bruynzeel account in a Brussels bank. Plus a Swiss account, which could belong to anyone.'

Their drinks came, delivered by a dark woman, slim, swift, wearing a waistcoat over a white shirt. Beer from Dresden, pils. They drank.

'Cowbarn?' said O'Malley.

He forgot nothing.

Anselm shook his head in pity. 'This is civilised beer, northern beer.'

'These banks, they offer much resistance?'

'Only the Swiss. Total resistance.'

'Secretive bastards.'

O'Malley drank again, a good inch, and wiped his lips with a paper napkin. 'A little mannered for me, this drop. But otherwise you're cooking with gas.'

'Not all good news. The Johannesburg accounts, no electronic records before 1992. Jersey and Brussels, scanned all paper accounts still active. So we have those Lourens and Bruynzeel transactions.'

'Yes?'

'Lourens. Twelve million through the Jersey account. Most of it spent on properties. Four in England, one in France.'

O'Malley held up his right hand. 'In what name?'

'In the name of Johanna Lourens.'

O'Malley closed his eyes and smiled, a look of bliss. 'Go on,' he said.

'He has two English accounts, that's been shopping money. About a million, it's in the report.'

'The properties. Currently held?'

'Unless she's sold and parked the money somewhere else.'

'What's the detail?'

'Enough for you to drive by and see what the doctor's money bought.'

O'Malley put his head back and made a humming sound through his nose. He brought his chin down and said, 'No doubt this little tavern would run to a decent bottle of champagne.'

'Who paid Lourens this kind of money?'

'Ours not to wonder,' said O'Malley. 'I feel the lovely chill of frozen assets coming on. And I taste Krug. Krugish, I feel Krugish. Join me?'

Anselm wasn't sure how to go on. He looked out of the window, he could see a piece of sky, nicotine-tinted grey. Across the street, a silversmith's display window glowed like a square-cut jewel. There was a burst of sound and the street was full of brightly coloured children tethered to young women: a nearby kindergarten had released the inmates into the custody of their mothers.

'I'll pass for the moment,' said Anselm. 'The film Serrano and Kael talk about, the one Lourens found …'

'Pass? I say again, Krug.'

'The man who's got the film, he's in England. People are trying to kill him.'

O'Malley tilted his head, his poet's head, ran a hand over the poodle curls. 'You learned this in your professional capacity, did you?'

He was saying: Do you tell other people about my business?

Anselm said, 'Do you know what Eleven Seventy means?'

'Eleven Seventy.' Not a question, just a repetition.

'Serrano said Lourens told him someone came to him with a film. Dynamite, he said. He said, tell them it's Eleven Seventy, they'll fucking understand. And then Serrano said, that was when he wanted us to go to the Americans.'

'I thought you had memory problems?' said O'Malley. He finished his beer, looked into the glass. 'Sure about the Krug?'

'A village in Angola. Wiped out. Does that have meaning?'

O'Malley looked up and sighed. 'Boyo, villages get the chop all the time. Afghanistan, Burundi, Macedonia, Iraq, a man can't keep track. They go, villages, that is the historical fate of villages. Across the centuries, they go more than they come.'

'This particular one.'

'No. It has no meaning.'

Anselm looked into the pale blue eyes and he thought, I don't know what this answer means. I don't know what he thinks about anything. I've never seen beyond his eyes.

'I've got to get back,' Anselm said. 'Instructions?'

O'Malley tapped the envelope. 'When I've read it. Tell your crack team I'll be sending around a little something of appreciation if this bears fruit.'

Anselm was getting up.

'Sit for a moment.'

He sat.

'I say this *en passant*,' said O'Malley. He was inserting his car key into the envelope, concentrating.

'Yes?'

'Lourens is messy. Even after death.'

He didn't look up, ran the key through the yellow paper, slowly.

'These smart boys,' said O'Malley. 'They had a lot of money lying around doing nothing, this is pre-Mandela South Africa. So they lent some to Lourens. Well, not to him personally, to a company owned by his wife, it's registered in the UK. Lourens is a chemist by training and he promised them big returns. Some story about a breakthrough drug delivery system. Well, they got bugger all, then the big white dream-time ended. These boys waited till the new mob, bribed to the earlobes, let them shift their ill-gotten out of the country and they were gone. They're in Australia now, big in bio-tech, cutting edge in the fight against snoring, hot flushes, jock itch. Also manufacturing, they're applying the old South African talents to a new labour force, chaining the Asian poor to the wheel.'

'They sold you the debt.'

'A fully documented debt. My point is, the Süd-Afs were scared of Lourens. One of the charmers said, this is after we've done the deal, bought the debt, he says, good luck and sooner you than me, pal, they call you pal this lot, he says Lourens is poison himself and he's been in bed with even more dangerous people.'

O'Malley had the report out, looking at the first page. 'That's it,' he said.

'Thanks for the background.'

Without looking up, O'Malley said, 'You aren't a journalist any more, John. That part of your life is over.'

Anselm walked down fume-acrid Sierichstrasse, thinking about what had been. Once his trade had been going to sad and violent places and telling their stories, telling stories of death and barbarism, selling the stories.

The occupation seemed to have chosen him and it was without glamour or reward. Still, there was a certain dirty-faced dignity and pride in being the person who went where other people didn't want to go, asked questions they wouldn't ask, saw things they would rather not see.

But that was gone forever. He didn't need O'Malley to tell him what he wasn't.

Kaskis once said of a famous *New York Times*

reporter, 'Covers wars from his hotel room. The dog's gun-shy.'

Gun-shy, that's what he was. He should leave Lourens and Niemand and films of Angolan villages alone.

As he walked down the howling street, he rubbed his useless fingers. My dead bits, he thought, the bits visibly and tangibly dead.

64

HAMBURG

INSKIP saw him coming in and raised an arm, the wrist cocked, a pale and bony index finger pointing. Anselm went to his side.

'I have entered the temple wherein all men's secrets are known,' said Inskip. 'It was a fucking doddle. But Joseph Elias Diab's file is marked "Out to Agency". Permanently removed.'

'What agency?'

'Defense Intelligence Agency.'

'There endeth the lesson,' said Anselm.

'Tilders wants you to call. Soonest. That's about ten minutes ago. Beate put him through to me, why I cannot think. Carla's here, she's the logical person to take your calls. The senior person.'

'Perhaps Beate favours you, dreams of the touch of your nicotine-scented fingers.'

He went to his office and rang Tilders. The line was strange, an echo, as if Tilders were in a tunnel.

Tilders said, 'The present matter, there is something …'

'Yes?'

'Brussels?'

'Yes?'

'That person is dead, a suicide, in his office. A gun. Our party called him, they told him that.'

Bruynzeel dead. Anselm remembered the man's voice, his wry, weary tone.

'Thank you,' he said.

Bruynzeel, the account in Serrano's Credit Raceberg, recipient of large loans.

A suicide.

He got up and found Tilders's audiotape, DT/HH/31/02, put it in the machine.

Serrano at his hotel, talking to the Bruynzeel of Bruynzeel & Speelman Chemicals in Brussels.

Bruynzeel: *They want what?*

Serrano: *Records. Anything. Everything.*

Bruynzeel: *You have records?*

Serrano: *No.*

Bruynzeel: *Well, just shut up. It's all bluff. These things pass. Just keep your mouth shut. Trilling's connections, there's no problem.*

Serrano: *You can talk to him?*

Bruynzeel: *I'll see. Things in the past, no one wants to talk about the past.*

Anselm sat, touching the lost fingers, the Beirut fingers. Cold, they were always cold, like Fräulein Einspenner's fingers when he held them.

Trilling's connections.

Trilling. Who was Trilling?

Anselm called up the search engine and typed in *trilling.*

There was no shortage of Trillings. The search engine found 21,700 references.

Bruynzeel & Speelman Chemicals.

Lourens is a chemist by training ...

O'Malley said that. Perhaps Trilling was in the same line ...

A long shot. Anselm added *chemicals* to the search.

Too many.

Try *drugs.*

The first reference said:

Pharmentis Corporation president Donald Trilling tonight defended his company's record on the pricing of drugs sold to the third world.

The phone.

Beate, sandpaper voice. 'A Dr Koenig for you.'

'Thank you.'

Alex.

'Is this a bad time?'

'How can that be?'

'Can I say ... what can I say?'

'Say I could come around and see you. Or the reverse. Or anything.'

'Come around and see me, I'll say that?'

Anselm's heart lifted and he closed his eyes.

'That's fine,' he said, 'that's very good. About when would that be? The time doesn't matter much to me.'

'Whenever your work is, well, after work, whenever. I'm at home, I'm here. So. Any time. From now.'

'From now is fine. I'll see you soon.'

'Yes. That's good.'

'I'll just settle the bill here, get going. Bye.'

'Bye.'

A moment.

'I could pick you up,' she said.

'No, I'll get a cab, it's easy.'

'Fine. See you soon.'

'Soon.'

He put the phone down.

This elation was stupid, he knew that. He saw her face. The phone rang again. Tilders, the dry voice:

'Our friends are meeting again. The same place. In an hour.'

Kael and Serrano.

'I have something new,' Tilders said. 'Worth trying perhaps.'

'Two minutes,' said Anselm. He rang O'Malley.

'The person in Brussels is dead,' Anselm said. 'Apparent suicide by gunshot. Our friends here are meeting again. We can try.'

There was a pause. Anselm could hear background noises. Perhaps O'Malley was drinking Krug alone. A voice said, 'British Airways flight 643 to London ...'

'Sad news,' said O'Malley. 'But no thanks. I'm happy to stick with what I've got.'

Anselm said goodbye, sat for a moment. The light was going. He rang Tilders.

'Yes,' he said. 'Go ahead.'

'It is the same as the first time. I'll call you.'

'I'd rather not wait.'

'Otto will pick you up outside in twenty minutes.'

65

HAMBURG

THEY SAT in the Mercedes, parked at almost exactly the same place as the first time.

'When?' said Anselm.

'Four forty-five,' said Fat Otto. 'A few minutes.'

Otto liked to speak English. He had once worked in England, in restaurants.

Under the ashen, dying sky, the lake was still, pewter, mist on the far shore. A lone swan came into view, imperious in its bearing.

The words came to Anselm from his father and he said, 'And always I think of my friend who/amid the apparition of bombs/saw on the lyric lake/the single perfect swan.'

Fat Otto looked at him. 'What?'

'Edwin Rolfe. A poem.'

Fat Otto looked away, looked at his watch.

'He almost missed this appointment,' he said.

'Who?'

'Serrano. There was trouble about the hotel safe.'

Anselm's mind had turned to Alex, the Italianate face, the full lower lip she sometimes bit when she was listening.

'What kind of trouble?'

'Something about the keys.'

'What's that got to do with Serrano?'

Fat Otto's mobile rang. He listened.

'*Ja. Ja, alles okay.*'

'Serrano's getting on,' he said.

'What have the keys got to do with Serrano?'

'His briefcase was in the safe. He couldn't get it while they were arguing about the keys.'

'Briefcase? The same one?'

'No, he has another.' Otto looked at his watch again. 'Paul has to get close with this new gadget.'

Anselm's mind had returned to Alex but something passed over his skin like a touch, like walking into a cobweb, cold.

Serrano's briefcase in the safe. Trouble over the safe keys. Bruynzeel dead.

There was something wrong here.

'Ring Tilders,' he said. 'Tell him not to get on.'

Fat Otto opened his mouth.

'Do it,' said Anselm. 'Now.'

Fat Otto closed his mouth, tapped a number into his mobile.

Anselm watched Otto's face. Otto's eyes flashed at him, away.

Anselm's mouth was dry. Something very wrong.

'It's off,' said Otto. 'He's switched it off. Interference, he's scared of that.'

Anselm closed his eyes. He felt sweat on his forehead, his skin was prickling, the car felt intolerably hot.

'*Was ist los?*'

Otto was looking at him. Anselm shook his head. '*Eine Vorahnung. Nur einen Augenblick lang.*'

Otto shrugged. 'I get them too,' he said. 'Before plane trips, I always get them.' He turned his attention to the black box.

They sat and listened to crackling, to static. Anselm was rubbing his fingers, the premonition wouldn't go away, he felt panic coming.

Sit up straight. Put your hands in your lap, palms up,

open. Breathe deeply, breathe regularly.

'From hearing-aid technology,' said Fat Otto. 'And the tuner you wear in your ear, like a hearing aid but tiny, invisible. Cordless. The mikes are in spectacles. Three mikes. You tune until you drop out everything you don't want. To six or seven metres, phenomenal, the clarity. I heard this couple in Spitalerstrasse talking dirty, whispers, whispering dirty, she said to him ...'

'This isn't phenomenal clarity,' said Anselm.

'We had no time to test transmitting.'

They sat for a long time listening to crackling and hissing, Fat Otto fiddled, Anselm tried to still his mind, slow the turning of the planet.

Serrano's briefcase in the safe. The keys to the safe. An argument about the keys to the safe.

Bruynzeel dead. Lourens dead. Falcontor. Credit Raceberg.

'The transmitter,' said Fat Otto. 'Still, we'll have it. Probably.'

The ferry came into view, sliding on glass, windows aglow, in the last moments of the day.

Anselm felt the panic recede. The beating in his chest was less insistent, his pulse rate was falling. He opened his mouth and his jaw muscles made a noise, relief from the clenching.

Kael's dark-blue Mercedes was in the same spot fifty metres from the landing, the driver leaning against it, looking at a hand, his nails, bored.

Calm. Anselm felt it come, his mouth was moist again, the salivary glands working.

All that troubled the lake was the ferry's wake, the chevron, corrugations expanding, dissipating.

The lyric lake.

Only the swan missing, alone and perfect. The swan had come along too early.

They would have to go somewhere to listen to Tilders's tape, ensure that there was something to listen to, that this hadn't been a complete fuck-up. Or they could listen in the car. This would have to be a separate bill, a private bill, this was not O'Malley work, O'Malley had his freezable assets, he had what he wanted. Not a bill, no, ask Tilders to name an amount for this evening's work, pay him in cash. Tilders would be impassive. But there would be something in his eyes.

In the distance, another Mercedes, black, parked illegally, there was no parking there. A wife, a driver, picking up the weary financial analyst, not parking, just waiting.

The day was dwindling, the far shore dark now.

Fat Otto switched off the noise, the crackling, the sibilance.

'We have to work on this,' he said.

Anselm ran hands up and down his cheeks, heard the sawing of the beard. He would ask Fat Otto for a lift to Alex's.

When they had heard the tape.

He thought about unbuttoning the shirt. She always wore shirts. Kissing the lower lip that she bit. Biting it for her.

He felt in his groin the possibility of an erection, perhaps more than a possibility. He moved his thighs apart, made room for possibility.

The ferry was about to dock, a handful of people waiting.

'An experiment,' said Fat Otto. 'Better next time.'

'Yes,' said Anselm.

Movement inside the ferry. Passengers getting up.

There was a sound, not loud.

The ferry lit up inside.

Light red as blood, dark streaks in it.

A hole appeared in the ferry roof, a huge scarlet spear through the roof.

The ferry lifted, not high, came down, settled on the water, listed, burning inside.

'*Um Gottes Willen*,' said Otto. '*Um Gottes Willen*.'

Anselm was out of the car and running for the landing when he looked for the black Mercedes.

It was gone.

66

HAMBURG

IT BEGAN to rain as Anselm neared home, cold sleet-like rain, but it didn't bother him. He had sent Tilders to his death. There would never be any escape from that fact.

On a whim. Not on business. Not on behalf of a client. On a personal whim.

For that, Tilders was dead.

The house seemed colder than usual, the rooms darker. He rang Alex.

'I was wondering about you,' she said.

'I won't be coming,' he said. 'Someone's been killed. A friend.'

A silence.

'I'm sorry. That's terrible. Of course, you must ... Whatever you have to do.'

'Nothing. There's nothing to do.'

'Where are you?'

'At home.'

'Well. I'll call you tomorrow.'

'Yes, I'll call you. I'm sorry.'

'No, please, don't be. These things, you need time.'

Anselm sat on the edge of the desk, looking at the carpet. He felt all his aches, no alcohol in the system to dull them.

A whim. Was it a whim?

No.

'You aren't a journalist any more, John,' O'Malley had said. 'That part of your life is over.'

It wasn't over. It had started again with the decision to put Tilders on the ferry. Sad-eyed Tilders, wry and icy-calm doer of the impossible, benchmark for reliability. It couldn't stop because he had been blown to pieces. The opposite. It had to go on because he was dead.

Dead. How many people in this unfathomable business were dead. Now Tilders by chance, Serrano and Kael murdered, Bruynzeel, probably murdered. Lourens, probably. Shawn.

And, long ago, Kaskis and Diab.

He thought about the Wishart woman. She connected Kaskis and Diab to the film shown to her by Mackie, who was Niemand, and that brought in Serrano and Kael and Shawn and Bruynzeel and Richler and Trilling, whoever he was.

Anselm went to the cold kitchen and poured half a glass of whisky, took the bottle back to the study, sat in the ancestral chair behind the desk. He found the number and dialled.

It rang and rang and cut out.

The other number, he dialled that, it was a mobile number.

It rang and rang.

She answered.

'John Anselm.'

'Hold on, I'm in the car, have to pull over, I don't have a hands-free.'

He waited.

'Hi, hello,' she said. 'Sorry, the traffic's terrible.'

He wasn't sure how to put it, then he said it. 'Mackie is a man called Constantine Niemand. He's a South African mercenary. The film comes from South Africa. He came upon it by chance, I think.'

A sound, a sigh, perhaps a passing vehicle, too close.

'Do you know what it's about?' Her tone was tentative, talking to a cat so as not to scare it away.

He didn't know what to say.

'No,' he said, 'but I think knowing about it is very dangerous.'

She said, 'Yes. I know that. They tried to kill him again. Last night.'

'Your paper knows what you're doing?'

'No. They don't. It's … well, it's complicated.'

'I'll call you if anything else comes up.'

'Please. I'm feeling desperate.'

He put the phone down. It rang.

'Anselm.'

'I'm outside your house. Yes or no?'

'Yes.'

He waited for a while, drank some whisky, and then he went to the front door and opened it. Alex was there, hands in the pockets of a trenchcoat, face impassive, beautiful, rain on her hair.

'I want you to fuck me,' she said.

'I ordered a pizza.'

'We're out of pizza.'

'Well, this is most unsatisfactory.'

'We'll see about that.'

She came inside, closed the door, came up to him, close, he could smell her perfume. He put his hands on her waist and drew her to him.

They kissed, softly. Then harder and she pressed against him. He could feel her ribs under his hands. He slid his hands to her buttocks.

'Do you have a bed?' she said, not her usual voice, throatier.

'We never sleep.'

'I wasn't thinking about sleeping.'

She put a hand on him but it was already happening.

'I think you're recovering,' she said.

'Only clinical trials can confirm that.' His breath was short.

'I'm a doctor.' She unzipped him, put her hand in.

He was unbuttoning her red shirt. 'A red bra,' he said. 'That's provocative.'

'White didn't work last night.' She squeezed him. 'This is promising.'

'Upstairs,' said Anselm. 'Quickly, I don't know how long it will last.'

He was awake, lying on his back, still in the afterglow, and he caught the phone on the first ring.

'Haven't woken you?' Inskip.

'What?'

Anselm could make out Alex's pale shoulders, the curve of the shoulder blades.

'I heard about Tilders. I'm really sorry.'

'Yes. Well.'

'This probably isn't of interest but that removed file, do you know ...'

'Yes.' He was talking about Diab's file.

'There was a number with the entry, a code. I didn't think anything at the time, but it nagged. I went back and fiddled, just curious, you understand, pure spirit of inquiry, and ...'

'What?'

'It was one of a group of files removed at the same time, a bulk buy. All gone for good. Same remover.'

Alex turned onto her back and he could see her left breast lolling, flat on the breastbone, the nipple prominent. She moved her head, disturbed, as if worried by a fly.

He said softly, 'How many?'

'Eight.'

He felt her hand on his thigh, the long fingers moving slowly. Slowly. It was happening again and he had no moisture in his mouth.

'Run the names,' he said. 'That's good work. And if you've got time, do a biog on a Donald Trilling, Pharmentis Corp, that's P-H-A-R.'

'Certainly, sir. Enjoy your rest.'

'Who said anything about rest?'

Her fingers were lying on him, doing nothing, he could feel each finger. Then they closed and she had him in her grip, a silken, strong grip. And there was something to grip.

'Calling for pizza again?' she said.

'A victim of night hunger.'

'Me too.'

He turned and she put her right hand to his head, he got his mouth on her breast, tried to engulf it, the whole breast, her, the whole of her.

67

HAMBURG

'THERE'S INSURANCE,' said Baader. 'Tilders's wife and children will be looked after, I'll make sure.'

Baader looked away, fleetingly touched his desk blotter, the computer mouse, pulled fingers away from them as if they were hot.

'I signed as a witness when they got married,' he said. 'He gave the boy my name. Well, he never said it was for me, but I always thought, well, you know ...'

Anselm wanted to tell him that Tilders had not been on the firm's business. He wanted to confess. But he could not bring himself to.

Later. He would tell him later.

Baader shook his head, gathered himself. 'What does O'Malley say? This is his business. Fucking around with Kael.'

'I'll find out today.'

'We've never ... This prick in Munich shot Fat Otto but that was a mistake ...'

Baader looked away again. It was a tired face, the signs of too much and too little. 'On the doorstep, too. That's so fucking, I don't know. I can't ...'

Baader shook his head. He made hand movements.

Anselm caught himself doing the same. Language has failed us, he thought. We have no way to express the ache. He went to his office.

The logs stood on his desk, high, two stacks, sixty or seventy files, the records of twenty-four hours, the doings of strangers, their comings and their goings, their gettings and their spendings. He sorted, found Inskip's pile, found the one he wanted.

The eight names.

Diab, Joseph Elias.

Fitzgerald, Wayne Arthur.

Gressor, Maurice Tennant.

Galuska, Benjamin Lincoln Garner.

Kaldor, Zoltan James.

Macken, Todd Garvey.

Rossi, Anthony Raimond.

Veldman, Elvis Aaron.

He felt something stir in a far corner of his mind, something in a crevice, stuck. He read the names again:

Diab, Joseph. Fitzgerald, Wayne.

Gressor, Maurice. Galuska, Benjamin. Kaldor, Zoltan. Macken, Todd. Rossi, Anthony. Veldman, Elvis.

Nothing came to him. He turned to the next page.

Inskip's notes, in his sloppy hand, ballpoint, some letters upright, some slanting to the right.

Found five. With Diab, six.

Fitzgerald. Dead, suicide, gunshot, Toronto, Canada, 9 October 1993.

Gressor. Dead, drug overdose, Los Angeles, California, 7 October 1993.

Galuska. No trace.

Kaldor. Dead, apparent road-rage victim, Miami, Florida, 8 October 1993.

Macken. No trace.

Rossi. Dead, motor accident, Dallas, Texas, 14 July 1989.

Veldman. Dead, shot by intruder, Raleigh, North Carolina, 7 October 1993.

Early October 1993 was a really bad hair time for this bunch. Have some birth dates, could check horoscopes. Is this unusual mortality for a group of soldiers of average age forty? How would I know?

A good thing Baader didn't read the logs any more. He disliked frivolity. Except in its place. Anselm looked at his slice of view, not seeing it. Early October 1993 was certainly a bad time. They had been kidnapped on 3 October. Within a few days, Kaskis, Diab, and these five American soldiers, probably ex-soldiers, died violently.

There were two more pages from Inskip. The abbreviated biography of Donald Trilling, president of Pharmentis Corporation, fourth largest US pharmaceutical company.

Born Boston 1942, graduate of Stanford, PhD Cambridge, chemist, military service in Vietnam, founder of Trilling Research Associates of Alexandria, Virginia, developer of anti-depressants Tranquinol and Calmerion, consultant to the US Defense Department. Many more achievements. It was an impressive career, capped by the Pharmentis takeover of Trilling Research in 1988 and Trilling's rise to head of the corporation. There was a quote from *Time* magazine in 1996: '... scientist, corporate strategist, and, as convenor of Republicans at Work, one of the most influential men in America'.

At the bottom of the page, Inskip had written:

Not just consultant to US Defense Department. Congressional hearing in 1989 told Trilling Research received Defense contracts worth more than $60 million between 1976 and 1984. No details. Classified.

May be more about this elsewhere.

Was this the Trilling? The only connection was that Bruynzeel and this Trilling were in the same trade, roughly. Bruynzeel and Speelman sold chemicals. Lourens was a chemist, like Trilling.

Bruynzeel said to Serrano:

Trilling's connections, there's no problem.

If it was this Trilling, what connections was Bruynzeel referring to? With the US Defense Department?

And Serrano had said something to Spence/Richler about needing to worry because 'the Belgian's one of yours'.

Bruynzeel and the Israelis? Was this the Trilling? It was a thicket, hard to get in, easy to be trapped, no way out.

What exactly did Lourens do? He'd never bothered to find out. He swivelled to the machine.

There wasn't much about Dr Carl Lourens on the electronic record. The Johannesburg *Weekly Mail & Guardian* had a 1992 story that the Office for Serious Economic Offences, a branch of the Attorney-General's Department, was investigating his company, TechPharma Global, for currency and other offences under the apartheid regime.

The Johannesburg *Star* reported his death. It called him an importer of chemicals 'with links to the South African Defence Force'. The report said:

The body was burnt beyond recognition in a fire that destroyed the premises of TechPharma Global outside Pretoria. Police said gas cylinders and chemicals exploded, making it too dangerous to approach the blaze. It had been allowed to burn out.

It was rumoured in 1993 that Dr Lourens would be charged with serious offences relating to the apartheid era, but these never eventuated.

A spokesman for the Attorney-General's Department said yesterday that Dr Lourens had been questioned in recent weeks over allegations made by a former employee of TechPharma Global.

There was one more reference.

A man found dead of a gunshot wound to the head in

a Sandton City car park yesterday has been identified as Dr Johan Scheepers, 56, a chemist of Craighall Park.

Dr Scheepers was found with a pistol. He was a former employee of TechPharma Global, whose director, Dr Carl Lourens, died in a fire two days ago. Dr Scheepers had been assisting the Attorney-General's Department with inquiries into the affairs of TechPharma.

Lourens, Shawn, this man, Serrano, Kael ... he didn't want to go through the list again. No end to the number of deaths. He was sick at heart and stomach and the twenty-four-hour logs were waiting.

Jessica Thomas, the name added to the Mackie file, had used a credit card to buy petrol at a stop on the A44.

TIME OF EVENT: *12.42 a.m., Thursday, 13/10.*

The CLIENT NOTIFIED box was ticked. TIME: *3.27 p.m., Thursday, 13/10.*

In the COMMENTS box, Jarl had written: *Checked long delay in central transaction recording – Amex computer problems, system down.*

Lafarge looking for Niemand. Was Niemand with Jessica Thomas? Why not, she had picked him up on her bike. Lafarge looking for the film Niemand had. Dead soldiers. Dead Tilders.

Anselm's mind was sick of the puzzle, slid away to Alex. She had left the bed before dawn. He had woken but kept still, lying on his side, eyes closed, listening to her dressing, the fabric sounds, pulling, sheathing. She had come to the bedside, bent over, tried to place a soft kiss on his face, and he had taken her, caught her, pulled her down to him.

'This is over-compensation,' she said in his chest, breathless. 'You don't have to prove anything. It works.'

'It's not doing anything.'

'Are you sure? Let me check ...'

Riccardi. He should have spoken to him earlier. What did Riccardi know?

68

LONDON

'WE'RE PRETTY much in a holding pattern,' said Palmer. The small windowless room on the top floor of the embassy was overheated, and it made him feel tight in the chest.

'It's getting close for me, Scottie. I'd hoped things would be tidy by now.'

'I'm not taking this lightly.'

'No, I know you're not. What help have our friends given you?'

'Some. They're on the case. Could hear something any time.'

'Not a big country.'

'Big enough. Plus there's water around it.'

'Is that a thought?'

'We've got it covered, I hope.'

'There was something in Hamburg.'

'Yes. People did some housekeeping.'

'Simpler ways, surely?'

'They apparently thought it would be more surgical.'

'They think Hiroshima was surgical. Sorted out the clown problem?'

'An all-professional show next time.'

'Call me any time.'

'I will.'

'And not a loose thread, Scottie. Not a fucking thing.'

'Understood, sir. Goodnight.'

'Goodnight, Scottie.'

Palmer dialled the other number. There were two rediallings.

'Yes.' It was Casca.

'Palmer. Anything of interest?'

'The present matter, sir,' said Casca. 'We put together a bunch of stuff, bits and pieces, mostly from the one place. It adds up and it's not helpful. You might want to do something about it, sir.'

'Tell me.'

69

HAMBURG

RICCARDI SOUNDED groggy, as if woken from a deep sleep.

'What time's it?' he said.

'It's morning,' said Anselm. 'What sort of hours are you keeping there? Still up all night?'

'Yup but now I'm getting paid for it. Got a job. Night job.'

'What kind of job?'

'In a call centre. I answer customers' questions about software problems. From all over the world.'

'What do you know about software?'

'Fuck all. I've got an FAQ sheet, that won't do it, I say we'll get back to them.'

'Do you?'

'No. How you been?'

'Alive. Listen, there's something I want to ask you. Kaskis had a photograph.' Anselm described it.

'Yup. I saw it. The guy, he was in it.'

'Diab?'

'Yup. Diab. That woman get hold of you?'

'In every sense. Did Kaskis say anything about the picture?'

He could hear Riccardi yawn, a sound a bear might make in spring.

'She'd be an A1 fuck, I thought. Good legs. See her legs?'

335

'She appeared to have legs. She was walking. What did Kaskis say about the picture?'

'I turned it over and on the back was written SD and a date, I can't remember, 1980-something, early eighties.'

'SD?'

'I asked him and he said, "Special Deployment, Sudden Death, the funny guys."'

'Slowly, I'm slow. Say that again.'

'Special Deployment, Sudden Death. That's what he said. And he said, "There but for the grace." It stuck in my mind.'

'I'm amazed. Drugs are doing you good. You asked what he meant?'

'He said, just people who don't exist.'

'That's all?'

'Yup. Wildly talkative, Kaskis, notice that?'

'I did. He said, "But for the grace"?'

'That's what he said. Listen, you raking over all the shit again? Baby, it's history. Get on with life. Take drugs. Get a job in a call centre.'

'I'll pencil that in for tomorrow. Anything else about the picture?'

'The one musclehead was called Elvis – not a name you forget.'

Elvis.

'How do you know that?'

Riccardi said, 'Written on the picture. Guy next to Diab. Elvis. On his big fucking chest.'

Anselm had the log open, he found Inskip's list. *Elvis Aaron Veldman. Dead, shot by intruder, Raleigh, North Carolina, 7 October 1993.*

This was the something that had moved in a crevice of his mind. The names on the list were the men in Kaskis's photograph.

Most of them dead. Five of them killed in the space of a few days in October 1993.

When the picture was taken, in the early 1980s, they belonged to Special Deployment – Sudden Death.

SD, some kind of special unit. Unit of what?

Sudden Death.

Not the Peace Corps.

70

WALES

THEY LAY in their sweat in the cold room, her head on his chest.

She had come to him in the early morning, light behind the curtains. He heard the door and he was moving, one leg off the bed.

'I dreamed you'd gone,' she said. 'I dreamed I came here and found you'd gone.'

He held out his arms. She came to him and he put his arms around her, put his head against the long white nightdress, against her stomach, smelled the clean cotton and her body, rubbed his face against her. She pushed him away gently, crossed her arms and lifted her garment over her head, revealed herself, lean, small breasts.

They made love slowly. He felt the hesitancy in her and he had it in himself, he did not deserve her, he was too crude a creature for her. But when he entered her, she became urgent, squeezed his flesh, made him roll, roll again, she bit him, scratched him, she groaned, and he could not maintain his silence.

Done, she was sleepy, languid, her body was aligned with him, her arm lay across him, a hand on his thigh.

Niemand spoke into her damp hair, softly, 'I want to say thank you. Better than I said it. I don't know why you did that for me.'

'I saw you coming,' she said. 'You had this look.'

He felt her words on his skin, the warm brush of her breath.

'I thought, shit, off his face, he shouldn't be in the traffic. And then I saw your eyes and I thought, no, not stoned, I didn't know what but I knew not stoned.'

He remembered the yellow helmet looking at him and the man coming from behind and the weak feeling.

'My brother died in Cardiff because no one would help him,' she said. 'They thought he was drunk but he was diabetic, he was having a hypo and people walked around him, walked away. So. No. Anyway, you looked so straight, your hair, the tan, and you looked hurt, there's a look you know, you see it in kids. And then I saw this guy coming, he was running. In a suit but not your suit person, like a bouncer, thug face, and I thought, fuck you, boyo, let's go, catch us if you can.'

She raised a hand, touched his lips, ran a finger along the thin ridge of cartilage on his broken nose.

'Do you have a job?' she said. 'Do something?'

How did you tell someone like this what you did, what you had done, without her rejecting you?

'A soldier,' he said. 'I used to be a soldier.'

71

HAMBURG

'TELL ME what the fuck you're doing,' said Baader. 'Just tell me.'

'What I'm doing?' The response of the guilty. Anselm turned his head to the window.

Baader looked down, tapped the edge of his desk with both sets of knuckles.

'I talked to O'Malley,' he said. 'Don't mess around with me, John. The boy's dead because of this. Paul's dead.'

Through the trees, Anselm could see a glass tourist boat going by, not so much a boat as a coach on water, light glinting on it.

How to tell this story to Baader? To anyone?

He tried. It took a while. Baader listened, head on hand, eyes closed.

When he'd finished, Anselm said, 'That's it. I'll take it to the grave. Sending Stefan.'

He felt relief. He had spoken of the weight on his heart.

There was a long silence. Baader didn't move, he didn't open his eyes, he could have died during the telling of the story.

'Say the word and I'm gone,' said Anselm. 'You are fully entitled.'

Baader opened his eyes, blinked several times. 'I

should say it. But what if he'd been on O'Malley's business? He'd still be dead. And you'll be dead if you go on with this. I think you're fucking around with stuff you can't begin to understand. Leave it alone. It's got nothing to do with you.'

'It goes back to Beirut. That's got something to do with me.'

Baader shook his head. 'You can't bring back the dead. You can't change anything. Be grateful you're alive.'

'I'm grateful,' said Anselm. 'I'm grateful.'

'Go away,' said Baader. 'You worry me. Go away.'

Anselm was leaving, he stopped when Baader said, 'If they killed Kaskis for what he knew, you're alive because you knew fuck all. Then. Now you might just know something. Something you don't even know you know.'

'I'll reflect on that,' said Anselm.

'So composed. So fucking composed.'

Anselm stopped, didn't turn, the desire to be punished fully risen in him. 'Sack me,' he said. 'Why don't you sack me?'

Nothing. He turned. Baader was looking out of the window and the view gave him no peace. He had tramlines down his forehead, deep between the eyebrows. Anselm had never noticed them.

'Being sacked is too good for you,' said Baader. 'Sack yourself. Stand on your pride and your honour and your fucking dignity.'

Anselm went to his office. I'm like a small dog, he thought, only bark and snarl. The logs were waiting. He was grateful that he had something to do, working out how much to charge people he did not know for spying on other people for reasons he did not want to know.

72

LONDON

FROM THE car park, Caroline rang Craig, Zampatti, the architects who employed Jess Thomas. She explained to the receptionist and was put through to a woman called Sandra Fox.

'I'm an old friend of Jess Thomas's, but I've been away, I've lost touch. I found her work address in the book but she's not there and the someone told me she did a lot of work for you and ...'

'She lives there,' said Fox. 'Battersea. In that last little pocket of ... well, if she's not there, I really can't help. The people who could are in Nepal, climbing, I gather you have to, it's all uphill in Nepal. So that's not much use.'

'Who are they, the people in Nepal?'

'Mark and Natalie. They're the Craig and the Zampatti, the principals here. Look, leave your number, I'll ask around. Umm.'

A wait.

'There is someone you might try called David Nunn. They came to our Christmas party together. An item, I thought, more than just good friends. You could try him. He's with Musgrove & Wolters, I can give you a number, it's here somewhere ...'

Caroline left her number and rang Musgrove & Wolters. David Nunn was in Singapore. It took almost an hour to reach him, late afternoon there.

Too late to stop lying.

'Mr Nunn, Detective Sergeant Moody, Battersea police. I'm hoping you might be able to help me locate someone called Jessica Thomas. I understand you know her well.'

'What's happened?' He was alarmed.

'Possibly nothing. There was some sort of disturbance at her place the other night and she hasn't been seen since earlier that evening. We'd like to be certain she's unharmed.'

'Well, I don't know. I haven't seen her for a while, not since January or February.'

'Close family?'

'She doesn't have any.'

'Friends?'

'Anne Cerchi, she's a good friend.'

'Do you have an address?'

'Not a number, no, it's in Ladbroke Grove.'

The old address.

'We've tried her. Anyone else?'

'Umm, she's friends with Natalie Zampatti. Natalie and Mark Craig. They're architects, the firm's ...'

'I know the firm.'

'Right. She goes back a long way with Natalie, with the family, I think.'

'They can't be contacted. They're in Nepal.'

'Shit.'

'Anywhere she might go? She might want to get away from everything?'

'Not that I know of, no.'

She said her thanks and sat for a long time with her eyes closed, slumped, an ache in her shoulders, in the back of her neck. Then, a man and a woman walked by, the woman laughed, a shrill birdlike sound.

What else to do, to try? Help me, McClatchie, she thought, wherever you are, help me.

73

WALES

NIEMAND GOT up early, left Jess asleep, innocent-faced, and went for a look around. They were high here, the farm buildings on a terrace cut into the hillside. Behind it, the slope was dotted with scrubby wind-whipped trees and then there were conifers, solid, dark.

Below the farm, the road twisted down the hill and crossed a small stone bridge over a stream. He couldn't see water but the stream's course was marked by dense vegetation. Low drystone walls flanked the road and all around on the slopes other walls marked out fields, nothing in them, no farm animals, no signs of tillage.

He could see where the road ended at a gate. From behind the barn, a track, deep wheel ruts, went around the side of the hill. There were no other buildings in sight, no power lines.

He went into the dark house and took the map off the corkboard in the kitchen, went outside and sat on an old bench beside the front door. It was large-scale, British Ordnance Survey, a decent map. He knew about maps, he had had maps beaten into him – reading them, memor-ising them, summoning them up on moonless nights in swampy tropical lowlands and high, hard, broken country.

Someone had marked the position of the farm in ball-point. He traced the road they'd come on, the village, some long name full of 'l's and 'm's, the other roads around them. There weren't many roads and most of them dead-ends. He studied the contours, the elevations, the beacons, the watercourses. A little peace began to fall on him. It would be hard for anyone to surprise them here.

'You sneaked away.'

Jess, still in her nightdress, arms folded against the cold, no make-up. She looked like a teenager, he thought. Beautiful. He looked away, shy.

'Nice country,' Niemand said. 'Looks like sheep country but no sheep.'

She came up behind the bench and kissed the back of his neck, put both hands on his forehead and pulled his head against her stomach. He felt the soft warmth of her and a lump rose in his throat.

Niemand made breakfast out of cans in the pantry: grilled tomatoes and pork sausages. There was mustard powder and he made some with water and a little dark fragrant vinegar.

'Useful around the house then,' she said when she came from the bathroom, shining clean, hair damp.

They ate.

'Good this,' she said. 'Who says you need fresh food? I could live out of cans.'

They were almost finished when he realised that he hadn't noticed her eating. His feeling about eating with other people seemed to have left him.

'There are clothes here,' she said. 'But you'll drown in them, he's big and overweight. Fat, actually.'

Niemand knew he should do what he had said he would do. Go. He had a chance of finding the Irishman and they could get him out of the country. But his fears had abated. How could they find them here, so far from London? He thought he knew how they'd found him at

Jess's place. The motorbike. The registration. It was obvious. The man chasing him had got the number, they could bribe the owner's address out of some clerk.

But now these people had nothing to go on. Jess had brought him to a remote farm owned by a sister of a friend and the friend was somewhere far away, Nepal, and the sister was in America.

These people didn't have supernatural powers. They'd had luck, that was all. Just luck.

They washed up, she said, let me do it, she pushed him with a hip, he pushed back, they bumped and jostled, laughing, at the end she rested her head on his arm for a few seconds. He kissed her hair. She turned her head and he was kissing her lips, faintly salty.

He broke away. Something said, she'll think that's all you want. 'Could we stay for a while?' he said. As he said the word, he thought, *we*, who am I to say, *we*?

Jess nodded. 'I've got nothing urgent.'

He showered and found clothes that hung on him. They went outside, walked down the track around the side of the hill, shoulders touching, hips touching. He found her hand, long fingers.

'Tell me about your life,' she said. 'We're like people who meet because they crash into each other.'

They walked in the wind, a sky to eternity, torn-tissue clouds. He talked, he told her. He had never told anyone. He couldn't remember anyone ever asking, but he wouldn't have told them.

'When I was a kid, my dad wouldn't come home for days. An alcoholic. Once my mother was in hospital and he wasn't there and the welfare took me, put me in this place. The man there tried to make me ... do things. He beat me with a belt, I was bleeding. The belt buckle. I remember later I could see the buckle on my legs. Anyway, I ran away, to the railway yards. My pants and my shirt stuck to me, the blood. I was there for weeks, hiding in the old carriages, the black men gave me food, the workers, they had nothing, they owed white people bugger all, they were treated like dirt, but they looked after me. That, I've never forgotten that. No. You end up with these pricks, they'd waste any black. Well, this white guard saw me one day, he chased me, he couldn't catch me, and the police came with a dog and it sniffed me out. They took me home. My dad was sober and my mother came back, so that was okay for a while.' He stopped. 'You don't want to hear this stuff.'

Jess swung their arms, bounced her right temple against his upper arm. 'Yes. I want to hear it.'

They walked, the rutted track turning north-east, the land bare, never cultivated, small huddles of trees.

'Anyway, he started drinking again, hitting my mom … next thing we were on Crete, me and my mom. I only had a bit of Greek but you learn quickly when you have to. I must've been ten, eleven. We were there for years, I kind of forgot about South Africa. When I thought about it, it was like something someone told me about, a story.'

The track ran out on the crest of the hill, just a circle where vehicles had turned, churned the thin topsoil, the far side in view, more of the same, farm buildings a long way away, perhaps five or six kilometres, it was difficult to judge, too much dead ground in between. Ahead was a low drystone wall. The farm boundary. They turned for home.

'Did you go back?'

'My mom had a fight with her family, I never worked it out, and my dad, he'd been writing to her about how he'd changed, how much money he had, that made her go back. So we went. It was all bullshit and we had no money to leave and she got sick again and she died.'

The landscape was spread before them – big fields,

walls, far below the wandering, bushy line of the stream, the land rising again, another hill, this one bare and rocky.

'I really loved her, you know,' said Niemand. 'She was such a brave person. She wouldn't give up ...'

'What about school?' said Jess. 'Didn't you go to school?'

'Always. I finished school, on the automatic pilot. I liked reading, that helped, the other kids read nothing, just comics, junk, and I finished and I joined the army.'

He felt a lightness. He wanted to go on talking about himself, but he knew he should stop.

'I've never really talked about it, I've never met anyone ... well, that's my little story.'

'And the army?' she said.

'I was happy there. I came from this life, nothing was certain, then I had ... you knew what was expected of you. They tried to kill you, run you to death, weed out people, but they looked after you. If you could take it, you had value. I got into the parachute battalion. Then I found out what hard was like, the stuff before, that was nothing.'

'It's about killing people, isn't it?' she said, letting go his hand. 'Being a soldier?'

How many people had he killed? He didn't want to look at her, looked away, at the valley, the upland, there was cover up there, a fold in the hill, going up, you would go for that, jinking, east to west, back again, use the patches of vegetation.

'Have you killed people?'

On the opposite slope, a long and bare slope running up to a wainy edge and a dull silver sky, halfway up a tree spat black specks, birds, a scattergun spit of birds, disturbed by something.

'Have you?'

'Yes,' said Niemand.

They walked in silence. Apart. He looked at her quickly, he knew that he had lost her, she was a dream, he had never had her.

'No pleasure in it,' he said. 'I'm not like that.'

She was far, far too good for anyone like him.

They walked for a distance. He could not look at her but he knew how far she was from him. To a tenth of a millimetre. Then she took his sleeve, his hand, she moved against him, rubbed her shoulder against him.

'No,' she said, 'no, I don't think you're like that.'

74

HAMBURG

BAADER WAS right, he should do it, quit. He had no right to stay in the job. He had sent Tilders to his death.

No, he hadn't. It was the work Tilders did that killed him. Baader was also right about that. Clients often left open authorisations, do whatever you have to. O'Malley had talked him into the job at the *Hauptbahnhof* and he had agreed because they needed the money. If someone had been hurt, killed that day, would he feel as he did now?

Perhaps. Probably.

The job was all he had. If he quit, what would he do? He was gun-shy, there was nothing he could do that he knew anything about.

Think about something else. Think about Special Deployment. Sudden Death. What did these names mean? Deployed to do what?

Kaskis had said: 'There but for the grace.'

Kaskis had been in Delta Force. He had gone from the Green Berets. Was Special Deployment a unit of Delta Force? Did he mean that he was lucky not to have ended up in Special Deployment?

Kaskis had said something else in Beirut, on the way from the airport. Anselm remembered he had thought it odd, but that was all he remembered.

He stared at a log recording emails sent by a Swiss

engineer from his home in Zurich to a company in Palo Alto.

Lourens in a hotel in Zurich with Serrano, snorting coke and meeting Croats. The Hotel Baur au Lac. Lourens burnt beyond recognition. His ex-employee dead in a car with a gun. What did Lourens have to do with all of this?

'That stuff from last night any use?' said Inskip from the doorway. 'The amazing disappearing soldiers and the drug czar?'

'Good stuff. You're early.'

'Can't stay away. I'm filling in for Kroger.'

'Any trace on the Lafarge file, bring it straight in. Don't send without having a word. And anything on Trilling and his Defense Department contracts.'

'As you wish, o masterful one.'

'Something else. In an idle minute, see if you can find a Dr Carl Lourens at the Hotel Baur au Lac in Zurich in 1992. Serrano should be there at the same time.'

'No minute shall be idle.'

The day went by. In mid-afternoon, Carla came in.

'Tilders,' she said. 'I'm sorry. I know you and Herr Baader were ...' She opened her hand on the stick for a moment.

'Thank you.'

'The English accounts of Dr Lourens, they were cleared yesterday. The money went to the Swiss account.'

'On whose authority?'

She shook her head, the swish of hair. 'There's no record, it must have been done on paper, personally.'

Mrs Johanna Lourens, probably. Had O'Malley got a court order on the properties?

It was almost dark when Alex rang. He had been on the point of ringing her several times.

'Are you going home on foot?'

'I am. Too little vertical exercise.'

She laughed. 'Does that mean too much horizontal? Would you like to stand up more?'

He had discovered that she was a laughing person, something her *Frau Doktor Koenig* persona tried to conceal.

'I suggest experimenting until a proper balance is found,' he said. 'I'm leaving in a few minutes.'

'Along the lake?'

'Yes.'

'I'll meet you. Look out for me. Don't let me pass in the dark.'

'No. I won't let you pass in the dark. Not if I can help it.'

75

HAMBURG

IT WAS cold outside but still. Just streaks of day left, lines of light running down the sky like the marks of raindrops down a dusty pane. His breath was mist as he did his rudimentary warm-up, his stretches.

The pain of the start, the complaints of the knees and ankles and hips, of ligaments and tendons and muscles. They did not want to do this any more.

Anselm got into his stride, no one on the path, a good time to be running, the day's traffic of walkers and runners and tourists and lovers and young mothers with high-speed babycarts and in-line skaters, all gone. Too cold, too dark.

You got used to running with a bag, passing it from hand to hand. It was heavier tonight, the bottle of Glen Morangie he'd bought from the supermarket in Hofweg. He reached the ferry landing, no sign now of what had happened, he shook the thought from his mind. Just run. Try to run at a decent pace. Don't slop along. Run. You used to be a runner. You could run.

It was dark now. Alex was somewhere ahead, coming towards him. Was she running? I'll meet you, she said.

A runner coming towards him.

Alex?

No. A thin man. They both grunted, runners' greeting grunts.

The path turned right, following the lake. There was a moment when he heard the sound of the city, when his brain for some reason registered the noise. A loud hum, a soup of a thousand sounds, like living in the innards of a machine.

Go away, he thought. Would she go away with me? Somewhere quiet. We could read. And make love. Then eat and read.

She would be coming towards him, not far away.

To kill Serrano and Kael, they would trigger a bomb in a ferry. Kill anyone near the pair. Tilders had been close. He had managed to get within two metres, a few seats. Wearing glasses and an invisible hearing aid.

Two figures ahead, coming towards him, walking, heads together.

He felt the familiar alarm, the signs of panic.

There was nowhere to go here, no sideways escape.

He slowed. Heart beating much faster than it should from running. Dry mouth, the tightness of skin.

Relax. The pair from the other night? He picked up his pace. No, it wasn't, just two people out for a walk. One medium, one small, they parted to let him through. He was close, he started to say *Guten Abend*.

The bigger one on the left had his right hand in his coat, high up, at his chest.

A few paces away. The smaller man smiled at Anselm, white teeth. Polite.

The bigger one's hand came out of his coat, something caught the light, a blade, Anselm saw it clearly, the man's arm was back.

He tried to get out of the way, go to the left, but the blade came across him, it felt as if an ice cube had been passed over his flesh. He looked down. The old tracksuit had opened across his chest, parted.

354

He had stopped. He had not intended to stop. He stood there, bag in hand.

The knife man had the blade upright. Just a sliver of steel.

A thin expressionless face. Moustache and eyebrows of thatch. The man was in no hurry.

He's cut me and now he's going to knife me, Anselm thought. The traditional way of doing things. Not a German tradition but this is the new Europe. He had no feeling of panic or fear. It had happened. He was glad. All the waiting was over.

The man said, '*Tschüs*.'

The cheerful chirping goodbye.

Anselm swung his bag at the man. It knocked the knife hand back, the full weight of the whisky bottle caught him in the face. He went backwards, his knees bending.

Anselm hit him with the bag again, heard the bottle meet bone, felt it, turned, saw at the edge his vision something in the smaller man's right hand – a pistol, a pistol with a silencer.

Awkwardly, off balance, Anselm swung the bag at him.

Missed.

The man had stepped back, out of range.

He raised the pistol.

Anselm heard nothing but he felt an impact against his chest.

The smell of something.

Whisky.

He had raised the bag without thinking and a bullet had hit the bottle of whisky.

'*Leg den Beutel fallen*,' said the man. He had both hands on the pistol now, but not sighting, holding it at his chest. Unhurried, confident.

Anselm threw the bag at him, it missed, went into the dark.

'*Stupide*,' said the man.

'Shit,' said Anselm and it came into his mind that it wasn't an awful thing to die here, in the open, beside the lake. He could have died in a stinking hole in Beirut.

'*Nochmals Tschüs*,' said the man.

He raised the pistol, sighted.

Nothing to do, thought Anselm.

The man grunted and pitched forward, came towards Anselm, falling, the pistol pointing down, someone behind him.

Alex. She'd hit the man with her left shoulder, run into him at full stride.

As the man fell, met the ground, Anselm, the calm still upon him, stamped on the hand holding the pistol. He wished he wasn't wearing running shoes.

The pistol came free.

Anselm picked it up and pointed it at the man's head. '*Bewegen Sie sich nicht*,' he said.

Alex was standing behind the man, winded, bent at the waist, holding her shoulder, looking up at Anselm.

'*O mein Gott*,' she said.

Anselm held the gun on the smaller man and walked backwards to the knife man, bent to look at him. He was breathing. There were blood bubbles at his nostrils, foamy blood bubbles.

'*Was is los?*' said Alex.

Anselm said to the gunman: '*Steh auf. Zieh die Hose aus*.'

'*Was?*'

'*Ziehen sie Sich aus oder ich töte sie*.'

The man had to take off his shoes to remove his trousers. He stood awkwardly, pale legs ending in short black socks.

'*Machen Sie schon,*' said Anselm, showing him the direction with the pistol. '*Bewegen Sie sich.*'

The man took off at a half-run.

'Come,' he said to Alex.

'What about him?' she said, pointing at the man on the ground.

'His friend will be back for him,' said Anselm. He took the pistol by the barrel and threw it into the lake.

They walked back towards the office. Anselm put his hand to his chest and it came away black with blood.

He was beginning to feel nausea rise.

She took his arm and they walked back along the lake shore towards the cheerful lights.

'Where'd you learn to knock someone like that?' he said.

'Gridiron. I played in the States.'

'We didn't pass in the dark,' he said.

She leaned towards him and touched the side of his face with her lips.

'No,' she said. 'But it was close.'

76

LONDON

CAROLINE FOUND the note on her desk:

See me soonest. Halligan.

End of the road. Goodbye Fleet Street, hello Leeds.

Family, McClatchie once said, you always start with the family. But Jess Thomas didn't have any family.

The architect in Singapore had said something.

She goes back a long way with Natalie, with the family, I think.

Natalie Zampatti had a family.

She rang Sandra Fox at Craig, Zampatti.

'Nat's got a sister somewhere, a doctor,' said Fox. 'Hang on I'll ask the secretary from whom no secrets are hidden.'

Caroline waited. The longest possible shot. The most fucking impossible shot.

'There? Try St Martin's Hospital. Apparently sister and husband are both doctors. Her sister's name's Virginia.'

It took a long time and she couldn't get hold of Virginia but she got the name of her mother. Finally she was speaking to Mrs Amanda Zampatti in Cardiff, a thin voice, uncertain.

Caroline gave her the Detective Sergeant Moody of Battersea police line.

'Oh my God, she's all right is she? Poor girl, she's got no one, you know.'

'We'd like to be sure. There's no actual cause for alarm at the moment. But we thought she might have gone somewhere to get away from everything.'

'Well, Virginia and David have a place, a farm sort of place. She's been there, I know that, Ginnie told me on the phone.'

'And where's that?'

'To tell you truth, I don't know. They wanted to take me but really I can't be ...'

'No idea where it is?'

'Well, Wales, but that's not much use is it? Up north, I think. She said it was away from anything, no phone or telly or anything. I can't think why you'd want to have a place ...'

'Thank you, Mrs Zampatti. I'll get back to you if we find out anything.'

Caroline slumped again. There was no quick way to do this.

77

HAMBURG

BAADER'S DOCTOR was in Mittelweg, a small, bald man, impassive. He looked at the wound under Anselm's pectorals and made clucking noises.

'*Das ist nicht übel*,' he said. '*Da können Sie von Glück reden.*'

Light-headed, Anselm watched as he cleaned the long cut, sprayed it with anaesthetic and stitched it up with the quick movements of a tailor. He wound a bandage around Anselm's body.

'Don't get it wet for forty-eight hours,' he said. 'Then change the bandage every day. Any sign of infection, come and see me straight away. Otherwise, in a week. Tell the receptionist you are Herr Baader's associate.'

He went to a cupboard and came back with two packets of tablets. 'This one twice a day. That's important. The others are for pain. If you have pain.'

Baader was waiting, sitting in an uncomfortable chair reading a fashion magazine. They walked to the car, drove in silence for a while.

'This is deep shit,' said Baader. 'Dieter says we've been opened. He doesn't know for how long.'

Anselm tried to focus on the meaning of this. 'What can they know?' he said.

'Where we go, what we want. Everything. Everything we know.'

'Won't make much sense.'

Baader turned into Schone Aussicht. 'In the end,' he said, 'everything makes sense if you've got enough of it.'

Not life, thought Anselm, not life. 'Who would they be?' he said

For a second, the sad wolf face looked at him. 'People who are offended,' Baader said. 'People who don't mind blowing up a ferry full of people to kill two men. The people who want to kill you.'

Baader turned into the driveway, parked outside the annexe. He put his head back against the rest, looked at the roof, said, 'I think you should go away for a while. Tonight. Just go. Fat Otto will get you out of here, we can switch transport a few times. Do a few things like that. Go to Italy. Rome. I'll give you an address, you can collect cash there.'

Anselm didn't argue. He felt sick, weak, tingling in his veins, the taste in his mouth he remembered from Beirut.

He was part of someone's problem now. Whatever the problem was and whoever the people who had it were. He had joined Lourens and his ex-employee, joined Serrano and Kael and Bruynzeel. Yes. And Kaskis and Diab and all the dead soldiers from Special Deployment. They had been a problem for someone and they had been killed for it. Tilders, he had been collateral damage. They hadn't cared whether they killed him or not.

And he was a target now. Two men sent to kill him. They would have killed Alex too, killed anyone who happened to be there, also collateral damage.

They would come for him again. Tonight. Tomorrow. He couldn't go home. He couldn't go anywhere.

At the annexe entrance, Baader rang the bell for Wolfgang to let them in. They were in Baader's office, both of them standing, when Inskip came to the door.

'Could I have a word?' he said to Anselm.

They went to Inskip's workstation. Inskip pointed at a screen.

'The Lafarge file. The woman, Thomas, she's used a card. Twice in the same place.'

'Where's that place?' Constantine Niemand and Jess Thomas. The film, Eleven Seventy.

'Some godforsaken Welsh hamlet.'

He needed to tell Caroline Wishart.

'There's something else,' said Inskip. He pressed a button on one of the recorders. A monitor came alive, a man in a military overcoat walking across tarmac. He wasn't smiling for the cameras.

The voiceover said:

General David Carbone, commander in chief of US Special Operations Command today denied the existence of a special unit of the US Special Forces' super-secret Delta Force called Sudden Death.

A woman was on screen, long grey hair, haggard, talking soundlessly, wiping her eyes with a tissue.

The voiceover said:

The mother of an ex-Delta Force soldier, Benjamin Galuska, found dead yesterday in Montana, has alleged that her son was haunted by things the Sudden Death unit had done but would never have taken his own life.

Soundbite from the woman:

Ben said they'd kill him, he said they'd killed the others. But we didn't believe him.

Cut to the man in the overcoat. He was shaking his head.

I'd like to say that I share Mrs Galuska's grief over the death of her son and I put out my hand to her. And I'd like to say that Benjamin Galuska served his country with courage and honour and pride. But I must also state categorically that the unit she speaks of did not and does not exist. Why Staff Sergeant Galuska invented this story we will never know. He seems to have been a troubled person. God rest his soul. Thank you.

'Galuska's one of the two I couldn't find,' said Inskip. 'Are we dealing with supernatural coincidence or what?'

'What,' said Anselm. 'Don't tell Lafarge anything. Even if they ask.'

He went to his office and rang Caroline Wishart's number. She picked up on the first ring.

'John Anselm. I've got something on Jessica Thomas.'

He heard her breathe in. 'Yes?'

He spelled out the name of the place, the business.

Breathe out, a sigh.

'Any use?'

'Yes. I think I know where she is.'

Anselm heard himself sigh in return. 'Listen,' he said. 'I'll come to England tonight. We might make sense of this if we find them.'

He went back to Baader's office and told him. Baader looked at him for a long time, a finger tracing the line of his upper lip.

'What the hell,' he said. 'Nothing to lose. Kill you here, kill you there. Not a fucking thing to lose.'

Anselm rang Alex.

'I wasn't pleased at being got off the premises as fast as possible,' she said. 'I have a small interest in whether you live or die.'

'He meant well. I have to go away for a day or two.'

'You're not going to tell me?'

'No. Would you like to go away for a while when I get back?'

'To do what?'

'Exercise in the morning, philosophise in the afternoon.'

'Leaving the nights free for ...?'

'Yes, that's what I thought.'

'I need to think about it. I've been behaving impulsively. It's a dangerous time.'

'I'm a dangerous man.'

'Much more than I thought. The answer is yes, call me.'

'I'll call you.'

'Be careful. Please.'

Baader made the arrangements. Anselm rang Caroline again. An hour later, tired, chest hurting, he walked across the tarmac at Fühlsbuttel to the executive jet.

78

WALES

NIEMAND SAT against the stone building in the last light, feeling the wall's warmth. He heard the car change gear to climb the hill, and he took the machine pistol and ran for the barn. He climbed the ladder into the loft and stood beside the dormer window looking down the hill at the twisting road. A hawk in the darkening sky rose and fell, planed sideways, watching for any small movement below.

The car came into view at the small stone bridge. It was the dark-green Audi. Jess coming back.

The gate was open. She drove up past the house and into the barn and he waited until she was out of the car and he was sure she was alone, no one crouching in the back, before he spoke.

She looked up, alarmed, then she smiled, the smile that changed her face. He climbed down and went to her and kissed her, took her head in his hands, ate her mouth, felt her hands on his back, on his buttocks, pressing him into her, pulling him.

When their mouths came apart, she said, thickly, 'Christ, is this allowed before lunch?'

They got as far as the sitting room. He had made a fire, the room was warm, and they fell on the sofa. He was underneath. They kissed, rolled, changed places. He found the button, the zip. She pulled her jeans off, he undid his button, she pulled the zip, dragged the jeans down, they lay and rubbed skin, making throat and nose sounds. She moved and sat on him, she was weightless. She put her right hand behind her and took him, held him, squeezed him, raised herself and came down on him. In that moment, he could have died of pleasure, he wanted to be as deep in her as was humanly impossible. She pulled her heavy jumper off, threw it away, the spencer gone too, ripped off, discarded. His hands went under her bra and it loosened, he had her breasts in his hands, the inexpressibly lovely weight and feel, and his face was on them, rubbing, a nipple in his lips, a small nipple, sucking it, the other one, back and forth between them. She was riding him, her head back, making sounds, a hand behind his head, a hand behind her scratching him, short nails scratching him.

The fire's light lay yellow and gentle and unstable on the things in the room, the room was smaller now, shrunk to the reach of the flames.

79

LONDON

PALMER SAT behind the desk, hands together, fingers steepled.

'Come in,' he said.

The man came in, looked at Palmer and Charlie Price and Martie and Carrick, looked around with an air of distaste, like a first class traveller allocated a seat in economy by mistake.

'Couldn't we have done this another way?' he said. 'I'm not ecstatic about coming here.'

'I don't have time for the cloak-and-dagger,' said Palmer. 'And I wanted to impress on you this business has been fucked up to high hell. There's shit flying, there's no error margin left.'

'You may consider me impressed,' said the man. His eyes panned over the three other men. 'The committee may also consider me impressed.'

Palmer thought he would like to kick the man's arsehole north of his eyebrows. He said, 'There are possible complications.'

'Life's a vale of possible complications.'

Palmer looked at his reflection in the glass door behind the man. He could just make out the furrows on his forehead and the deep folds flanking his mouth. When the kick urge had subsided, he told him about the problem.

'Well,' said the man, 'that's a pity. And it'll make the laundry work troublesome. Where are we talking about?'

'Right here,' said Carrick.

He had the maps out on the table. 'It's difficult country,' he said. 'I'll talk you through the ...'

'Just point, darling,' said the man. 'I was reading maps when you were doing wee-wees and poo-poos.'

80

WALES

HE WAS IN the kitchen, filling the kettle. Jess came up behind him and ran a hand up the back of his head, from nape to crown. He shivered like a puppy.

'I meant to say,' she said, 'before you grabbed me and did those awful things to me, Dai at the garage says he'll ring if anyone asks the way here. I gave him my cell-phone number.'

'You know him?'

'From the other times I've been here. Four slices be enough?'

He loved her lilting voice. He loved everything about her.

Nothing in his life had prepared him for her. He could not believe that she had happened to him. He knew about luck. He had survived things by luck and chance and fate, if there were such things, Greeks seemed to think so.

He turned and grabbed her by the hips and kissed her.

It went on for a time, it could go on forever. They parted and she drew the back of her right hand across her lips.

'Good kisser. I've been meaning to ask, what does your name mean? Does it have a meaning?'

'It means no one.'

'No one?'

'No one, nobody.'

She raised her right hand and drew her fingers across his mouth.

'Good mouth,' she said. 'You have a very good mouth. Good for many things. You'll never be no one to me. Well, never's a long time. Let me work now. We have a long afternoon ahead. And then there's the night.'

She went to the bench top beside the stove. She was spreading bread when she said: 'Dai at the garage says the bank thinks my card's been stolen.'

Niemand thought the room seemed dimmer, the light through the small windows seemed to have faded.

'Why?' he said.

'What?'

'Why would the bank think that?'

'Don't know.'

'When did you use it?'

'When I filled up. Then I went to the shop and when I was coming out Dai came over and said the bank rang and asked if he knew the person, the cardholder. He said yes, so they said that was fine.'

Niemand went to her, stood behind her, put his hands on her shoulders.

He felt no alarm, no urgency, only a terrible certainty of what his stupidity had wrought and a terrible sadness.

'Jess,' he said, 'you have to go now, soon. Get in the car and go.'

She turned, mouth open. 'Why?'

'They've found us. Your card. They'll be on the way here now.'

She closed her eyes. 'What about you?'

'I'll try to do a deal with them.'

'Then I'll stay.'

Niemand put fingers to her lips. 'No. I can't take that chance. I'll tell you what to do and when it's over, I'll come to you.'

She put her right hand under his chin, pushed his head back.

'I'm in love with you,' she said. Her eyes were closed. 'That's pretty stupid, isn't it?'

His chest was full, his throat was full. He found it hard to speak. He kissed her closed eyes, so soft, so silky, he could have died in the moment, been spared the rest.

'We'll go to Crete,' he said. 'You'll like it.'

81

WALES

WHEN THE old Morris Countryman was out of sight, Niemand reversed the Audi out and parked it in plain sight. He had to assume that there was time, that they were not already there, watching the farmhouse, waiting for dark.

He went back into the barn and took a reel of nylon fishing line off its peg under the rods. He closed the barn doors and went inside the house, put on his own clothes. There was a dark-blue jersey in the dressing table drawer and he put that on. He went to the fireplace and reached in for soot, rubbed it on his face, his throat, his neck, his ears, on his eyelids, into his hair.

He left his hands clean. That would be the last thing.

The gun cupboard Jess had shown him was in the smallest bedroom. He unlocked it and took out the shotgun, a double-barrelled Brno, and the old .303, a Lee Enfield bolt-action with a ten-round magazine. It would have been better to have the machine-pistol he had taken from the man on the roof but Jess needed a weapon in case they were lying in wait along the narrow road. There was an unopened box of shotgun cartridges and five clips of .303 rounds. He filled the magazine, pressing in the cold brass-jacketed shells with a thumb. The other clips he put in his jacket pockets.

The sitting-room furniture had to be rearranged, curtains drawn. After that, he rubbed soap on the barrel of the .303. He found the small sewing-machine screw-driver in the kitchen drawer. He sat at the kitchen table and worked on the shotgun, testing until both triggers were as he wanted them to be.

The light was going fast. He pumped a lamp and lit it, took it into the sitting room, tried several resting places for it until the shadows were right. Then he did the delicate work, not hurrying.

It was dark when he finished. He went to the bedroom and put on the bulletproof apron, adjusted it until it was comfortable. Second-last thing: pocket the packet of nuts and raisins Jess had bought.

Last thing: he went to the fireplace again and blackened his hands, blackened his wrists and forearms. He rubbed soot into the soap on the .303 barrel

Then he put on the black rolled-up balaclava, took the old .303 and went out the back door.

He went around the barn and up the cold slope into the dark, dark conifer wood. At the place he had chosen earlier, he sat, leaned against the tree, listened to the sounds of the night.

It was a pity it had to end here, like this. But you couldn't keep running away. He thought fleetingly about running away from the boys' home to the railway yards, about the blood, dried black and crusted, that was still on his filthy legs and buttocks and back when the police took him home.

No more running. He had told Jess to wait until morning, then take the film and Shawn's documents to a television station. He should have done that after he was shot.

No point in regret.

He tried not to think about Jess, not to think about anything but to go into the empty trance of waiting and listening.

82

HAMBURG–ENGLAND

THE ONLY passenger in an eight-seater jet, sitting in a leather chair in the hushed and hissing projectile.

The co-pilot came out, young, short dark hair, released the crackling, buzzing sounds of the cockpit.

'Clear night,' he said. 'That's Gronigen below us. We'll be over the North Sea in a minute. Can I get you anything, sir?'

Anselm shook his head and the man went back.

Sliding on the night towards England. With luck, towards Constantine Niemand and his film. What did it show that made it so sought after? Was it the end of the long line that Caroline Wishart had drawn from Kaskis's reference to a village in Angola?

Anselm closed his eyes. The only sound in the capsule was a gentle sibilance, a steady watery murmur. His mind drifted on the current.

Kill you here, kill you there. Not a fucking thing to lose.

The words of Baader. He was right. It was better to die trying to find out what these people had done than to die ignorant.

The firm's layers of disguise penetrated, their mosaic of inquiries known to someone, laid out somewhere, piece by piece, until the picture appeared. What else had Baader said?

In the end, everything makes sense. You just need enough of it.

He fell asleep and then the co-pilot was saying, 'Starting our descent, sir, would you mind fastening your belt?'

83

WALES

NIEMAND HEARD the sound.

A small sound, a tap.

Close behind him, on the path, a foot had touched something. Perhaps knocked one solid pine cone into another, the path was littered with fallen cones.

Silence.

Niemand rose against the broad tree trunk, inch by inch, not touching it, breathed as shallowly as possible, regularly, just enough oxygen to sustain life.

A breath, a quiet expulsion of air, a hiss.

Someone was almost close enough to touch him. He didn't move his head, kept it back, didn't look sideways. The yellow night glasses might glint, catch some light from a star a trillion miles away and betray him.

The figure was beside him, an arm's length away. He held his breath.

Passing him, moving slowly.

A figure as black as he was, bent forward.

Let him be alone.

Niemand didn't breathe, bent a little at the knees.

He pushed off, swung the Kevlar knife in his right hand. Around and down.

There was an instant when the man's head was turning, disturbed, then the narrow blade entered the side of his throat above the collarbone, penetrated downwards.

The man made a hawking noise, not loud, and Niemand pulled him to earth, dropped him softly, held the knife in him, moved it.

Waited until he was sure.

Then he took the man's weapon out of his left hand, ran his fingers over it. Heckler & Koch machine pistol, MP5K, three-round burst trigger group, he knew the weapon. He wouldn't be needing the old .303. He ran his hands over the man's clothing, felt his footwear.

How many would there be?

Not too many. This man was a soldier. By his weapon and his clothing and his ankle-holster and his knife and his silky night-fighting boots. That was good. Trained to kill, he had been killed. No hard feelings. Soldiers took their chances with death.

How many? Soldiers, trained killers, perhaps four or five, no more. Two from the back, two from the sides, the doorkeeper at the front. One front door, one doorkeeper.

Niemand moved forward, the dead man's black-bladed knife in his mouth, machine-pistol in hand. They would not be able to pick him from the dead man. Just a black figure carrying a weapon coming from where they expected someone to come.

He waited at the forest's dark edge, looking back and forth. A wind from the north now, not much, just enough to disturb the scrubby trees on the slope.

There.

A shadow moved. On his right.

Again.

Keeping low, hugging the shadow of the conifers, not too concerned about being seen from the house, the big barn blocking the line of sight.

Niemand looked to his left. Another one should come from there, around the corner of the trees.

He didn't. He came around the stock pen, near the rough path they had taken on their walk. Just his shoulder and his head in view. He had come up from the stream, crawled up, lots of cover, dead ground.

That was three. Three and the doorkeeper. They were confident, they knew they were good. Just two to take out and one of them a woman.

He waited. He couldn't move first.

The other men weren't moving, frozen. Were they waiting for him?

Did I kill the leader? Am I the leader now? Are they waiting for my signal?

Shit.

No. The man on his left came out from behind the stock pen and ran for the side of the barn.

The shadow on the right was moving too, coming down the slope, heading fast for the other side of the barn.

Niemand stepped out of the trees, moved down the slope in a crouch, reached the wall. The man on the right was around the corner. He would be waiting for him now.

He put the H&K in his left hand, took the knife out of his teeth.

He went around the corner fast, bent low.

The man was waiting at the corner, back to the wall, machine-pistol up, at head height.

He turned his head, looked past his upraised arm at Niemand.

He was wearing sleek night-vision goggles.

Oh Jesus, he can see me, he can see a man in a black leather jacket.

The man's weapon was coming down.

Niemand fired the pistol one-handed, fired two bursts at the middle of the body, bullets hit the brick wall, screeched, the man's knees went, he sat down, he didn't get off a shot.

Niemand ran past him, didn't stop at the corner, went around it, got halfway along the barn, at the doors.

The other one appeared, night-vision goggles too, Niemand was running straight for him, the man hesitated for a moment, uncertain, he would have recognised the sound of the H&K.

Niemand shot him at point-blank range, in the chest, a three-round burst, gave him the double tap, the man went backwards and sideways, not dramatically, met the barn and slid.

Two bangs in the house, an instant apart.

The shotgun tripwire.

Someone in the house, the doorkeeper had left his position, come through the front door, into the sitting room.

Four down, that would be it.

Make sure. If I come from the back, he'll think I'm one of them.

Niemand ran for the back door, wrenched it open, ran through the room, through the sitting room door in a crouch, the dim lamplight, a figure on the floor ...

Little pops of flame, he didn't hear the sound, he was punched in the chest, more than once, it was hard to tell, so quick, he stopped in his tracks.

Niemand emptied the magazine into the man on the floor, firing bursts as he went to his knees.

Silence.

No pain.

Not gut-shot anyway, the BB. Good thing I found that in the car. And the knife. That's something positive.

He fell over sideways, felt his head hit the stone floor. As if it belonged to someone else.

Breathing was a problem. Something stuck in his throat.

Funny place to die. Up here in English mountains. Hated the English, the old man. Dumb to take on four of them. Still. Know they've been in a fight. Jess. So lovely. So good.

84

WALES

THE FARM gate was open and they drove up the steep drive and turned left, stopped in front of the low stone farmhouse. In the lights, they could see the front door – open, not fully open, ajar.

'Well,' said Caroline. 'It's the place. Here's hoping.'

'Yes. There's a light on.' They sat for a moment.

'Cold to have the front door open,' said Anselm.

'Yes.' She shivered. Her clothes made a sound, her chin against the fabric of her coat.

'Well,' he said. 'Since we're here.'

He got out. Black night, cold wind whining in trees somewhere nearby. They were high here, clean air, it felt like the Balkans.

He went to the front door, reached across the threshold, held the doorknob and knocked.

Nothing. Not a sound.

'Mr Niemand,' he said loudly.

Nothing.

'Jessica.' Louder.

Nothing. Just the wind, the keening wind.

He felt the hair on his neck. He looked around. He could see Caroline in the car, her outline. His chest hurt.

She saw him looking at her and got out, came across the gravel, a tall woman, not unhandsome.

He tried again.

'Mr Niemand. Constantine.'

Nothing.

He pushed open the door and went in. A small hallway, coats and hats. The light was coming from a door to the left.

A smell of something. Not quite of burning, something more acrid. He looked around. Caroline was biting her lower lip.

'I don't know about this,' she said quietly.

Anselm thought he would like to turn and leave, drive down the hill, along the winding road, through the cluster of buildings, get back to the highway.

Too late for that. It occurred to him that he had no panic symptoms. He was uneasy, he was close to fearful, but he was not showing the symptoms.

Caused by fear and violence, cured by the same.

Hair of the dog.

He went through the door, saw the legs first.

A figure in black, absolutely dull black, no head. No, a hood on his head, face down, his black hands around a black weapon, a machine-pistol.

In the middle of the room, a shotgun tied to a chair was pointing at him. Anselm was too shocked to move.

Caroline made a noise, a deep, sobbing intake of breath.

On the other side of the room lay another figure in dark clothing, a man lying on his side, blood run from him over the stone floor to the edge of the carpet, soaked up by the carpet, blotted, blackish blood.

The man made a sound like a hiccup. Again.

Anselm did not think, he went to the man, pulled his poloneck down, put an index finger against his throat, in the collarbone cavity. The faintest pulse.

'He's alive,' he said. 'We'd better do something.'

For want of anything better to do, he took off the man's rolled-up balaclava.

'It's him,' said Caroline in a voice without timbre. 'It's Mackie. Niemand.'

'And a terrible fucking nuisance the man is too,' said O'Malley from the doorway.

85

WALES

HE CAME into the dim room, bent over and picked up the machine-pistol lying near Niemand's head.

Anselm stood up. 'Jesus, Michael,' he said. 'What the fuck is this? What exactly the fuck is this?'

O'Malley had the magazine out, looking into it. He dropped it on the floor and took another one out of his coat pocket. It made a precise snick as it locked in.

'What the fuck is this, John?' echoed O'Malley, looking around the room like a real estate agent being asked to sell something nasty. 'Why do rich people crave this sort of thing? A croft in the Welsh wilderness, wind never stops howling, natives slathered in sheepshit and woad, incomprehensible tongue, nasty secessionist tendencies.'

O'Malley walked over to the shotgun tied to the chair, ran a hand over the trigger guard, pulled at something. It caught the lamplight and Anselm saw that it was nylon fishing line that ran to the leg of an armchair.

'A booby trap so cheap, so primitive, so old. And here lies dead of it a killer with the most expensive and sophisticated training the modern world can provide.'

He tested the triggers with a black-gloved finger. 'Ah,' he said. 'Knew how to make this work, did your Mr Niemand. Breathe hárd on the buggers and bang.'

'Michael, what?' said Anselm. 'Tell me. It's late, I'm

tired and sober and I've got a knife wound nine inches long. What?'

O'Malley had the Heckler & Koch in his left hand. He transferred it to his right.

'I'm sorry about that,' he said. 'Sorry about this too.' He ran a hand over his curly head. 'Truly, I wish it were another way.'

It came to Anselm, as it had come to him in Beirut, that something had ended, something was over and gone. A still moment, the highest point of the pendulum's swing, the end of momentum, the dead point.

'Kaskis,' he said.

O'Malley was looking at Caroline. She was frozen, hands at her sides, holding herself like a Guardsman on parade, waiting for the Queen.

'I saved you, John,' said O'Malley. 'You and Riccardi. They wanted to kill all three of you, I talked them out of it. I said it wasn't necessary, you knew nothing, the idiot Riccardi less. I've given you eight good years. Well, eight years. Think of it that way. And I told you you weren't a journalist any more. I tried to warn you off.'

Anselm thought that he had never seen this look on O'Malley's face. His handsome poet's face was sad. He was going to kill both of them and he was sad that he had to do it.

O'Malley raised the weapon, held it on its side, weighed it in his hand, bounced it.

'This is awkward,' he said. 'I would really rather not. But. *Necessitas non habet legum.* Know the expression, boyo?'

Anselm nodded. He felt nothing. No panic this time.

'Yes, well ...' O'Malley raised the weapon and pointed it at Caroline.

'Sorry, darling,' he said. 'But think what you did to that poor old bugger Brechan on behalf of MI5.'

Grunts, not loud, several quick grunts.

O'Malley's face below the high cheekbone blew apart, his face seemed to break in two, divide, an aerosol spray of red in the air around his head, a piece of scarlet veil floating.

They stood.

The woman came in, went to Niemand, put her head down to his head, seemed to kiss him.

She jerked her head up.

'He's alive,' she said. 'For fuck's sake do something.'

Anselm looked at Caroline. She was grey-white, the colour of cemetery gravel. She shook her head and put her hand in a coat pocket and took out a cellphone.

'Right,' she said. 'Right.'

And then Caroline, holding the tiny device towards the light to see the keys, she moved her head, her long hair moved, she looked up and said to Jess in her upper-class voice:

'I don't suppose, I don't suppose you know where the film is?'

86

HAMBURG

IN THE BLUE underwater gloom of the workroom, Anselm and Baader and Inskip and Carla watched the big monitor.

The television anchor was too old to pull her hair back like a twelve-year-old Russian gymnast. She tested her lips swiftly. They worked. Collagen and cocaine did terrible things to lips.

All front teeth showing, she went through the preamble. Then she said:

We warn that the film contains images of violence that will shock. Please ensure that children are not watching.

The aerial view of wooded sub-tropical country, late in the day.

Angola, 1983. The oil-rich African country is in the grip of a long-running civil war in which the United States has intervened, spending millions of dollars in an attempt to counter Russian influence. This film was taken from a helicopter. Analysts say from the co-pilot's seat. They believe the film was unauthorised and the person filming took care not to be seen.

A village burning, thatched huts burning, several dozen huts, cultivated fields around them marked by sticks.

This nameless village is in northern Angola. There is no evidence of military activity.

On the ground now, another helicopter in view, no markings visible.

The filming is through the open door of the helicopter. Notice the dark edge to the right. The other helicopter is a Puma of a type used by the South African Defence Force.

Now a long panning shot, bodies everywhere, dozens and dozens of bodies. An enlarged still of a group of bodies.

These people have been overcome by something. There are signs of vomiting, stomach cramps and diarrhoea.

Another enlarged still. At least a dozen people lying near a crude water trough. Black people in ragged clothes, mostly women and children, a baby. Some have their hands held to their faces, some are face down on the packed dirt.

Medical experts say the signs of poisoning are even more apparent here. They are consistent with those produced by the biological poison ricin, which is made from a toxic protein found in castor oil seed.

Motion again, white men in combat gear carrying automatic weapons, standing around, six of them, relaxed, weapons cradled.

The frame held still, enlarged.

These men are American soldiers, part of a super-secret unit called Special Deployment, also known as Sudden Death. They were drawn from Special Forces Operational Detachment Delta Airborne stationed at Fort Bragg, North Carolina. Although they wear no insignia, they are armed with the Heckler & Koch MP5K, first issued in 1977. The man on the left carries a Mossberg Cruiser 500 shotgun, and Beretta 9mm handguns are visible on three of them. Their boots are Special Forces tropical issue.

We also know the names of four of these soldiers.

Circles around four heads.

Enlargements.

From the left, Maurice Tennant Gressor, Zoltan James Kaldor, Wayne Arthur Fitzgerald, and Joseph Elias Diab. These men are all dead, in circumstances that can only be called suspicious. It is thought that all except two of the Special Deployment members in this shot are dead.

The film moving again, two men in coveralls talking to a tall soldier, the only one without headgear, his back to the camera. The camera zooms in on the group, the soldier is talking to one of the civilians, a man with a moustache.

Freeze.

Enlargement.

This man is Dr Carl Wepener Lourens, then head of a South African company called TechPharma Global, an importer of chemicals. Lourens moved in white South Africa's highest military and political circles and travelled the world, frequently visiting Britain, the United States and Israel. His death in a fire at his company's premises outside Pretoria was reported recently. He was under investigation for currency and other offences committed under the apartheid regime.

Dr Lourens is also linked with an Israeli company called Ashken, said to be an Israeli military front engaged in defence research.

The film moving again. Lourens is speaking to the person next to him, a short man, balding, a mole on his cheek. The man shakes his head, gestures, palms upward.

Freeze. Enlargement.

This man is Donald Trilling, president of Pharmentis Corporation, fourth largest US pharmaceutical company, convenor of Republicans at Work. He is often described as one of the most influential men in America.

When this film was taken, Trilling, a Vietnam veteran, was head of Trilling Research Associates of Alexandria, Virginia. Trilling Research was taken over by Pharmentis Corporation in 1988 and Trilling became head of Pharmentis. In 1989, a Congressional hearing was told that Trilling Research received US Defense Department contracts worth more than $60 million between 1976 and 1984. The details remain classified. These contracts are now believed to have been for research into chemical weapons, including one called Eleven Seventy, apparently a ricin-like poison.

It is now clear that millions of dollars found their way from the US Defense Department to Trilling Research and then to bank accounts linked to Dr Carl Lourens.

They are thought to be payment for the manufacture and testing of chemical weapons developed by Trilling.

The film moving again. The soldier is turning towards the camera when the picture goes dark.

Here film analysts think that the cameraman is trying to avoid being seen.

When the film resumes, the tall soldier is standing at the bodies lying around the water trough. He moves a man's head with his boot.

The man on the ground is alive.

The man moves his arm, his fingers move. The soldier shoots him in the head from a few inches, gestures with his left hand, a summoning gesture.

The soldier takes off his dark glasses, wipes his eyes with the knuckle of his index finger. His face is seen clearly.

Freeze.

Enlargement.

This is the Special Forces Delta Force officer in command of Special Deployment on this mission.

A still photograph of five smiling young soldiers in dress uniform. One head is circled.

This is the same young soldier photographed on graduation day with other members of his West Point class.

A montage, the soldier in the film side by side with the smiling West Point graduate.

This young American soldier is Michael Patrick Denoon, later a four-star general and, until three days ago, US Defense Secretary and aspirant presidential candidate.

Michael Denoon resigned as Defense Secretary of State shortly after being shown parts of this program. He will not be seeking the Republican nomination.

The Angolan film running again, Denoon and the soldiers going around shooting people where they lie, shooting them in the head – men, women, children, a baby.

The Angolan village is believed to have been targeted by mistake. Fifteen kilometres away was an encampment housing hundreds of military personnel. It is believed that no one in the village survived, dying either from the chemical weapon used or executed by the men of Sudden Death. The bodies are thought to have been loaded onto C-47 transport aircraft by the unit and dropped at sea off the South-West African coast.

There is today no trace of the nameless village. Not a sign that people, families, lived there. The victims have no monument. Documents we have seen place the blame for this terrible experiment, this atrocity, squarely with the military in the United States, South Africa and Israel.

The program went on, putting together the pieces. Kaskis, Diab, Bruynzeel, Kael, Serrano, Shawn, all had their moments.

'No mention of O'Malley,' said Baader. 'Why am I not surprised?'

In the last minutes of the television special, they watched Caroline Wishart, tall and elegant in chinos and a leather jacket. Ringing a bell in a white wall beside a wooden gate. No one comes but the camera peers over the wall and, for a moment, captures a picture of a tall, grey-haired man with a moustache standing by a swimming pool and shouting something, angry.

Then Caroline:

This millionaire's villa in Madeira is owned by a company called Claradine. Its directors are two Swiss lawyers. The man in the picture calls himself Jürgen Kleeberg. His real name is Dr Carl Lourens and he has been staying in this luxury home since shortly after his death in a fire was reported in South Africa.

'I take it that's the Jürgen Kleeberg once a guest at the Hotel Baur au Lac, Zurich,' said Inskip.

'That is the Jürgen,' said Anselm.

The program finished. The credits described Caroline Wishart as the chief investigative reporter of her newspaper.

'Well, you'll probably live,' said Baader. 'For a while.'

He left the room.

'Sound of polite cough,' said Inskip. 'What did that mean?'

'He thinks I may see Christmas,' said Anselm.

'I wasn't told this job was life-threatening.'

'Only for the living,' said Carla. 'You have nothing to fear.'

87

BIRMINGHAM

HE WAS dreaming about walking down a mountain path. There was someone ahead of him, talking to him in Greek, a boy, his cousin Dimi. And then Dimi started speaking in Afrikaans. He stopped and turned, and it wasn't Dimi. It was his father, the lined brown adult face on a boy's body. The sight frightened Niemand, brought him awake. He opened his eyes, blinked, his vision blurred.

For a moment, he was without memory. Then he saw the tubes in his arms and chest, tubes taped down, realised. Joy at being alive flooded him until he thought of Jess. He had sent her away, hoping that they were not watching the farmhouse, not waiting beside the lane. But even if she had got away from the farm, they would have found her. They could find anyone.

He closed his eyes and tears welled behind the lids, broke through the lashes, ran down his face, down his neck.

'You're crying,' said the voice, the lilting voice. He could not believe he was hearing it. He opened his wet eyes and she was there, leaning over him, inches from him, and then she was kissing his eyes, kissing his tears, he felt her lips and he hoped he was not dreaming. Life could not be that cruel.

'Crete,' said Jess. 'I'm going to take you to Crete. Get you well.'

'Yes,' said Niemand. 'I love you. You can take me to Crete.'

88

HAMBURG

FRÄULEIN EINSPENNER'S last rites were at the crematorium in Billstedt. Anselm, four elderly women, and a middle-aged man were the only mourners. He knew one of them, Fräulein Einspenner's neighbour, Frau Ebeling.

Afterwards, she came up to him and they shook hands. She was carrying a parcel wrapped in brown paper.

'It was very peaceful,' she said. She had a round face, curiously unlined.

'I'm glad,' said Anselm.

'She went to the doctor and in the waiting room, she was sitting there, and she closed her eyes and she died. They didn't notice for a while. Her heart.'

Anselm nodded.

'It was as if she didn't expect to come home again. Everything was packed. Her clothes, everything.'

Anselm didn't know what to say.

'She was so fond of you,' said Frau Ebeling, putting her head to one side and studying him as if to find the reason.

'I was very fond of her,' said Anselm. 'I loved her.'

'Yes. Your whole family was very dear to her. She spoke often of them. Frau Pauline and Herr Lucas. Frau Anne and Herr Gunther and Herr Stefan and Fräulein Elizabeth and Herr Oskar. I know all the names, I heard them so often.'

'Did she ever speak of Moritz?'

'Moritz? No, not that I can recall.' She held out the package. 'This has your name on it. Perhaps she was going to give it to you when you visited again.'

Herr John Anselm was written on the top in a fine crabby hand, big letters.

It was almost dark when he got back to the office. He parked outside the annexe. Cold but no wind, it was going to be a clear night.

In his office, he unwrapped the parcel. A cardboard box, the size of two shoeboxes. It held five framed photographs of different sizes, unframed photographs, a dozen or more, old letters tied with a blue ribbon.

The face jumped out of all the photographs. A blond boy growing into a tall, fair-haired young man. In one of the framed pictures, he was in a dinner jacket, elegant, laughing, cigarette between long fingers. The dark-haired young woman at his side had a nervous look, as if she wasn't quite sure what was happening.

The unframed pictures would fit the empty spaces in the old albums, fit neatly back into the corners that once held them.

It would be restoring the albums, Anselm thought, filling the gaps, making the record whole. He could put Moritz back into the family memory.

He untied the ribbon around the letters. They were all addressed to Fräulein Erika Einspenner in a slashing hand.

Not only letters. There was a photograph.

A group of soldiers, hands on each other's shoulders, a truck behind them.

Moritz was in the centre, bare-headed, smiling.

Anselm turned the picture over. On the back was written in the same bold handwriting:

Dienst bei die Fahne. Riga, August 1943. Moritz.

On service with the colours.

What colours?

He went down the passage. Baader, one leg on his desk, was reading a file.

'What do you know about World War Two uniforms?' said Anselm.

Baader looked at him, at the picture he was holding. 'What's that?' he said.

'A photograph.'

Baader held out his hand, looked at the picture. 'Himmler's scum,' he said. '*Waffen SS SD*. See the collar tabs on the *Sturmbahnführer*, this blond one in the middle? Black felt with silver piping.'

He turned the photograph over. 'Even worse. *Einsatzkommando*. Extermination squad. Scum's scum.'

He turned it back, studied it, looked at Anselm, back at the photograph. 'Looks a bit like you, the blond major. What's the interest in these murderers?'

Anselm held out his hand, took the photograph.

'Just something I found,' he said.

He went onto the balcony and smoked a cigarette. He stood in the corner, looked at the winter city, the white tower and the glowing skyscraper, the low lights of the Pöseldorf shore, a ferry heading for the Rabenstrasse landing. The light from Beate's desklamp lay across the balcony in a shaft, lay on him. His smoke drifted across it, sheet white, met the darkness, vanished in a straight line.

He took the final draw, arched the stub into the night, a dying star falling on the old, forgotten roses. Roses without names.

In his office, the phone rang.

'Are you running?' she said.

'I'm running.'

'When?'

'Five minutes.'
He waited for her to say it.
'Don't let me pass in the dark,' she said.
'Not if I can help it.'
'You can,' she said. 'You can.'